Jane de La Vaudère

RAPID TALES

Translated and with an Introduction by
BRIAN STABLEFORD

RAPID TALES

JANE DE LA VAUDÈRE (1857-1908) was baptized Jeanne Scrive and was married to Camille Gaston Crapez, who began styling himself Crapez de La Vaudère after inheriting the Château de La Vaudère from his mother. Her prolific literary work is very various but she was assimilated to the Decadent Movement firstly because of two scandalously scabrous Parisian novels, *Les Demi-Sexes* (1897) and *Les Androgynes*(1903), and, more pertinently, because of a series of accounts of moeurs antiques, some of which—notably *Le Mystère de Kama* (1901)—set new standards of excess.

BRIAN STABLEFORD's scholarly work includes *New Atlantis: A Narrative History of Scientific Romance* (Wildside Press, 2016), *The Plurality of Imaginary Worlds: The Evolution of French roman scientifique* (Black Coat Press, 2017) and *Tales of Enchantment and Disenchantment: A History of Faerie* (Black Coat Press, 2019). He has translated more than three hundred volumes from the French, mostly in the genres of *roman scientifique, contes de fées* and Romantic and Symbolist fiction. His recent fiction includes the visionary science fiction novel *The Revelations of Time and Space* (2020) and its sequel *After the Revelation* (2021); the last in his long series of "Tales of the Genetic Revolution," *The Elusive Shadows* (2020); and the comedy fantasy *Meat on the Bone* (2021), all published by Snuggly Books.

CONTENTS

INTRODUCTION

The series of vignettes by Jane de La Vaudère (1857-1908) translated in the present volume began publication in the Parisian evening newspaper *La Presse* in 1897 under the heading *Contes Rapides*. That heading was dropped in 1899 and replaced by a variety of others, but the nature of the items did not change. The vignettes continued to appear, usually at approximately weekly or fortnightly intervals, with several longer interruptions in the sequence, until July 1900. The feature was restored in January 1901 but terminated again in May of that year. Many of the stories in the series were reprinted in the weekly supplement to another newspaper, *La Lanterne* between 1901 and 1908, sometimes under different titles, and five stories in a similar format appeared therein that had not been published in *La Presse*, perhaps rejected by the editor of that paper. The series was never reprinted in book form, in spite of the fact that Jane de La Vaudère was already a popular author when the series began, and by the time it ended she had risen to best-seller status.

The series is, of course, interesting as an example of an aspect of La Vaudère's work, more closely allied with the many vaudevilles and skits that she wrote for the stage than with her novels, and also contrasting with the longer stories featured in a previous collection of translations, *The Double Star and Other Occult Fantasies* (2018). The series is perhaps even more interesting as a pivotal contribution to a strange and short-lived subgenre of short fiction "mass-produced" by writers commissioned to produce such stories on a regular basis, in

the same way that some newspapers commissioned "colum-
nists" to produce articles on a regular basis. La Vaudère was
one of half a dozen female writers who attempted such regular
production for a brief period of time, and the first to succeed;
all but one of the others were leading contributors to the feminist newspaper *La Fronde* during an experimental dalliance
with the subgenre in 1899-1901, the exception being Lucie
Delarue-Mardrus, who wrote her series of short stories for *Le
Journal* in 1906-8. The present volume of translations thus
forms part of a select group whose other volumes are *The Path
of Amour* by Marie Krysinska, *The Last Rendezvous* by May
Armand Blanc, *The Inn of Tears* by Alice Télot, alias "Jacques
Fréhel," and *The Last Siren and Other Stories* by Delarue-
Mardrus. All of those volumes contain an abundance of material never collected in book form in the original versions,
although a good deal of the material written in the subgenre
by male writers was routinely and swiftly collected.

French newspapers had carried occasional items of short
fiction since their foundation, but from the mid-1830s onwards the principal form of fiction they featured consisted
of "feuilleton" serials, so-called because they were separated
from the other contents of the paper by a *feuilleton*, a line
drawn across the page a couple of inches from the bottom.
The *feuilleton* was an invention of Émile Girardin, the great
pioneer of the French popular press, in *La Presse*—which still
bore his name on its masthead while the paper was publish-
ing the *Contes Rapides*, although he was long dead—but it
was in rival papers that *feuilleton* serials enjoyed their first
heyday in the 1840s, when long novels by Eugène Sue and
Alexandre Dumas became important circulation-builders
and useful devices for maintaining reader loyalty. From then
until the end of the century, *feuilleton* fiction became a key
feature of many French newspapers, and a prolific supplier of
popular material to book publishers. Although short stories
and novelettes sometimes appeared beneath the *feuilleton*,

editors greatly favored long, potentially interminable serials that might help to ensure that readers bought the paper every day, or took out a subscription for its delivery by mail, with the result that much nineteenth-century French fiction was written in episodes of approximately 2,000 words, devised and delivered on a daily basis.

When new technologies of printing and paper manufacture permitted French newspapers to undergo a spectacular economic boom in the 1880s, competition to find new ways of interesting readers and maintaining their loyalty led to wide experimentation and rapid evolution, which reached its peak in the 1890s and gradually tailed off after 1900, when the results of the various experiments were weighed and evaluated. Half a dozen editors of major daily newspapers experimented with additional short fiction; although they did not put it under the *feuilleton* they initially tended to favor stories of similar length to the episodes of *feuilleton* serials. At first, such stories were produced and published haphazardly, but a number of professional writers, finding it a convenient and lucrative market, soon began to cultivate a particular expertise in work of that kind, notably Catulle Mendès and Guy de Maupassant.

Toward the end of the decade, the editor-in-chief of the *Écho de Paris*, Valentin Simond, decided to make such fiction a routine feature, using it as the lead item on page one (of four, daily newspapers routinely being printed on a single sheet folded down the middle). He hired Catulle Mendès to work as his "literary editor" and Mendès assembled a "stable" of writers commissioned to produce stories on a weekly or fortnightly basis, thus maintaining a continuity of product. The initial members of the stable included two of the *Écho*'s staff journalists, Armand Silvestre and Marcel Schwob, supplemented by freelancers, including "Montjoyeux" (Jules Poignard), Octave Mirbeau and Jean Reibrach; the stable was subsequently enlarged to take aboard Jean Lorrain, Paul Arène, Paul Margueritte and others. In the mid 1890s, however, most of the members of the group moved to a stable formed by the rival paper *Le Journal*, which then replaced the *Écho* as the leading Parisian market for short fiction of the relevant length.

The *Écho* and the *Journal* were both relatively pretentious periodicals, considerably upmarket of *La Presse*, which, while by no means part of the "gutter press," was pitched at a more working-class audience, conscientiously carrying forward Émile Girardin's crusade to make literacy universal in France. While the *Écho* and the *Journal* covered daily fluctuations on the Bourse, *La Presse* routinely devoted the entirety of page two to horse racing results and associated advertisements. Émile Girardin had, however, been a very active member of the French Romantic Movement, and his various publications had offered useful markets to many of the ambitious writers associated with that movement, including Théophile Gautier, Honoré de Balzac and Jules Janin. There was, therefore, a certain residual incentive for the editor of *La Presse* to join in with the *Écho*'s experiment, all of whose contributors of fiction were associated with a burgeoning neo-Romantic Movement in contemporary literature sometimes classified by its detractors and adherents, the latter using the term ironically, as "decadent." The *La Presse* venture was, however, tentative and distinctly half-hearted. Its fiction feature was a one-horse stable that never expanded; it set a much lower word-limit—a maximum of 1,000 words rather than 2,000, and an average of 800 words—and it placed the feature on page three rather than page one (an example followed by *Le Journal* in the genre's twilight, as a reluctant but perhaps inevitable admission of the feature's lack of success as a marketing tool).

Jane de La Vaudère began working for *La Presse* in September 1896, initially as an orthodox columnist commenting on current affairs or producing items of criticism, and all her contributions until the end of March 1897 were articles. It is possible that the decision to switch to the *Contes Rapides* at that point (with the occasional interjection of an article) was actually hers rather than her editor's, but wherever the initial suggestion came from, she approached the new brief very methodically, evidently well aware of the progress already made by members of the Mendès stable in refining the art and craft of writing very short stories in quantity, and ready to carry strategies of narrative minimalism to a new level, halving the standard wordage adopted by her rivals. She was undoubtedly well aware too, of the fact that the fledgling subgenre had previously been almost entirely a male preserve, into which female writers had previously had great difficulty in breaking.

It is probably not irrelevant to that difficulty that Catulle Mendès was a notorious womanizer. It might or might not be purely coincidental that "Georges de Peyrebrune," the only woman who contributed stories (only three of them) to the *Écho* while he was running his stable was one of two female authors who managed to publish a novel complaining bitterly about the handicap placed on French female writers by the tendency of Parisian editors to expect and demand "payment in kind" for accepting their work. (The other was Rachilde, who was pursued relentlessly by Mendès for six months, apparently unsuccessfully; he never published any of her work.) At any rate, it is not surprising that La Vaudère's work in the genre, like that of the members of *La Fronde*'s stable, differs considerably in tone from that of the writers of the *Écho* and *Journal* stables, in spite of being forced to adopt very similar narrative strategies. The decision of *La Fronde*'s editor, Marguerite Durand, to imitate her perceived rivals by introducing a fiction feature and placing it, while it lasted, at the head of page one, surely involved a deliberate reaction to the evident sexism of the genre dominated by the Mendès stable, and La Vaudère had set an important example in that regard, albeit working in more restricted circumstances.

The narrative strategies applicable to *feuilleton* fiction and newspaper short fiction were, inevitably, poles apart. A *feuilleton* serial consisted of a long series of incidents in which the same limited cast of characters pursue a few simple goals, continually harassed and handicapped by obstacles placed in their path by hazard and their adversaries. The "natural" conclusion of a story of that sort consists of the sympathetic characters eventually attaining their hard-fought goals while their enemies are thwarted: a stereotyped "happy ending". That is difficult to achieve in a short story, and the shorter a story is, the harder it is to contrive, because there is no space for the necessary build-up and expansion of narrative tension. The "natural" story-arc of a vignette of less than 2,000 words is therefore a matter of sketching a situation whose innate tension is resolved, not by a simple fulfillment of ambition that would inevitably lack drama, but by some kind of cynical summation or ironic twist.

Ultra-short stories inevitably overlap with the oral genre of humorous anecdotes, of which they often seem to be a variant. The dominant form of the short story has, therefore, always been what was frequently characterized in France as a *conte cruel*. Whereas long fiction seems to be so naturally orientated toward "happy endings" that any deliberate violation of that expectation often disappoints or annoys readers—and thus swiftly became anathema to editors courting popularity—short fiction routinely carries no such expectation, and, viewed *en masse*, can easily be seen as an infinitely repetitive recognition of the inherent perversity or tragedy of life—or, as it is sometimes expressed, "the irony of fate."

It was more difficult for writers in a stable like the *Écho*'s to produce a new short story once a week, or once a fortnight, than it was for a *feuilletoniste* to grind out episodes of the same ongoing story every day. Not only had they to construct a new beginning every time but also a new ending, producing a sense of conclusion without the convenience of the ritualistic "happy endings" of enrichment and marriage. "Fate"—not a great creative artist, by any means—only has a limited repertoire of conclusions, and it is not easy for writers commissioned to produce a short story a week to find a great deal of terminal variation in their ironic themes. It is also necessary for them to compete or compromise with the elementary fact that most readers delight in happy endings, with a seemingly infinite appetite, while the minority who appreciate cruel twists are soon sated. It is probable, in consequence, that the subgenre of mass-produced newspaper short stories was doomed from the start as a means of courting lasting reader enthusiasm, and that the experiments of the *fin-de-siècle* were bound to fail in a relatively short period of time—and inevitable, too, that even the most expert writers would not be able to keep up that pace of production for very long. Jane de La Vaudère, whose total production amounted to more a hundred items,[1] was one of only a handful of writers to attain such a milestone.

The pattern of reader appreciation, as filtered through editorial demand, generally required writers to use the soft pedal when playing the scales of cruelty in their *contes cruels*. Most of those featured in newspapers were teasing rather than intense, and the tone of most of the stories produced by the *Écho*'s stable was maliciously witty rather than tragic. Its two most prolific members, Silvestre and Mendès, specialized in salacious stories with a conspicuously light and amiable tone, and were greatly aided in producing conclusions by the same resources that have always abundantly supplied comedians with lewd material. With regard to more intense stories, the pace was set by Marcel Schwob and Octave Mirbeau, with the important difference that they deployed the cruelty of their narratives in markedly different ways. Mirbeau, a resolute misanthrope

---

1 The present volume contains 111, but might not be complete; several issues are missing from the file of *La Presse* reproduced on *gallica*, from which all the translations were made, and it is possible that my search of the issues overlooked one or two items.

and a virulent misogynist, often seemed to be relishing, and even applauding, the cruelties devised in his stories; Schwob, by contrast, stated explicitly in the introduction to the first collection of stories drawn from his newspaper column, *Coeur double* (1891; tr. as *Double Heart*), that his purpose was to emphasize the cruelty of fate in order to stimulate the readers' pity for its victims—and, indeed, that that ought to be the fundamental purpose of literary art. In all probability, Mirbeau would have endorsed that claim, and Mendès too—but neither of them would have been convincing, and even Schwob might have occasioned a certain skepticism in regard to his more brutal stories. La Vaudère softened the cruelty of her *contes cruels* considerably more than Mirbeau (a writer she admired greatly) and Schwob, probably in response to editorial instruction, but it is worth noting that in her novels, at least when she was allowed free license, the cruelty of her characters and her plots is remarkably unrestrained, always with the ostensible purpose of exciting pity for its victims.

The cruelties of "fate" featured in newspaper short fiction, as delivered via human agents, inevitably occasioned an evident difference between stories written by male writers, whose vignettes often took it for granted that fate's most cunning agents of cruelty were *femmes fatales* and harridans, and those penned by female writers, who often took it for granted that systemic male brutality toward women was far more to be regretted. It is not surprising, therefore, that much fiction of this kind written by women exhibits a distinct misandry, frequently velvet-gloved for diplomatic reasons and generally less vitriolic than the naked misogyny of much fiction by male writers, but often deeply felt. In that context, the work that Jane de La Vaudère did in the subgenre—which is conspicuously even-handed by comparison with the work of the *Fronde* stable, exhibiting a wry misogyny as well as a contemptuous misandry—is of particular interest, and it clearly connected with her own experience of life and her particular position in Parisian society, where she was a maverick in more ways than one.

Baptized Jeanne Scrive, Jane de La Vaudére was the younger daughter of the surgeon-general of the French Army, and belonged by birth to the "second tier" of French high society, immediately below that of the true aristocracy. Orphaned at a young age, she and her sister suffered the conventional fate of orphans in that stratum of society: she was placed in a convent where she could receive a good education, and was only taken out when a "suitable" marriage could be arranged for her within her family's social circle. She was married in her teens to Gaston Crapez, whose family had aristocratic connections on his mother's side, and who inherited the Château de La Vaudère from her, after which he began styling himself Gaston Crapez de La Vaudère, although it is likely that members of the topmost tier of French high society regarded him as a *parvenu* and a *poseur*, and that they considered his wife in the same light.

The marriage produced a son, but does not appear to have been happy. Jane left her husband and son in their provincial château and went to Paris while still in her twenties, where she lived alone for the rest of her life. Initially she attempted to cultivate a career as a painter, and exhibited at the Salon, but soon switched to literature, first as a poet and a dramatist, and eventually making her reputation as a novelist, her greatest successes being obtained with novels of a calculatedly scandalous "decadent" nature. Her work for *La Presse* was bracketed by her first and second spectacular achievements in *succès de scandale*, *Les Demi-Sexes* (1897; tr, as "The Demi-Sexes") and *Le Mystère de Kama* (1901; tr. as "The Mystery of Kama"), both of which are eccentrically "sampled" in her short fiction. If her career is considered simply in terms of the quantity and range of her publications and dramatic productions, it might seem to have been spectacularly successful, but it is significant that the only brief notice of her death that was written by a journalist who had known her personally for a long time concluded with the bitter observation that "she never encountered anything but obstacles in her literary vocation."

In order fully to appreciate the spectrum and attitude of the *Contes Rapides* it is worth bearing in mind the situation in which the author must have found herself when she moved to Paris, already a scandalous figure simply by virtue of having deserted her husband and child. As a slight, seemingly frail, but very pretty married woman separated from her husband, she might as well have had a figurative target instead of a fig leaf below her waist, which must have drawn the attention of every rake in Paris, in an era when rakes were as common as dead leaves, especially in the society of sub-aristocratic salons in which she moved. By the time she began writing the *Contes Rapides*, however, she was nearing the age of forty and much of that experience would have been behind her, having left a sour legacy clearly reflected in the cynicism of the vignettes.

La Vaudère does not appear to have frequented specifically literary salons and gatherings; she probably would not have been seen dead at the Chat Noir or any other literary café, and she does not seem to have associated with any of the *littérateurs* in her own stratum of society. She was certainly acquainted with the leading female writers of the capital; she was an active member of the *Societé des gens de lettres*, she served on charitable committees with the likes of Georges de Peyrebrune and "Séverine" (Caroline Rémy de Guebhard), and she was also acquainted with Rachilde, but she does not appear to have attended any of their salons. She actively distanced herself from the moderate feminist writers of *La Fronde*; an assembly of the Societé des gens de lettres in 1900, at which the situation of female members was placed on the agenda and La Vaudère was one of the principal speakers, attracted a good deal of comment in the press because of a fierce dispute that broke out between allies of the *Fronde* contingent and an opposed group; the reportage did not specify what the bone of contention was, but in lists of the adversaries La Vaudère was cited among the opposition to the *Fronde*'s supporters, in the same camp as Camille Pert, the most outspokenly radical of the Societé's feminist members.

Like Rachilde, La Vaudère appears to have refused to define herself as a feminist, but only because she similarly considered herself to be independent of all coteries. In the same spirit, she refused to associate herself with Natalie Barney's pretentious coterie of female poets, although she would surely have been invited to join it, insisting on plowing her own scandalous furrow. The image of a particular sector of Parisian society presented in collage in the *Contes Rapides* is, therefore, seen from an idiosyncratic viewpoint—but one with which many of her female readers, similarly considering themselves to be isolated and badly-done-to outsiders, would have been easily able to sympathize. Although her particular cynicism has much in common with the work of such maverick feminists as May Armand Blanc and Lucie Delarue-Mardrus, who might have taken some inspiration from it, La Vaudère's black comedy is distinctive in the character of its customary diplomacy and its occasional frank brutality—a distinction partly occasioned by the exiguity of the narrative space allotted to her by *La Presse*, but undoubtedly also reflective of the uniqueness of her attitude.

Reading the stories in sequence, as they were presumably written, is interesting as an illustration of the development of the author's narrative technique, which makes extravagant use of several techniques cultivated by Catulle Mendès—especially a quasi-dramatic format—but is genuinely experimental in its deliberately cursory strategies of termination. The series begins in a carefully professional vein, slanted to a hypothetical audience and wary of a censorious editorial eye, with occasional deliberate sidesteps into prose poetry, Symbolist allegory and even crude sentimentality expressed in happy endings (which never ring true). By the later months of 1897, however, the cautious professionalism had loosened up and the work had developed a greater freedom of expression and enterprise, although it is significant that two items, "Dompteuse" ("Tamer") and "Le Départ" ("The Depature") were rewritten for republication—the former in the *Lanterne* supplement—in order to make them much sharper and more cynical in tone. The last few vignettes published in that year, notably "L'Accident" ("The Accident") and "Un Fou" ("A Madman"), are among her most brutal, and it seems probable that she received an editorial instruction at that point to rein herself in and maintain a more reader-friendly balance—which she did, faitly conscientiously, until she let herself go again in 1900, after the feature was dropped for six months, and when she could presumably see the writing on the wall with regard to its lack of a future.

The series is by no means even in its quality; there are intervals when the author's enthusiasm and creativity flag—twice, in 1899 and 1900, she supplied reprints of early short stories in lieu of new material and often relaxed into tired repetition—but that is typical of work produced for the subgenre, and even Marcel Schwob, the titan of the format, occasionally "phoned in" his performances in order to meet his deadlines. Many of the items resemble comedy skits rather than short stories, and some of them were adapted for use on the stage in her many vaudevilles, but their slightness should not be mistaken for laziness; the best of them are fine examples of narrative compaction and subtlety of implication. A mastery of understatement is a necessary concomitant of the genre, but there is a range of styles in understatement, as there are in cynicism and misanthropy, and La Vaudère's was distinctive, breaking new ground in the male-dominated subgenre, whose prevailing styles of understatement, cynicism and misanthropy all tended to be conspicuously masculinized.

The great majority of the vignettes deal necessarily and deliberately with the trivial rather than the grandiose, but the best of them make the trivial work hard as aspects of the entire collage. Many readers will undoubtedly feel that La Vaudère was a far more effective writer when she had the narrative space to give her particular brand of cruelty free and phantasmagoric rein, most obviously in the series of exotic novels begun with *Le Mystère de Kama*, and there is no cause for surprise in the fact that she chose to concentrate in such substantial work in the final phase of her career, but the *Contes Rapides* do have a fugitive charm of their own and do offer an interesting insight into the complexity of her character and the calculated perversity of her attitude to life. They represent a curious episode in the evolution of a genre whose contributions by female writers were almost entirely neglected in their day, and whose omission from conventional literary history has left a significant gap.

This collection offers the first opportunity that anyone has ever had to read the series of rapid tales *as a series* and to asses it as a collage; as a bird's eye view of contemporary Parisian society it is highly selective and idiosyncratic, but that only serves to make it more interesting, and as a pioneering adventure in narrative minimalization it offers a significant exemplar to modern writers' workshops.

—Brian Stableford, August 2020

RAPID TALES

JUMPING FENCES
(*La Presse* 5 April 1897)

Augusta Durand: twenty-two years old, brunette, slim, pretty. Dress of periwinkle-blue woolen cloth, immense hat ornamented with black feathers.

Madame Durand: fifty years old; hooded mantlet sumptuously decorated; skirt of aubergine silk ornamented with old lace.

It is five o'clock; they are crammed into the stands of the show jumping arena, and it is with great difficulty that the ladies in question succeed in reaching the first row of banquettes. In front of them is a spectrum of pastel colors, a profusion of primroses, hyacinths and anemones, celebrating spring in women's hats, and red coats resembling, at a distance, large poppies detached from their stems. The trials have been brilliant and a thousand quivering little fingers stab the program with enthusiastic thrusts of a pencil. But Augusta and her mother turn their backs resolutely on the course and set about inspecting the strollers.

Augusta: I think the Messieurs will soon come; let's try to stop them as they go past.

Madame Durand: Be exceedingly amiable, and decently cheerful. Only laugh in order to show your teeth, and blush if you can . . .

Augusta: Understood, Maman. I'll have the modesty of a marriageable girl. Anyway, with a few adroitly presented flatteries, one always gets out of difficulty with men. I'm ecstatic for a painter's daubs, I wax lyrical for a musician's quacking and I weep for a poet's symbol; all three are content.

Madam Durand: And which one do you prefer?

Augusta: The banker.

Madame Durand: Bravo, my daughter! Your ideas are sound; you have judgment and reason . . . everything you need to succeed.

Loud applause bursts forth; number thirteen has jumped the fences without the slightest hesitation; horse and rider are only one and cut through the air like a dragonfly. Number thirteen will be the day's great triumph.

Augusta: Look at Madame Chapuzon . . . is that allowed? With her belly and the green sides of her dress, she looks like a melon.

Madame Durand: And her daughter Caroline is a pip . . . If I'm not mistaken that's Isidore, your latest flirt!

Isidore goes past without appearing to notice the ladies. That casts a chill.

Augusta: He looks even more like a musician than usual!

Madame Durand: He's saluting Madame Chapuzon

Augusta: That's because Caroline had a fit of nerves the other evening, when he did his burglar trick; personally, in spite of my efforts, I've only ever been able to attain bewilderment.

Madame Durand: Musicians are so demanding.

Augusta: He's the least rich of the four; let's not be nasty. Here comes Monsieur Raphael . . . but he isn't alone. That woman is . . .

Madame Durand: What horror! It's his model!

Augusta: A creature who doesn't hide anything!

Madame Durand: Turn away, my daughter!

An emotion agitates the crowd; a few screams are heard.

Augusta, indifferently: A man in the river. We're wasting our time.

Madame Durand: We still have the poet and the banker.

Augusta: I feel sick . . . how ugly life is!

Madame Durand: You'll have your revenge later; it's necessary to be patient.

Augusta: I promise you that the one who marries me will pay for the others.

Madame Durand: You'll be for your husband what I was for your father. The late Durand, in sum, gave me nothing but satisfactions. It's just a pity that he didn't leave you a larger dowry. What do you expect? He was a man of mediocre intelligence, an honest man! He was never able to profit from opportunities . . .

Augusta: Oh!

Madame Durand: What's the matter?

Augusta: Can't you see? It's Edgard, the poet . . . Edgard, who's giving his arm to his friend Oscar. They have Botticellian hats, pale green waistcoats and mutton-chop sleeves. It's insensate! Let's not talk to them . . . they'll cover us with ridicule. Let's dive, Maman, dive!

The two women disappear and the poets draw away, in search of a rhyme to murder.

Madame Durand: They look like consumptive she-monkeys. Where are we with the trials?

Augusta: I haven't been looking. We didn't come here for the horses, did we? Victory! Here comes Bertillon, Bertillon the banker? He's alone, and he's seen us . . . he's coming!

An immense clamor resounds; women faint. A rider who has been thrown and trampled by his horse is carried away. His eyes are closed, his face livid, and a trickle of blood is running down his forehead.

Augusta and Madame Durand, smiling at Bertillon: Oh, my dear Monsieur, we're delighted . . . !

LENT SERMONS
(*La Presse*, 8 April 1897)

Yvonne and Lise are coming back from the sermon.

Along the route, in the damp moss of the ditches, violets are accumulated under the golden feathers of the first cowslips; behind the great beeches, the countryside is perceptible: a vast plain with occasional clumps of trees, farm buildings and groups of distant workers as big as a finger. Under the grass, the earth, impregnated with recent rain, is moist, and sinks underfoot with a watery sound. However, the bitter wind, the cold and the sufferings of winter have left beings and things with a charming fragility, a kind of ingenuous mildness. Spring, charged with effluvia, is warming and swelling the buds and insinuating itself into the heart of plants, encouraging in their song the eternal hymn of resurrection.

All the languor of renewal cradles and penetrates the two young peasants marching side by side along the road, who are not speaking, in order better to savor the tender charm of their sensations. They have scarves folded over their breasts, new skirts gathered over their hips and little embroidered muslin bonnets over their smooth chestnut tresses.

The village church, with its red and blue windows, its golden paper roses and, on the altar misted by incense the pale gleam of candles, seemed to them more attractive than on other days. Abbé Pistache, who comes from the town and has erudition, had never been as eloquent. Never had his unctuous speech made such an impression on his flock. Never had his broad enveloping gesture, which seems to caress souls, rounded out with so much forbearance.

Yvonne, the more enthusiastic, breaks the silence.

"As beautiful sermons go, that was a beautiful sermon."

"Oh, for sure," declares Lise in her turn. "Abbé Bridelle, the poor saintly man, may God have his soul, didn't make any like it."

"Repeat a little, to see? Grandmother, who's infirm, always wants to know what Monsieur le curé has said."

"I don't have a good memory. I know the basics well, but as for the words, it's too difficult."

The two young women meditate again, seeking in their memory for the edifying and sonorous phrases that they have just heard. Gradually, their thoughts drift, and the tenderness of matters of religion and nature lead them to talk about their amours.

"Oh," says Lise, sighing. "mine is a soldier. It's hard, all the same, not to see him."

"Since he's promised to marry you, you can be patient."

"Does one know what's passing through their heads when they're far away from us? You have your Pierre; at least he's done his time."

"All the girls run after him. Such a handsome fellow! I'm always tormented."

"Perhaps you're too stern, then? He might look elsewhere."

"You think so?"

"Since you love him, he must be worth the trouble, that man."

"You're right."

And Yvonne, suddenly becoming pensive, exclaimed volubly: "Everything that M'sieu le curé said is coming back to me now. Here, I'll recite it for you, like the catechism."

With a joyful expression, the peasant girl repeated Abbé Pistache's sermon faithfully, in a vibrant voice, while the terrible and gentle sun drowned her in its great radiance, rolling her in a river of hopes and desires, giving her the joy of living in the expansion of her young dream.

The courtyard of the farm now extended before her: a courtyard surrounded by trees with a pond in which ducks were splashing. The thatched roofs of the buildings were fuming slightly, and pigeons were shifting their backs with metallic reflections and their necks of bright silver with a pink luster.

The young women had stopped, intoxicated by words and pure air.

"The best part of the sermon was the end," said Yvonne. "'My brethren,' said M'sieu le curé, 'in these times of Lent, it's necessary to have pity on all suffering; it's necessary to open our hearts to mercy, in memory of the Passion of Our Lord. Don't reject any supplication, for whoever gives to the poor gives to God! Be charitable, my brethren, give without counting, give, give and Heaven will recompense you.'"

"Yes, yes, that's right!"

"And do you know, Lise, it's been a long time since Pierre has asked me for anything; in order to obey M'sieur le Curé, I'll give him everything tonight!"

THE BRANCHES
(*La Presse*, 16 April 1897)

Night was falling, and a bitter wind was blowing through the streets. Little Etienne picked up the box-wood twigs that had fallen to the ground during his brief nap and resumed his route.

All day long he had offered his branches at the doors of churches, but his poor dusty foliage had not tempted anyone. Now he could no longer hope to sell them, but he kept them, hugging them against him with a feverish effort of his feeble arms.

At an uncertain pace he drew away through the narrow streets, the passages warmed by the warm breath of subterranean kitchens. At intervals, he stopped under porches to get his breath back, and his gaze rose up to the row of windows with closed shutters, where the gleam of the gas lamp often picked out a mascaron sculpted above a pot-bellied balcony in flamboyant ironwork.

But the chill of the paving stones extracted him from his contemplation and he set off again, staggering, rounding his back in order to offer less purchase to the whips of the icy evening air. He went at random, with the futile desire to find a shelter or to interest the passers-by in his fate. He lingered outside the doors of taverns, having noticed that every time customers went in or out, a little of the good warm within reached him.

He had not eaten for two days and hunger was burning his stomach, twisting his guts, gnawing and clawing at him.

When he did not bring anything back to the lodgings the old folk chased him away, and he dragged out his vagabond existence on the roads, too proud to beg and too ignorant to lament . . .

At present he no longer had the strength to climb his calvary; a flood of mist drowned his wandering thought, preventing him from thinking about his frightful misery. Haggard, he dragged himself along, only stopping mechanically outside the displays of rotisserie; his taste buds quivered with covetousness and his eyes vacillated, hypnotized by the long pink flames inside.

Soon, the shops closed; he no longer had the resource of doors flapping under the coming-and-going of clients. The air became increasingly damp; everything fell into a mortuary silence, with the vague trembling of gas jets burning like candles along the deserted sidewalks. He did not think of returning to the lodgings. What was the point, since he had no money? In any case, he was too weak; the lodgings were too far away.

A great frisson ran through his bones, and, his soul in pain, his legs weary and his belly empty, he set forth again.

Houses became sparse; soon, there were no longer any, and he found himself in the country.

Gray clouds were rolling in the sky under the enraged pressure of the wind. The bare trees twisted in the darkness with a noise of rattling bones in the frail skeletons of their branches.

He was now terribly hungry: one of those hungers that throw wolf-cubs on to any errant prey. Exhausted, he stretched his legs and, his head heavy, blood buzzing in his temples and his eyes red, he spoke aloud, under the obsession of incoherent ideas. Then his throat contracted in barking coughs; his uncovered breast tore all the way to the liver, as if under the bite of ferocious jaws. He gasped; the clappers of bells were hammering his temples; there was a tumultuous racket of forges around him, the noise of a train running at top speed, the sound of the sea submerging a world . . .

Rain started to fall, urgent, cold and penetrating, and a thousand terrified voices howled in the treetops, colliding in the tempest. Everything was confounded in the bewildered mind of the child, who fell upon the soaked ground and remained motionless.

Miraculously, though, while he agonized, the box-wood that he was still holding took root and extended toward the sky heavy branches charged with flowers, the flowers of dreams, such as he had never seen. And he rose up with the perfumed flow, sustained by foliage gentler than feather pillows. Songs of an infinite purity resounded, and he did not know whether they came from the mystery of the box-wood or the mystery of the heavens. The clouds dissipated, torn apart by the victorious branches; he rose up and up, irresistibly, invincibly, in his nest of verdure toward the stars.

The cradling of the branches was a caress, the vertigo of the abyss became an ecstasy. Etienne's soul was filled with light and joy . . .

Suddenly, he uttered a cry and put his little hands together, for the last silver clouds, like the curtains of a tabernacle, were unraveling in wide spirals, and he saw Paradise.

DOSIE'S EASTER
(*La Presse*, 22 April 1897)

On Easter Day, Dosie went to sit in the haunted room, the chamber hung with mauve silk that had been her mother's bedroom. She loved that solitary place, where she hid her troubles, her anguish and her disappointments of a disdained and mistreated little girl.

With a complexion still indecisive, mingling amber and honey, Dosie had long, scattered hair. Her little dress, crumpled and too large, hid the slender lines of her body; her sad, melancholy face, scarcely tinted under the rings of her eyes, resembled the pale roses of October that only have a vague perfume of flowers in pain and shed their petals when touched by the hand. Since her mother's death she had languished thus, like a plant deprived of care and light. Who would love her now?

A stranger had come into the house in mourning; another young and beautiful woman, who had taken her name and directed everything in accordance with her caprice, with the unconscious cruelty of frivolous, egotistical and vain individuals. The daughter of the dead woman had displeased her immediately by virtue of the fixity of her long reproachful gaze, the coldness of her attitude and a kind of hostility that children are able to put into their slightest actions and words. Now, there was open warfare between the stepmother and the child, before the silence of the father, who dared not intervene.

Oh, how pretty it was, the late mother's bedroom, with its heavy silky curtains, its large bed in the form of a gondola, draped with a coverlet that scintillated like a firmament dotted with golden roses. There were the most various styles in the furniture: a superb Louis XIV chest of drawers armored with gleaming brass, Louis XV armchairs clad in their green damask with mauve bouquets, and on the side-tables, works of embroidery that death had interrupted, which had never been completed.

Her face bathed with tears—for she never received a kiss or a caress for Easter—Dosie went to sit down in one of the armchairs near the widow, which she opened. Flowering trees, aurified by a gentle light, shook their embalmed snow nearby, which swirled as it descended. Everything in nature spoke of happiness and renewal, next to her mute despair. Slowly, she tipped her head backwards on to the back of the armchair and thought . . .

Next to the casement, in front of her, a mandora was hanging on a yellow satin ribbon, and the child remembered that her first dreams had been lulled by the melodies of the old instrument, the strings of which were vibrated by a light and tender hand.

Then, the little guzla had exhaled its soul in quivering chords, with a flight of faith and hope in its songs. With the melancholy of the present, Dosie rediscovered her beautiful dreams of old, the memory of joys that were too brief and long kisses, passionately given and rendered. She was then in a nest of amour; she never had a chill in her little heart in the down of cares and smiles. Now, a great glacial breath fell upon her; she shivered in the indifference of people and things.

"Oh, darling guzla, will you no longer sing for poor Dosie the melodies that warm up little girls and baby birds?"

New tears streamed over the child's feverish cheeks; but, as she did not yet have the habitude or the strength of suffering, her eyelids lowered gradually, while one last limpid droplet trembled in the golden thread of her eyelashes, and her mind flew away to the land of dreams, where there are still a few choice grains to be gleaned by those disinherited down here.

A thousand confused visions haunt her thought; it seems to her that the door opens mysteriously without making any sound and that a dear phantom advances, gliding, in an apotheosis of light . . .

The phantom has blonde hair like her, limpid eyes of faith and goodness; its arms extend in a gesture of caress . . .

But Dosie is nailed to her armchair; in any case, she knows full well that the specter would close its maternal arms of light upon her in vain, and that she would not feel the beating of the heart asleep under the cypresses of the little cemetery. Dosie is very reasonable in spite of her youth, and she has already learned to doubt things.

However, the phantom contemplates her with its shining eyes, which resemble two stars detached from the vault of the heavens; and, taking the forgotten mandora, it plays a prelude of a few light chords. Now the requested song rises, the celestial song that carries souls toward the blue immensities. The melody become precise, makes itself consoling and seductive, stirs the air with a murmur that is scarcely perceptible, swelling in sonorous waves, rolling in cascades of pearly notes, only to fade away gradually and become as tenuous as a thread of spidersilk suspended from the calyx of a flower . . .

And the phantom starts to sing:

"Dosie, little Dosie, the sky is blue, the road is white. It is only necessary to see the gifts that God makes us . . . Humans are wicked? What does that matter too is, if nature is gentle . . . ? It is necessary to live with the trees, the flowers, the singing waves and the stars . . . When you are sad, little Dosie, go down into the garden. I will take you by the hand, and we will visit together all the riches of odorous roads, with their joyous little flowers and their familiar mosses. The flowers of bindweed will perfume the wind with an almond incense, the clusters of gorse will cover the slopes of the valleys with a broad golden cloak. Their strong and persistent odor will intoxicate you like a new wine. You will sow memories everywhere as one throws seeds to the earth, and the roots of those memories will hold fast until death! You will see that life is the same for everyone, made of brief joys and long dolors; that it is necessary not to ask of it more than it can give. Mothers must die before their children, and sooner or later, you would have lost me. Don't cry; I'm very happy, little Dosie; the sufferings of the earth cannot attain me . . ."

The song continues over the hum of the vibrant strings, and the child wakes up, listens again, passes her hand over her forehead with intoxication and fear . . .

But yes, the melody is still vibrating . . . so it was not a dream?

Dosie opens her astonished eyes wide and gazes without moving her head: a bee, its wings quivering, is caught in the strings of the mandora, and a tiny bird, perched on the neck, is singing recklessly; and the child understands the bee and the bird.

One is saying: "I am the light hand of death," and the other: "I am its faithful voice . . . don't tremble, for the flowers that the wind brings through this window are kisses, and the ray of sunlight that envelops you, caresses and warms you is the maternal soul . . .

"Nothing dies, little Dosie, and mothers return in flowers, bees and birds to console beloved children."

JUVENILITY
(*La Presse*, 29 April 1897)

The fête unfurls like an apotheosis of enchantment in the immense hall decorated with bright estival drapes, gauze blinds, foliage and garlands of roses. A blue light falls from electric tulips with radiant pistils, frosting faces and bare shoulders with lunar light. An entire phantasmagoria of lace, ribbons, feathers and straw wrapping agitates and rubs together in the noisy measure of a quadrille. A little to one side, on a divan, a middle-aged Isabeau de Bavière clad in yellow damask blazoned in black, with a pearly hennin on her head, is chatting with a Charles Quint, dazzlingly helmeted and armored. A few paces away, near a door, two young people are watching them and speaking in low voices:

Edmée is eighteen years old, costumed as an "Aesthete's Mistress." A long frog-green stain sheath clings to her slim body; sprays of violet leaves and stems are embroidered on her skirt and rise like Roman candles all the way to her bodice, where they burst forth in superb silver calices. Long black tresses are compressed by a gold circlet posed on her forehead in an aureole.

Raymond is twenty-five years old, costumed as a "Gypsy Lover." A jacket with enormous Brandenburg fastenings, a symbolic bow ornamented with flowers and diagonally-crossed ribbons.

Raymond: Adorable! A real find, that sheath with glaucous tints, which espouses your contours devotedly and makes you a great animate flower: my lovely flower of mysterious pools . . .

Edmée: No compliments! They're unnecessary between us, my good Raymond. And don't come too close. Don't forget that, so far as everyone knows, we're talking for the first time. Don't let anyone suspect our prior arrangements. Oh, if they knew that, contrary to what is done in such cases, it's us who have contrived an interview between our parents and that we hope that it will establish a sympathetic current between them of which we can take advantage!

Raymond: Well, thus far nothing has been established between them! They have a desolating coldness and are yawning like fish out of water!

Edmée: I have, however, adorned Maman carefully. I've curled and waved her hair, made her up, dressed her tightly and perfumed her. I've sewed all the family pearls on to her hennin!

Raymond: Papa has cost me no less effort. I've done my best to render him seductive and bellicose.

Edmée: I assure you that Maman is entirely organized to her advantage; I've extracted the best from her and she ought to please a serious man. She has read all of Lord Byron and she plucks the zither. She also sang once, but now her voice loses its tone slightly when it rains.

Raymond: In his normal state, Papa hasn't much conversation, but his silence can pass for profundity.

Edmée: Oh, what men ordinarily say to women doesn't convey a very elevated idea of their superiority. Mundane gossip, warmth . . . amour . . . I'm certain that the most stupid get away with it!

Raymond: Except that it requires a certain audacity, and my father is so timid!

Edmée: That's unfortunate.

Raymond: I've never been able to launch him in business . . . his favorite occupations have a sweet innocence. Can you imagine that he employs a great part of his leisure building fortresses with old corks. He has such a great quantity of them in our villa in Cabourg that if the house were borne away by a flood it would certainly float.

Edmée: When we're married, our parents won't trouble us much.

Raymond: It's still necessary that they consent to our marriage.

Edmée: I was counting on the thunderbolt. If they reflect, we're doomed. Our notaries can't remain in the dark forever . . . and between ourselves, it's all façade, your luxury?

Raymond: Your lands and ours are mortgaged and we only have unproductive immovable property. So, we're living on the capital!

Edmée: And in spite of everything, we've been very cunning in choosing one another, for you have determination and I have cleverness. With perseverance, intrigue and flexibility one always succeeds. You don't possess special knowledge, your opinions aren't tenacious, but they give the illusion. You'll thrive in politics! I'd rather have a wily man without money than a simpleton clad in gold! The former enriches himself and the latter ruins himself. I've reflected maturely, my friend; you'll suit me marvelously.

Raymond: The two of us will be *somebody!*

Edmée: And the association will give marvelous results, you'll see!

Raymond: Yes, we're very strong. (*Pointing at Charles Quint and Isabeau.*) It'll be necessary for us to talk to them about our plans with the greatest reserve.

Edmée: They're so stupid!

Raymond: Veritable children. (*Anxiously.*) In the meantime, they're not hooking up. It seems to me that Madame Isabeau would like to go to sleep?

Edmée: But your father's Charles Quint is made of cardboard!

Raymond: Oh, if only Madame your mother had the same liking for fortresses made of corks!

Edmée: Perhaps it will come. Have you noticed that when one puts together an aging gentleman and lady, they no longer have anything to say to one another?

Raymond: Yes . . . but eloquence doesn't take long to come. I'm counting a great deal on the buffet. Would you care, pretty aesthete flower, to take a turn at the boston? Attention is beginning to fix on us.

He puts his arm around Edmée's waist and moves away with her. The waltz draws them in; they disappear into the crowd of costumes while serenely settling the bases of their future association. On the divan, Charles Quint has offered Isabeau a cup of tea accompanied by a little foie gras *on toast. They talk about Lord Byron and corks; a certain entente is produced. When the young folk return, the Queen of France's hennin is slightly tilted over her ear, and the King of Spain has removed his helmet.*

Edmée, *joyfully*: It's not an illusion! They're thawing out! They're exchanging sympathetic quips!

Raymond: They're caressing one another with their voices . . .

Edmée: Maman is lowering her eyes . . .

Raymond: Papa is becoming animated . . .

Edmée: We're saved! Our parents are flirting!

THE MYSTERY WOMAN[1]
(*La Presse*, 12 May 1897)

One day, while he was playing in the path, she came to take him by the hand and led him to her palace of dreams . . .

He had visited with her the beds of lively springs where flowering herbs grow, cathedrals of foliage where nightingales intone amorous hosannas and the damp blue-tinted corners where evil spirits reside in hemlocks and foxgloves.

When they returned, in the frisson of twilights, the landscape appeared to deepen in the distance and mingle with the sky, filled with metamorphoses. Its distant hills surged from the azure like floating white ships ready to set forth for the country of the stars. And he huddled against his little friend, whispering words of ecstasy and terror in her ears.

Who was she? Where did she come from? He could not say, but she scarcely quit him, watching over him like a sister, enveloping him with affection and caresses.

"What is your name, benevolent little fay?" he often asked her. But she laughed, put her arms around him, and kissed him with her fresh lips, without ever replying to him.

On the horizon, of the transparent gray of an old road, flakes flew up like feathers lost by swans gliding over water, and everything in life seemed as lovely and snowy as that heavenly down. Melodies trailed in the air, stretching out, putting light chords into his joy. There was the quivering of foliage and the chirping of birds, so numerous and so hectic that he thought

---

1 This story appeared with a footnote acknowledging its previous appearance in La Vaudère's collection *Les Sataniques* (1897).

he was in an enchanted wood in which the flowers and trees talked. And he only thought about his infantile companions, naïve and tender, whom he found again in his path every day, and whom he loved more every day.

He grew up with her, saw her put on her first long dress and wished, not having any money, that he could collect lunar droplets in order to suspend them from her pink earlobes. But she could only make his presents: her skirts, her shoulders and arms shook, in the dust of the roads, an entire constellation of unknown gems, and efflorescence of the Milky Way.

Her beauty became sovereign; the charm of her voice had no equal, similar to the sound of a silver bell vibrating in the belfry of some distant church.

He wanted to possess her, and she gave herself, unfastening for him alone her long golden tresses, unlacing in the dark her corselet of fine pearls. He shuddered recklessly when she brushed him with her mouth, enveloped him with the perfume of her flesh and intoxicated him to the point of dementia with her insatiable kisses.

Many years passed without altering her powerful beauty. He had built her a regal dwelling for which she hardly ever emerged, and he always rediscovered her there, seductive and supple, in her amorous adornments.

"You are the divine mistress that one only encounters once," he said, kissing her lips. "You are the woman that one adores in a holy and exclusive fashion, the one who renews herself incessantly and never changes. Let me plunge my forehead into the radiance of your hair; let me go to sleep on your heart, after the dear fatigue of enlacements. I shall always possess you!"

"Who can tell?" she responded.

But he became indignant.

"How could I forget you, when I truly have no desire but you on earth?"

"We'll grow old, my friend; those eyes that shine with amour will no longer have any but glimmers of fever in their desiccated eyelids. Beneath the flesh of caresses the hideous skeleton will stand out, and our thought itself will no longer be anything but a cemetery in which sinister crosses mark memories . . ."

"No, no, life is sweet! Who are you? Where do you come from? I've hidden nothing from you but I know nothing about you! When I encountered you, you were alone, lost, like a little flower in a rut in the road, and anyone might have plucked you and caressed you."

"I was waiting for you."

"So you knew that I would come?"

"Don't ask me any more."

"Why not?"

"When you know me, I'll no longer exist. Let me live on in your amour. Let me sing the divine canticle amid the suffering and moans of beings. Every minute that goes by marks an agony, and our feet, on the ground, stir the dust of the dead. Let me forget, in giving you my soul, that the soul itself is only a tiny flame, and that one day you'll blow on it in order to return to your darkness."

"What are you saying?"

"I'm saying that you're worth more than other men, because I've lived without and within you for such a long time. Oh, how ardent your embraces are, and how good I feel in your arms!"

However, the years passed, and as their gazes weakened they were gripped by a vague malaise, an indefinable anxiety. He discovered signs in his friend that announced the twilight of her beauty and the decline of her strength. He counted the first wrinkles on her forehead and plunged his saddened gaze into the snow of her hair. Soon, old age curbed her, enveloping her with the desolation of its shadow. She oppressed him, as an enormous weight pushed her toward the earth.

He still sought her kisses, but they were indifferent and no longer consoled him. Kneeling before her he contemplated her passionately, appealing to her and imploring her in the great silence of the night. Then, desperately, he pressed her to his bosom, insufflating her with his soul in furious caresses.

"Oh, don't leave me! Don't abandon me! I love you . . . ! I love you . . . ! I don't see your old age . . . you're always the unique, the sovereign! I only have you . . . I only desire you . . . ! What will become of my existence when you're gone? At least tell me your name, in order that I can engrave it in my memory . . ."

She raised her withered eyelids, still smiling her equivocal, agonizing smile.

"Soon; soon, you'll know who I am."

Immediately, a great calm filled her lover's soul. He leaned over her, in order to see her one last time, and he rediscovered everything that she had been in the most beautiful years of her youth, with her soft visage, her flowery lips and her honeyed hair. But she seemed to recoil in reality, to be no more than a distant dream image, a pure and pale fiction . . .

How had he ever possessed her? He took what remained of her: a little perfume and light; and he buried it piously in his heart, for he knew her now that she was dead; she was Illusion.

FOR YOUR BIRTHDAY . . .
(*La Presse*, 21 May 1897)

A severe bedroom hung with old Flemish tapestries depicting singular and slightly disquieting individuals. Furniture in various styles, bought at the hazard of sales: a Louis XIV chest of drawers armored with shiny brass; Louis XV armchairs with faded little bouquets on a background of "water-lily" satin; a sculpted oak bed, almost black, with four columns terminated by Corinthian capitals, under a cornice lined with roses and amours.

In the bed, buried under a coverlet of faded old brocade, Monsieur is sleeping like an honest magistrate. He is not snoring; he is suave and collected. His guardian angel is quite content and is preparing to make an excellent report to the good God. The door opens, quietly Madame enters, walking on tiptoe, pulls back the curtains abruptly and kisses Monsieur, who wakes up with a start.

Madame is twenty-two years old, blonde, slim and curvaceous, with lovely dark eyes huddling like birds in a nest of golden lashes. Her peignoir of soft silk, loosely fastened, partly disappears under the mantle of her hair.

Monsieur is thirty-six, myopic, grave, replete, going bald.

Monsieur: Awake already?

Madame: I was in a hurry, this morning, to come and kiss you.

Monsieur: You're not ill?

Madame: I'm marvelously well. Only, for some time, I've been troubled, discontented . . .

Monsieur: Well, with all these horrible events, the nerves end up breaking down . . .

Madame: I don't want to think about those poor people; it makes me feel ill. And then, we've done our duty by giving a thousand francs to the *Figaro*'s subscription.[1] Our friends are edified. I beg you, don't talk to me any more about that catastrophe. No, my preoccupation today has another cause.

Monsieur: Your cycling, hunting or walking costume fits too tightly, or not tightly enough?

Madame: You don't understand; you never understand anything! The day after tomorrow is your birthday, my friend, and I want to give you a surprise.

Monsieur: Oh, my dear little wife.

Madame: I'm putting my imagination to the torture in order to make an idea of genius spring forth. Let's see, what do you desire?

Monsieur: Nothing, my Thérèse, nothing but your kiss and your smile . . .

Madame: You'll have those into the bargain; I'm not half-generous. Come on, let's seek together in the simple objects of common custom; for I'd blush to give you a gift of money. I want you to feel that it's my heart that I'm giving you in the smallest things . . .

Monsieur: My Thérèsine!

Madame: What would you say to a morocco briefcase, stitched all around, to carry your files?

Monsieur: I take pride in handling them, and the dignity of a magistrate can bear it!

---

1 *Le Figaro* raised money in May 1897 for the victims of a fire at a charity bazaar on the fourth of the month. Many people were trampled in the panic as the crowd attempted to get out of the wooden building. 126 people died and 150 were seriously injured.

Madame: A portfolio with compartments and leather gussets, then, for your correspondence?

Monsieur: You do it too much honor; a simple drawer suffices.

Madame: A cigar case with your monogram in silver? Something sober and in good taste?

Monsieur: You gave me one last year, and I offered you, in exchange, a blue hussar card-holder with a winding watch surrounded by turquoises.

Madame: Yes, yes, I'm foolish. But what, then? I've made you tobacco-pouches in all colors; Maman has given you flannel waistcoats and incombustible underpants, a photographic apparatus, a music box . . . (*With discouragement.*) My God, send me a delicate, original, charming inspiration, which will be able to reflect my ardent affection! When we married, my family truly provided for everything.

Monsieur: Mine too.

Madame: Oh, for me, it's different. It requires so many things for women to maintain their reputation for beauty and elegance. There's so much competition, and the man becomes so disdainful.

Monsieur: Not so! I paid court to you for six months. Well, I've never seen the dress that you wore!

Madame: You didn't study it in detail, I agree; but the ensemble charmed you by virtue of the skill of the cut, the softness of the fabrics, the harmony of the shades. It's precisely because nothing shocked your very refined and very reliable taste that you didn't seek to analyze it, and that pretended indifference was a discreet eulogy of which I was proud. (*Seductively.*) Oh, tell me that I'm still the Thérèsine of before the marriage.

Monsieur, *his eyes moist*: You're the Thérèsine of before, after and forever . . . the awaited, the desired, the cherished, the unique . . . !

Madame: Truly?

Monsieur: How can I prove it? I only have one ambition: to make you happy. I only have one good fortune: to know that I've succeeded.

Madame, *faintly*: Then my gift is found.

Monsieur: Impossible.

Madame: It's quite simple. I offer you joy by furnishing you with the opportunity to make me happy. For your birthday, you can give me a diamond necklace!

STRAWBERRIES
(*La Presse*, 29 May)

The current is carrying spangles of starlight and moonlight, the rising breeze is sighing and murmuring its mysterious and monotonous song in the trees. A boat glides slowly between the two banks, seemingly following an avenue of azure and gold.

Lili, sitting at the prow, lets a bunch of red roses that she is holding in her hand dangle in the water; shedding their petals one by one, they leave behind a trail of murder.

Totor, standing at the stern, is leaning effortfully and straightening up again over a long pole, which is propelling the smooth and silent progress of the boat.

Brushing the sands of the borders, they pass over the reeds, imprisoned in the midst of the aquatic vegetation and shuddering over a white tree-trunk, stripped of bark and polished by the current, reminiscent of a cadaver lying in the mud.

Lili shakes her curly hair, of which starlight has taken hold, like a spider-web, and her girlish face appears very white, contracted by fear.

"It's bad, what we're doing."

But Totor, two years older than her, looks at her, laughing.

"Bah! Our parents don't know anything; they think we're busy studying our lessons. I'll show you the hole with the strawberries, near the grotto."

"We could go during the day."

"During the day your governess, Miss Mabel, never leaves you alone."

"There are werewolves in the bushes at this hour!"

"You still believe in such stories at your age?"

"I tell you that I saw one last year. It had phosphorescent eyes, a long goat's beard, and black horns on its head!"

"You were dreaming!"

"No, I saw it."

Totor remains pensive; a little frisson runs between his shoulder-blades, but he doesn't want to agree.

"Miss Mabel and Monsieur Charles," he says, "went for an excursion in the boat yesterday evening."

"That's what you were told?"

"You can't say that it isn't true. I saw them."

"Sly rogue!"

"And Monsieur Charles kept repeating: 'Sit still, Miss Mabel; you'll make us capsize,' while she sighed with the voice of a fairground ventriloquist: 'Oh, that was the emotion . . .'"

"That's why she had a funny look when she put me to bed and her chignon was full of leaves. For sure she'd seen the devil!"

"You always believe things! Anyway, if there are ghosts in the grotto, we'll talk to them. Oh, the pretty grotto, covered in jasmine and honeysuckle! You'll see how nice it is."

"No, no, they return there every night; it's an accursed place. The gardener told me that witches hold their sabbat there. What's a sabbat?"

"I don't know."

"They arrive on broomsticks and they dance around a big cauldron in which there are toads, vipers and the heads of children."

"The gardener is making fun of you because you're a little girl. With me, he wouldn't have dared."

"Oh, Totor, I'm scared!"

Totor shrugs his shoulders and pushes the boat more vigorously, while Lili hides her face in her bouquet of roses.

They pass alongside little cliffs, steep veined slopes of beautiful yellow sand, which extend very straightly and from which soft herbs hang down. They brush hedges of clematis florid with mauve stars, ramparts of plush irises and reds whose menacing leaves rise up like sabers. Alders and willows show the undersides of their leaves, frosted with silver.

Lili is no longer talking; her dark eyes gaze at the confused silhouettes of the trees; it seems to her that arms are agitating, that fleshless bodies are leaning over, and that clenched fingers armed with claws are reaching out behind her back. Totor is no more reassured than her, but he doesn't want to retreat, and maneuvers his long pole more rapidly in order to give himself courage.

Oh, how Lili would flee, returning to the house in order to learn her lessons meekly, if she were not in this wretched boat, which doesn't want to stop.

Now there is the entrance to a stream as dark and profound as the mouth of an urn tilted by a naiad, and the water, gliding over the pebbles, seems to be laughing madly at their fears. Leaves are floating in the current, accumulating in ocher masses in the clumps of rushes floating in blue vapors.

"It's there," says Totor. "Let's not make any sound."

"I want to go home."

"You'll see the beautiful jasmine and honeysuckle!"

"I prefer the roses in the garden."

"Come on! We'll eat strawberries. There are lots of them . . . lots . . . and sweet!"

Lili decides in favor of the strawberries. Very gently, like sylphs, they file through grass so tall that their little pale faces can no longer be seen, approaching the grotto. The perfumes of honeysuckle and strawberries combine delectably, singing a passionate duet punctuated by the suave note of jasmine . . .

Totor kneels down, taking care not to stain his short trousers. But with an abrupt movement he gets to his feet again, while Lili utters a cry of anguish. A shadow has suddenly loomed up in front of them: a bizarre, fantastic, frightful shadow, which dominates the hole of the strawberries and seems to touch the sky; a shadow that does not recall any human form, but which might be that of a giant mushroom. It elongates, bends over, collapses into itself like a jack-in-a-box.

Abandoning their boat, Totor and Lili run through the fields, at a frantic pace. To the left and the right, before and behind them, there are phantoms galloping through the countryside. It is a formidable troop, and army of hideous skeletons escaped from cemeteries, whose tibias are clicking in a sinister fashion; and the cows that are following them in the night are putting black mantles over their white shrouds!

Near the grotto, meanwhile, Monsieur Charles and Miss Mabel have recovered from their surprise.

"Oh," she says. "They've gone!"

And putting his arm around her, he says: "Don't fold up your umbrella, darling. They might come back."

DEBUTANTE
(*La Presse*, 2 June 1897)

The study of a great critic. On the walls, paintings by friends; scattered around, bronzes and *objects d'art*, photographs of women with admiring, grateful and tender dedications: *To a dear friend; To the respected master; To the impeccable judge. Tulu to her old penguin*, etc. Various animal hides, low furniture, a profound divan. One respires a perfume of incense, dust and cooking. The mocking valet pinches a little maid in the antechamber.

Alfred: The profile of an ancient medal, a thoughtful and distinguished expression. He is sitting at the desk and arranging various shiny objects on a foolscap piece of paper,

The debutante: Twenty-one years old. Her hennaed hair falls in russet cascades over her cheeks. She is wearing a short guipure bolero over a pale dahlia dress that molds her hips. The pretty head of a successful whore; gilded eyes and white teeth always on display; kohl on her eyelids. She enters and approaches Alfred.

Alfred, *bowing*: Madame . . .

The debutante, *aside*:He's a scribbler; it's him! (*Aloud.*) My God, Monsieur you don't know me.

Alfred: Indeed.

The debutante: But you're good, and I've come without dread.

Alfred: Don't be shy; put yourself at your ease.

The debutante: Those encouraging words fill me with emotion. Such an honor!

Alfred: I treat ladies thus. They all have confidence in addressing themselves to me. Although still young, my reputation is well-established.

The debutante: And I feared this first interview so much. How mistaken one can be, and how necessary it is to mistrust what people say.

Alfred: Do they say things?

The debutante: Yes, it's claimed that you're unjust and a lunatic. Oh, pardon me! To repeat those vile things . . .

Alfred, *laughing*: Me, a lunatic?

The debutante: That you're trenchant and that you cut to the quick.

Alfred, *indignantly*: It's an infamous calumny! I've never even broken the skin!

The debutante: Then, dear Master, you promise to be clement with me?

Alfred, *with grace*: I don't touch, I brush . . . a butterfly on a rose!

The debutante: Oh, you'll appreciate me.

Alfred: I'm certain of it.

The debutante: First of all, I know how to walk . . .

Alfred: That's the essential thing. Everything is there, you see: the foot straight, the tread light, the heel very straight, in shoes from a good maker. The toes must be maintained without violence, so that the supple leather espouses all the contours faithfully and gently.

The debutante: The voice isn't very good. Will you give me some advice?

Alfred: The voice? The voice is insignificant.

The debutante: But . . .

Alfred: No, a pretty foot and a pretty hand are sufficient.

The debutante: Many thanks! You are talking about me?

Alfred: Of course.

The debutante: You'll come to see me perform?

Alfred: More than once.

The debutante, *tenderly*: How happy Maman will be!

Alfred: Madam your mother too? It's necessary to bring her to me; I have a specialty in older women . . .

The debutante: Oh?

Alfred: Because of my extreme gentleness . . .

The debutante: Yes, I understand. That's why there's no one else for the great tragedienne?

Alfred: Only, for her, *noblesse oblige*, I ask for a slightly higher fee . . ."

The debutante, *admiringly*: You charge a fee?

Alfred, *gallantly*: For you, I won't ask for any.

The debutante: How nice you are! (*Sitting on Alfred's knees.*) Do you know that I that you'd be quite different . . . physically.

Alfred. Why is that?

The debutante: I was assured that you were somewhat fatigued . . . demanding and . . . a trifle neglected . . .

Alfred, *furiously*: That's not true!

The debutante, *seductively*: Great fool! You're charming! You please me more than I can say. I belong to you body and soul.

Alfred: The soul too?

The debutante: Yes, my Master, everything!

Alfred, delightedly: Then let's hurry; someone might come!

The debutante: Bah! Are you not at home? Let's close the doors.

Alfred: Come on!

The debutante, *very crumpled, remaking her chignon*: What will Maman say?

Alfred: I shall never forget!

The debutante: You'll think about me?

Alfred: In the most critical cases!

The debutante, *delicately*: But without criticism? Adieu, my king!

Alfred: Call me Alfred.

The debutante, *astonished*: Alfred?

Alfred, *triumphantly*: Yes, didn't you know that? Every day from two to five, at the back of the courtyard, in the entresol. Having only the service staircase to traverse, I'm quite at home here.

The debutante: I don't understand.

Alfred, *very gravely*: Enough chat. Here comes the old man, who has finished taking his bath.

The debutante: !!

Alfred: Duty before all . . .

The debutante: !!!

Alfred: I'm the pedicurist.

A JUNE NIGHT
(*La Presse*, 2 June 1897)

The moon's rays enter softly through the window of the high-ceilinged room. Down below, motionless branches extend veils of green silk, the clumps of odorous plants that are climbing the walls, exhaling an ardent breath, cause a kind of perfumed soul to float in the mysterious evening.

Yvonne has lifted the curtains; pensive, she gazes into the distance at the pale gleams that frost the foliage with a dream-like light. Yvonne is small, ageless, and pale, with a pitiable and morbid thinness. She has nothing womanly about her but an ardent and dolorous thirst for tenderness. She feels the immense need for abnegation that curbs Sisters of Charity over feverish couches, and she suffers from not being able to devote her paltry existence to a work of bounty and nobility. Very rich, she was married for her dowry. She knows that and does not bear a grudge.

Comte Etienne, her husband, let things proceed while his parents consulted physicians and weighed the fortune. Now, the humble amour that he had initially suffered indifferently has become a burden, and his cold gaze and curt words fall on to the enchained, humiliated and quivering heart of the wife, bruising it.

For a fortnight, a childhood friend, a relative devoid of birth and fortune, has been installed with Yvonne and has tried, by means of the cheerfulness of her character, her nice smile and the caress of her gaze to distract the invalid. Suzanne is all charm and youth, with her wavy hair, her dark blue eyes, in which the languor of temptations floats, and her fleshy mouth, as attractive as a fruit.

At first, Yvonne allowed herself to be vaguely rocked by that spring-like dream, that renewal of a voluptuous dream; she thought that she was rising up in the roses on the threshold of the tomb, and she shrugged the icy shroud of ennui from her shoulders. But the happy dreams faded away in tears. That very morning, the postman had handed her a letter, whose disguised handwriting, awkward in design, revealed the odious goal, the infamous intention.

That letter, which she has been rereading all day with sobs and somersaults of despair, has informed her that her husband has a mistress whom he loves enough openly to brave the opinion of society, and that the mistress in question is her relative, Suzanne, the friend who lives by her side, consoles her with her lying voice and embraces her with her criminal arms.

Yvonne is swollen with indignation and anger; she is thinking about the vengeance, which will not be difficult, for the lovers, encouraged by their impunity, scarcely hide. To the fury of the deceived wife is added the exasperation of a soulful elder sister, mocked and robbed, tricked by a child! What a bleak existence! What lies, succeeding other lies! What crumbled hopes! What anguish of expiring belief she is evoking in that deserted bedroom in which her pride of an abandoned woman is bleeding.

She tells herself that the comte has no fortune and that divorce, for him, would be inconvenience, almost penury. A bitter smile of triumph creases her lips, shining in the midst of her tears. Then that smile gradually pales and fades way. Her gaze is transported to a long mirror that reflects her from head to foot; she contemplates herself at length and shivers before the shadow of a shadow that the mirror sends back to her. In her livid face with pinched nostrils and prominent cheekbones the eyes alone are alive, strange and supernatural: eyes of desolation and prayer in which her bewildered soul is transparent. Her loose dress hides the cemetery of her ribs, but on her dangling hands, as fragile as those of a statuette, the delicate clasp of the bones stands out. Consumption, slowly pursuing its work, is extinguishing the body that can no longer defend itself.

Trembling, Yvonne returns to the window in order to try to distract her mind by means of contemplation, and she applies herself to the penetration of the mystery of the somnolent park. For a long time, avidly, she respires, inhaling the perfumed air full of the voluptuousness of plants. Nature is inundated with blue light, drowned in the tender charm of spring evenings. After the sun, the night star reigns over the earth, spreading a frosty sheet over the meadows, animating the pathways with the light course of its radiance, allowing its fluid tresses to hang down through the branches and drinking from the pond with pale lips that ripple the water. In the distance, a line of poplars snakes like the columns of a fantastic city and a fine white iridescent mist remains suspended around them, like a gigantic web on which the moon, a golden spider, seems to be climbing toward the stars.

Yvonne listens to the multitudinous sounds of the countryside, which, suddenly animated, vibrates and whispers vague and tender words; increasingly, she senses herself weakening under the ardent magnetism of things . . . the veil rips and she understands . . .

She understands that the world is banishing the frailty and sadness from her breast in order to continue eternally in its fecund and cruel splendor. By what right can she rise up against the immutable law that has governed us for so many centuries? Is it just that she should rebel, she who can neither be a lover not a mother? It is not on earth that she ought to seek the reason for her abandonment but in the eternal calm where the soul is liberated from all miseries and is transfigured gloriously . . .

Out there, under the vault of trees, trembling with gleaming mist, Etienne and Suzanne are walking side by side. They animate the motionless landscape that envelops them like an amorous flame made for their youth; the two of them appear to be a single being of strength and mildness. The splendor of the night covers them quite naturally, like a hyacinth and silver robe made for their royalty.

Yvonne remains standing, her arteries throbbing, in that atmosphere of felicity in which, over the ungraspable friction of plants, the trees extent their protective arms; in that languid alcove atmosphere in which the gleam of the stars presides over eternal kisses and eternal embraces . . .

From the flower-beds, the woods, the meadows, and the ponds, the hot breath arrives that sows over nature entire an ardent dust of fecundation.

The abandoned woman comprehends the cruel logic of terrestrial destinies; she thinks that her life is nothing in universal life and that she ought not to trouble the unconscious joy and harmony of things.

Then, as the enlaced couple of Etienne and Suzanne slowly come closer, she closes the window again gently and removes herself, submissively, from the field of amour in which she can neither sow nor reap.

A SERIOUS AMOUR
(*La Presse*, 18 June 1897)

The Following Day

My adored! How many caresses! How many embraces! And yet, my lips are thirsty for more kisses, my heart is avid for new transports! I would give ten years of my life for one night like the last one! Oh, my darling, love me as I love you, for such an amour must be the prelude to divine ecstasies! Repeat to yourself often that I belong to you until death! My eyes closed on my hectic dream, I see again all the little corners of your beauty: your pale hair, so fine, so fine that my fingers, in that golden distaff, seem to be spinning light; your voluptuous arms, your soft and firm breast . . . [*ten pages of varied and ardent citations*]. Thank you for the unforgettable infinite happiness! Thank you for the inexpressible delirium of my senses! To you, heart, body, soul, everything! To you, eternally!

René de Hyacinthe

A Month Later

My beloved! The more I see you the more adorable I find you! You are the amorous ideal, the ever exquisite and new woman who is able to vary her caresses as much as her dresses. Before, I did not know what tenderness was. Now, my sole occupation will be to think of you every moment of my life. I only want to be an emanation of your soul, a brightness of the luminous hearth that I contemplate! Oh, my Sylvie, when I am dead, take back and guard very preciously that miniature that you gave me, and which I am pressing to my lips at this moment. Later you will rediscover, on this portrait, a little of my passion, when I can no longer tell you, as today: "I love you! I love you! I love you!" Yes, death alone can separate me from you

René de Hyacinthe

Six months later

Château de Verjus

My Sylvie, what had happened to me is very annoying. I counted on taking the first train in order to come to embrace you, but a family of chimpanzees has fallen upon us at Verjus, escaped from the menagerie—about which it is necessary for me to say a few words to you. Thomas Pomaré, the eldest of the anthropmorphs, gained his immense fortune in flannel waistcoats, and his entire person is soft, flaccid, damp, greasy and dull, like flannel worn for too long. As for his wife, who is much taller, she is comically thin: no belly, no bosom, no back and hips made of cast iron. The face is gray and hairy with hair tending to green and a neck like the neck of a guitar . . .

Shall I tell you about Mademoiselle Joséphine Pomaré, the worthy product of that cruel coupling? Could my dear little Sylvie, so fine, so aristocratic, so perfect in all her poses, be interested in so much vulgarity? To say everything, Mademoiselle Pomaré does not resemble either Papa or Maman; she possesses big feet, big hands, a big nose cleaving through excessively narrow skin and a dirty apricot complexion. My heart sickens in witnessing the family dinner and I cannot help thinking of everything that I'm losing far from you. Will you, at least, stockpile kisses for me in order to compensate me for such a harsh privation?

René de Hyacinthe

Château de Verjus

Dear Sylvie, the Pomarés have definitely got a taste for the country. I shall end up reeking of flannel like the father and speaking in pidgin like the mother. Didn't she say, yesterday, on seeing her daughter's face grotesquely tumefied by mosquito bites, "that one could no longer take the fresh air in the evening in front of the perron because these were too many *insests*?" These things are not invented. You can imagine how I laughed. My poor mother is sick with it. Joséphine guzzles cream cheese and does crochet. She is odiously ridiculous. Sylvie, Sylvie, don't forget that your letters alone give me the courage to support such cruel proofs, and don't spare your ink or your paper.

René de Hyacinthe

Eight Months Later

Since my return, my dear Sylvie, you're no longer the same; you only have words of doubt and reproach in your mouth. Is it my fault if my parents have cut off my allowance for two months and imposed Verjus and the Pomarés on me? Your jealousy? It's me who ought to be jealous, for, after all, I don't know what has happened in my absence. The thought that you might have deceived me is frightfully painful. Oh, be careful . . .

Your friend, nevertheless,
René de Hyacinthe

It's over! I know everything! Don't ask me for details, I don't have the strength to give you any. Me, who loved you so much, who would have sacrificed my entire life to a single one of your desires! You'll never know what you have lost! During these none months of amour I have given you the best of myself, without ceasing for a minute to think about you. If circumstances stronger than my will have separated us, I've deplored it, believe me! Now, what have you done during that cruel ordeal? No, no, don't deny it; I know everything, I tell you. Everything, everything, everything! Adieu, Sylvie; I shall retain the memory of our too brief moments of intoxication in the solitude of my existence . . . Adieu, Sylvie . . . A Dieu! [*Here, three tears, expertly grouped.*]

René de Hyacinthe

Ten months later

Le Comte et la Comtesse d'Hyacinthe have the honor of informing you of the marriage of their son, Vicomte René d'Hyacinthe, with Mademoiselle Joséphine Pomaré.

A REVOLUTION
(*La Presse*, 23 June 1897)

Crespeline des Orgelets, one of the most ardent proponents of female emancipation, finished preparing her notes for the imminent conference of the Union of Mature Virgins, covering several pages with cabalistic signs destined to guide her in the labyrinth of her arguments, and, exhausted by that effort, fell into a feverish slumber . . .

Her ideas, vague at first, gradually became more precise, and she dreamed . . . she dreamed that all men had been put to death!

Women, having recognized that their worst enemies were precisely those who pretended to defend them, had finally risen up, and by gentle means, such as asphyxia or poison, had annihilated the stronger sex.

It is in vain that a few of the condemned might attempt to corrupt their guardians; the latter, indignant at having allowed themselves, for centuries, to be classed as inferior beings, intend to reign alone, administrating, voting, presiding, healing, perorating, duping, stealing, murdering and making war!

In truth, that great revolution did not happen all at once. The timid protested at first, while taking account of the prevailing injustices; but Crespeline des Orgelets appeared, and her vibrant speech awakened consciences.

After the men, all the children of the male sex were sacrificed, with the exception of the best-made and strongest, who were set apart and brought up carefully in order to preserve the race. In the most useful animal species, only the female is esteemed, for her intelligence, her mildness and the innumerable services that she never ceases to render; the sanguinary, capricious and encumbering male is immolated at the most tender age; henceforth, it would be the same for the human species.

And the execution took place!

The rare survivors were surrounded by delicate attentions; nothing was neglected to soften their fate. Only captivity and ignorance remained obligatory; the revolutionary ferment of the masculine mind only sought to break out at the slightest pretext. By way of compensation, they had fine wines, choice cigars, soft furnishings and padded cells.

After ten years of submission and exactitude, the prisoner was suppressed and replaced by an entirely new subject . . .

Other nations having followed the good example of France, the world finally knew long years of calm and prosperity. By virtue of the enormous diminution of the terrestrial population, there was no more poverty. The wealth that humankind had amassed, the great employment of machines, and the products obtained every day were amply sufficient to nourish all women.

The capital of cities, houses, fields, factories, systems of transportation and schools became common property instead of belonging to a few privileged individuals. All forces, combined, were applied to augment general wellbeing, to favor the study of the sciences and the cultivation of the arts. That happened simply and naturally, without false anarchist theories, without grand gestures and bombs, women always being just and disinterested.

There were amities and associations that nothing could trouble. Marriage, that baroque and vexatious institution, ceased to enchain the convicts of amour for life. Individuals loved purely and nobly, the ancient and unique cause of discord—men—no longer existing, except in the state of necessary exceptions. Carnal and unhealthy evocations were banished forever from literature and painting. The theater was metamorphosed. The crises of insipid adultery ceased to trouble public digestion, and the new art was finally found!

No more jealousy, treason or lies! Happiness expanded visages, pity reigned in the courts and the Society for the Protection of Animals no longer had any reason to exist. Silk, velvet and lace replaced the horrible suits of English tailors; sight was no longer troubled by the aggressive ugliness of top hats.

When a daughter was born it was a great subject of rejoicing for the mother and her friends; she was congratulated, embraced and fêted for weeks. When a boy came into the world, he was immediately sacrificed, unless he possessed a perfect vigor and beauty—in which case, he was destined for prison service.

Crespeline was triumphant! But Heaven, jealous of a felicity that it had not foreseen, sent a new microbe to earth, which attacked the captive males and was given a barbaric and terrifying name. The subjects suddenly etiolated and ceased to fulfill their mission, in spite of the most energetic remedies. In a short time, death scythed down the most remarkable livestock. Young newborns, it is true, were waiting in special establishments destined uniquely to favor their physical development; they were isolated from the contaminated prisons, but the most intelligent care did not succeed in preserving them.

Then the women, abandoned to their own resources, died without progeniture, and it was thus that the world ended.

Crespedline des Orgelets uttered a profound sigh and woke up. Her gaze, still blurred by the dream, wandered over the surrounding objects with an unspeakable terror.

Everything in her modest lodgings was, however, in its place. The same disorder combined, in a touching fraternity, the remains of her breakfast, her hat, her hairpins and the pages of her lecture. The stewpot simmering harmoniously in the kitchen spread the comforting scents of leeks and cabbages.

She pinched herself, and established that she really was alive.

But then, what had become of the prisoners—the pretty, obedient, dainty prisoners?

She got up, her heart filled with anguish, and opened the window in the hope of perceiving the male silhouette of her concierge.

The courtyard was empty, and abnormally neat. Père Rodrigue must have been sacked, as unfit for service. Unless the homicidal microbe . . .

The uncertainty became horrible.

Suddenly, a hoarse voice rose up to her, barking the latest news. "Demand *Le Prodigieux!* Five issues for a sou! Read about the frightful explosion of dynamite, with all the details! Six dead! Twenty-four wounded! Arrest of the guilty parties!"

Intoxicated by joy, Crespeline fell to her knees and put her hands together. There were still men on the earth!

LUCETTE
(*La Presse*, 12 July 1897)

The child, her gaze lowered over the necklace that she was sliding between her slender fingers, made no response.

"Who gave you that?"

"Oh, Papa," she said, finally, "it was at the Neuilly fair. As we were walking past the stalls, Madame Palmyre, the patronne, bought us all a little souvenir. It isn't gold, you know."

Reassured, the father did not persist.

Lucette put the necklace around her neck again, taking down a little mirror, and moved closer to the window in order to judge the effect that the jewel produced on her blonde skin. She had naïve blue eyes with shiny black pupils, round and dilated; her thin face, with the transparency of wax, had a delicate charm, and her long hair haloed her with fine gold.

When she could no longer hear her father's footsteps she put on her best dress, ornamented herself with a ribbon, and went downstairs. At the street corner Mére Brulot, the second-hand dealer with the profile of a screech-owl, interrogated her:

"Where are you going, Lucette?"

"I'm going to the store, Mère Brulot."

"But it's Sunday, Lucette."

"An urgent order. No time to lose."

"Well, child, would you like to sell me your necklace?"

Lucette shrugged her shoulders disdainfully and drew away without looking back.

The little girl has gone into a house of well-to-do appearance; she has climbed the stairs covered with a thick scarlet carpet, holding on to the banisters with a clenched hand. Her heart is beating rapidly; in spite of her decisive attitude, her courage is beginning to abandon her.

She has rung a bell on the first floor; the door opens and she finds herself in the presence of a black-clad valet, grave, clean-shaven and perfectly dressed, who introduces her into a drawing room and withdraws without saying a word. The vast room, surrounded by soft divans, is impregnated with an indefinable musky odor, as overwhelming as that of steam-baths in which human bodies are massaged. The little girl lets herself fall into a plush elastic armchair, which grips her gently, and she closes her eyes wearily.

Around her, engravings of the last century represent half-naked women surprised by gallant messieurs. Something suspect emanates from the walls, from the fabrics, from the exaggerated luxury, from everything.

A decorated old monsieur has approached the little girl and shown her a bag of bonbons in a pink ribbon. Through the door, which he has left open, a bed is visible, with a brocade awning, and behind it, a large bright patch gives the impression of a lake seen through a window; it is a discreet mirror that seems to be gazing at the couch, its accomplice . . .

✳

In the evening, Lucette is wearing a glass medallion suspended from a copper chain, but the indulgent father does not even interrogate her again. He spoils the child, whom he loves madly, in memory of his wife, who died the previous year, and also for her mildness and politeness. In any case, Lucette has only one fault: a taste for dresses and trinkets, which keep her immobile for long minutes before window displays. She clings obstinately to her chrysocolla ornament, and Mère Brulot, the old second-hand dealer with the screech-owl profile, asks her every morning:

"Hey, child, do you want to sell me your necklace?"

But Lucette shrugs her shoulders disdainfully and draws away without turning her head.

Now Mère Brulot, mocking, is with the workman.

"Monsieur Vincent, do you remember the bauble that Lucette lost a little while ago on the sidewalk. One is honest, isn't one?"

"This, Mère Brulot, is similar, a gift from the patronne."

"Indeed. Would you like a hundred francs for it right away?"

White with stupor, the workman does not reply.

"Don't look so disgusted. Didn't you know that the child goes with old men . . . ?"

But the old woman is already outside, her wrist clasped by iron fingers, and her clamors fill the staircase.

"Yes, old men!" she howls. "And she's not the only one! There are some even younger! If I wanted to talk . . . for sure they'd be able to catch them . . . it's a whole organized gang. And the police shut their eyes, you know, because they're high-ups . . . You can't do anything about it. And then, perhaps you profit from it . . ."

When Lucette comes back, her soul sad because of her lost chain, a cold hand slaps her in the dark, and she bumps into a black body that is swinging behind the door.

IN THE CARRIAGE
(*La Presse*, 20 July 1897)

Julien looked at his neighbor. She was a thin, pale brunette with large golden eyes drowned in amber. With her slender, ungloved hand she was leafing through a volume distractedly, but her gaze suddenly lifted, lost in the contemplation of the landscape.

They had been alone in the carriage for an hour, and, brought together by a kind of instinctive sympathy, they dared not speak as yet, searching for a pretext.

Perhaps deliberately, she dropped her book, and he bent down to pick it up.

"Verses," he said. "Do people still read verses?"

She smiled and, encouraged, he said: "You like them?"

"Very much."

"They console or they despair, but they often contain a great thought, delicately expressed. Only poets don't fear the ridicule of certain confessions; only poets still know how to believe and to love."

She did not reply. In a lower voice, he asked: "Are you going to see your family?"

"No."

"Friends, then? Forgive me if I'm indiscreet."

But she shook her head sadly. "I have no friends."

"What, at your age?"

She indicated her black garment. "I'm in mourning for my father, I no longer had anyone but him. He has left me without a fortune, and I obtained a position as a governess. It's necessary to live, isn't it?"

"You're going to join your pupil?"

"Yes, a girl of fifteen or sixteen, who won't need my lessons for very long. Her sister is going to marry soon, I'm told, and as there's a large fortune to divide between them, it's probable that there'll be no more lack of suitors for the second than there was for the first. Then I'll try to find a new place. It's my fate now, no longer to settle anywhere."

"And no one is interested in you?"

"No one."

He dared not interrogate her any further, and she lowered her head in discouragement.

The train was traveling rapidly. A fresh and powerful odor of aromatic herbs entered through the lowered window: the strong odor that plants spread at the end of the day, as penetrating as the scent of a body, like the sweat of green earth impregnated with perfumes that the soil emits, which evaporates in the passing wind. The meadows starred with buttercups and campions, the streams singing behind curtains of willows and, as tiny as playthings, the spotted cows with shiny muzzles lying in the lush grass, fled before their eyes. Then, in the distance the profound valleys, the hills glazed with pink and blue, like the throats of pigeons, closed the landscape.

Julien resumed speaking, without really knowing what he was saying, for the pleasure of feeling the gilded gaze of his companion upon him. She listened to him with a serious attention that flattered him, and ended up rendering him eloquent. Sometimes, she supported his reflections with an apt word, an intelligent and delicate remark.

Night was falling gradually, and he saw the white face of the young woman paling further against the faded gray of the cushions. He thought about his fiancée, whom he would soon see again: an insignificant blonde whom he scarcely loved, but whom he was taking without regret because she was rich and because his parents desired the marriage.

This one, certainly, was better. He felt mysteriously attracted to her, as toward a danger. It seemed to him that he had known her for a long time, that she was returning from a long voyage in order to save him, to defend him against himself. He was not sad and he was not joyful; he did not how to say what he felt; it was something that had suddenly hooked on to his soul and was troubling it delightfully. Did he love her already, then?

Amour substituted for long memories by virtue of a sort of magic.

They were talking now like two friends, recounting their future projects, their fears and their hopes. For a long time they told them like the beads of a precious rosary: the secret enthusiasms and secret tendernesses of their young hearts . . .

But the hours went by, and they were about to reach the end of their journey.

"We shan't see one another again," she said, with a hint of melancholy. "I'm going to try to earn my living, and you're going to get married. Let's forget these futile confidences."

"That's true; you're joining your pupil and I'm joining my fiancée. The idea of not seeing you again troubles me strangely. In a few moments we'll have arrived. At least give me your hand!"

"Oh, gladly."

But he drew her toward him, and for a moment he held her in his arms, sought her lips . . .

The train stopped. They got down, very gravely, like two strangers. Their gazes scarcely met one last time; they were about to separate forever . . .

A nondescript man of about fifty, red-faced, bald and replete, stopped them in passing.

"Bonsoir, Julien . . . Bonsoir, Mademoiselle . . . Come along, quickly . . . it's late, and my daughters are impatient.

And as the young people, astonished, remained motionless, he went on: "Oh, yes, you don't know one another. I haven't told you, my dear Julien, about the departure of the former governess of my younger daughter. Your fiancée will explain that to you; it's her who summoned Mademoiselle . . ."

Julien was in a daze; he had just understood that the strange encounter—hazard or fatality—was about to change his entire life.

THE GARDEN OF AMOUR
(*La Presse*, 8 August 1897)

Etienne marched straight ahead through the sunlit country-side. The slow hour was still chiming on the church clock with the quavering voice of an old man at prayer; dangling clumps of embalmed foliage and avalanches of roses buried the walls of the presbytery; bats were flapping their velvet wings silently in the warm and humid atmosphere, skimming the roofs, the casements and the well-head. They chased one another, fluttering madly, as if gripped by vertigo, drunk on amour. And everything seemed to be in love, swooning in indescribable celebrations: the great trees by the roadside, the distant hills, the earth and the sky.

Suddenly, from the music of the silence, sprang something akin to the sound of a crystal flute: the shrill lament of a nightingale. Its voice awoke the mocking joy of echoes, rising in savant trills, and dying away in sighs, vibrations of an infinite softness. And in the distance, scarcely perceptible in the mysterious foliage, in the enclosure of the dream of darkness, other nightingale songs responded. It was a fervent litany celebrating the renewal of beings and things, the delight of plants at the hour when the stars were circling like golden bees over the closed calyx of the earth.

Slowly, Etienne went on his way. He was happy, but his human happiness lacked a human vision, a cry of passion in the universal harmony.

Now, at a bend in the road, a garden appeared to him: a large garden filled with trees, in which he distinguished confused silhouettes, and invisible flowers that exhaled their souls of perfume behind the railings. There must be enchanted flower-beds there, an ocean of ardent corollas, but a cloud had veiled the moon and he no longer perceived anything but a bright patch under the branches.

The form became more precise; it was an amorous couple. He could not doubt it: two young people, tender and strong, whom the beautiful night had charmed and who believed themselves free in the sleeping countryside.

It is good, when people adore one another, to have a frame of solitude and silence around themselves. Behind the trees, a warm nest awaited them, a silky nest where freshly cut flowers would be reminiscent of the beautiful garden. They were holding one another by the waist, doubtless whispering the countless trivia that the heart finds for the heart, and have no meaning otherwise. They were holding one another tightly, so absorbed by their dream that they did not even hear the creaking of the sand.

And the traveler, as he advanced, thought about the fiancée that he would soon see again, the friend who was waiting for him and whom he loved as on the first day. For weeks he had been without news, but he had communicated with her mouth, and the sweetness of her kisses could not lie.

He recalled their last meeting, on the eve of departure; it was a night like this one. She told him about her profound and faithful love, and he had responded with such devotion and tenderness of the voice and the heart that she had thrown herself into his arms, sobbing. And while their lips mingled in an action of grace, the nightingales had intoned a triumphant hosanna, as they were doing now.

The lovers remained immobile. Etienne stopped in order not to trouble them. Yes, this garden was similar to the one he would soon see again, the one that she illuminated with the sunlight of her hair, the promise of her smile and the aurora of her blue eyes. She appeared to him, the delicate fiancée, in the veiled sanctuary of his memory, with the supple line of her body and the lilial clarity of her face and her hands. How sweet it would be to remain with her in the old provincial dwelling. Their similar days would not know autumns or winters, cares or weaknesses.

The future belongs to those who believe, happiness is always present. It is sufficient to see . . . Etienne is young, life will be clement, good and generous . . . it will keep all its promises . . .

A ray of moonlight glides over the beautiful garden. It is the cemetery. And what he has mistaken for an enlaced couple is only a tombstone a little higher than the rest. Two words still stand out under the moss by which it is corroded:

Here lies . . .

TAMER
(*La Presse*, 13 August 1897)

"Oh," said Maud, "I'd like so much to see blood flow."

She was very young, with calm bright eyes in a pale face, and her physiognomy had the disdainful assurance that beauty and money give. A governess, ageless and sexless, followed her meekly.

"To see blood flow!" Maud repeated.

The acrid odor of beasts stung the nostrils. A tamer had just entered a cage . . .

Around the two women were the usual public of menageries: the special public composed of socialites and workers in quest of distractions: simple but strong emotions. Men were amusing themselves by tormenting, with the tip of a cane, the nonchalance of crouching wild beasts; a laughing little girl was throwing almond shells and bread crusts at the monkeys. Bears were swaying persistently behind the railings; tigers and hyenas were looking at the visitors slyly. But everyone hastened to see the black panther perform. With her paws stretched out before her, her head erect and her emerald eyes motionless, she seemed indifferent to the cracks of the whip.

No patch starred her dark velvet fur, of a hue so profound and so mat that the light did not even raise a frisson of luster thereon. And the tamer, supple and brave, leaned over her, appealing to her in a curt voice.

"Ah!" said Maud, contemplating the indifferent beast scornfully. "Servitude has robbed it even of the idea of revolt.

Everything will happen as usual. What's the point of that ridiculous parade?"

"However," the governess objected, "that panther has already wounded two men. Look how big and strong she is, Mademoiselle."

Maud smiled and her imperious gaze fixed upon that of the tamer, descending into him as if into a mysterious well, and made all the fibers of his being shudder. He went pale, and the fearful expression of his features revealed that he was conscious of her desire. His will capsized in that of the enemy he did not know, he lost the personality of his free and thinking self.

"Coward!" murmured Maud, so quietly that only he heard it.

Meanwhile, the panther seemed to sink further and further into her rigid immobility, and, like a cat dazzled by the light, she extinguished beneath her weary eyelids the double star of her metallic eyes. The unknown woman standing before her cage resembled a human panther more implacable than the imprisoned wild beast.

"Coward!" repeated Maud, and, with the golden shaft of her umbrella, she struck the muzzle of the beast, which only made a single bound and launched herself upon the disarmed man. The two bodies rolled, embracing and biting, amid gasps and roars. Women fainted, while the employees, armed with pitchforks and iron bars, hastened to the bars.

Maud detached the pearl necklace that she was wearing around her neck and held it out to the tamer, who had been pulled out, quivering, from the cage.

"To remember me by," she said.

ON THE BEACH
(*La Presse*, 21 August 1897)

Pierre and Marthe had hired a boat for an excursion at sea. In the distance, the beach at Trouville was reminiscent of a flowery garden. On the great yellow sand dune, from the jetty to the Roches Noires, shiny umbrellas, bright dresses and beribboned hats resembled splendid flowers on a golden meadow; and confused voices threaded in the pure air—appeals, cries of children and laughter, made a slight rumor that passed with the breeze.

Marthe was blonde with gray eyes and a cloud of strands of hair fluttering around her delicate face. He was as blond as her, tall, slim and elegant.

Since the departure she had abandoned herself entirely to that soft glide over the calm green water. She was not thinking, was not stirring any memory or hope; it seemed to her that her mind was floating, like her body, on something fluid and delightful, which was rocking her. Her entire amorous past retreated into the mist. Nothing existed any longer but the present moment.

"What are you thinking about, Marthe?" he asked, tenderly, leaning toward the young woman.

"Nothing, I'm happy."

"Really? You've forgotten that man who made you weep so much?"

"Yes."

"You're never going to see him again?"

"Never."

"Could you love me a little? Only a little? Oh, tell me . . ."

"Yes, my friend, I love you. It seems to me that I've had a bad dream. Certainly, it was only a dream . . ."

They returned slowly toward the shore, and he took her hand, which she did not withdraw. At intervals, the red sail of a heavy fishing boat, immobile on the sea, resembled a rock projecting from the water. Suddenly, he made a sharper movement. Long and low, with two yellow paddle-wheels and two chimneys inclined backwards, a boat laden with passengers was arriving at full steam. Its rapid wheels were beating the water noisily, which fell back in foam, and the straight prow cut the water into thin slices, which ran along its sides. A man on the steamboat was gazing at them curiously.

Marthe paled and turned away.

"Is it him?" asked Pierre.

"I don't know. What does it matter?"

"Let's depart, shall we? Let's depart this evening."

She responded, mildly: "What are you afraid of, Pierre? Since I only love you!"

"You swear it?"

"I swear it."

Now the waltz is drawing the couples beneath the harsh electric light, in a flutter of light skirts. Slender waists undulate to the rhythms of the voluptuous orchestra. On the benches, young men take their places next to their dancing-partners, gazing into their eyes, speaking to them with their mouths close to their mouths, caressing them with their voices and desire.

In a corner, Pierre observes sadly. It seems to him that the vast beach, with its hotels and its casino, is nothing but a hall of amour in which all the women have only one thought: to offer their flesh, already given, already sold, already promised or taken back. They are agitating to please, seduce and tempt someone. They are making themselves beautiful for today's elect and that of tomorrow, for the stranger encountered, remarked and perhaps awaited.

Marthe goes back and forth on the arm of her former lover. Her eyelids flutter in the ecstasy of the dream, a happy smile parting her lips. As in the boat, she murmurs in a fractured voice, in a voice into which her entire unconscious soul passes, tender and deceptive:

"I love you! I love you! I've never loved anyone but you!"

Like a madman, Pierre has fled on to the strand. His throat contracts in a sob, his hands tense in a desire for murder.

On the profound water, the limitless water, darker than the sky, multicolored stars run into the distance. They are the lights of moving boats in search of a mooring. And up above, the moon, which is rising, resembles a divine lighthouse illuminated in the firmament in order to guide the infinite light of the stars.

Before the mysterious immensity of the waves and the heavens, Pierre thinks bitterly that a human amour is a very little thing, and that men are quite despicable for suffering so much.

FISHING
(*La Presse*, 28 August 1897)

During the fortnight that he had been staying in the Dhervillys' elegant villa on the edge of the sea, Jacques had been wondering whether he ought to marry the eldest of their daughters. Every time he saw the cheerful and lively brunette Louise he decided to make her his wife, but then, as soon as he found himself alone, further hesitations paralyzed his will. She was richer than him, possessing beautiful farms in Normandy with lush meadows and apple orchards. His family desired the union and there was no impediment on either side.

That day, watching the two young women walking in front of him, he thought: *Come on, it's necessary that I speak; I won't find anything better.*

His gaze thoughtful, Jacques saw fleeing before him the frail figure of Renée, the supple hips of Louise, and the large hats of white gauze that danced in the light. His desire, suddenly activated, impelled him to the decisive resolutions that grip the hesitant and the timid abruptly.

The warm odor of grass, gorse and clover mingled with the marine scent of the rocks, intoxicating him mildly, and truly felt amour in his heart for the beautiful, provocative and cheerful young woman. Renée, on the contrary, discouraged him because of her mutism and the melancholy of her large dark eyes. He only accorded her a distracted attention, did not pause to scrutinize her soul, had never even examined her closely.

After walking for half an hour, the young woman stopped and sat down on the sand.

"Continue your walk," she said, with a pale smile. "I'm tired today." She turned away, her eyes fleeing Jacques' gaze.

Although secretly satisfied with the tête-à-tête that was being contrived for him, he insisted politely: "Come on, a little effort; your sister will sustain you."

"No, I don't want to."

Her voice trembled, a fog of sadness drowned her delicate face, but the lovers paid no heed to it and continued their route.

A narrow path descended along the cliff and was lost in the sand. They started to run in order to reach the rocks, which extended over a long surface covered with thick grass, in which innumerable pools of water shone. The sea undulated in the distance, behind the sticky gray plain of wrack.

Jacques tucked up his trousers above the calf and extended his net to catch shrimps. Mademoiselle Dhervilly, laughing, tucked up her skirts and leaned over a profound fissure in which pink and green tresses floated, which seemed to be swimming,

"Look, look—I can see three big ones at the very bottom!"

The three animals were already in the net, and Louise, pinching the tapering end of their tail between her fingers, slid them into her basket. She was adroit and cunning, with the necessary hunter's flair. Jacques did not catch anything, but he followed her meekly, brushing her, impregnating himself with her perfume.

Abruptly, he declared himself: "Would you like to be my wife, Louise?"

And as she had anticipated that confession, she let her little wet hand fall into the young man's hand. That calmness surprised him. He had expected blushes, refusals that said yes, an entire coquettish comedy of tenderness . . . And it was over; he felt bound, married, in a few banal, almost involuntary words. They were standing face to face, examining one another curiously, no longer knowing what to say.

Finally, he murmured: "Thank you; I'm very happy."

When they returned they found Renée lying in the sand with her handkerchief over her lips. The setting sun covered the whiteness of her neck delicately and put tawny reflections in her hair. She got up; her dark eyes had only one gaze and were dolorously veiled. She had understood . . .

He had also understood, and with clarity; a furious despair entered his heart, for he sensed now that it was not the other, but this one, that he loved.

THE DEPARTURE
(*La Presse*, 7 September 1897)

Jean was about to depart. His first emotion was that of someone condemned to death to whom a commutation of his sentence had been announced; he felt his torture slightly lessened by the thought of the distant journey over the waves, the exile from which he might never return. Oh, if only the old man could change his soul and metamorphose, like the water, the sky and the shore as the wandering great ship passed by!

He thought that the last rent had been made, that he no longer had anything to hold on to, since Suzanne did not love him and was marrying someone else. However, in his hours of struggle, he had never felt plunged like this into a cloaca of misery. It was no longer an obsessive mental pain, but the madness of a beast devoid of shelter, the anguish of a lost individual who no longer has a roof, and whom all the brutal forces in the world come to assail.

On setting foot on the steamer and going into the cabin rocked by the waves, a more profound distress had drowned his heart. Then, his aggressive and vengeful dolor wearied; he no longer blamed Suzanne for her treason. What was the point? Was she not similar to all the women he had known? Ought he to charge her with a crime for having preferred to his amour the luxury that would make her more beautiful and happier? He had deceived himself, that was all, and his torture was merited. His revolt was going downstream, like his existence. He was weary of struggling, striking, detesting; he tried to numb his reason in forgetfulness, as one falls asleep.

Flight! Flight! Flight or death . . . later, if his wound remained incurable.

The boat train arrived at the quay, bringing travelers from Paris. Jean wandered around the ship in the midst of those busy, anxious people searching for their cabins, calling to one another, questioning one another, responding at hazard, in the bustle of the commencing voyage.

The immense steamer emerged slowly from the harbor, drawn by a powerful tug, and the people of Le Havre, massed on the sea-walls on the beach and in the windows, acclaimed its departure. As soon as the ship had passed through the narrow passage enclosed between two granite walls, however, finally feeling free, it departed under its own steam like an enormous monster running over the water. It drew away at top speed after its emergence from the port, in beautiful clear weather, and from the shore it soon seemed very small, as if it had dissolved in the Ocean.

On that vessel, which nothing could stop, Jean felt once again that he was dying of anguish. He had a desire to talk to the strangers who were rubbing shoulders with him, to tell them his troubles, in order to be listened to and consoled. He had, deep down, a shameful need, like a pauper holding out his hand, an irresistible need to feel someone suffering his pain. No one turned round toward his misery; he remained desperately alone, and it seemed to him that his whole wounded heart had remained back there, on the shore that he might never see again.

He made an effort and went into the lounge, where a few passengers were already asleep in the corners. It was in that vast floating cosmopolitan hall that well-to-do people of all continents would live in common. Its garish luxury resembled that of large hotels, theaters and all the public places in the world where money was not counted.

Suddenly, a frisson ran from his head to his feet and his blood was chilled. A woman he had not yet seen was weeping silently to one side. He approached her and murmured, with an unspeakable emotion: "Suzanne!"

Immediately, she uncovered her pale face.

"Yes, it's me."

"Suzanne! Suzanne!"

She wiped her eyes and looked at him, all the way to the depths of his soul.

"How could you believe that I loved another, or that I would give myself for a little gold? Undeceive yourself; I have come, in spite of my relatives, in spite of society, in spite of everything . . . and I'm departing with you! And we'll no longer quit one another. And you'll make of me whatever you please . . . speak . . . speak . . . do you want to?"

With a cry of supreme joy he took her in his arms and the long martyrdom was forgotten.

THE EYES
(*La Presse*, 23 September 1897)

Having landed on the island, the stranger found himself in the midst of the women, who had been lying in wait for him for some time. As he was handsome, they made a fuss of him and adorned themselves with their finest jewels in order to please him. He was surprised to see that they resembled one another strangely in their voluptuous grace, and that they all had ardent and curious eyes, which desire caused to vacillate. And those large eyes with changing hues, eyes in which the enchantment of the sea, the sky and the abyss revived, fluid eyes sown with unknown gems, searched his heart and anguished him with their obsessive pursuit. Their fire penetrated him; he absorbed the burn with a kind of unhealthy voluptuousness. At the same time, the voices clarified, melting into a faint vibration of harps, a tender and seductive lament, in order to vanquish his last resistance.

A blonde approached, svelte, supple and haughty, like the mystic virgins who lean backwards in efflorescences of lilies in old stained-glass windows. She had eyes as profound and vague as the mists of summer evenings.

"Do you want me?" she said.

Her mouth was offered but her eyes remained fixed and dull in their deceptive languor, and he recoiled before that glaucous gaze, in which the mystery of waves and virgin immensities took fright.

A brunette emerged from the ranks.

"Is it me that you will choose?"

Her unfastened hair fell over her cheeks and her gleaming, staring eyes were as disquieting as beacons in darkness. She extended her arms, offering the polished roundness of her breasts, but her eyes, before being veiled by the intoxication of a dream, had a glimmer of hatred. He was afraid of their menace and refused.

Then a gamine with golden eyes started laughing. She showed, against her white skin, a fleshy, flavorsome mouth, and in her rutilant fleece with coppery reflections, a red rose was shedding its petals one by one, like a murderous flower.

"I'd love you well," she said.

She rubbed against him like a fond cat, but her gaze, like that of felines, seemed to be lined by a metal sheet.

"No, no," he said, again.

Others presented themselves, brunette, blonde and red-haired, frail or robust, aggressive or timid, cheerful or grave. And before the spell-casting eyes of those young women, as beautiful as temptation and sin, who had in their attitudes the undulating grace of reeds and young shrubs, and in their voices the deceptive plaint of waves and the wind, he understood that they were all deceptive and that he would never know the divine sensuality of confidence. Tears moistened his cheeks and he trembled like a child abandoned all alone in darkness. And yet, the large eyes were as radiant as a sky florid with stars, the lips smiled, and the arms opened for the embrace and the caress. He had only to choose from the regal flock . . .

All those gazes became animated, radiant with their deadly gazes. They unhinged and maddened him, making him ill. But he did not have the strength to flee them and continued to absorb the malevolent gleam throughout his being, with a morbid pleasure.

Finally, he uttered a cry of joy. In the last rank of the crowd, a young woman was holding the arm of a child. Her heavy eyelids fell over her gaze, and only the silky border of their golden lashes was visible.

"She's the one I want," he said, after a moment of profound emotion.

All the women uttered an exclamation: "But she's blind!"

And he said, sadly: "I want her . . . because I shall never see in her eyes the lie of amour."

CLAUDIE
(*La Presse*, 24 October 1897)

The countryside is somnolent in the crimson and gold of the sunset, which puts a last frisson of life over the large silent pond, starring the autumnal rust of the trees with light gleams. A gentle breeze wanders in the roadway, bringing the feverish soul of shredded roses with the sylvan perfumes of lavender and marjoram. A fine mist rises from the earth; a hoarse breath emerges from the stables and the pig-sties, with the panting grunts of sleeping and sated beasts. The voice of cicadas in the warm grass resembles the voice of gentle waves upon shingle.

Claudie, hoisted on to the wall of the farm, her legs dangling, is gazing at the setting sun. She is dazzling in youth and strength, with her clear complexion, her unkempt hair, in which the last rays have taken hold like a spider web, and her avid mouth.

"Bonsoir, Claudie!"

"Bonsoir, Dominique!"

A moue of discontentment darkens Claudie's features, and it is with constraint that she has put her hand in that of the young man.

Without being put off, he has jumped on to the wall and is sitting next to her in the moss and the ivy. Their harmonious silhouettes are outlined against the crimson sky; they complete the landscape, seemingly made to live in that calm and healthy nature with the trees, the plants and the birds.

"When is the marriage, Claudie?"

She has closed her eyes, and her thoughts seem to be following a mysterious dream, which she does not betray. Anxiously, he has leaned toward her and has slid his arm around her waist in order to draw her closer.

"When?" he repeats, in a lower voice, with a suppliant and tender intonation. "You know that I have some property, and will have more later? By working hard, we certainly won't be the least in the neighborhood. Your father said yes a long time ago, and we're only waiting for your pleasure. Do you want to? Respond, Claudie! I love you dearly . . . as much as one can love, I think. You wouldn't be unhappy."

"Yes, Dominique, I wouldn't be unhappy."

"The farm is poorly cultivated, it can be made to yield more, but your father is too old, too bowed down by dolors. We'll make meadows, fields, vines. With courage, we'll get out of difficulty. Your people have struggled like us. You've been raised in a hard school, and you're familiar with poverty."

"Yes, Dominique, I'm familiar with poverty."

"In spite of everything, there are good days, days of repose and celebration when you'll dress up a little to show your beauty. And also think that a child might be born, a dainty pink and white child that you can bounce on your knees with laughter and caresses. How you'd love him, Claudie! How well you'd be between the two of us! How good life would be!"

"Yes, Dominique, life would be good."

"Then . . . you say yes?"

And the young man, in a surge of tenderness, has taken Claudie against his heart, has covered her forehead and cheeks with kisses, has hidden his face in the tawny fleece of her hair.

But she pulls away.

"No, I'll never be yours. I'm leaving, and you'll never see me again, and you'll never hear any mention of me."

He fixes her with a gaze full of fear and distress.

"Where are you going?"

"How do I know? Into the unknown, toward good or evil, to the great city where girls like me go who want to know everything and possess everything."

"You're going to the big city, to that inferno of lies and vice! You're going toward the enemy who exploits us, scorns us and kills us! But you'll perish like the rest, Claudie, you'll perish in shame and misery! What do you hope for, then?"

And she, in her disquieting nonchalance of a young she-wolf: "To avenge you, perhaps."

THE WILD BOAR
(*La Presse*, 17 November 1897)

Ludovic, however, wanted to put an end to it.

The season of hunts was beginning and his, very much in fashion, were justly renowned. He sent an invitation to the Comte de Farges, who was careful not to refuse.

At Valembois, the unleashed dogs ran over trails, giving voice, rushing in pursuit of foxes and wild boar. In the countryside, frosted with mauve by the autumnal mists, the sadness of agonies took on more acuity; a wind of murder passed through the desolate branches of the oaks. Along the russet avenues the somber leaves swirled, the air carrying more penetrating and more acrid odors.

Ludovic accompanied his beaters, disposed the relays and organized everything personally, until dawn.

When Lauriane de Farges appeared with her father the horns sounded and the signal to depart was immediately given, for they were the only ones awaited. A wild boar, flushed out and running, was followed by the dogs through the ferns, and the horses started to gallop, carrying the horsemen and horsewomen along mossy paths, while the carriages accompanying the hunt at a distance rolled more slowly along the gray road.

Lauriane's father, as if by chance, retained his horse and allowed himself to be outdistanced by the young woman and Ludovic.

Lauriane, straight in the saddle, pale and slender, was listening simultaneously to the slightly breathless voice of her cavalier and the song of the horns, mingled with the barking of the pack, which was drawing away.

"Yes," said the Seigneur de Valombois, "this solitary life weighs upon me. In the evening, the empty house makes me think of everything that we don't see, everything that lies in wait for us in the shadows; about mournings, rancors, treasons and the vague hostility of things . . ."

As she did not respond, he added: "I've spent without counting; I've wanted to know everything and I'm weary of everything. A lovely young woman like you would be very welcome here. What do you think of this domain, Mademoiselle?"

Lauriane thought that Ludovic was rich, and that she possessed nothing. But a glance cast covertly at her companion caused her to judge that the sacrifice was beyond her strength. She also felt slightly offended, without knowing why. It seemed to her that this was not the way that he ought to be expressing himself. The request was too brutal and too cold. A kind of susceptibility protested within her, a susceptibility that did not come from her pride but from an overly delicate sentiment of nuances.

With an effort, she said: "Let's rejoin the hunt, shall we?"

He whipped the flank of his horse, which departed at a fast gallop. They went thus through the trees, sometimes leaping over some trivial obstacle. The tumult of the hunt drew nearer. The bushes seemed to quiver. Suddenly, breaking branches, covered with blood, shaking the dogs that were clinging to it, the wild boar went past.

Ludovic, who was an audacious fellow, disappeared into the thicket uttering a cry of victory, and when Lauriane arrived, a few moments later, curious and fearful, he stood up again, his garments in tatters and his hands bloody, while the beast, a knife plunged to the hilt in its shoulder, was gasping in front of him.

The young woman quivered in admiration, and a kind of veil passed before her eyes.

The curée was made by torchlight under the noisy flutter of the last leaves. The flames of the torches rose up, crackling, yellowing in the lunar radiance, and resinous smoke caught in the throat.

The beaters and the gentlemen hunters, in a circle around the curée, sounded the horn frenetically, while the howling and ferocious pack fought over the entrails.

The savage clamor rose above the woods, repeated by the echoes of distant clearings, awakening the mysterious beasts of the shadows. Nocturnal birds skimmed the branches in their hectic flight, and the troubled women also felt, in that décor, their thoughts reeling and struggling.

Now Ludovic and Lauriane were going at a walking pace through pathways felted with dead leaves. He looked at her, so frail and charming, her knee folded over the mane of her mare, still vibrant with emotion. Without speaking, he put his arm around her waist, and drew her toward him slightly. The complicit night made him romantic, seductive and passionate . . .

The young woman closed her eyes, intoxicated by the open air and delectable dread; her lips did not slip away.

And it was thus that Lauriane de Farges became the wife of the Seigneur de Valombois, whom she did not love and whom she deceived frightfully.

THE ACCIDENT
(*La Presse*, 27 November 1897)

In her large bedroom hung with white satin Claire straightened up, shivering. Passers-by were assembling at the door of the town house, and the domestics were agitating in the corridor, as if to announce some misfortune.

What had happened, then?

She dared not approach the window to part the curtains; an anguish paralyzed her, gripping her heart. Finally, she made an effort and advanced on to the landing, but she had no sooner seen and understood than she recoiled, crying out.

With infinite precaution, and stopping at every step, men were climbing the stairway, sustaining in their arms an inert body, dislocated and crushed, covered in dust and blood, large red drops of which were wrung from garments, making a murderous trail on the blue carpet.

"Dead? Dead?" demanded Claire.

The *valet de chambre* replied, hesitantly: "We don't know, Madame. Perhaps Monsieur has only lost consciousness."

"What has happened to him? Speak . . . speak, quickly!"

"He's just been brought back . . . an accident . . ."

The young woman was sobbing.

"He wasn't cured! Why was he allowed to go out?"

Gently, Claude was laid on the silky bed, and a physician examined the wound in his chest, from which the thick blood was only emerging drop by drop, as if regretfully. The wounded man's eyes were revulsed, his mouth open in a sigh of agony, and a final spasm ran through his flesh.

"Well?" demanded Claire, going pale.

The physician turned round, hiding his red fingers.

"Courage, Madame."

She understood, and let herself fall to her knees. Sobs lifted her shoulders convulsively; a cold sweat moistened her body; words rose to her lips, mingling names with explosions of despair.

She was left alone, and the crisis gradually died down. She had no chagrin, but only a frightful anguish, a kind of remorse that tore and crushed her. It was over, then? The man that she had unconsciously martyrized with her disdain would no longer stand before her with the painful exigency of his tenderness; she would no longer have to play the odious comedy of affection and gratitude.

She recalled the tormented visage of her husband, his pale lips always avid for kisses and the somber fire of his gaze, which dilated in a morbid expression of covetousness. She had only ever ceded while trembling when his feverish hands, placed on her body, had passed from caress to brutalization. All her vague virginal desires had suddenly disappeared, leaving nothing but a singular physical coldness, an increasing repulsion that chilled her limbs dolorously. Her forehead had turned away from Claude's burning forehead, her eyes obstinately closed, her loins stiffening under the embrace. From the realities of amour that he had taught her, a mortal foam of disgust had risen, and all her rancor of disappointment had been concentrated on that man. His presence had been so painful that she had wanted to flee with the first comer, abandoning forever the sumptuous dwelling that he had given her, with her clothes and jewels, all the superfluities of the devoted luxury with which he heaped her.

He divined in her, at the slightest touch, an almost insurmountable shame. In the tragic silence of their days, an increasingly profound abyss was hollowed out between them, distancing them from tender confidences and the exquisite communion of the body and mind that is the whole of existence for the privileged. They mourned their inaptitude to understand one another; they were only conscious of the terrible fatality of human amour and the certainty that a malevolent will was driving them and playing with them.

And Claude, already ill, had no longer reacted, had let himself go to the ravages of obsession and hypochondria.

She did not find herself culpable, having done what was in her power to reduce his revolted nerves.

No, it was over, never again would he approach his mouth to hers, never again would she feel the heavy burn of his body against her. It was over!

Claire's eyes interrogated the face of the dead man avidly, and in that unrecognizable face with pinched nostrils and twisted lips she sought an expression of malediction, a supreme accusation hurled from beyond the tomb at the ingrate woman who had had no amour, nor any pity.

And she recalled words spoken by Claude, who allowed himself to be a little more downcast every morning by the sickness of living.

The fits of spleen had become gradually more frequent. Chagrin accomplished, surely and terribly, the long destruction of his physical and mental being. And she had loved another, who did not love her but who had tamed her with the brutal and scornful force of conquerors; another, who had insulted her in his desires, in his actions and in his speech. She had loved him uniquely, jealously, passionately, for his vices as for his disdain. And it was of that, undoubtedly, that Claude had died, after an anonymous denunciation.

Accident, they said? Accident, or suicide?

And she sobbed uncontrollably at the thought that she would never know, and that perhaps a malediction from beyond the grave would poison all her joys.

A MADMAN
(*La Presse*, 8 December 1897)

Claude could not dissimulate from himself that his family had always shown a sort of coldness, almost repulsion, in his regard; that even his mother, so weak and so tender, had always kept him at a distance with a singular persistence. Even when she held him in her arms, he sensed that her caresses were not exempt from a certain dread, that they did not have the spontaneity of his own caresses. It was to that involuntary repulsion in the sentiments of others that he owed always having felt the isolation and the sadness of his long hours of reverie.

For a long time he turned over in his head the question that preoccupied him, for he sensed that his future might depend on the response that would be made to it. It was during recreation that he decided to interrogate another, a collegian like himself, and knew that, without deploying a great deal of skill, he had to succeed in confessing that tall, egotistical and loquacious fellow.

But the cries of comrades, their noisy gaiety, took away the courage of any effort. That became a veritable anguish, sudden and unexpected. Confusedly, he suffered from having so many painful things to stir, when everything around him respired youth and insouciance. He found his reflections discordant with the ambient spirit, and pitied himself for being so scantly of his age, for having such dolorous preoccupations.

"There's my Claude in the clouds again!" said André, imitating his friend's vague gaze, in which thought, turned inwards, was disinterested in things. "Come on, old man, return to yourself! You'll prove your enemies' predictions right."

"What predictions?"

André, fearing that he had said too much, bit his lip and talked about less dangerous subjects. He was not a malevolent fellow, that André. He was too amiable to do anyone any harm, fearing to sense a reprisal. By virtue of his extreme lightness, however, he was bound, in a moment of boastful or angry expansion, to reveal everything he knew about Claude's unhappiness. It was in consequence of an assignment confided to the latter and voluntarily forgotten, that the thunderbolt burst.

"Why didn't you work for me today?"

"Because I didn't have the courage . . . I'm suffering, devoid of energy."

"Oh, truly? And I have to have it for you! I have to defend you in all the scuffles, to take your part against the comrades' attacks . . ."

"Don't take that trouble any longer. If I'm not strong enough to defend myself, I'll allow myself to be beaten to death. What does it matter to me?"

"Then you'll give more and more reason to what they say . . ."

"What do they say?"

"Oh, well, it doesn't concern me; but, as you'll learn sooner of later, I'm only anticipating events. And then, that way, you'll watch yourself, you'll try not to give purchase to malevolence and suppositions."

"What suppositions? Come on André, I beg you, explain yourself. Don't leave me any longer in the anguish of indecision. Whatever you tell me, I can't be any more unhappy."

"It's that . . . it's very difficult . . . I don't know where to begin."

"Well, I'll help you. One word, only, to put me on the track. I'm puny, I know; sad, concentrated . . . but I try, by my efforts and my application to study, to redeem my faults. In spite of everything, I find nothing but indifference or hatred. Even Maman is uninterested in me . . . I haven't seen her for more than a year. That does me so much harm. For what do people reproach me? My God, what have I done?"

André was not wicked, he merely liked to toy with the dolor of others.

"What a funny head you have" he went on, laughing brightly and frankly. "Don't turn your brain upside down, old man! That would spoil your affairs utterly. Madame your Maman doesn't come to see you because she's afraid of you."

"Afraid of me?"

"Listen: the son of a madman who has tried to kill her isn't very reassuring . . ."

"A madman . . . ! Mad! My father was mad? André, don't deceive me!"

A flash passed through Claude's eyes, a flash so terrible that his comrade became very serious again.

"I never lie," he murmured, annoyed. "I'm assured that your father was mad. I'm only repeating the rumors that are going round."

"Oh, the wretches!" sobbed the child, raising his arms in a gesture of malediction and rage. "So that's the explanation of all the infamous jokes of which I've been the object! Is that my fault? Is there any shame in that?"

Claude held back his tears. It would have cost him to show his suffering to that stranger who had just broken his heart, and taken away his joy and security forever. He sensed that the completion of his despair would only be one more subject of mocking amusement for that laughing schoolboy, that the flame shining slyly in his brown eyes came from curiosity rather than interest.

How lugubrious for poor Claude were the hours that followed! Thus, it was true, he would carry the hereditary stain forever, his existence could only by haunted miserably by memories and apprehensions. He could not marry . . . no. The happiness of companionship would be refused to him. He did not want to become the root of misfortune, to perpetuate the curse of his race.

He did not appear in the refectory; in the dormitory, his bed remained empty. It was not until the following morning that the little boys, playing in a courtyard, found him hanging from the strongest branch of a chestnut tree, his stiff body swinging in the meager foliage.

THE LAST ROSES
(*La Presse*, 19 December 1897)

In the little garden all bathed in pale light, the shrubs design their frail skeletons, still covered with a few shreds of gold, in the autumnal night. An odor of apples, mint and dry leaves floats in the air; on the walls, the last roses are losing their tender petals, of a delicate white of agonizing flowers. It is warm; a kind of caressant soul is passing over things.

"Look, Colette, see how pretty it is!"

Climbing up a ladder, Dominique is cutting roses and throwing them down to his companion, who is holding out her skirt and laughing.

"That's enough, Dominique. Where do you expect me to put them?"

"You can make a big bouquet with them for your bedroom. There won't be any more next week. In any case, in a week you'll be far away."

"Yes, we're returning to Paris."

"How bored I'm going to be!"

"You'll work hard in order to come to Paris in your turn, to choose a career."

Dominique, scarcely any older than Colette, had been a precocious and charming child. One would have said that all the affective faculties and all the exaltations of thought had developed in him. Timid, and slightly unhealthy, he did not like his companions' games and preferred to take refuge with the girls, who teased him more gently, with mild scolding and name-calling. Idly, his soul still torpid, he did not want to emerge from that restful fog. He liked women, whom he divined to be fearful and timid beings, like him, very close to nature but also to charity, pity and devotion. He felt attached to them already by the need for expansion that quivered within him. He sought the mercy of their extended arms and seductive eyes,

Every year, during the vacation, he saw Colette again, a genteel Parisienne attracted invincibly by the little corner of flowery verdure, and then, his happiness knew no bounds.

How had he got to know her? Quite simply: one morning, after one of the bouts of illness that suddenly afflict children without cause, he had perceived on opening his eyes a child's head leaning over him. It was a joyful little girl, and his first movement had been to extend his arms to her. He could not weary of admiring her delicate features, aureoled by hair floating in the light. Without knowing her yet, he was grateful to her for her beauty, her smile, and the tender charm that she brought to his awakening.

Dominique's recovery had been fairly rapid. After a few days he was able to walk in the garden, and Colette came to take him by the hand in order to take him on a tour of the flower-beds. He awaited her coming with a delectable anguish, and when he finally perceived her he was faint with excitement. But she scolded him for being so feeble.

"You'll never be completely cured, then? What do you lack? Personally, I've never been ill."

He lowered his head in confusion, without responding, The presence of the little girl was his entire life now. He fixed his wide-eyed, slightly feverish gaze upon her, and when she went away he remained motionless for hours, becalmed in the memory of her.

They had grown up almost without perceiving it, and had ceased to be children. Colette, now in the flower of her spring, was charming, with her aquamarine eyes, in which magic was legible, and the splendor of her hair, in which there were flames, amber and honey. During the winter months, Dominique saw her again in dreams, in the glory of her lily-white dresses, with an enigmatic smile on her lips, already ripe for kissing. He did not scrutinize the secret contours of her shoulders or her hips, but he caressed her soul divinely with a young amour that he sensed palpitating within him like a bird in the sunlight.

This evening he was picking roses, and it was the moment of separation.

Standing on his ladder, Dominique turned round in order to contemplate his friend in the moonlight. He could not get a grip on himself; it was like an ecstasy, an ecstasy similar to that of the nearness of God that young priests experience.

He believed in her; he felt strong in his faith, as in armor, and all the rest no longer mattered.

He picked the last rose and came down to her.

Her face buried in the large bouquet that she was holding, she was sniffing the flowers voluptuously. He could see her head tilting and the aureole of her hair, aurified by lunar reflections. Abruptly, he seized her fingers.

She looked at him, laughing.

"How hot you are, my dear Dominique. Always that nasty fever! It's necessary to go back inside."

"No, no, I beg you, don't go away!"

He stopped, trembling.

"Well," she said, "you can write to me, and I'll answer."

"You won't forget me?"

"Certainly not."

"Never?"

"Never."

He fell to his knees and, kissing the hem of her dress with a furious impetus. He repeated: "I love you! I love you! I love you as if to die of it."

She stammered: "Let's go back inside, let's go back inside!"

There was no longer anything above the wood but a kind of metallic gleam, a pale steely reflection. He lay down at the place she had just quit and, putting his face in the grass trodden by her feet, he wept for a long time, while the rumble of the carriage that was carrying his heart slowly died away on the road.

And Doninique never saw Colette again.

ROSELINE
(*La Presse*, 24 December 1897)

It is dark and it is cold. Behind the windows of the cottage, heavy white moths are fluttering incessantly, and while the wind howls under the disjointed door, the little children are sitting round the hearth with Roseline, their elder sister, whom a secret trouble is rendering silent and somber.

"Roseline, Roseline, tell us a Christmas story!"

"Roseline, pray to baby Jesus for us, so that he won't forget us!"

"I'd like a porcelain doll with hair the color of honey."

"I'd like transparent colored marbles to play with in the courtyard of the château."

"I'd like a missal with Holy Virgins like those in the stained-glass windows in the church, Holy Virgins in gold and silver."

Roseline, puts another log in the hearth and leans over to stimulate the flames. Her face remains sad and a slight tremor agitates her fingers.

The children consult one another with their gazes, understanding that their sister has some chagrin, and that it is necessary not to insist.

"Myself," says the smallest, "I'm certain that Jesus will be obliging. For a week I haven't been disobedient; I've said my prayers and the jam pot has remained on the dresser."

"Me, I've gone into the wood and brought back a large bundle of dead branches to cook the goose with chestnuts."

"I've collected mistletoe for the beautiful ladies of the town. There are more than twenty well-furnished bunches, with fruits that shine like pearls."

"Roseline, tell us that we've been good!"

A frisson runs through the young woman's body; she does not try to dissimulate her suffering, and sobs recklessly.

That is because Benedict has not returned for a month, and, that same morning, she had learned that he is courting Françoise Brichaut, the daughter of the Brichauts, who have land and money. The lads of the neighborhood have seen the lovers behind a hedge. They talk in low voices, very close to one another, and seem to be in accord. It's a good match for Benedict, who only possesses his arms and his courage. What can Roseline do? For a dowry she only has her seventeen years and her prettiness. Everyone knows that, as time goes by, it needs more than that to retain a boy.

The adorable dream dissipates in the mist. It is as cold in Roseline's heart as in the garden of the farm, and the shroud of her despair is like the shroud of frost that covers the seeds. It seems to her that the flowers of amour will never resuscitate within or around her, that it will snow eternally in her life.

The three children have taken their sister by the hand and have led her to her cold bedroom, her poor tiled bedroom, as neat and white as a nun's cell. They have undressed her and tucked her into her virginal bed, as she has the custom of doing every evening for them; then, politely, they have wished her goodnight, kissed her on her cheeks, shiny with tears, and returned to huddle by the fire. Each of them has taken off a shoe and placed it on the flagstones, saying a prayer to merciful Jesus in order not to be forgotten in his terrestrial tour.

"Oh," says the youngest, "I have an idea. What if we were to put Rosaline's shoe by the fire? Perhaps Jesus will also console her with a gift?"

"Yes, yes, let's put Roseline's shoe by the fire."

And softly, softly, in order not to disturb the afflicted young woman, who is still weeping, her head buried in her sheets, the smallest child has gone to look for the humble shoe and has put it next to the others, making a large sign of the cross.

Now, everything is asleep in the cottage. The clock with the quavering voice sounds the fateful hours, while the snowy moths outside chase one another madly against the windows and the wind plays Wagner on the great organ of the denuded branches. The earth is white, the woods are white, and the children have dreams as white as the earth and the woods.

They see luminous angels pushing the door of the dwelling with their long wings, in order to make way for the celestial Child, who is carrying the porcelain doll, the shiny marbles and the book of images. The brand new gifts adorn the poor shoes, putting a festival air into the smoky room. Between the rows of silver tunics and immaculate wings, Jesus seems to be walking on a moonbeam, and the aureole of his forehead is like a little star fallen from the heavens.

The escort has resumed its flight in the square of azure designed by the wide open door. The three children hear the light beating of wings and the murmur of seraphic litanies shivering in the peace of things.

Roseline, too, has had a beautiful dream; but her awakening is full of anguish, and forgotten momentarily, nothing remains to her but a greater pain. It is late; her heavy and painful slumber has been traversed by brief visions. Slackly, she gets up, puts the room in order, goes to fetch the milk and brown bread for breakfast, and breaks thin dry branches in order to light the fire.

The children are waiting mysteriously beside the hearth.

"Oh, Roseline, I have my doll!"

"I have my marbles!"

"I have my book! What about your shoe? Look to see what there is in your shoe?"

"Nothing, doubtless, my darlings; I didn't ask for anything, and the good God hasn't given me anything . . ."

The mother and the father laugh silently. They have come in stealthily and their clogs, caked with snow, have not made any sound. Roseline throws herself into their arms and her sobs increase.

"Don't cry any more, daughter. Don't cry any longer . . ."

"Oh, Mother! You have news? Benedict . . ."

"Yes, Benedict . . ."

"He's marrying the Brichauts' daughter . . ."

"You're mad, Roseline."

"Isn't that what they're saying in the village?"

"They were saying it yesterday, but they're no longer saying it today. Look, look what there is in your shoe!"

And while the bells sound the hosanna of amour, and the snow, falling more gently, seems to be no more than the falling petals of an immense virginal crown, Roseline kneels down on the flagstones and, very pale, withdraws from her shoe the blessed ring, the beautiful golden ring of betrothal!

FAITH
(*La Presse*, 27 December 1897)

After a week of struggles and tears, at the moment when the young man was thinking seriously about suicide, his door opened suddenly and Georgette came in, with the lovely undulating gait that he knew so well. He wanted to be indignant, but she threw her arms around his neck, with tender words of contrition that left no room for reproaches, reflection or second thoughts.

She told him that she was foolish, that she had tried to forget him because their amour was culpable, but that she had not been able to succeed and that she had come back, more loving than ever. Tears, promises and confessions were punctuated by kisses and smiles, which seemed to them to be sunlight after a downpour. Feline, she coaxed him, extending the crimson fruit of her lips to him and the blue flower of her eyes with golden lashes. Then, when she saw her lover's last rancor melt under her caresses, the prayers that had disarmed him were succeeded by the gaiety that forgetfulness brings.

"Why didn't you come for an entire week?" he asked, with a hint of suspicion.

"I had to care for a friend."

"You could have written to me, to explain . . ."

"I was so busy that I couldn't think about anything else. But I love you, I love you! You can see that, since I'm here."

"And you still love me?"

"Until death!"

"And I'll be the only one?"

She laughed, mocking his fears, when he had every reason to be content, reassured and liberated, with the future of amour that she would make for him. How foolish he had been to create torments for himself when he only had to let himself live; to let the rosy hours pass, even in the mists of winter . . .

And the flow never dried up of those sweet words that sing in the hearts of the amorous the eternal hymn of resurrection.

Their beautiful romance recommenced.

Georgette's entire occupation during the days that followed was to love René. She even had the illusion of a unique tenderness. She no longer looked at, and seemed no longer to think about, anyone but him. They shut themselves away in their room, made countless plans, and never wearied of proving their mutual folly.

In spite of his meager resources, René had created a charming interior. He had bought from a second-hand dealer a delicate Chinese silk, slightly passé, decorated with golden butterflies and mauve flowers, to cover the walls of his bachelor pad. Tables frilled with lace bore a whole set of brushes and blond tortoiseshell boxes for Georgette's toilette, and enormous bunches of the pale violets that she liked were steeped in crystal cups.

He only lived in his memory and his expectation, heaping her with caresses, kisses and sensuality when she was there . . . Every day, all their felicity returned in an instant and possessed them, while, bound to one another, they smiled at one another before looking at one another, slowly renascent within themselves and taking care not to lose the slightest flutter of the fleeing ecstasy.

It was such a sweet embrace! Half-dressed, still quivering, her hair undone, she nibbled the cakes that he had prepared. Their chairs soon came together; he took her waist and she held out some perfumed fruit to him between her lips. Her moist mouth fled René, attacked him, and fled again. Finally, almost caught, she put her cheek on his and slowly, in a kiss, abandoned herself to him.

Those insatiable delights filled the little apartment entirely. Their Paradise was scarcely large enough for their amour, and the world was distant enough for their happiness. There was nothing around them that was not theirs; there was no gaze other than their gazes, no voice other than their voices.

Outside, the bad weather—days devoid of light when the sun seemed drowned in a muddy pond, glacial rain and wind that whipped the widows—left them indifferent.

He no longer went out, spending his time waiting for her. In the evening, when she left, his heart cradled him softly. The fire had filled the room with a mild warmth; the lamp poured out a white light, illuminating a corner of the table, an armchair, a patch of carpet . . . The rest was in warm shadow, cheered up here and there by a golden glint on a picture frame, a glimmer of silk or a coppery reflection.

Could he ask for anything more? Every day he undressed her, pin by pin, lingering over the light whiteness of her lace, her silk stocking, which could he held in the palm of his hand, and when, of all her costume, nothing any longer remained but the woman, he picked her up and carried her to the bed like a child.

When she was weary of his caresses he gazed at her, remaining in contemplation: in the lamplight, her fine cloudy hair had the radiance of dust in moonlight; her face was languid in the whiteness of the pillow, and nothing could be seen of it any longer but the long somber eyelids lowered over the ecstasy of the dream . . .

Time, for them, fled like water between open hands. The hours pressed one another; memory succeeded anticipation, and in the instant of the dear presence everything else was abolished. No bitterness, no dread, no cares, no doubt and no threat! René believed in his mistress as he believed in God.

And when she emerged from his embraces, Georgette, all pink and quivering, gave herself to someone else.

THE FESTIVAL OF THE ROSES
(*La Presse*, 18 January 1898)

The costume ball of the Princesse de X*** was a worthy conclusion for the series of white and rose balls that she had given in her splendid town house on the Parc Monceau. It was midnight, and the most elegant crowd was packed into the drawing rooms when Madame de Bryas, as Minerva, and her son Amaury, as a Vendean chief, made their entrance.

The diamonds were sparkling; the spectacle of all the marvels heaped up pell-mell under the colored glass of the Venetian chandeliers seemed a magical apotheosis. An immense hall opened at the bottom of a marble staircase with a double revolution, on which were stacked Pierrettes, marquises, queens and goddesses streaming with jewels, as immaterial, as monstrous dream flowers grown in a spring night. On each step stood Japanese vases, porphyry flower-pots in cloisonné enamel containing camellias, lataniers and delicate ferns: an entire somber forest rising toward a mysterious paradise. The banisters disappeared under a trellis of multicolored roses: a rain, a cascade, an ocean of embalmed petals.

The Comtesse de Bryas drew her delighted son along, as mad with pleasure as a girl at her first ball.

They went into a hall of light, estival hangings, sewn with a flock of birds and giant butterflies. Everywhere there were roses and more roses, running over the old paneling, the mirrors, the tall Renaissance chimney-breasts, the gauze blinds and the lacquer awnings. A network of green branches dangled from the ceiling, florid lianas were traversed by garlands of white, brown and red tea-roses: an orgy, a downpour of heavy corollas, as heavy as the raindrops of a storm, which made pools of perfume on the floor.

But Amaury, already fatigued, stopped.

"Where is Mademoiselle de Verneuil, then?"

"In the upstairs drawing rooms, no doubt. Come on, come on; it's absolutely necessary to arrange the affair tonight."

"I'm not in a sentimental humor."

"Bah! A little schoolgirl isn't difficult to seduce, that one less than any other. She must be waiting, and her seventeen-year-old imagination has done half the work. Remember that she's a superb catch and you'll scarcely need your handsome face."

Mademoiselle de Verneuil was in a separate drawing room with a view over the garden of the house and the Parc Monceau. Leaning on the balcony, the young woman was gazing distractedly into the night, and her bright eyes had an expression of tenderness and anxiety.

While her mother delivered herself to demonstrations of the most affectionate solicitude, Amaury listened with an interested ear to Clotilde's ingenuous responses, and gazed at her shoulders, slightly frail above the nascent roundness of her breasts.

She was truly charming in her Royal Lily costume in white damask and her blue velvet mantle sewn with golden flowers. A narrow diadem of peals crowned her ash-blonde hair, which spread fluid waves over her shoulders.

Beyond the park, frosted with moonlight by electric bulbs, the darkness was triumphant. Certain leafy corners, closer to her, and certain patches of lawn also resembled a somber gulf, from which the treetops loomed up like the arms of shipwreck victims.

The young people were now left alone, and Amaury, very close to Clotilde, spoke to her in the warm and captivating voice that he adopted with all women: those in society, those

in the theater and those of the street. He brushed her with his
knee, with his arm and with his breath, and the naïve virgin,
divinely intoxicated, listened to his amorous words as she had
listened in chapel, only yesterday, to the words of the priest.
Never had the Song of Songs resonated more adorably in her
ear, never had pious ecstasy curbed her thus with an offering
of faith, in an abandonment of her entire being. What was
he saying? It hardly mattered. It was the music of her hope
to which she was listening, the harmonious awakening of her
woman's heart, the hosanna of a tenderness already ripe for
disillusionment and suffering.

At their feet, in the florid garden, the garish costumes
passed: all the characters of the Italian comedy, a roaring menagerie, a Japanese wedding with delicate mousmés dressed
in bright colors, and, springing from the branches, bright
beams of electric light caught and set light to bare shoulders,
straw wrapping and accessories of painted cardboard. In the
hall, people were no longer dancing; gypsy music, as light and
sweet as a buzzing beehive, emerged through the wide-open
windows and seemed to wake the torpid soul of the plants.
Gusts of cool matinal air were agitating the curtains and
making the light of the dying candles tremble. The domestics
were setting up little tables for the supper, and couples were
searching for one another, calling out.

Amaury quit Clotilde after a passionate handshake into
which he put what he had the custom of putting for all wom-
en ripe for the taking, and when his mother asked him what
stage his matrimonial campaign had reached he declared:
"Affair concluded," with a little scorn for his facile triumph.

Meanwhile, the young woman, in her white bed, was em-
broidering the canvas of the future with the golden thread
of her dream, surrounding the evoked image of her fiancé
with chaste adoration, confidence and devotion, and telling
herself that her entire life would not be enough to prove her
gratitude to him.

A DEBUT
(*La Presse*, 29 January 1898)

Louise Laval, a young woman devoid of fortune but educated in a bourgeois fashion in a small provincial town had, to the scorn of all dignity and reason, followed her lover into the Parisian furnace, where so many poor girls go to expiate the folly of a first amour.

Lucien was already fatigued by her caresses and adorations, ever the same, but as she was pretty and well made to satisfy the vanity of a man, he had taken her to the theater that evening and then to the cabaret, where his friends were waiting.

Two black suits and two fashionable good-time girls, Camille de Paros and Lia Raphael, were laughing noisily when they made their entrance into the brightly-lit and florid little drawing-room. Half-lying on the buttercup-yellow divan, the young women were showing off their jewels, so close to one another that their supple, undulating and powdered hair mingled their metallic reflections. They were resplendent in similar exquisite and savant arachnean dresses, veiled by long panels of inestimable Venetian guipure, and their bare arms shone silkily in the light under the trellis of multicolored bracelets. Thus adorned, with their glittering eyes and their faunesque smiles, they were truly intoxicating and attractive. Louise, in her thin silk dress, felt cruelly humiliated. She was installed on the divan between Lucien and Camille, while one of the black suits assured himself that the silk had been dressed in accordance with his instructions. Lia Raphael was already tucking into the hors-d'oeuvres: enormous pink crayfish elevating their antennae on a bed of parsley with yellow roundels of butter and a blue varnish of granulated caviar. Violent scents of agonizing flowers floated in the air.

The light of candles coiffed with minuscule pink lampshades was reflected in flashes on the silver buckets in which Aï wine was chilling; orchids overflowed the cups, and rubies and amethysts, suspended like golden spiders from silky threads, were trembling over the table at the end of long stems. Thick curtains were carefully draped over the closed windows. Outside, a fine drizzle was streaming over the panes, and Louise, who had not unsealed her lips, saw through a fog the made-up faces of the two women at the same time as the discontented gaze of Lucien, which occasionally turned toward her. He poured champagne for her; she drank in order to stun herself, in order to try to put herself in unison; but the sonorous waves of her nervous system had intolerable vibrations, the smile on her lips grimaced, her hand trembled and the glass she was holding fell and broke with a clear sound.

The older of the black suits had taken Camille's place next to her and, speaking to her at very close range, brushed her elbow and caressed her cheek with the pointed tip of his moustache.

As she recoiled, Lucien said: "Don't worry, I'm not jealous."

The baskets of fruits had been ransacked. The coffee was now going cold in the cups. Lia, laughing like a lunatic at her neighbor's sallies, was enveloped in clouds of white smoke and dipping her red lips into a glass of kummel. The conversations became strangely free, and Lia's dress had slid from her shoulders, only retained by a string of pearls. Although Louise still retained a sort of deceptive lucidity in her ideas and sensations, a final imperfect simulacrum of life, it was difficult for her to recognize what was real in the fantasies and what was possible in the strange caprices that were accomplished before her weary eyes. The stifling sky of her dreams weighed so heavily over her thought that she took the play of those embraces for the lies of a nightmare in which movement is soundless and cries are lost for the ears.

But she experienced a revolt. Lucien had just placed his lips on Lia's shoulder. Louise stood up, trembling; two arms surrounded her waist and tipped her back on the divan. Pale with indignation, she pulled away with an exclamation of pain and anger.

"Uh oh!" said the older black suit. "So we've had the honor of supping with a rosebush?"

"It's her debut," replied Lucien, with a hint of scorn. "Bah! We'll knock her into shape."

HOME VISIT
(*La Presse*, 6 February 1898)

Le Vicomte de Sainte-Daivène: twenty-five years old; in evening dress, with an orchid in his buttonhole and black silk socks; he is varnishing his patent leather shoes, which he is holding in his hand.

La Marquise des Etendards: thirty-five years old, very elegant, thin everywhere. Robe and bolero of scabious velvet garnished with chinchilla. Brown hair tinted with henna.

The Vicomte (*sadly drawing his brush, coated with varnish, over the sole of his shoe*): When one has no valet de chambre, eh . . . ?

The Marquise (*knocking on the door*): May one come in, Monsieur de Sainte-Daivène . . . ?

The Vicomte: Oh! Sapristi! (*He puts on his shoes precipitately with a cry of pain and hides the varnish and the brush under a table.*)

The Marquise (*coming in*): I see that I've taken you by surprise. It's strange, what I'm doing! Damn! The intention excuses everything.

The Vicomte (*kissing her hand*): You have intentions in my regard? Oh, what a dream! What felicity! What excess of intoxication! What . . .

The Marquise: Don't wear yourself out, my friend, and let's talk seriously. I haven't come, as you seem to think, in order to deceive the poor marquis.

The Vicomte (*conceitedly*): He won a great deal yesterday though, at the Esbrouffant.

The Marquise: Get it into your head that husbands, even those who are lucky at cards, deceive lovers more often than lovers deceive them. I have no lover; adventures of that sort have become damnably bourgeois. There's no petty wife of an employee earning three thousand francs a year who doesn't offer herself the luxury of bad taste. Amour? Oh, no—the very word is ridiculous and out of fashion.

The Vicomte: I don't deny it; however, as long as you haven't found anything to put in its place . . .

The Marquise: I have, in fact, found something much better.

The Vicomte: What's that?

The Marquise: Charity.

The Vicomte: That's still amour.

The Marquise: Yes, but amour . . . at a distance.

The Vicomte: The definition is nice; only, that love at a distance represents to me dinner at a distance; one is hungry, one sees blonde quail and red partridges on their tempting vine leaves, little pink woodcock in canapés, big black turkeys in truffles, and it's all inaccessible!

The Marquise: Bah! I'm talking about charity in the noblest sense of the word, the charity that is only addressed to genuine misfortunes, and which elevates the soul . . .

The Vicomte: So be it, send your soul to the sixth floor, but leave your heart at the entresol, if there isn't an elevator in the house.

The Marquise: "Do you call that wit? Truly, you're not difficult.

The Vicomte: Does one have wit when one's in love? And then, when a woman comes to a man's home, it's not, I suppose, to talk to him about the last interpellation in the Chambre?

The Marquise (*ironically*): I wanted to inform myself as to the state of your health.

The Vicomte (*surprised*): Of my health? Have I been ill?

The Marquise: Well, for two years, that's the response you've sent me whenever I've sent you my card to beg you to attend my charity sale.

The Vicomte: This year, you haven't sent me anything.

The Marquise: I wanted to spare you another lie, and I've come in person.

The Vicomte (*anxiously*): Then it's for . . .

The Marquise: Yes, it's for a contribution, and I'll add that I'd be grateful for the smallest offering . . .

The Vicomte: A year ago you were, I believe, patronizing the elevation of cripples . . .

The Marquise: That's correct.

The Vicomte: The year before, it was for the flattening of hunchbacks . . . and this time?

The Marquise: This time, I'm asking on behalf of parricidal children. It's a pity! Think of those poor children, who have unwittingly deprived themselves of their support, and who will henceforth drag the burden of their solitude and misery through life!

The Vicomte: One can't offer them too much protection.

The Marquise: The little darlings! They know neither religion nor good examples. The parents have been very culpable to have left them in such ignorance. But what a funny face you're pulling!

The Vicomte (*admiringly*): Oh, Berthe, my charming Berthe! Will you reserve for me a little of the benevolence that you experience for the little parricides?

The Marquise: I'm entirely devoted to my pious mission.

The Vicomte: The encouragement of crime?

The Marquise: Get away! That which is unconscious doesn't count.

The Vicomte: Let's be unconscious, Berthe. It's night; my concierge won't come up before one o'clock. Let's be delightfully unconscious!

The Marquise (*very dignified*): You're despicable.

The Vicomte: Ought you not to relieve all the unfortunate? After having lifted up the crippled, flattened the hunchbacked and encouraged the little parricides, give a crumb of amour to the starveling who's begging you . . .

The Marquise: You're causing me to waste precious time; I have other visits to make this evening. (*Extending her hand*): For the poor, if you please.

The Vicomte (*with a sigh*): So be it. (*He gives a hundred-franc bill to the Marquise.*)

The Marquise: Thank you, (*Ironically*): And admire my generosity; by coming to see you, I've spared you a malady. Well, adieu, my friend, I need a thousand francs today, and I only have your hundred as yet. (*She goes out, laughing.*)

The Vicomte (*after having rummaged in his pockets for a long time and ending up discovering two sous caught in the lining, taking them and contemplating them, sadly*): I'll dine on a small loaf . . . oh, the old nag!

THE LOVER
(*La Presse*, 13 February 1898)

A bedroom hung with mauve velvet veiled with broad sheets of old Venetian guipure. Pale green lacquer Louis XVI furniture covered with mauve brocade and silver florets. A bed in the middle surrounded by similar curtains, crumpled, draped and raised by silver cords with multiple tassels. Escutcheoned and fleurdelysed white silk foot-cover, as stiff as a chasuble. On the steps of the platform that supports the bed, a dozen polar bear skins make a snowfall.

Lucienne (*Eighteen years old, blonde, slim, very hieratical in her slightly awkward grace of a missal figurine; she opens a small door slightly and calls in a low voice*): Hector, are you there?

Hector (*Thirty years old, very chic, a trifle world-weary*): Dear Lucienne! (*He tries to embrace her.*)

Lucienne: Soon . . . You say that my husband is deceiving me?

Hector: Terribly.

Lucienne: How do you know?

Hector: It's not a secret for anyone. The liaison between your husband and Lolo is even known to my hairdresser, and if I were to ask my shirt-maker . . .

Lucienne: Oh, shut up! What does that woman have that I don't, then?

Hector: Twenty years, at least . . . For you, I'd give my situation, my happiness, my life . . . even more, if I could.

Lucienne: Shh! Someone's coming . . . it's my husband.

Quickly, quickly, disappear. In case of emergency, the service staircase is at the end of the corridor. (*Sending him kisses.*) Have no fear, Hector; I love you!

Hector: I adore you! In an instant . . . oh, how long the time will seem to me!

(*She closes the door again; Pierre enters from the opposite side.*)

Lucienne: I thought you were at the club . . . or with your mistress . . .

Piere: My mistress!

Lucienne (*bitterly*): I don't blame that creature. She's following her métier as a courtesan, and even employs a certain discretion. She has taken my husband; that's her right, she doesn't owe me anything. But you, Pierre, you whom I chose with love, you to whom I've given the best of my being . . .

Pierre: I haven't demerited it, believe me. There's a misunderstanding between us . . . forgive me!

Lucienne (*volubly*): Forgive you? Tomorrow, you'll recommence, and we'll be at the same point.

Pierre: Circumstances are overwhelming me.

Lucienne: Oh, yes, overwhelming you terribly. Once, you would have thrown yourself into my arms with tears of repentance; today, you argue like a businessman over a question of interest. And then—it's not out of jealousy that I'm saying this—the choice you've made is particularly humiliating. We've been married for eleven months, I'm only eighteen years old, and your mistress is a person of rather mature age . . .

Pierre (*vexed*): The person about whom you're talking doesn't interest me in any fashion. I merely observe that, like all women, Lolo is only as old as she appears to be.

Lucienne (*ferociously*): I thought she was younger. Well, I'll make you suffer all that I've suffered.

Pierre: The ordeal won't be very arduous, then.

Lucienne: That depends on the manner of envisaging things. An eye for an eye: I shall take a lover.

Pierre (*violently*): You'd dare! (*He seizes her arm brutally.*)

Lucienne: You're hurting me horribly!

Pierre: Listen to me carefully, and, whatever happens, only accuse yourself. I always do what I've resolved. If you take a lover, I'll kill you. Yes, I'll be able to catch you and I'll kill both of you . . . but him first! And I'll be cruel, you hear? And I'll plunge my hands into his wounds, and I'll strangle you with my warm hands!

Lucienne (*laughing*): Ha ha! How amusing that will be!

Pierre: Try, then, a little. If you like blood, screams and dying gasps, you'll be satisfied. Bonsoir, Madame. (*He goes out.*)

Lucienne (*opening the door to the corridor and calling*): Hector, you can come back now, my dear lover! Do with me what you please; I'm yours! (*She waits a moment and then, stupefied*) Why, there's no longer anyone there!

PRELUDE
(*La Presse*, 20 February 1898)

In a young woman's bedroom, all white: Marthe, eighteen years old, pretty, blonde and delicate; hair flying madly in an aureole; ingenuous gaze; Louise, nineteen years old, mat complexion, more expansive beauty; expertly powdered tresses framing a pure oval; large velvety brow eyes.

Marthe (*holding Louise's hand, confidentially*): Yes, an entire romance, my dear . . . he adores me. It's a violent passion, but contained and respectful. We've sworn an eternal fidelity to one another in spite of society, obstacles and separations; if necessary, we'll fight.

Louise: Oh, how closely your story resembles mine. And that handsome blond . . . where did you meet him?

Marthe: At the Malpertuis'. It was hot and my head was spinning slightly because I'd danced six waltzes with him—six slow waltzes of which the refrain pursued me with an obsessive sweetness! A strange fog drowned things, but I could see him quite clearly, with his empty cup in his hand and the orchid in his buttonhole, with the stem soaking in a little silver tube. He talked for ten minutes, and I felt that my life was linked to his for eternity. Since then, we've seen one another regularly every Wednesday, in the same house, and when the sky is starry and the moon is doing its Loie Fuller, we go down into the garden at eleven o'clock. Oh, if you knew . . .

Louise: I know. The same adventure happened to me while my mother was sleeping with yours. My flirt, who will soon be my fiancé, offered to take me to the buffet, here I took something cold, but mediocre—the Malpertuis economize on everything! Like you, I was delightfully moved; I closed my eyes languorously, listening, as to a divine litany, to the thousand foolish things he said to me in his warm and captivating voice. Everything dissolved around me into a mist of dream in which I could no longer see anything but the conquering tips of his moustache and the stars of his eyes!

Marthe: Oh, you love him! You love him!

Louise: Toward midnight, hypnotized by the amour that I felt beating wings in my heart like a bird in the sunlight, I went down into the garden. We were sitting next to the goldfish pond; he put his arm around my waist and kissed me for a long time . . .

Marthe (*severely*): That kiss enchains you forever. A kiss! And you haven't told your mother anything?

Louise: No. When Maman woke up, she told me that she was sleepy, and we went home and went to bed. I remained alone with my dream, which rocked me all night.

Marthe: When we're married, we'll see one another often. My fiancé is so seductive! He writes free verse, my dear, and is descended from Crusaders!

Louise: Mine too. He bears "*gules* traversed by *argent*" accompanied by four gold shields, each one charged. He explained that to me, in accordance with the setting of his ring,

Marthe: Mine also bears *gules* with something very good above . . . oh, tell me the name of your fiancé?

Louise: Certainly; it's Vicomte Raoul de Boisflotté.

Marthe *utters a cry and falls backwards into her friend's arms; after a moment of suffocation, her voice intercut with sobs:* That's my Raoul . . . oh, the traitor!

Louise (*forcefully*): That's impossible! You're lying!

Marthe: No, it's him, I tell you! He's deceiving us both! He's laughing at our credulity, our candor and our stupidity!

Louise: Well, I can confess to you now that Raoul de Boisflotté doesn't have a sou! His real name is Tripard and his poetry comes from a fraudulent poet strangled to death by a line that had too many feet!

Marthe: A millipede, then! How right our mothers are to be scornful of men!

Louie: Dear Maman! They've doubtless encountered Boisflottés in their youth!

Marthe: One has no idea of that! A monsieur neither handsome nor ugly—for there's nothing remarkable about him, is there?

Louise: Let's say a rather bad monsieur: a hypocrite, a poseur, a grotesque! I assure you that he's grotesque, with his porcelain plastrons, his orchids and his pretensions!

Marthe: Grotesque is too weak; he's odious! And yet, we loved him anyway, we were ready to forgive him his ridiculousness, to marry him, to enrich him and to rehabilitate him for a little amour!

Louise: We were ready to link our existence with his, to console him, to cherish him, go make him a pleasant future of tranquil happiness . . .

Marthe: That cries vengeance! Let's avenge ourselves!

Louise: Undoubtedly . . . but how? What can a poor young woman do against those monsters, men?

Marthe: Bah! Since they're all the same, we'll avenge ourselves on our husbands!

IN THE PARC MONCEAU
(*La Presse*, 6 March 1898)

Josette d'Argis has given a rendezvous to the Baron de Vanfreleuse after the Princesse de X***'s sale. It is her first encounter and she is trembling all the more because the Parc Monceau, where the skirmishes of the two lovers are to be exchanged, is full of people. She has already recognized several of her friends, returning from the Bois, and the old Comte d'Ossur, who pursues pretty nursemaids. Although night has almost completely fallen, numerous carriages are circulating at walking pace. Inside, on the padded cushions, couples are drawing together and whispering caressant words. Something like a river of amour is flowing in the discreet pathways under the cloudy sky. Josette, very troubled, has headed toward the Guy de Maupassant monument. Vanfreleuse, under a willow, his collar raised, is stamping his feet furiously and consulting his watch.

Vanfreleuse: Finally! What happened to you, then? Does it take so much time to get here? I'm dying of cold.

Josette: Really? I find it quite pleasant.

Vanfreleuse: You're lucky. I've spent my afternoon searching for old engravings and autograph manuscripts, and this evening, in my haste to see you, I neglected to take my chamomile . . .

Josette: Poor friend! It's the successes of the collector that have put you in this state?

Vanfreleuse: You're laughing? Know that I only show my riches to women of the highest society. I possess the rarest pieces . . . you can judge for yourself tomorrow.

Josette: No, let's leave it there and return to your house. I find you a mine of buried information.

Vanfreleuse: That's because I'm an intellectual . . . and the slightest contradiction . . . (*Trying to pull himself together.*) If you knew how I love you . . .

Josette: Oh, I don't doubt it.

Vanfreleuse (*remembering fragments of his reading*): It's necessary that I tell you what I have in my heart. It's necessary that I tell you with all the ardor of a reckless amour. No, I've never felt anything similar! We're both young, and we adore one another.

Josette: I never said that.

Vanfreleuse: Don't interrupt; you'll make me lose the thread . . . We adore one another . . . I must live for you, since the miracle of my cure is accomplished . . .

Josette: You've been ill, then?

Vanfreleuse: Don't interrupt; it's an English author.

Josette (*anxiously*): What are you saying?

Vanfreleuse (*who has remembered the whole passage*): We'll belong to one another; our destiny is to fuse into a single being, for you penetrate my tenderness irresistibly; you vibrate in unison with the trees and the flowers . . .

Josette: Flowers? There aren't any.

Vanfreleuse: That doesn't matter. You understand this silence and this solitude . . .

Josette: There are people everywhere!

Vanfreleuse: This solitude, this merciful sky, this caress and the nocturnal warmth . . .

Josette: You're freezing!

Vanfreleuse: . . . of the night . . . In this décor of amour we have our place. I am the man who weeps and implores . . . Julie.

Josette: Julie? Shut up; you're being ridiculous. Go and take your chamomile.

Vanfreleuse: That's all right. I won't tell you the name of your husband's new mistress, then.

Josette (*begging*): Yes! Tomorrow, I'll come to see your autographs . . .

Vanfreleuse: All right; tomorrow, at three o'clock. And don't make me wait, for I'm an intellectual, you know . . .

He draws away to the right, in an indifferent manner, and Josette goes into a lateral avenue to the left.

Baron d'Ossur (*emerging from a clump of bushes*): Why, what a fortunate chance!

Josette: I've caught you bothering nursemaids?

Ossur; The snows of yesteryear have left no traces, alas! (*He points to his bald head.*)

Josette: You still have a little flake at the back, and it goes very well with your genre of beauty. Would you care to escort me back to my carriage?

Couples pass by. A few maids are looking for their gallants, vagabonds are half-asleep on the benches; the last leaves are falling, one by one, from the lugubrious trees, like tears of gold and blood, on to the mourning dress of the earth. In the far distance a piano is accompanying a shrill soprano voice that rises dolorously in an infinite lament, like the desperate appeal of a soul silent for too long.

Ossur: That's coming from the house of the beautiful Madame Samuel. It's said that her husband has been ruined in a false speculation . . . once and for all! It's a swan song . . . or a sign,[1] for the consoler is waiting behind the gate . . . To love or not to love; it appears that everything is therein. Myself, I find that hope and memory are worth more.

Josette: Undoubtedly, before or after, when one can't yet or can't any more . . . But to feel in the heart all tenderness

---

1 The common wordplay linking *chant du cygne* with (*chant du) signe* does not translate.

all aspiration, all devotion . . . to be possessed of a desire to sacrifice oneself beyond human strength for an individual adored among all . . .

Ossur (*anxiously*): Are you suffering?

Josette (*laughing feverishly*): Do you take me seriously? I'm only joking! It's funny . . . extremely funny . . .

(*Her laughter terminates in a sob.*)

TO BE LOVED
(*La Presse*, 10 March 1898)

That evening, Emmeline felt a humiliation more bitter than the rest. Georges, her husband, had not ceased since the commencement of the ball to flirt with the beautiful Madame Larivière, who, her eyes drowned in an ecstatic softness and her fingers unquiet under the quivering wing of her fan, seemed to be taking an extreme pleasure in that game.

Emmeline, too overtly disdained and profoundly wounded in her womanly pride, wanted to know everything that the felony of Georges' plump, cold regular and slyly sensual mask—which had been able to conquer her heart and her dowry two years before—was hiding from her

Enveloping herself in her thirty-six-tail zibeline mantle lined with equally-tailed ermine, she returned to her carriage and had herself taken back to the conjugal abode in all haste. There, her eyes troubled, her throat contracted and her hands febrile, she sprung the lock of the little chest of drawers in which her husband hid his letters and, leafing through the pile, she read avidly, with sighs of anguish and cries of rage, the pink, blue and mauve notes with stimulating perfumes, which she scattered on the floor like cut flowers.

Here are a few specimens of that gallant correspondence:

My darling,

I'll wait for you at the theater exit, as usual. I hope for a great success in my poisoning scene: a real find! I've imagined a fashion of falling while pirouetting on the left leg and agitating the right arm that will stimulate enthusiasm. I've been studying before my mirror all day long. What diction! What mime! It's better than art, it's genius! Don't forget to send my six big bouquets of orchids and roses. It's necessary that I crush Lucie Dorgeville, whose lover doesn't have a sou!

One kiss per orchid . . . try to see that there are a lot of them!

Your great artiste.

My dear,

Until tomorrow, in our love nest. Oh, how sweet our embraces are! You can't imagine all the adorable surprises and exquisite discoveries I have in store for you. I tremble at every rendezvous, and that emotion doubles the perverse charm. What if my husband caught us! What would become of me, with the ten thousand francs that I owe? The situation is frightful! I need five thousand francs right away, and you'll give them to me, my darling, for you love me as I love you!

Your lover, who covers you with kisses,

Angèle

Mossieu,

You have turned an honest girl from her duty. It is very pinful for me to deceive madamme, who is so good. Be generus, or I tell all.

Joséphine

My old rat,

Certainly the necklace you gave me is nice, but it only has two rows of pearls, when Liane's—who is not worth as much as me—has three. You can't be less chic than her fellow, can you? You'll add the third row, my pink mule; that's why I adore you and embrace you . . . inexhaustibly!

Nini d'Arvers

Dear Georges,

A woman like me only has her word; it is gold and diamond. Bring what you know, in order not to remain behindhand, and I shall be yours.

Marquise de XXX

Friend,

Yes, this evening, outside the omnibus bureau at Saint-Philippe-du-Roule. Don't forget that the rent is due tomorrow . . . and I won't put an end to my caresses.

Your Marguerite

There were longer ones, more passionate ones, more amusing ones, brisker ones more imperious ones and more frivolous ones, all of which demanded something. The eloquence of the words was matched by the eloquence of the figures in the billets-doux, which reeked of the woods and the fields: wild heather and freshly-cut hay mingled with the aristocratic aromas of hothouse plants.

After having sobbed recklessly for an hour, Emmeline wiped her bruised eyes and, her heart mutilated forever, traced these few lines, which she put in evidence on the open chest of drawers:

Adieu, Georges; after what I've just read, any reconciliation is impossible. My astonishment surpasses my suffering. Is it a dream, a frightful nightmare? My poor head is spinning. I make vain efforts and try to understand. Why do our families inform us so poorly about life? Goodness! Virtue! Frankness! Devotion! Grandeur of soul! Get away . . . it's entirely the opposite that is necessary to succeed! I brought you my affection, without division, my beauty in flower and a million in dowry . . . you might have loved me!

THE SUITOR
(*La Presse*, 19 March 1898)

Ernest Dupont had been nurturing matrimonial projects for some time. He was scarcely worn away by life, but his rational mind and simple tastes made him desire the tranquil joys of the hearth. His more than adequate fortune allowed him to make a choice; he frequented salons and, although timid and even a trifle gauche, he risked himself with young women.

After a few agreeable researches, he honored with his preference Victorine Costard, a pretty blonde twenty years old with a narrow waist and lively and inviting eyes. Madame Costard, having sought information, authorized the suitor to present himself at her home and pay his court officially.

He already loved Victorine ardently. Merely on seeing her, so gracious and so delicate, he had the emotion of his entire being that precipitates the heartbeat, and he sank into long silent contemplations. She retained a charming moue while smiling vaguely and staring with interest at the patterns on the carpet.

It was the beginning of the season of renewal. The Parisian sparrows were chirping frenziedly in the branches of the chestnut trees with pale closed flowers; carts full of hyacinths and wallflowers were circulating in the streets, soothing the idyllic souls of the strollers.

Ernest felt an intoxication of tenderness throughout his flesh, and when he arrived at the young woman's house a kind of unaccustomed eloquence inspired his words. She listened to him without responding, with astonishment, but Madame

Costard, setting down her crochet hook, exhibited polite approvals and encouraging words.

That day he had brought a bouquet of white carnations, and, having deposited it in Victorine's lap, he expressed his amour tenderly.

"You'll see that we'll make a charming little household, Mademoiselle. I'm an orderly man, devoid of surprises and caprices of the imagination, and I understand the pleasure of long tête-à-têtes with a beloved wife. I'm ignorant of the club and the café, political meetings and racecourses. We'll spend our evenings together, me with a newspaper in hand and you with some fragile needlework between your dainty fingers, which will play in gold and silks. You'll make music for me and sing sentimental ballads. I also adore waltzes, languorous waltzes that carry you away in a whirlwind of dreams, until the moment when eyelids close delectably; good old waltzes with old-fashioned but enveloping rhythms, which are exquisite cradles . . . I'll fall sleep to the sound of your piano and I'll accompany you on the flute, for I once studied that instrument. On Sunday, we'll go to eat fried fish on the bank of the Seine; we'll go cycling and canoeing. I have an even and cheerful temperament, good health and an affectionate nature . . ."

He was sitting on the divan beside her, and holding her hand, which he was patting gently. A ray of sunlight entered through the window, playing over the curtains and making a golden trail on the bright carpet.

Ernest waited for a sign of assent and leaned forward with a tender grimace. He had a rosy complexion, blue eyes protruding slightly from his head, and a curly down on his chin. His entire replete person respired the serenity of a pure conscience.

"I would make the happiness of a wife," he repeated, daring, this time, to plant a sonorous kiss on his fiancée's cheek.

A vivid blush invaded Victorine's face; she suddenly shuddered and let herself fall on the divan, her head buried in the cushions. A kind of spasm ran over her shoulders, which lifted up convulsively.

Madame Costard had risen to her feet fearfully.

"Leave us," she said. "Your presence is troubling my daughter more than I could have believed. Do you not hear her sobs? Can't you see her emotion? Please don't abuse your power by remaining here any longer. Have pity on a poor child, who will recover possession of herself in her mother's arms."

Ernest searched for his hat and, too upset to express his sentiments, he withdrew, wiping away a tear.

As he went past the threshold of the chamber in which such an ardent tenderness had been revealed to him, he stopped in order to enjoy his triumph momentarily. She was his, the dear adored, the sweet and candid virgin! An immense pride inflated his breast; he drew his small stature up to its full height and raised his head in a halo of glory.

But suddenly, the irritated voice of Madame Costard struck his ear.

"What's all this stupidity?"

And the angelic Victorine replied, in a final fit of gaiety: "What a cretin that fellow is! I've never laughed so much . . ."

ADULTERY
(*La Presse*, 27 March 1898)

In a room in a banal hotel, with a pendulum clock in gilded zinc representing the three Graces, curling wallpaper with a yellow flower-pattern and faded green curtains. He and She were sitting on a divan that resembled the humped back of a camel, contemplating one another silently. He had come on foot, three-quarters of an hour late. She had left her coupé en route and taken a fiacre.

He: Twenty-five years old, robust, tall, supple, a trifle vulgar. Abundant curly hair and a long silky moustache. Convinced that one must treat women roughly in order to be adored. That attitude does not cost him anything; he has a vocation. It is to amuse himself, first of all, that he pays court to them, randomly, and then because he is very chic, very rich and possesses nothing; because he has not yet had a woman of the world, because her husband occupies an elevated situation, and because he hopes vaguely that that might be useful to him.

She: Thirty years old, pretty, delicate, distinguished, a little timid and weary. Determined to do anything to keep her lover, because it would be too painful to give him to another and because she does not want to live without amour.

He (*indifferently*): It's finished, the sulk?

She: I'm not sulking; I'm sad.

He: Oh, you're not amusing every day. Regrets, remorse, reproaches! There's such beautiful sunshine outside . . . if I'd known, I wouldn't have come.

She: You already come so rarely, my dear. Understand that I would be cheerful and confident, like anyone else, if you didn't torture me so cruelly.

He (*disdainfully*): Yes, you're sentimental, moonlight and little blue flowers. I don't make small talk, myself. We know one another too well; we have nothing more to say to one another, that's all.

She: Isn't it sufficient for two lovers to be together to be happy?

He: A turn around the Bois would suit me better. What if you were to take me in your carriage a few more times?

She: I can't. We'd be noticed. You know very well that I'm surrounded by enemies, who are watching me.

He: A truly devoted mistress ought to brave opinion and compromise herself for the man she loves. Isn't fortune on your side? Couldn't you, in case of divorce, live independently and in luxury, as in the past?

She: That situation . . .

He: Well, I can see that I'm wasting my time.

She: You have nothing to do.

He: I have the club, friends, the walk that is necessary for my health. Can women understand? It's always necessary to occupy oneself with them, their stupidity and their egotism . . .

She: Me, egotistical? I've sacrificed everything for you!

He: That's what gives you pleasure. It certainly gives you more pleasure than me.

She: In my existence there's no thought of anything but you.

He: If there were another, you'd be more amusing.

She: Why that passion at the outset, that persistence, that ardor in pursuing me? Why those tears, those pleas, those supplications? Didn't I resist as much as I could?

He: It's always necessary to resist. All the charm of amour is in the resistance.

She: Yes, I've been maladroit; but I'm alone in suffering from it. Don't quit me like this. Let's spend the evening together, shall we?

He (*consulting his watch*): Impossible; I have a rendezvous . . . a business meeting.

She (*resignedly*): When shall I see you?

He: Soon, no doubt . . . I'll write . . .

As she hesitates to go, he holds out her mantle and hat, and on the threshold, he kisses her coldly through her veil.

She: Oh, how I'll hate you when I no longer love you!

EQUINE COMPETITION
(*La Presse,* 16 April 1898)

Under a raw, terrible light that exasperates and makes the most pacific colors howl, socialites and good time girls are rubbing elbows, jostling one another and studying one another. A glacial impression: it's the province, exile deportation! Even the Butte is no longer the Butte! There, as on the track, the thoroughbred mares and ponies with elegant harness, presented in pairs, the fine fillies disembarked from all regions, do not attract the amateurs overmuch. The financial crash has been followed by a crash in gallantry. A few former lovers of those ladies are astray in the sumptuous stands of the committee. They have passed over the Seine bridges regretfully and shelter gladly under the peak of a helmet. Is that a consequence of feminism? At any rate, the weather is overcast and so are spirits.

Gisele des Abrusses, in a good place to be noticed, tries to smile at Marion d'Angora in order to show her teeth in public. Once, it was because she had less wealth in the face; now it's because she has more. One can see and touch—not the slightest trace of artifice. In any case, all the dear beauties know Doctor James Williams, American artist, who puts gold into his speech and into jaws, and even more in his pockets.

Gisele (*bitterly*): This isn't going well; I have a cloud in my soul.

Marion (*yawning*) There are no more except in the reserved stands, where there are fewer and fewer women.

Gisele: Dishonest competition. Economic reasons, my dear.

A fanfare of horns. A few minutes of sustained attention for a rider who masters his nervous and irritable beast and makes it jump obstacles with forceful thrusts of his spurs. Then exclamations and cries, a general tumult.

Marion (*turning away indifferently.*) On the ground, number thirty-two. I think he's had his lot.

Gisele (*ferociously*): Bah! They always get up; it's a waste of emotion. I prefer bullfights; there, at least, one sees blood, small intestines fuming.

Marion (*enthusiastically*): And the guillotine! That's worth the trouble.

Gisele: Pooh! Over too quickly. Once, one saw tortures that were much more chic. They knew how to make the pleasure last.

Marion: Oh, personally, I'm tired of always laughing; I'd rather weep at a good black drama. I really only have an appetite for fiction.

Gisele: *Les Deux orphelines,*[1] that's fine work, which makes the tears flow.

Marion: Look, Beatrix de Flotteville.

Gisele. Damn! She's come here to humiliate us! A hundred thousand francs in pearls on her fur! I knew her when she was broke. She went out in the morning to fetch a small loaf and three sous' worth of milk, feet bare in babouches!

Marion: Do you think she's pretty?

Gisele: No, she's been lucky, that's all. It's an old rake that launched her and a spoiled young fop who maintains her.

Marion: She's lifted a definitive type now.

Gisele: A famous type?

Marion: He thinks she's virtuous?

---

1 *Les Deux orphelines* (1874; tr. as *The Two Orphans*) by Adolphe d'Ennery and Eugène Cormon was the most popular theatrical melodrama of the last quarter of the nineteenth century, still running all over France and America in 1900.

Gisele: You're telling me! She's spun him a fine line: daughter of a colonel killed in Tonkin, Christian education, good, devoted, talented . . . what do I know?

Marion: He's in contemplation before her as before a Madonna.

Gisele: She's certainly seen faithful ones. There are plenty of people disposed to offerings and burning candles before her altar. The carpet on the steps must be worn away. Well, my dear, he's marrying her!

Marion: Damn! That's a man of cathedrals!

THE NEW TARIFF
(*La Presse*, 27 April 1898)

The sun, like a golden spider, has remade its web on the morose sky, and its rays, ardent threads, are caressing us and enveloping us. The buds, swollen with sap, and making the chilly hawthorn burst forth, and the lilial cluster that preludes, with timid arpeggios, the splendid symphony of summer.

The Vicomte des Herbages and the Marquise de La Roche are pedaling in a discreet path in the Bois. The steel of their bicycles launches rapid sparks, and the branches, dotted with nascent leaves cover them with very fine green lace, which designs complicated networks on the azure of the sky.

The marquise, slim and supple in her long skirt and blue-gray blouse, tightened at the waist by a narrow silver belt, seems to have wings. Like a dragonfly she flits, turns, appears and disappears, and the vicomte, who only got home at seven o'clock in the morning from the redoubt most beloved by gypsies, is having difficulty keeping up with her.

Finally, capriciously, she stops, and, looking at him with a mocking expression, she says: "You have hamstrings of cotton today, my dear!"

He does nor riposte, and assumes the hypocritically modest expression that signifies: "I'll employ condescension; it's necessary to be gallant with women, isn't it?"

"Tell me," the marquise goes on, adjusting her cloth toque over her black tresses, slightly deranged by the rapidity of her course, "Are you as dull when you accompany the Baronne des Ombelles?"

"When I'm with the Baronne I launch myself impetuously, and keep my distance at all times."

"But why?"

"Because the Baronne leaves me cold."

"It's a proof of amour that you're giving me, then, by dragging the pedals behind me?"

"Certainly; I'm bathing in your splendor, in the wake of your glory. You're a star that one never wearies of contemplating. The Baronne is a mature star that is devouring itself, having no more fuel: a globe that will soon cease to be anything but a heap of ash drifting in space . . . a phantom vessel of the sidereal waves."

"Brr!"

"Yes, dear friend, let's rather sing about the primrose pink of your lips and the hyacinth blue of your eyes, which I'd love to pluck in a kiss!"

The birds are singing amorously, while a jealous and solitary blackbird whistles in the shadow. Timid new grass with an infantile freshness is growing at the feet of trees whose bark is covered with a rutilant moss that is beginning to peel away. The earth, still in mourning yesterday, is reanimating, and feeling the sap of ardent roots flowing within it like a generous blood. It makes one good to be alive, to forget and to dream!

The marquise and the vicomte have returned their bicycles to the garage at the entrance to the Bois, but their inexact coachmen—as befits the coachmen of grand houses—have not yet arrived. The Vicomte, after a few remarks on the failing of domestics, omnipotent nowadays—the true kings of the world—hazards a proposition:

"What if we were to take a fiacre?"

"I'd like that. It would be charming."

They choose green lanterns on a yellow carcass—hope in adultery—and install themselves with difficulty. The faded fabric reeks of benzene, the cushions are stuffed with coconuts, the trimmings resemble the grass of the fortifications, but the marquise is drunk on pure air and the vicomte no longer has any memory of the favorite redoubt of gypsies.

The coachman leans over and declares, firmly: "If it's the new tariff, bourgeois, you can get out. I'm for established custom."[1]

Two emotional voices respond from the interior: "Us too, friend. Get going, at a walk, and go the long way round!"

---

[1] The taximeter, which calculated fares based on a combination of distance travelled and waiting time, met considerable opposition when it was introduced in Paris in the 1890s, partly because it was a German invention and partly because fiacre drivers, naturally resistant to regulation, preferred to make their arrangements independently.

TO GET IN![1]
(*La Presse*, 5 May 1898)

Rich interior; objects d'art, master paintings. Ancient tapestries authentically worm-eaten. Silky and low quilted furniture. Flowers everywhere in baskets, in bunches, in clusters and strewn around. Dying daylight, still filtered by pale-hued silk blinds, adroitly combined. Lolo, in a mauve crepe and soft malines peignoir dotted with turquoise scarabs, is chatting with Baron Huguonet. Lolo is no longer very young, but still fresh in her chosen frame. The baron is not very old, but already wrinkled like a dried cherry.

Lolo (*after having lit a cigarette*): Yes, my friend, those who want to get in come to find me, because I'm the prince's official mistress and his best counselor.

Baron Huguonet: Well, the prince is the most influential member of the Centaure, and the Centaure is the most chic club in France.

Lolo: There's no cheating there, then?

Baron Hugonet (*laughing*): As much as elsewhere. The Centaure has had the Duc de B, who played with loaded dice, as the Grand-Cercle has had Colonel G, who was an inveterate hustler. Need I cite others?

Lolo: Go on, you're exaggerating. Les Farineux has always maintained a perfect correction; no card sharp has ever crossed the threshold.

---

1 A version of this vignette was reprinted in the 13 April 1899 issue of *Gil Blas* as "Le Rendezvous," stripped of everything but the dialogue and with the names of the interlocutors changed to "Hector" and "Lucienne."

Baron Hugeuonet: I admit that no one has ever been caught, but one doesn't play there! And tell me, exquisite Lolo, I suppose that you'll recommend me to the prince as a choice candidate? I've been told that you've been terrible for a very grand individual of my acquaintance?

Lolo: Yes, at the last moment, at the second enquiry, a slight peccadillo was discovered, which prevented the vote.

Baron Huguonet: And it's you who had exhumed that little peccadillo?

Lolo: This is my excuse, and I guarantee the perfect exactitude of the story! I had a lovely little bitch of an absolutely rare species, which one can only procure for its weight in gold: enormous eyes, a little nose, all black, drowned in a long yellow moustache and paws as big as a penholder. But Lolotte was bored; Lolotte dreamed of a free union on beautiful spring evenings, and implored me with the gaze of an amorous woman. Then I set out on campaign to find her a worthy husband, a handsome, aristocratic husband as pure-bred as herself. It was only after long research that I ended up unearthing an accomplished male. Oh, he was handsome—the same enormous eyes as my Lolotte, the same impertinent little nose, the same yellow moustache drooping on either side of the witty mouth. I believe they were the only ideal couple in all Paris. You can imagine how happy I was. Immediately, I made overtures to the owner of that marvel, our gentleman in question, and begged him to accord to the pooch a few hours of conjugal joy. I didn't have excessive pretensions, did I? And any gallant man would have granted them in haste?

Baron Huguonet: Certainly.

Lolo: Well, he refused flatly, under the fallacious pretext that it was necessary not to spread products as precious. Then I said to myself: Lolotte will die a virgin and martyr, but you, my lad, will never play at the Centaure.

Baron Huguonet: What destinies hold! I knew the importance of the affairs of women, but I was ignorant of the affairs of bitches.

Lolo: There you go! Otherwise I'm a good girl, and as my already long career and my profound experience have taught me to judge men, I'll recommend you . . . and good luck!

A TRIPLETTE[1]
(*La Presse*, 12 May 1898)

It is an odorous scatter,
A carpet of pink velours,
On which the sun has reposed
Its errant splendor softly.

Under your pure bright veils,
Trees and flowers of gray roads,
You seem, in the incense of breezes
To lead to the sprees of spring.

Five leagues from Paris; on a road bordered by hawthorn hedges and apple trees in flower. In the fine, silky grass that seems to emerge from the canvas of some fay, dainty daisies and sumptuous buttercups are huddled in the necklaces of gamines. The air is pure, the landscape silent . . . Suddenly, a triplette appears at a bend in the road, advancing vertiginously in a cloud of white dust, like a frenetic, fantastic and maleficent beast. On the front saddle, Adolphe, while directing the machine, is chatting with Julia Morin, who is behind him. Auguste Morin, the husband, occupies the third place.

Auguste Morin: There was a second ballot, but I prevailed.

Adolphe (*in a low voice, to Julia*): My God, what a bore he

---

1 A triplette is a three-seater tandem bicycle; they were first marketed in France in 1895 or thereabouts, but only survived as novelties; one was featured in André Maréchal's one-act comedy "La Triplette," (1897), which La Vaudère might have seen.

is! It wasn't worth the trouble of quitting Paris to bring that old electoral poster on our back.

Julia Morin (*quietly*) What does it matter? Let him talk.

Auguste Morin (*declaiming*): Messieurs and dear fellow citizens, it's necessary that France rids herself of politicians who cheat her and break the ancient molds . . .

Adolphe (*quietly*): Oh, what an idea! Shall we break Auguste to see what there is inside?

Julia (*quietly*): No, no—no accidents, I beg you!

Auguste Morin: French and sovereign people, my candidature is not the egotistical action of an ambitious man; it is the disinterested protestation of a man of courage, merit and intelligence, who would like to give the Republic a new and durable foundation, to purge it of . . .

Adolphe: He'll certainly succeed in that! Make him shut up, Julia, or I'll tip us over!

Julia (*to her husband*): You're swallowing a lot of dust, Auguste, be careful.

Auguste (*stubbornly*): No, let me finish.

But the triplette has lurched over a heap of stones, has jumped and, after a few swerves, tottering like a drunkard, has spilled Auguste so awkwardly that his skull has hit a sharp stone.

Julia (*lifting the head of the injured man*): Is he dead?

Adolphe: Oh! No! A candidate for parliament can't die . . .

Julia: It doesn't matter; he's well-insured.

Adolphe: Why was he so obstinate? Politics bores me in Paris; in the country it renders me rabid. At first I tried to cut his speech short by going at a diabolical speed . . . he just got louder. The more I pedaled, the more he perorated, and my toes were curling. Then, seeing that he wouldn't switch off his machine, I've broken mine!

Julia: How red he is!

Adolphe: It's nothing. A little fracture. In the Chambre he'll see many others. Veil his face with his handkerchief and come and kiss me, Julia!

Julia: My Adolphe!

NEW GAME
(*La Presse*, 21 May 1898)

A guinguette in Bas-Meudon, Max and Sylvie are finishing dinner on the edge of the water, in a pavilion veiled by virgin vines, the nascent foliage of which still resembles frail green spiders. It is raining, and they can only perceive the far bank of the Seine vaguely, blurred by a mist of powdered glass, a Japanese curtain of glaucous pearls that a pale radiance aurifies at intervals. Sylvie has rolled a cigarette of fine blond tobacco and has her elbows on the tablecloth, making the emerald on her little finger glint. Max has yawned discreetly in the middle of a sentence that remains unfinished.

Sylvie (*in a soft voice*): In fact, the tête-à-tête only suggests to us things taken up again many times . . . we know one another too well, even our lies are not unforeseen. It's better not to go on.

Max: You think so? I'd like to, though.

Sylvie (*her gaze distant*): You love me, as I love you, with the indifference of inevitable tomorrows, the certainty of the futility of serious effort and the humiliating condescension of habit.

Max: Perhaps. Our liaison hasn't been able to last because we were too experienced, and also too indulgent. Neither of us has been able to impose on the other.

Sylvie: Indulgence kills amour! In that game, the man who has no fault for which to reproach his partner inevitably drifts away. The superiority of the other becomes injurious to him.

Impossible to pose as a victim, to moan and feel sorry for oneself. What remains of amour without blasphemies, tortures and agonies?

Max: Ennui, somber ennui . . .

Sylvie: It's raining in our spirit as in the country. Everything is cold, brackish and reeks of mildew. Our thoughts are worm-infested; viscous creatures, slugs, are crawling there, rendering enthusiasms sticky . . . if only I still had a husband! If only you had a wife! We'd have the resource of deceiving them, and that would be a measure of emotion in our life . . . but no, we're free, free to adore one another all day long! What a cruel fate!

Max: The situation is intolerable.

Sylvie: Intolerable. What are we going to do?

Max: It doesn't seem to me that I'm ripe for retirement. I'll push myself by means of a chic marriage.

Sylvie: Yes, a fine gift to make to a youngster! I know one whose parents would be realizable in short order.

Max: It's just that I can scarcely support investigation . . .

Sylvie: Don't worry; trust me. I'll cover you with flowers.

Max: You're an angel! But what will become of you?

Sylvie: I've already thought about that, and I'm counting on your good offices to come to my aid.

Max: How?

Sylvie: You know my tastes, my desires, my annoyances, and also my physical and moral qualities . . .

Max: Certainly.

Sylvie: So I can't address anyone better, in the circumstance. Among your friends, your sure and devoted friends—in sum, your best friends—I beg you, my dear Max, to choose a replacement for yourself.

A LOTTERY
(*La Presse*, 1 June 1898)

The home of Madame Séné on the fourth floor of an old house in the Rue de Clichy. Furniture in mahogany and yellow Utrecht velvet; gray wallpaper with gilded stripes; aggressive color prints; little tapestry stools, the backs of the armchairs crocheted; crochet-work also in front of the fire, with long slack fringes that resemble green macaroni. A great many artificial flowers and a few photographs in pretentious frames bought at hazard from shops of novelties.

Madame Séné, in a monastic costume, is hosting a tombola for her friends. Her daughter Charlotte, a thin blonde whose virginal dress is as blue as a ball of detergent, is distributing tea with the maid, who is holding a plate of treats. Alfred, who has not wanted to go to bed in spite of his youth—he is ten years old—is slyly keeping watch on a cream baba that has been left imprudently within his reach. Some fifty people are admiring an antique brooch ornamented with a large ruby and four small diamonds, in a white satin jewel-case placed on the table.

Madame Séné: That jewel, which the late Séné gave me for our betrothal, is very valuable. Look at the purity of the stones . . .

A Guest: Ten francs a ticket isn't sufficient. You ought to have asked more, Madame, for such a precious object.

Madame Séné (*amiably*): It is, so to speak, a gift that I wanted to make to my good friends, a pretext for a gathering . . .

A Lady: You have all the delicacies.

An Aging Demoiselle: And what modesty! Is the charm of your conversation not sufficient to fill your drawing rooms?

Madame Séné: I want to leave a durable souvenir to those I love. And then, the poor will lose nothing by it. It's so pleasant to do a little good!

The Aged Demoiselle: Those sentiments honor you.

A Monsieur with a green and violet palm: Isn't your demoiselle going to play the piano for us? She must certainly know something?

Madame Séné (*simultaneously tender and authoritarian*): Go on, my child, play us your latest novelties: "The Burglars' Dance" or "The Virgin's Bedtime."

Charlotte (*blushing*): Oh, Maman, I'm afraid!

Madame Séné: That child is a shrinking violet! (*Severely*): Play, Charlotte; I want you to.

Charlotte runs through her repertoire. After "The Burglars' Dance" comes "The Bride's Bath," then "Foolish Love," "The Negro's Kiss," etc. etc. The mothers doze off in their seats, the young folk exchange consternated glances. Alfred had slipped into the dining room and has emptied two large glasses of punch without urgency, perfectly at ease under the table beside Bismarck, the philosophical household dog. Now, his thoughts vague and his expression beaming, he resumes his place in the drawing room and seems to be listening very sagely to his sister's final chords. A bald monsieur sings "The Fallen Angel" with disquieting tremolos in his throat; an aesthete gone astray in that unworthy milieu recites an amorphous poem that no one likes. But it is time to draw the tombola; naturally, it is Alfred who has the honor.

A Lady (*affectionately*): Go on, little man, think of me as you put your hand into the hat!

A Young Woman: I'll win! I'll win!

Various voices: It's me! It's me!

Alfred (*completely drunk*): Don't get so excited. All the little pieces of paper have the same number, and in the five years that we've been doing this, it's always Maman who wins!

BETWEEN LOVERS
(*La Presse*, 28 June 1898)

Adrienne adjusts her veil tranquilly before the mirror. Her eyes, behind half-closed eyelids, have a curious and ironic gaze. Robert, with an extinct cigarette between his teeth, is chewing it furiously.

Adrienne (*disdainfully*): As you please.

Robert (*feverishly*): You've never loved me; your egotism is revolting.

Adrienne: What about yours? A woman of the world . . . I'm a woman of the world. Your vanity was flattered, that's all. Only a coward abuses his masculine strength like you, and his baseness, with the assurance of impunity!

Robert (*seizing her arms*): Shut up!

Adrienne: For a quarter of an hour I've been listening to your recriminations, and I've had enough, you hear? I've had too much! I've had it up to here!

Robert: What! I surprise you almost in a lover's arms; I prove to you that you've been deceiving me since the first day, that you've played with my stupid credulity as with my tenderness; I render any lie impossible, and you stand up to me and insult me again?

Adrienne: I pity you.

Robert: Go on, get out!

Adrienne: You're throwing me out? That puts the lid on it.

Robert: If you stayed any longer, I'd no longer be master of myself; I'd do something bad. Yes, my fingers are clenched, and there are red patches before my eyes!

Adrienne: Very well, I'll go. You'll never see me again.

Robert: It wasn't money, since you're rich, it was vice, uniquely, that threw you into another man's arms . . . and also the pleasure of bruising and torturing a heart entirely filled with you. Oh, how I've suffered!

Adrienne (*flattered*): Really?

Robert: Yes, I've suffered, but I'll recover. It's all over, finished forever!

Robert and Adrienne contemplate one another at length, with amour and ferocity. The little room in which they have loved one another is as florid as before. The silky curtains let nothing penetrate from outside; an odor of tuberoses and irises—the odor of the adored—floats indecisively, like the sad memory of defunct joys. Golden pins with golden heads star a little cushion that she has given him, bits of lace and ribbon trail over the furniture; a large blonde tortoiseshell comb that sustained the twisted mass of her tawny hair has fallen on to the carpet. Indifferently, she has buttoned her gloves and picked up her cat's-head umbrella—an ebony shaft studded with two glaucous eyes with feline gleams— from the divan. Robert has stood up in order to open the door to the antechamber for her.

Adrienne: Don't hold it against me too much, my friend. I am, in fact, light, capricious and inconstant, and we're not made to understand one another. Existence has become hellish recently. God knows what else our jealous hatred would have found. For half an hour you've been insulting me, with a crazy desire to strangle me and throw me down panting at your feet like an evil beast. Adieu, Robert!

Robert: You *have* deceived me, then?

Adrienne: Since we won't be seeing one another again, I might as well confess it to you. Adieu, Robert.

Robert: Ah, wretch! Wretch! (*He raises his arms recklessly in a furious gesture of menace. After a moment of tragic silence*): Until tomorrow, then? And above all, be on time.

EVOCATION
(*La Presse*, 10 July 1898)

Monsieur Sosthène, widowed eighteen months before, could not console himself for the loss of his Aurélie. Fortunately, spiritism, of which he was one of the most fervent devotees, permitted him to have tender conversations with his defunct wife, which often did not terminate until daybreak.

In those "caresses of the soul" Aurélie never offended her husband's sentimentalities any longer; her teasing character, which had once been given free rein, had become as sweet as honey in the other world; her eccentric humor had been amended to the point of being conciliating and charming.

Still amorous, Sosthène, gathered a few friends every week, and in the mysterious light of an oil lamp veiled with green gauze—like a ballerina in a phosphorescent tutu—he evoked the astral form of the dear dead woman.

Under the passionate desires of mediums, the latter did not take long to manifest herself in a table-leg or a frolicking pencil that only stopped when its lead ran out.

"I'm here," she said. "Interrogate me."

"Are you happy?" the husband asked.

"I'm happy," the table replied, delivering itself to a gyratory movement that communicated to the initiate the epileptic joy of a whirling dervish.

It was almost always Adolphe—Sosthène's best friend—who directed the choreographic gambols of the rapping spirit, or who was holding the pencil. Adolphe was full of good will, and traced with ardor, in letters flowing over the inciting slate, the most dythrambic eulogies of conjugal life.

Aurélie often repeated the same things, the adorably child-ish things of which a truly smitten husband never wearies.

"Do you love me, Aurélie?"

"I love you, Sosthène."

"Do you always think of me?"

"Morning and evening, in the midst of a beautiful garden full of lilies, in which I stroll in the costume of Eve. At all times I ask myself: "What is my Bibi, my Coco, my Curly Cabbage doing? Has he put on his flannel vest and taken his Janos?[1] Has he made a tour of the column twenty-two times before breakfast, as his homeopathic physician recommended? Has he added a drop of kirsch to his chamomile in order to give him phlogiston?"

"Phlogiston?" asked Sosthène.

"Yes," said Adolphe, who had studied medicine, and added: "It's a term that I've taught her."

Thanks to the frequent presence of Aurélie's astral form, life was bearable for the unconsoled widower. Adolphe excelled in the routine evocation of the adored; he even abused it slightly, almost always finding himself short of money, and Sosthène having a generous emotion.

The dead woman was reporting the great benefits that the future seemed sure to ensure him when, one evening in December, after a day's hunting and a few excessively copious libations, sweet memories suddenly palpitated in the heart of the former lover. He remembered that on similar nights, via the complicit slate, behind the husband's back, he had given many a rendezvous to the tender Aurélie. Perhaps the latter, avid for vengeance, was indeed guiding the hand of the trickster; at any rate, he forgot reality and traced on the slate—as he had done many times before—these words, which Sosthène read with amazement:

"Your old imbecile of a husband is falling asleep. When he's gone to bed, come to my room. There'll be a good fire there, and Malaga."

------

1 Hunyadi Janos mineral water—a popular laxative in the latter part of the nineteenth century.

CHAUFFEUSE[1]
(*La Presse*, 27 July 1898)

The linden trees along the road are shaking their pale florets with heady perfumes; the braches enlace and overlap, forming a thick vault that a few golden arrows pierce at intervals before going to die on the ground in sheaves of little yellow gleams amid the grass and moss. Everything seems to be asleep on the warm July day; except for the hum of mosquitoes vibrating insatiably, like the tremulous note of a violin, sometimes supported by the sonorous drone of a bee or the languorous appeal of a turtle-dove.

Suddenly, in the calm of the countryside, a forceful respiration makes itself heard. The breath grows and is magnified, seeming to fill space with its hoarse panting, and the fantastic, terrifying, indomitable beast goes past in a cloud of dust. It is Comte Arthold's automobile, a newly improved and extremely powerful machine, which can be steered with one finger and can attain an unequaled speed. The comte is sitting in the car with his young wife, who is motionless and thoughtful, her expression vague, seemingly indifferent to people and things.

---

1 This title has a double meaning. By 1898 the term "chauffeuse" was beginning to be adopted with reference to a female driver of automobiles, but it had long been used in a familiar fashion to refer to a provocative woman who stirs up trouble. Some secondary sources allege that Jane de La Vaudère generated scandalized comment because she drove her own carriage in the Bois de Bologne and the streets of Paris, instead of having a coachman drive her, as convention required. This story was reprinted twice in *La Lanterne*'s supplement, first under its original title and then as "Teuf! Teuf!"

"Guy," she says, eventually, "you won't do it; it would be a horrible crime!"

And he replied, in a blank voice, a changed voice that she does not recognize: "Yes, Maud, I'll do it. I've supported this existence of lies and shame for too long; it's necessary to end it."

"You can't condemn me on the basis of an anonymous letter. What proof do you have?"

A disdainful smile creases the comte's lips; he shrugs his shoulders without responding.

"Yes," she goes on, "what does it prove . . ."

But her voice catches in her throat; hear features contract and it seems to her that the blood withdraws from her face and that a little earth appears under the skin.

"Look," says Guy, with a cold rage, "that's proof you're giving me at this moment. Can you deny your emotion, your anguish? That's the undeniable proof of your treason!"

At the end of the road another breath is rumbling dully: a black beast, feverish and hoarse, is racing toward them. It's the motorcycle of Pierre Léris, the comte's best friend and a regular visitor to the house.

Pierre has recognized the couple and his hand is raised for an affectionate salute.

"What a pleasant surprise! You, here, so early?"

But Maud has straightened up in the unconsciousness of a woman and a lover.

"Save yourself! Save yourself!" she shouts to him, her gaze crazed and her gesture imperious.

Before that white, suppliant face, Léris has suddenly understood the danger that is threatening him. A few more meters and it is death for him: a stupid, almost ridiculous death. Stopping abruptly, he calls to the comte: "Come on, you're not serous! A duel, rather . . . I'm at your orders."

"Yes," Guy replies, "a duel, but right away, you on your machine and me on mine."

"Get away! What an idea!"

"We're too closely linked to fight one another; it's necessary that people can believe in an accident."

"A contest is impossible."

"You won't compete . . . I'll simply try to overtake you. So much the better if you can get away. Do you understand?"

"Let's go," said Pierre, "since that's what you want." And, coming around meekly, he takes the lead, drawing away at top speed, straight ahead.

Along the road the two beasts race hectically, hatefully, coughing convulsively. Maud, her eyes closed, clings to her husband, trying to paralyze his arm, which is as taut as a steel spring. She pleads, begs and sobs, carried away involuntarily toward the murder that appears to her in a terrifying vision.

The avenue of lindens is traversed, there is the plain now, the luminous road through the golden wheat, the pale oats, the meadows bordered by apple trees and willows. The course changes into an infernal gallop, an increasing, unprecedented vertigo contemplated by frightened peasants. The two machines are coming apart, rattling furiously, making epileptic bounds like wounded wild beasts, digging into the soil, seemingly fraying a passage into the entrails of the earth, in order to disappear into the eternal darkness of inviolate depths.

Pierre senses that he is beaten, in spite of his drunken ruses, which cause him to totter in the ruts and trace complicated zigzags in the lateral paths. Soon, the formidable impact will be produced; then the ignoble crush in a red pool, a mire of muscle and flesh . . .

Maud utters a heart-rending scream and . . . wakes up! A mocking sunbeam plays on the edge of her sheets. It was all a dream!

Pierre has not ceased to be a friend of the household and Guy is to try out, this very day, an admirable automobile that he bought at the last exhibition.

The young woman dresses in haste, her eyes shining with a great resolution; and when her husband comes to take her

for the morning excursion, she says, kissing him seductively: "You know, it seems to me that for a long time, you've
been . . ."

"That I've been what?" he asks, full of candor.

"A chauffeur! Chauffeurs have had their day. It's the turn
of chauffeuses! You'll show me how, won't you?"

THE POULTRY-YARD[1]
(*La Presse*, 3 August 1898)

It is a sunny day, a day of idleness and splendor. In the little garden the roses are blooming, all together, as if for a belated Fête-Dieu, and velvety petals are falling from excessively heavy stems, so numerous that they cause a perfumed downpour under each rose-bush.

Black butterflies with orange- and crimson-fringed wings settle on lilies; an active buzzing—the golden bells of the estival festival—is putting a rapid sonorous frisson into the swooning corollas. In the distance, the hoarse voice of a pastor is repeating some fairground song with a brutal, obsessive rhythm.

In the poultry-yard the hens, numbed by the heat, are scratching the ground lazily and calling to their chicks with light clucks; the ducks are fidgeting next to a minuscule pond, plunging their yellow beaks delightedly into the brackish water.

It is a beautiful day, full of the calm of beings in the calm of things, a day of truce and reverie, like an armistice accorded by victorious nature to terrestrial suffering . . .

---

1 Instead of bearing the usual heading of "Contes Rapides," this item is headed "Sanguines"—a heading employed by Catulle Mendès on aggregations of "prose poems" in more than one periodical. La Vaudère did not use it again in the pages of *La Presse*, although she published other vignettes—most obviously the one translated herein as "Sunset"— in evident imitation of the prose poems that many writers in the subgenre produced, especially those who worked for *La Fronde* when Marguerite Durand joined the editorial contest.

But trailing footfalls make the gravel creak, and a skirt, in passing, discrowns the regal heads of roses. It is Phémie, the cook, who, knife in hand, has penetrated into the poultry-yard. Phémie is not malevolent; her rude hair is raised up in discolored locks over a narrow forehead; her fat cheeks stained with bran resemble wild nectarines, and her pale eyes, with narrow irises, have a gaze of passive ingenuousness.

The young woman, one fist on her hip, makes her choice among the birds that hasten to contemplate her, with the ardent hope of a supplementary pittance. Already, she has trapped, without any great effort, the tame duck with the snowy plumage, the preponderant duck with the silk collar that leads the band. The attentive hens gather around Phemie, while she lifts the head of her victim, putting its body between her knees, and she saws through the neck slowly, because the knife is slightly chipped.

Blood, in an impetuous jet, splashes her face and hair; then the red rain falls into the litter, drop by drop, making a pool that spreads out, tinting the sticky straw, escaping in vermilion threads over the brown earth. The feet of the agonizing bird stiffen, its wings have one last beat of anguish, the black pearls of its eyes are veiled, and become extinct . . .

Serenely, Phémie resumes the route to the kitchen, carrying the twitching corpse, between the double hedge of the roses of the little garden, under the sky lightly drowned with blonde light, in the midst of the Fête-Dieu of blooming corollas.

And in the distance, in the poultry-yard, the avid ducks, the greedy chicks and the clucking hens have precipitated themselves on the curée, with fluffed-up feathers and joyous cries. Their beaks plunge ardently into the fetid dung-heap in order to drink the blood, still alive, the warm sweet blood of the executed animal . . .

POMPONNET[1]
(*La Presse*, 17 August 1898)

Avenue de Messie, a bachelor pad on the ground floor: nothing but a bedroom and a dressing-room, but very elegant, garnished with the necessary, and even the superfluous. Bright Liberty wall-hanging with yellow and mauve flower-patterns, curtains, little curtains and complicated blinds that only allow a mysterious light akin go that of a chapel to penetrate. On the walls, a few gallant pastels of the last century and a multitude of photographs of pupils of the Conservatoire, dancers, acrobats, traveling princesses, snobbish women and upmarket whores, fixed by gold pins. For the pretentious, a marble miniature of *The Kiss* and the polar bear that represented the author of the *Comédie humaine* at the last salon.[2] Grrreat Art above all, my dear!

Pomponnet, the handsome Pomponnet, feminist, socialite, journalistic, critic, novelist and dramatic author, is no longer young, but he refrains, like a brave man, from using any creams or cosmetics, and sweeps back insidiously three hairs that are worth twenty. His moustache is, depending on the weather, shiny, gilded, coppery or azure-tinted; thanks to the Liberty blinds, however, it can still play "the crow's wing."

It the hour of the shepherdess, the hour of little Madame

---

1 This item too carried a variant heading: "Les Conquerants" [The Conquerors].

2 The reference is to Rodin's statue of Balzac, described by the critic Bernard Berenson when it was first exhibited as looking like "a polar bear standing on its hind legs." Other contemporary critics were not as kind.

Barbarin, who is in her first fall—the fall of flowers, not of leaves; the fall of a conjugal fidelity thus far intact, although mitigated by sentimental reveries and romantic reading.

Pomponnet has disposed on the table, alongside a superb ledger with a silver clasp, two glasses, a bottle of Spanish wine, dry cakes and Khedive cigarettes. A perfume-burner spreads archaic vapors of sandalwood and myrrh. Before the bed and the divan—sacrificial altars (and how!)—velvet cushions await delicate knees and dainty feet.

Pomponnet is walking back and forth patiently, sure of success, for little Madame Barnarin cannot resist the prestige of feminist writers—undressers of souls and drinkers of consciences—in the troubled hours of the dog days.

A light knock on the door, and Hortense Barbarin, veiled, helmed, cravated and draped in black lace, as befits this solemn moment, makes a timid entrance.

Pomponnet (*pressing her in his arms*): Oh, dear angel!

Hortense: I'm very culpable! If my husband knew!

Pomponnet: He won't know . . . I love you! (*He takes off her shoes with a flick of the wrist and kisses her expertly on the lips.*)

Hortense (*very emotional*): Let me go! I'm afraid!

Pomponnet (*kissing her even more expertly*): Afraid of what? Am I not your friend, your best as well as your most tender friend?

Hortense: What must you think of my step?

Pomponnet (*simultaneously brutal and insinuating, with all the virtuosity of which he is capable*): Child! I adore you!

Hortense: I beg you . . .

Pomponnet: Oh, say, say that you love me!

Hortense (*weakly*): Would I be here if I didn't love you?

Pomponnet: You love me? You love me? Repeat it again! You see, there's only amour, true, faithful, ardent, passionate amour . . . the amour of two young individuals who have met and united irresistibly, in spite of envious, unjust and cruel society! Amour, amour!

(*Pomponnet has eloquence; he punctuates his statement—pronounced many times in similar situations—with embraces, kisses, charming flatteries and graduated, irresistible caresses. Little Madame Barbarin, completely maddened, abandons herself with a great sigh.*

On the walls, the commemorative photographs seem to smile; a pale sunbeam traverses the superimposed blinds and animates the group of The Kiss *and the Balzacian bear; an apposite piano begins to play on the entresol.*)

Hortense (*very red, her eyes moistened by happy tears*): You'll never forget me?

Pomponnet (*coolly*): Never.

Hortense (*in an increasing exaltation*): My master! My king! My lover! My everything!

Pomponnet (*politely*): My dear Hortense!

Hortense: Now we belong to one another for life. We'll no longer be apart . . . oh, death . . . yes, death alone . . .

Pomponnet (*glacially*): I have proofs to correct . . . you'll pardon me.

(*He presents her with her hat, her long collar draped with black lace, and her gloves.*)

Hortense (*anxiously*): When shall I see you again?

Pomponnet: Soon.

Hortense: I'll be so unhappy apart from you, my love! Tomorrow . . . would you like tomorrow?

Pomponnet: Urgent work . . . I'll write to you.

Hortense (*who scents misfortune in the air*): You swear? You'll write to me?

Pomponnet: Certainly.

Hortense: In fact, there's divorce . . . I . . .

Pomponnet (*pushing her gently toward the door*): Adieu, mon amour!

Hortense (*suppliant*): Tomorrow, isn't it? Tomorrow?

Pomponnet: Yes, yes, yes.

Tuesday ninth of August, five o'clock in the afternoon. Madame Hortense B, twenty-three years old, brunette, plump, pretty, honest. Extremities slightly strong. Nature loving, credulous, naïve, even simple-minded, but of particularly signal temperament. In sum, flattering conquest. Number nine hundred and ninety-eight. Oof! At the round figure, I'll take a rest.

THE REMEDY
(*La Presse*, 28 August 1898)

> *Les Amants:*
> *Amantes, divine goldsmiths*
> *Have woven the gold of your hair,*
> *For the warm ruby of your lips,*
> *And the glaucous gems of your eyes.*
>
> *Your flesh is Saxe or Sèvres,*
> *Amantes with radiant bodies,*
> *Eyes more loving than the lips,*
> *And the heart more loving than the eyes.*
>
> *Les Amantes:*
> *You are the pride of our fevers.*
> *Lovers, with glorious kisses,*
> *Eyes that lie more than the lips,*
> *And hearts that lie more than the eyes.*

Geneviève and Raymond are sitting under a large parasol with gray and red stripes, by the seaside. Thin plashing waves come to die at their feet, covering and uncovering two opaline jellyfish on pink seashells, as delicate as nascent flowers. It is five o'clock. The sun is shining obliquely upon the flap of the tent; faint harmonies are escaping from the casino in trills and early notes that seem to dance on the waves. It is the hour of worldly gossip, flirtation and little horses.

Genevieve, a pale, supple brunette with an ardent gaze, remains thoughtful beside Raymond, who is nervously drawing stick figures in the sand with the tip of his cane. She has exhausted the chapter of confidences, has related, almost involuntarily, in an invincible need for frankness, her fears, her rancor and her disappointments of a disdained and betrayed lover. Raymond, discontented, wounded in his self-respect without quite knowing why—since he is as yet only a friend—interrogates her almost brutally:

"In sum, you still love him?"

"The swan song, my friend."

"You miss him?"

"I don't know. That depends on moments. Believe that I aspire to deliverance with all the forces of my being."

"And you have some hope of success?"

"Certainly. I even have a treatment, as you can see. The separation, the change, the new horizons . . ."

"Is the rupture definitive?"

"I hope so. We quit one another having no more to tell, he to take a rest from me—for I'm conscious of having wearied him with my mildness, my docility and my devotion—and me to try to pull myself together, to rediscover a little dignity."

"You're still quite ill, my dear Geneviève."

"Yes, it's a neuralgia of the soul, if I can put it like that. The pain comes and goes, sometimes dull, sometimes stabbing. Sometimes, I no longer feel anything and think I'm cured; then, suddenly, for a cause that remains mysterious—perhaps a mental draught—the pain reappears, fulgurant and intolerable. Oh, a singular suffering that takes away all life and flees one day without leaving any trace."

"You're still at the sharp crisis?"

"Yes, it's a haunting of every instant that I curse and seek . . . and then, most of all, I despise myself infinitely."

Geneviève tries to smile at the young man, inclining her languid pretty head on his shoulder. In the warm light her hair is coppery; her eyes sparkle through the moist fringe of lowered lashes, a little tear glides over the meager cheek and descends to the corner of the lip, and Raymond collects that diamantine pearl tenderly, hugging the desperate woman forcefully, who does not put up any resistance.

"Oh," she says, "don't abandon me! It seems to me that I'll get better. Let me weep in your arms, I beg you . . . for a long time . . . a long time . . ."

"You'll love me, then," he says, joyfully.

"It's necessary . . . you're the remedy."

"The remedy?"

"Amour, my friend, is only cured by amour. Cure me of Ernest!"

THE NECKLACE
(*La Presse*, 9 September 1898)

Gontran and Georges are at table outside a café on the beach, while gypsies scrape away fashionably, and good-time girls in red jackets and white dresses pass back and forth in the swing, provocative in their narrow skirts, buttoned at the back.

Gontran: Nice, the blonde in the black boater.

Georges: You haven't looked very closely; she's only held together by paint.

Gontran: What about the redhead with mauve shoes?

Georges: Leave me tranquil with regard to women; I've many other things on my mind.

Gontran: Gambling?

Georges: Yes, gambling. Nothing left again. Cleaned out, scraped and hung out to dry, as on the best days of the feast.

Gontran (*anxiously*): Alas! Personally . . .

Gontran: Yes, yes, don't worry, I'm not asking you for anything. Only, I don't know how I'll get out of this hole. Usually, my wife comes to my aid.

Gontran: You're lucky. You simply ask her for the sum you've lost, then?

Georges: No, I detach one or two pearls from her necklace. You know her five-row necklace, which excites admiration in the casinos?

Gontran: Certainly. I've even quarreled about it with Fichette, who asked me for one like it. Well, this time, again, you can take a pearl from the famous necklace.

Georges: I've thought of that. Oh, my dear, what a pickle!

And Georges, who has spent the night playing baccarat, can no longer contain his emotion, in the release of his sick nerves. He leans his elbows on the dusty little table and passes a tremulous hand over his dark-ringed eyes with rare lashes and red eyelids.

Gontran (*with a slightly disdainful commiseration*): Come on, old man, pull yourself together.

Georges (*increasingly feverish*): Do you know Paul?

Gontran: Paul Dartoys your best friend?

Georges (*bitterly*): My best friend—oh, if you knew!

Gontran: Explain yourself.

Georges: Listen. Anyway, it will relieve me to tell you these things. Yesterday, therefore, I had taken Mathilde's necklace in order to take it to the jeweler. Three rows already being false; I deplored it, but what do you expect? Bad luck, black bad luck! Fortunately, the largest pearls remained: round, clear, iridescent pearls with an incomparable orient, which had to be very valuable. The jeweler took the necklace, examined it with his magnifying glass from every angle, tested the beads between his teeth and looked at me, smiling.

"How much will you give me?" I asked, impatiently.

He laughed lightly. "Nothing at all, Monsieur. These pearls are false, like the others."

"What do you mean, false?" I was perfectly certain that I'd only sold the first three rows, and I thought the man was mocking me.

Gontran: Then, it was your wife who . . .

Georges: No, my dear, my wife values her necklace more than her skin; she clings to it the way a poet clings to his glory and a speculator to his money. My wife would never have made such a sacrifice for herself or for me.

Gntran: Then?

Georges: I interrogated the jeweler adroitly, and as he had nothing more to expect from my distress, he identified the guilty party to me without too much difficulty.

Gontran: Well?

Georges: Well, old chap, it was Paul Dartoys.

THE FOLLOWER
(*La Presse*, 19 September 1898)

The home of Vicomtesse Anne de Haute-Roche. Pure and sumptuous Renaissance style, in contrast with the white lacquer drawing rooms and pacotille muslins that seem nowadays too vulgar in their effect to our elegant snobs. Old-fashioned fabrics, embroidered and re-embroidered in silk and gold thread, as stiff as chasubles. Florentine sculptures by Donatello, paintings by Giotto, Cimabue and Fra Angelico, gold ornaments by Cellini. The vicomtesse, in an incarnadine brocade dress trimmed with silver-goffered velvet and a large collar of precious guipure, in leafing through the works of Marot and Ronsard. As that reading is a trifle monotonous for her, her forehead inclines over the perfumed starch of her lace and her lovely eyes close slowly. Her frivolous mind is beginning to flutter in the land of dreams when a loud burst of laughter wakes her up abruptly and brings her back to reality.

"Gillette!" she cries, joyfully.

"Yes, Gillette, who forbids you to stuff your head with all this nonsense."

"They're classics."

"Look, this is what I think of your classics . . ."

And Gillette des Cinq-Amants, devoid of pity for the madrigals, elegies and ballads of Marot and Ronsard, sends the two volumes out of the window with a flick of her hand.

"Oh, villain!"

"My word, there's a whiff of mildew in here that saddens the sense of smell."

"I've put on vetiver, bergamot and benzoin."

"That preserves furs and virtue. Personally, I've simply sprinkled a few drops of a new Russian aphrodisiac perfume over my hair, and I've had a great success."

"What kind of success?"

"Followers, all along the road."

"They spoke to you?"

"Only one of them dared, but he avenged the others."

"A chic type?"

"Alas!"

"It's necessary to sow . . ."

"If you think it's easy to sow men! And it's almost always the old ones who are the most ardent. First, they examine your face, at an angle, in profile, from behind; touch you, step in front of you, move back, execute complicated maneuvers, stop in front of shop windows at random, contemplating with an extraordinary interest tapeworms in alcohol or women's hats, penetrate into coaching entrances, and then, finally, speak to you."

"What do they say?"

"It doesn't vary much. 'You're charming, What little feet! Oh, what a pretty waist . . .' The cunning employ a trick that sometimes works for them. A Monsieur approaches you with a profound respect and murmurs, in a minor key: 'It seems to me, Madame, that you have been presented in society this winter.' Or, if he has a great habitude of such operations: 'Would you permit me to accompany you? A turn around the Bois, my beautiful child . . . ? Private booth . . . ? Discreet ground floor . . . ? You'll see, you'll see!' There's also the Monsieur who has flirted with you at Vichy or Trouville and who gives you a few vague details, for form's sake. There's the well-brought-up man who excuses himself: 'Oh, pardon me if I'm importuning you . . . ' And finally, there's the lout who . . . I won't go on."

Anne de Haute-Roche remains silent, absorbed and languorous, her gaze distant. Gillette resumes, volubly: "I never respond, of course. When the quarter is deserted, I amuse myself momentarily; if not, I put on my air of an outraged infanta and cross from one sidewalk to the other without turning my head. Almost all of them understand."

"However . . ."

"Yes, today I was unlucky—and in the middle of the boulevard, no less! In front of a heap of people who might have known me and made hay with my adventure . . . He was a dark-haired fellow with a moustache, rather good looking, but reeking of flashy foreigner at twenty paces. He followed my detours and my circuits with a geometrical precision, stopped when I stopped and, from time to time, addressed a few words to me in some gibberish. I was as red as a poppy, and so angry that tears rose to my eyes. I know that there's a *sergent de ville* there, but we all recoil before the extremity of an explanation that provokes perfectly ridiculous gatherings."

"So, my poor Gillette?"

"As I was arranging and pulling myself together, I suddenly had a providential inspiration, a luminous idea, a stroke of genius. My flashy foreigner is still running!"

"Oh, do tell!"

And Gillette, with a soft smile, said: "It's quite simple. I went into a jeweler's shop."

FIAMETTE[1]
(*La Presse*, 2 October 1898)

"I'm bored," she said.

She was dainty, curvaceous, slightly plump under the old flower-patterned silk of her dress, with a frail figure tightened by a silver belt with glass beads. An immense black hat was lifted up over her short hair, so curly that her delicate face seemed to be huddling in a nest of golden foam.

With the slightly theatrical arrangement of her costume she was delightful in her youth and strangeness.

He was sitting on the edge of the water, fishing with a line. He had pink cheeks, pink eyelids, pink ears and a short beard that, at a certain distance, also seemed pink. And his speech, his reflections and his character were the same tender and candid color.

He was hypnotizing himself following with his eyes the little red cork that was gliding in the eddies of the current and dancing on the waves. All around, the long grass, where the umbels of hemlock trembled, was a potent green color, a green nurtured on fat mud, in the thin shade of willows.

"I'm bored," the child repeated.

He shook his head without responding.

Then she stamped her foot impatiently.

"I'm bored! I'm bored, I'm bored! Let's go!"

He turned round and looked behind him, between two branches, at the landscape that was delicately nuanced, in the distance, by the pale green of rye and the lilac of lucerne.

---

1 This story appeared under a heading that translates as "For Anglers."

"Go for a little walk . . . a voyage of discovery. You can pick flowers."

"No, no, I have enough of them. We've been here for two hours, and you're stupefying yourself spying on your hook."

"Go," he said. "Don't worry about me." But as she drew away, sulking, he shouted at her, in a fit of remorse: "Don't be long, though . . ."

She marched nonchalantly, making her hips sway under her metal belt. The earth was dry, crackling with the songs of crickets; the sand was aurified by gleams and flew up in light clouds around her skirts. The odor of a cowshed reached her, warmed by the sheet metal of a brilliant sky. White hens were clucking, pecking the ground with brief thrusts, followed by a troop of downy chicks: yellow cocoons in which the black pearls of eyes shone. On the roofs, pigeons were moving their backs with metallic reflections and their quicksilver necks with crimson sheens.

Curiously, she leaned on a fence. In the midst of convolvulus, whose flowers incensed her with an almond perfume, and she looked.

In the courtyard, a young man with long hair, his hands spattered with colors, was drinking a bowl of milk.

"Fiamette!" he said. "What a surprise!"

She went in, and darted a glance at the canvas that he had posed beside him. The fresh paint, applied in luminous layers, represented a pink fisherman fishing in violet water.

"Why," she said, "that's Hippolyte!"

"Who's Hippolyte? The fellow with the tiddlers?" Then, stopping: "Oh, pardon me, perhaps he's your friend?"

They started to laugh, and she told him how she had met Hippolyte—who had come in search of matches, as a neighbor—in the studio of a great artist who painted candy-floss women sitting on Savoy cakes in front of a bubble-gum moon: a reserve, for lean days!

She was posing in a suggestive costume, which impressed
the naïve fellow: her delicate neck, plump and white, remained
naked under the short curly mane that put a nimbus around
her head; then, from the shoulders to the heels, a sheath of
gemmed brocade, ocellated like a peacock's tail with glass eyes
with golden eyelids, enveloped her, making her resemble a
charming and magnificent idol. He had fallen in love with
her immediately and had told her so, in spite of the green
and blue phantoms that were floating, from the wainscot to
the friezes, like the nightmares of hashish. He took her to his
modest lodgings of three-hundred-francs-a-month employee
and they were happy for a while. But she was already missing
the fallacious art-students and pale aesthetes with crazed gazes
and vibrant speech who perpetrated immortal masterpieces
with a goose-quill.

"You're bored, then?" asked the painter.

"And how!" sighed Fiamette.

"And you'd renounce the opulence of three hundred francs
a month?"

"Yes," she said, nobly. "I'd love you for yourself. Come on"

"That's perfect; you can pose for me as Loie Fuller's Salome.
A delightful canvas—you'll see!"

And they left, while Hippolyte, ignorant of his misfortune,
continued to hypnotize himself with a little red cork that was
gliding in the eddies of the current and dancing on the waves,
as fragile and vagabond as Fiamette's heart.

UNDERGROWTH
(*La Presse*, 20 October 1898)

Jean Fremel, the last poet, has brought his young friend, Mademoiselle Georgette, into the autumnal countryside, which a languid sun is caressing with its lukewarm and melancholy radiance. With his arm passed around the waist of the darling, he talks to her about his aspirations, his projects and his dreams of the future—the beautiful dreams that blossom in the imagination of a few poor devils destined for the worst disappointments.

Georgette is scarcely listening, her mind haunted by the memory of a mauve surah dress in the form of a bell with little pleats, which she has seen in a shop window. With all the resources of her feminine cunning she is searching mentally for the means of procuring the fortune item, which, provided with a frilly lawn underskirt with ribbons and lace trimmings, would ensure her success at the Moulin Rouge.

Jean, with a benevolent candid smile and countless amorous flatteries, draws the girl into the metallic foliage fringed with rust, the leaves of which are detaching one by one, reminiscent of gold and silver tears against the sadness of a faded and chilly water-color backcloth.

For him, the old trees, the disjointed grilles and the stones ravaged by moss are adorned with unexpected seductions. His enfevered desires are projected upon them like a fragile loom, and he embroiders the fantasies of his brain thereon, with silk thread and pearls that the sumptuous caprice of a rajah would envy.

Georgette yawns and makes no response.

"What do you call a sonnet? It isn't too long, I hope?"

"Listen:

> *Words have their color, and kisses too,*
> *Some, already faded, pale under the leaf,*
> *Fly away sadly toward mourning summits*
> *Weeping the remorse of merciless farewells.*
>
> *Others, like April snow in the sunlit wood,*
> *Expand suddenly in fresh clusters*
> *Of amber and honey, which, in the evening*
> *Intoxicate the light hearts of carefree lovers.*
>
> *Some have the discreet hue of violets;*
> *Others, almost effaced, soft frail skeletons*
> *Seem to me a swarm of dying butterflies.*
>
> *The black kiss of evil bites a whore thus,*
> *But the sovereign kiss of which my being is fond*
> *Is your joyful kiss, your ardent red kiss."*

Georgette, who thinks she has found a means of obliging Jean to offer her the mauve surah dress in the form of a bell with little pleats, utters an approving burst of laughter that charms the vanity of the poet.

"Oh," he says, "you understand me and you love me, Georgette. With your tenderness I will do great and noble things! I've formed an entire magnificent plan, which will ensure our happiness."

"You can tell me about it another day, my dear Jean. Yesterday, I saw a pretty, pretty skirt, with a bodice . . ."

But Jean, once launched, no longer stops. He talks for an hour, with an enthusiasm and an eloquence that even astonishes him.

"Yes," he says, in conclusion, "I feel an energy capable of stirring the world, and scaling its highest summits."

Then Georgette says, disdainfully: "Do you think you're delighting me? I too have scaled many mattresses."[1]

---

1 Unfortunately, the wordplay linking *sommets* [summits] with Georgette's misapprehended *sommiers* [mattresses] loses a great deal in literal translation.

THE DRUNKARD
(*La Presse*, 6 November 1898)

Mélie has returned home with her man, Mélo, to the little
apartment on the sixth floor, composed of a bedroom and a
half, and a quarter of a kitchen, with a skylight looking over
the roofs. In the bedroom, the bed, with a guipure coverlet
against a backcloth of scarlet andrinople, recalls the roulette
of an extra-lucid somnambulist; on the walls, salmon pink
paper with green tulips is ornamented by three aggressive
chromolithographs and a few photographs of friends in plush
frames. A felt carpet, a chest of drawers, a table and four mahogany chairs complete the "furniture" of the narrow room.
The window, with a light wooden balustrade, is open upon the
starry sky; on leaning out, one perceives, as if at the bottom of
a well, the incessantly-swarming street and the curved file of
gas jets illuminating vague signs. It is with an indefinable sentiment of malaise that one approaches that window, which,
attracting like a gulf, seems a perpetual danger, an invitation
to suicide and criminal vertigo.

Mélie has taken off her mantle of black cloth and turned
toward Mélo, who has collapsed on a chair, already somnolent.

"Drunk again!" she says, vehemently. "I did myself an
injury hoisting you up this far! You were at the bottom of the
stairs, stumbling over the steps, for an hour! What have you
been doing all day?"

In a thick voice, he replies: "Well, isn't it Sunday? One can
amuse oneself a little."

"You call that amusing yourself?"

"Well, it's one way . . . and if I think it's the best?"

"You go out drinking when we no longer have a sou, when we owe the baker and the butcher, not to mention two months' rent, which the porter has told me will soon get us thrown out!"

Mélo utters a laugh of scornful superiority.

"A blockhead, the porter. The landlord will be paid, and the other oafs too."

"With what?"

"With this."

And Mélo takes out of his pocket a brand new hundred-franc bill, which seems to Mélie, in the candlelight, to be an opaline pink and blue flower, blooming prettily, a flower of paradise. Swiftly, she extends her head to take possession of the marvelous corolla, which, as in *contes de fées*, will grant her desires simply by blowing on it. But her man looks at her suspiciously and puts the bill back in his pocket.

"Hold on! I earned it, didn't I?"

Trembling, she seizes his arm. "How did you earn it, then?"

"I certainly haven't murdered anyone! With a comrade's money I bet on the races. That's my share. It's a bonus in recognition . . ."

"A bonus? You were both on strike, without a brass farthing!"

"It's an inheritance that big Auguste came into. Anyway, you're annoying me. That's enough."

"You were gambling on the races? You had a good tip, then?"

"You said it."

"Give me your winnings, Mélo, there's a good lad!"

With a mocking expression, Mélo fishes the bill out of his pocket again and turns it in front of the candle like a huge moth with extended wings.

"You're killing the kid!"

Mélie puts her hands tighter, in anguish, imploring with word and gesture, and bends her knees as if before an omnipotent and mocking divinity that it is necessary to cherish and fear.

"Will you give me your little banknote to look at, my darling; will you give it to me to buy goodies . . . ?"

Gravely, Mélo has brought out his pipe, has stuffed it methodically, and, having approached the candle, is holding out the bill so the tremulous flame.

Mélie utters a piercing scream and throws herself on the drunkard.

"You can't do that!"

"Why can't I do that?"

"It's a crime, you hear? A crime! Oh, the wretch . . . !"

"You're not funny, kid! Look and see . . . it'll make a lovely fire!"

One edge of the bill has caught fire. The woman, with the growl of a wild beast disputing a prey, throws herself on Mélo, brings nails and teeth into play, clings to him, succeeds in tearing away the burning paper, and extinguishes it in her clenched hands. But the man, with an evil gaze striped with red threads seizes her by the nape of the neck and tips her over, in spite of her gasps.

"Necessary to finish it!"

Now she howls with fear, pummeling the furious male with her fists, who drags her to the window, lifts her up, pushes her over the frail bar and dangles her in the void.

While she spins, tragic and feeble, her breath extinct, before flattening on the sidewalk—her limbs pulped, her skull emptied like a coconut—Mélo, tranquilly, presents the reconquered banknote to the flame, watches it burn while exhaling a few puffs of good pipe smoke, and then leans out of the widow with a gross laugh of satisfaction.

"Well, Mélie, you did your best—but I lit it anyway!"

MONSIEUR, MADAME . . .
(*La Presse*, 11 November 1898)

Max and Genevieve have been married for eighteen months, but they love one another enormously, while affecting before society an indifference in the best taste. However—still for the sake of society—Monsieur, who has acquired a large dowry, believes that he ought to offer himself a chic conquest from time to time: an expert old lady, highly quoted, or a young person still intact, making her debut. It is thus that he meets, at an intimate supper in the home of Cora de Namur, a charming child, as candid and pretty as one could wish, whose fall—her initial fall—is tariffed at five hundred louis by a lady in a red wig whom she calls her mother.

Lise Michon—pronounced Lisa Michaël—has to create a small role in the pantomime of the *Frantic Sprees*, and she would like to make the two "affairs" coincide in order to clothe herself prestigiously above and beneath. Max has appeared to fulfill the desired conditions to operate the sensational launch; so he finds himself addressed, for some time, with very amiable letters accompanied by suggestive photographs, in which Lise Michon risks herself under veil of her modesty alone. It is one of those photographs that Geneviève has found in Max's dinner jacket, and she has been stifled by sobs since the morning; it seems to her that furious wild beasts are tearing apart and devouring her heart. She has never suffered as much!

Max, his trousers hanging well over his varnished shoes, his slim waist in a white waistcoat buckled and strapped inexorably—his festival strapping—is curling his moustache with little iron tongs.

Geneviève (*attempting to adopt a detached air*): You're going to leave me alone again this evening?

Max: It's necessary. Heavy losses at the club yesterday, you understand?

Geneviève (*weakly*): You're lying! No, no, don't deny it! (*Holding out the photograph.*) Your club is called Lise Michon. According to this portrait dedicated by 'Lise to her first conqueror, tomorrow's conqueror!' and this letter: 'This evening at ten o'clock Maman will be at Mademoiselle Couesdon's consulting the Angel[1] and I'll be waiting for you,' no doubt is any longer permitted to me . . . Shut up! I know other things too. Yesterday, you were chatting in the drawing room with Guy d'Étoiles, and as the lamps hadn't been brought I was listening invisibly behind the piano. 'Oh, the bitch.' said d'Étoiles in his falsetto voice, 'her success in the *Frantic Sprees* will be colossal. That girl sings with her legs. Then, what's splendid my dear, is that she's new, quite new! The price? A pittance! But it needs a man, young, handsome, elegant, worldly, titled . . . you, for example, if you hadn't married the most adorable of wives.' Then you started to laugh, flattered in your self esteem, and you riposted: 'Geneviève? She'll love me all the more afterwards. I could make her mistake the sun for the beacon of the Eiffel Tower! She's as innocent as a garden rabbit!'

Max (*profoundly troubled*): Calm down, darling!

Geneviève: Never! We'll divorce, my good friend, and if you don't want to, I'll deceive you in my turn; I'll take a lover . . . two, so there! I'll render you utterly ridiculous. What has that brazen hussy got that I haven't? I too was new when you married me. A fine merit! I thought that kids bought

---

1 Mademoiselle Couesdon, who began to channel the angel Gabriel in 1896, soon cultivated a great reputation in Parisian occult circles.

a Christmas present—and for the initiation, it was me who paid the fat dowry!

Max: You're mistaken; d'Étoiles will tell you . . .

Geneviève: D'Étoiles? He's told me everything, and it isn't the first time. I find him charming! He loves me!

Max (*furiously*): What, you've listened to that ridiculous aesthete, who calls himself a feminist and defends women, doubtless because he can't attack them? But it's him who did all the harm, by trying to debauch me in order to worm his way into your good graces! Forgive me, darling. We're both at fault, let's leave it there. Anyway, little Michon was just for posing . . . a kid whose virginity only holds by persuasion. Less pretty than you and who scarcely tempted me. It's d'Étoiles who . . . and he did it in order . . . oh, he'll pay for it!

Geneviève: Yes, let's avenge ourselves.

Max: How?

Geneviève: Of course! By sending him the portrait of Michon with the letter: 'This evening at ten o'clock . . .' Lisette's flower will cost him dear!

Max: He doesn't have a sou; what a rabbit-hole for the poor child!

Geneviève (*laughing*): D'Étioles' child? Have you never looked at him? Ah! Well, certainly . . .

Max: Yes I believe that she'll be able to repeat the five hundred louis coup!

ZIZI, ZOZO
(*La Presse*, 25 November 1898)

> *I should like to distil in subtle perfumes*
> *All the enchantments of my defunct amours,*
> *And in my uncertain and fragile memory*
> *Retain them like a balm in a clay vase*
>
> *They would fume, as light as celestial gold;*
> *An insatiable lover, I would respire them.*
> *And intoxicate myself with them in morose hours,*
> *Inclining my heart over them, as over roses.*

Zizi is fifteen years old, Zozo is ten. With their parents, every summer, they come to spend their vacations in a nicely feathered little nest in the country, on the edge of the woods, where they can twitter and frolic like sparrows all day long. But for some time, Zizi has replaced her childish dress with a "formal" skirt, which forms over her contours an amorous calyx that causes the voluptuous corolla of her breasts and hips to creak. Zizi is a newly opened flower who wants her share of the sunlight and who is opening generously—poor thing!—on the road of life. The sun, personified by Célestin Chazotte, the son of the Maire, has launched a few rays in her direction, and she nestles in their soft warmth with the innocence of the flowers and beasts of the good God.

Célestin is a tall boy with curly blond hair, and the advantageous manners that succeed with women. He is consciously "doing finger exercises," preluding with a few sylvan chords before playing Wagner in salons. Last Sunday, Zizi listened to the melody in the woods, and the tune, which has become an amorous obsession, is singing recklessly in her memory. She recalls that she and Célestin left Zozo in a hedge of plum trees and mulberry bushes and found themselves, as if by chance, in the depths of a mysterious hiding-place resembling the golden grille of a confessional, in the middle of a cathedral of sunlit verdure. The student recited Verlaine and collected forget-me-nots, the ingenuous eyes of which were gazing at them in the grass. Zizi, blushing, shredded the petals of daisies, which have been polite oracles.

On returning home, after that first intoxication, she piously placed her little bouquet in a Japanese vase splashed with ocher, cinnabar and aquamarine. The little blue flowers mutated into brown threads as thin as Spanish tobacco under her mad kisses, but, still cherishing them, she comes every evening to make her devotions before the funereal vase: "Lord! Virgin Mary! I have given my heart to Célestin! Enable him to be worthy of it! Enable me to marry him and love him forever!"

Water has been droning in the gutters since morning, the thousand little fingers of the rain drumming a murderous march against the windows sustained by the great organs of the wind, unleashed in the branches. Célestin has written that he will not come, and Zizi has replied that she is very sad, while Zozo makes paper boats and locomotives. But Zozo does not linger for long in the same pleasures, and his absurd imagination is never at a loss.

"Sister," he says, "I have an idea. We're going to play at the Deluge in the garden, and when we've very wet, we'll dry ourselves in the roadman's hut with Mirza and Tom. That will be the Ark. You don't want to? Let's play soldiers, then. I'll be the poor wounded man and you can be the canteen lady. You can give me little glasses of cassis, which is in the cupboard. No? What if we were to organize a great hunt, then? We'll let the cockatoo out and we'll chase it in the apartment imitating the hiss of a serpent. When it has cried out a lot and raised its crest, we'll take it prisoner with a chain on its foot. You can put the chain on. There are also the gardener's canaries, which we could bombard with beans."

Zizi shrugs her shoulders. "Shut up! You're nothing but an insupportable nuisance!"

"I'm a man! I'm a man!"

"Zut!"

"A man! A man!"

She writes to her dear Célestin that the time seems mortally long to her and that there is not a minute when she does not think about him.

I'm afraid of not seeing you again. It's stupid, isn't it? There's no reason for you to forget me, since we've sworn to marry when we're old enough. I've put the forget-me-nots you gave me in a vase on the mantelpiece. They're no longer anything but a little lace of withered and ragged flowers, a pale dust that I kiss piously after saying my prayers. Sweet forget-me-nots, I'll conserve you forever . . .

But Zizi utters a shrill scream; Zozo, with the vase on his lap, is fabricating a cigarette with the frail bouquet rolled in the wrapper of a chocolate pastille. Sprawling on the divan, he is drawing enormous draughts, as he has seen Célestin do, but he cannot succeed in making the smoke come out through his nose. All the flowers have gone into it, and the room is filled by an acrid odor of roasted herbs.

"Oh, the wretch! The wretch!"

Before his sister's tearful eyes and desolate expression, he understands that he has done something bad, and is glorious in consequence, in spite of his imminent nausea.

"Hey, Zizi, I'm smoking too! You can see that I'm a man!"

IN THE CABARET
(*La Presse*, 10 December 1898)

An unimportant tea in the home of the young Baronne de Ravenel.

A few extra-smart socialites have come to exhibit tomorrow's fashions. Weary of Venetian henna and oxygenated water, they are sporting tresses of royal blue and celadon green. It is the last cry of the exposition.

The men are wearing orchids of an as-yet-unknown species in their buttonholes. Flirtation is triumphant in every corner. Everyone is repeating the "adorable" trivia that express so many things, and the habitual nonsense is being trotted out: frictions of the hand, glowing gazes, provocative smiles showing all the teeth, fearful little laughs, sustained from time to time by the vibrant contralto of the beautiful Madame Pinsonner; upright, vibrant with passion, her eyes capsized, with her hands feverishly joined, as if in ecstasy, she is clamoring:

> *Yes, I am your slave*
> *My roaring lion!*
> *Aaah!*

It is the yawn of a wild beast lurking in the savannah, and the audience has a hot flush in its marrow-bones. On a low divan covered with a Japanese Mikado robe and crowned with a silky awning with multiple drapes that sustains three golden mousmés, Lola Robin and Vicomte Ramone are entirely emancipated. The Vicomte, hussar-style, is requesting a rendezvous for tomorrow in a hidden place, and she responds with a little phrase that all her friends know very well.

"Come on, my dear, enough! No stupidities!"

She has even been nicknamed "No stupidities." That immediately puts an amiable note into the most banal conversations.

Behind a screen, Mademoiselle Paule Lampion, the pretentious and malevolent young woman with a diploma whom one encounters in all salons, is discussing literature with Oscar de Ravenel, the master of the house. Mademoiselle Lampion is a tall, poorly-groomed individual with strangely mobile simian eyes under harsh eyebrows with a disquietingly large ferrety nose. While all the other women are displaying milky, pearly or diamante shoulders, she is sporting a kind of carcan, which is said to hide a chronic birthmark. Her underclothes are generally unknown; those who have had a little peek maintain a rare discretion.

Baronne de Ravenel seems to be unmoved by her husband's flirtation. She has found herself, as if by chance, beside the handsome Serge Nangis, who has been soliciting her for six months. Serge has slyly taken a soft hand, ringed all the way to the little finger and rubbed with the subtlest essences.

"Oh, say that it's for tomorrow?" he implores, with all the ardor of a long-delayed desire . . . "Tomorrow, no? I know a discreet little cabaret on the heights of Montmartre, at the end of the world. No one will know, I swear!"

And with a consenting smile, she says: "Oh well, yes. Tomorrow my husband has his headache."

"His headache and Mademoiselle Lampion! That's a serious influenza. He won't be on his feet for a week . . . you'd like that, dear angel?"

The beautiful Madame Pinsonnet has left the grand piano, and Pierre Laval, the lover of chanteuses—no one knows why—has escorted her back to her place and is whispering something in her ear.

Under the Japanese silk awning, Lola is defending herself ever more slackly.

"Come on, my dear, enough! No stupidities!"

And the rendezvous that Ramone's fingers, knees and varnished shoes are soliciting is finally granted.

In the discreet cabaret on the heights of Montmartre, Baronne de Ravenel is sitting next to Serge in a charming intimacy. The crayfish and the partridges were a mistake, but the champagne is bubbling in three glasses and the baronne has sacked the rose-basked in order to make a large sash of the Légion d'amour.

"You can see that we have nothing to fear, my adored," murmurs the young man, caressing his friend's minuscule ears with the tip of his moustache.

"Oh yes—alone finally alone, my love. Let's thank Mademoiselle Lampion, who has exasperated Oscar's neuralgia. He's been shut in his room since seven o'clock, giving me leave until midnight. He thinks I'm at a concert of the *Arts ingénus*. How nice it is, my love, to deceive one's husband!"

Suddenly, the young baronne goes frightfully pale; in the booth to the right crystal laughter has burst forth like a string of small pearls, and these typical words have made themselves heard:

"Come on, my dear, enough! No stupidities!"

Serge, slightly ruffled, reassures the baronne: "You must be mistaken. It's not possible." And his lips attempt to stifle the last scruples on the lips of the darling.

The fidelity of Madame de Ravenel is only holding on any longer by a single blonde hair when, in the booth to the left, a Vesuvian contralto quivers:

Everything is there, even the nostalgic yawn of the wild beast lurking in the savannah.

The young baronne has risen to her feet as if moved by a spring.

"Come on, Serge, come on! They might hear us and betray us! Oscar is so jealous!"

Rapidly, they descend the spiral staircase and head for a fiacre providentially halted outside the door. It is salvation; the baronne rushes forward, but recoils almost immediately, tottering, speechless and breathless.

On the cushions of the yellow fiacre Oscar and Paule Lampion are clutched in a tight embrace. In their ecstasy they have not even perceived that they have arrived. Oscar's eyes are closed and Paule's big nose is quivering with pleasure.

A thrust of the outraged woman's umbrella recalls them to a sentiment of decency. Alas, this is the headache. Oh, these discreet Montmartrean cabarets!

The Baron and the Baronne de Ravenel are applying for a divorce.

BURGLAR!
(*La Presse*, 17 December 1898)

Everything is silent and dormant in the abode of the blonde Madame des Ablettes. A night-light in an opaline glass, which presents an amour crowned with roses, discreetly illuminates the lovers who are holding one another in an embrace on a polar bear-skin and whispering their ecstasies lip to lip. Aline des Ablettes, whom a long corridor separates from her husband, is still trembling, and that invincible dread puts a sort of impetuous feverishness into her effusions, which has a great charm for blasé individuals.

"You can't hear anything, Victor?"

"No. How can he have come back? I left him at the club not an hour ago, in the process of dealing a bank. He'd had bad luck, and will be obstinate. Bad luck is like a mistress who deceives you: one rages, and remains."

"How do you know?"

"From a friend. Before you, my adored, I didn't know what a woman was."

"And before you, my dear, I didn't know what a man was. Hold on; I'll open the window a little so that we can see the stars and breathe the spring air . . . Oh, how good it is to be alive! I love you! You love me! We love one another!

Suddenly, Aline sits up straight, fearfully. A door grates, a match is struck, and an authoritarian tread . . .

"It's him! That's Théophile's tread! Wait; I'll go prepare his chamomile for him . . . the affair of a moment, and with a little chloral . . ."

The beloved blonde flees, lightly, in her mauve peplum, a provocative and serpentine blur.

On the bear-skin, where he remains buried like an explorer in the snow, Victor tickles his palms vaguely with the long, rough hairs, changes position, yawns, rubs his nose, and finds the time long . . .

How difficult can it be to swallow that chamomile? In the warm atmosphere, under the opaline gleam of the night-light, an irresistible somnolence is about to close his eyes when an apprehension makes him turn them toward the window-door that gives access to the balcony. Is it a fit of madness? A nightmare? A hallucination? The curtain has trembled and a hand, which seems immense, has moved the silky fabric aside.

That hairy hand, deformed and hideous, with fingers crushed into spatulas, hard nails, horny and as if blood-stained, seems to grow and, like a dream tarantula, tries to traverse the bedroom in order to grip Victor's foot. Livid, he watches the murderous spider, which clenches the curtain, as if indecisive, before gathering itself in order to hurl itself on its prey. A minute passes in those Hoffmannesque sensations, and it is almost with relief that the lover sees an arm emerge from the shadow, a torso, and finally, the hirsute head of a sinister rogue, an assassin or burglar.

The man looks around anxiously, scrutinizing all the corners, while neglecting the candid whiteness of the bear-skin, listens momentarily, snaffles a few jewels, a purse of gold, and sets about breaking into a pretty Pomapadour secretaire, which is imprudently displaying its rosewood paunch. The item of furniture resists, the thief works harder, and Victor launches forward to punish the wretch. His avenging fist advances, strikes, strikes again, when a similar tread resonates in the long corridor. The husband!

Victor has no more blood in his veins; and it is while quivering that he is now striking the burglar on the shoulder.

The other has turned round, ready for murder.

But Victor understands, suddenly, that his presence in the room is inexplicable, even to arrest a burglar, and that if Monsieur des Ablettes surprises them thus, he is doomed and will doom his adored Aline with him! What a situation! My God, what to do? What to do?

"My friend," he murmurs, his voice suppliant, "have pity on me! Don't betray me!"

The man, rendered speechless by an excess of bewilderment, looks at him, wide-eyed.

And the husband's footsteps come closer.

"Comrade," says Victor, with the energy of despair, "I'll compensate you generously. Come, let's flee! Yes, by the same route!"

"?"

And the lover, in a luminous inspiration:

"You've guessed it; I'm a burglar!"

RESCUE
(*La Presse*, 27 December 1898)

The passers-by linger on the bridge to watch the boats gliding indefatigably. The yellow water, eddying lightly near the piles, has silver gleams; beautiful autumn sunlight illuminates the curb-chains of the horses, strikes sparks from the buttons of the coachmen and the grooms, caresses the braid of military trousers and the whiteness of little patissiers out for a stroll. There are three of them, full baskets on their heads, considering the maneuvers of a tug, as large as a fly, which is spitting its black smoke breathlessly, panting at the head of barges.

Two young women clad in long sixty-nine-tail zibeline mantles are lifting up the snow of their Malines underskirts over arachnean silk stockings. A matron, florid and plumed like a rich wedding-basket, goes past them, looking them over with an expert eye. Then there are bourgeois, notable merchants, idlers and prostitutes. In the sumptuously harnessed carriages guided by disdainful ephebes with crushing opinions, the handsome messieurs and the beautiful madames stretch out for a tour of the Bois. Handcarts overflowing with violets, pomegranates, apples and oranges incense the air with a heady perfume, mingled with the bitter odor of the Parisian pavement.

At the corner of the bridge, crouching in a pose of fatigue and resignation, a little old woman is holding out her hand. Her cheeks are wrinkled, bronzed and pitted like a road-map, and in the depths of her somber orbits, hollowed out like niches, the blue eyes—oil-lamp night-lights—are vacillating and distant.

From dawn till dusk the beggar-woman, immobile and silent, awaits from the munificence of passers-by the few sous that allow her to live. But she scarcely sees any, for the sous of the passers-by go to others: to street charlatans, clowns, cheats and thieves; to the poseurs of the sidewalk who augment themselves with humps, make themselves up with ulcers and leprosies, support themselves on crutches, or surround themselves with advertising posters and the lachrymatory urns of the maws of dogs.

Indifferent to discreet poverty, the florid matrons, the bourgeois, the notable merchants, the idlers and the prostitutes draw away. The pauperess does not complain, however. A thought has germinated within her, and has become an obsession that she takes up, turns over and caresses at every moment of the day like a rare collector's item: the unique exhibit in the museum of observations and disillusionment that forms her existence.

Night falls. The old woman, resolutely, puts her leg over the parapet of the bridge and lets herself fall into the water.

Her fall has made no more noise than that of a dead branch detached from the trunk; no one, doubtless, has heard it. Around her, Paris is singing, quivering, having fun, plotting and numbing itself. The sky is starless, but the Seine, with the red and green lights of its boats, takes on the appearance of a great Venetian canal, of a river with gondolas and serenades. To either side of the quays, the gas lamps extend to infinity under the skeletons of meager trees, corroded by rust and dust; orchestral strains emerge through the windows of a gipsy café surrounded by bare-headed waitresses.

However, the accident has not passed unperceived. A rescuer has raced forward and dived several times, and after a feeble struggle, has brought out the desperate woman, so thin and lamentable in her ragged skirt, who appears hardly human. Immediately, a crowd has formed of people avid for emotions. With curiosity, the florid matrons, the bourgeois, the notable merchants, the idlers and the prostitutes interrogate one another.

The old woman, turned over and over, rubbed and massaged, opens a dolorous eye. Slowly, her gaze scans the crowd and, in the vacillating flame of her blue night-light, a tear dries up.

"Oh, my worthy people," she says, so quietly that no one hears her, "what have I done that you should be so wicked? I haven't had the right to live; now I don't even have the right to die."

THE PASSER-BY
(*La Presse*, 10 January 1899)

Subject for placing above the clock

A mysterious landscape, an operetta palace, a flowery balcony, moonlight. Vanitza, in a white brocade robe with a serpentine train, her hair in hectic powdered curls under a bonnet gemmed with turquoises and amethysts, sends a last kiss to a female friend who is going away.

Vanitza: Don't worry, Nanie; I will carry out the commission, and since your gallant has ceased to please you I shall try to cure him of his amour. You say that he will die of it? Bah! Do men die of love? You will marry Signor Perduccio, old Perduccio, who displays his ugliness and his wealth in the sunlight. Perhaps you're right to prefer to the ruined youth the rich old man who will shower you with presents. Lorenzo would only bring you his pretty face, and he would have deceived you with all the courtesans. Perduccio might want to, but he no longer can! Adieu, Nanie, be well. You'll invite me to the wedding?

Lorenzo (*singing in the distance*):

> *Here comes spring, my charmer*
> *The snows of winter are ended,*
> *The branches and nest are flourishing;*
> *It is raining happiness, my love,*
>   *In the nests.*

Vanitza: Too much guitar, Lorenzo! Nanie has just departed and I already have something to say on her behalf.

Lorenzo (*in a cherry-colored mantle and a black cap with a cock's feather*): Nanie was to wait for me in your house . . .

Vanitza: She preferred to confide to me what she desired to tell you. Bad news, Lorenzo . . . courage! The child no longer loves you.

Lorenzo (*laughing disdainfully*): You're joking, and it's a game that scarcely befits your honest soul. Why would Nanie no longer love me? Have I been lacking in some duty of tact or tenderness? Have I not sent her flowers every morning? Have I not given her serenades every evening? There is no lover more attentive than me, and I will even confide to you, in secret, that I'm beginning to weary of my constancy.

Vanitza: Then all is for the best.

Lorenzo: No, for I don't believe you. A woman never ceases to cherish her first love, and if you're trying to excite my jealousy, you're wasting your time.

Vanitza: Since that's what you think, I'll speak to you frankly. Not two months ago I saw your beauty in Giomo's arms, at the gate of her garden. They were kissing one another on the lips. Cordiani has given her pink pearls and Perduccio is marrying her.

Lorenzo (*white with rage*): I'll kill Nanie's three lovers!

Vanitza: There are too many; wait a while. In any case, your love is cooling . . .

Lorenzo (*brandishing a stiletto*): It's reigniting! I curse the infidel, and never have I loved her so much! I feel that I have the strength to kill a wild beast . . . I shall kill or be killed, but there will be blood . . . a lake of blood! Oh, the perfidious woman! The traitress! The wretch! I adore her!

Vanitza (*aside*): It's necessary to avoid a disaster; let's try to lie brazenly. (*She bursts out laughing.*)

Lorenzo: Why are you laughing?

Vanitza: I've never been so amused.

Lorenzo (*vexed*): It's not funny.

Vanitza: If you could see yourself, you wouldn't think that. Come on, keep your fury for a better occasion. None of that is true. Time seemed long to me, today; I wanted to offer myself the comedy of your jealous wrath.

Lorenzo: Then, Nanie . . . ?

Vanitza: Is the model of all the virtues and has never ceased to think of you. She's an angel!

Lorenzo: But the presents, the kisses . . .

Vanitza: They were for me, as well as the request for marriage. Perduccio is committing follies to please me.

Lorenzo (*incredulously*): You're boasting. Nanie is the prettiest girl in the village.

Vanitza: So you say.

Lorenzo: A man has thrown himself out of the window of his palace for her.

Vanitza: No, he lost his balance; he was drunk.

Lorenzo: He was a poet.

Vanitza: Not at all; he was a mason.

Lorenzo (*yawning*): Oh, how insipid life is! Now I have nothing to occupy the rest of my day. It's singular, but I've never really looked at you, Vanitza. Do you know that you're quite lovely? Anyway, you must be, since all the men are at your feet. By my eternal salvation, I want to do likewise! (*He steals a kiss.*)

Vanitza: And Nanie, who has remained faithful to you and cherishes you with all her heart?

Lorenzo: Since she's so perfect, she has only to take the veil.

WINTER SUN
(*La Presse*, 1 February 1899)

It is three o'clock. A languid sun caresses the denuded trees with moss-covered trunks of the Champs-Élysées. It is almost warm, and not a branch is stirring, so the benches are invaded by the poor, idlers and nursemaids crested with blue and pink ribbons, who are turning babies back and forth and clucking like hens. Several modest mamans are devoting themselves to little items of crochet-work or knitting, while Zizi and Zozo are launching whiplashes between the legs of passers-by in order to activate their tops. A young seigneur, very Regency in a costume decorated with white paduasoy is conscientiously filling his pockets with damp soil, while his nursemaid, Mademoiselle Phémie, is making eyes at an old Monsieur. Bicycles are passing along the pavement of the Bois like frail crane-flies, along with dawdling fiacres, their philosophical coachmen sitting obliquely, the reins dangling between their hands, and also automobiles, whose raucous panting of rolling, fantastic, indomitable beasts covers the other sounds. And the horses, surprised and terrified, curb their heads, as if before an invasion of wild beasts.

Mademoiselles Poupette Avril and Cleo de Cerfeuil have taken chairs at the edge of the sidewalk and are showing, with savant tucks, embroidered silk stockings and underskirts with a sufficiently suggestive fluidity.

Poupette (*nervously*): I assure you that we're wasting our time. No one worthwhile will pass by today.

Cléo: I told you so. Those fellows only show themselves in spring.

Poupette: For once, I got up before nightfall; I have no luck.

Cléo: Bah! We'll rest today. We've earned a day's vacation.

Young Madame Francouer has given a rendezvous behind the circus to Baron des Obonnes. It is her first slightly serious flirtation, so she has not wanted to go to the entresol in the Avenue Matignon, where the baron shows off his autographs. Later, perhaps, one would see . . .

The Baron: Finally, it's you . . . it's you . . . Léonie . . . Madame . . .

Léonie: Shhh! You're quite certain that my husband isn't here?

The Baron: Why would your husband be here? There's no appearance . . .

Léonie: I've been told that he chases the nursemaids. I'm trembling like a leaf. If he found out . . .

The Baron: Instead of inventing, one would tell the truth, that's all.

Léonie: My God, that's Clara I can see at the end of the pathway . . . Clara, my best friend . . . I'm doomed!

The Baron: She's myopic . . .

 Léonie: But she has an infallible nose for these things. Look, she's heading straight for us. Save me, my dear Obonnes!

The Baron: Just come to my entresol.

Léonie (*frightened*): Yes, yes, but you'll only show me the autographs?

*Madame Francoeur and the baron draw away in haste, and Clara, who has recognized them perfectly, retraces her steps in order to convey the hot news to Madame de V***, who will confide it to Mademoiselle de P***, who will whisper it to Monsieur C. C., who . . . In brief, the fortunate Francoeur will find all the faces beaming this evening at his club, and it will augur well for the bit of ribbon he has solicited.*

Meanwhile, Mademoiselle Phémie has emptied the pockets of the very Regency young seigneur, and has made his plumed fur bonnet jump with a resounding slap. The young seigneur utters howls, and Monsieur Joseph who is carrying an urgent letter to a friend of his master's stops, smiling.

Joseph: How severe you are to that beautiful child, Mademoiselle!

Phémie: You wouldn't believe how naughty he is! I'm going to be reprimanded because he's made a mess of his new clothes! Dirty and sly, I tell you!

Joseph: They're tight, the bosses? A nice place, eh?

Phémie: Everything to spoil him, and no money!

Joseph: Blockheads, eh?

And Joseph pours into Mademoiselle Phémie's heart the overflow of his own, while his master, who needs to pay a debt of honor before four o'clock, is tearing his hair out waiting.

A little further away, Monsieur and Madame Duflot occupy a bench in the full sunlight. They have tremulous heads and limbs swollen by rheumatism. Monsieur Duflot is smoking his pipe and his wife is yielding to a vague somnolence while hugging an old shopping-basket whose contents are mysterious.

Monsieur Duflot: A beautiful day. It seems to me, all the same, that my pain is climbing back into my shoulder again.

Madame Duflot: It's so damp in our lodge. It's truly hard for poor folk to live in such hovels. Fortunately, our daughter is willing to stand in for us from time to time. What about your asthma, Isidore? How is it?

Monsieur Duflot (*as if in a dream*): Ah, Coralie . . . when one of us dies . . . I'll retire to the country!

THE PROOF
(*La Presse*, 12 February, 1899)

Colette had a lover and a female friend. Every self-respecting woman has a female friend and a lover. As usual, the lover courted the friend, who was dainty and blonde, and the friend had her eye on the lover, a handsome dark-haired fellow. The friend would have stolen the lover, but the lover was poor, which maintained the friend within the loyal and pure bounds of amity . . . scarcely a hand-grip here and there, a stolen kiss on the corner of the lips, and all the more delicious for it—grips and kisses don't count! She and he were ripe, nevertheless, for the fault, and Colette witnessed the crystallization of the obsession, her heart crucified but her lips mute. The fall was imminent; a few more days, perhaps a few hours, and it would happen. Such was the confession of Gabrielle's gaze, filled with the luminous vagueness that is the precursor of sin.

"My darling," said Colette, politely, placing her burning hand on the dreamer's shoulder, "I know what you're thinking."

The darling started in alarm and formulated the anticipated lie, fixing Colette with her big blue eyes of a charming ingenuousness.

"I'm not thinking about anything."

"Yes, you're thinking about Victor."

Gabrielle burst out laughing: light laughter similar to the fall of pearls down a crystal staircase.

"You're mad, Colette, quite mad!"

"No, I know what I'm saying, don't interrupt. Victor finds you to his taste because you're pretty, refined, intelligently perverse and because you'd be a nice specimen to add to his collection."

"Oh!"

"Yes, darling, nothing more, for fundamentally, he's very attached to me and always comes back to me. In his escapades he combines a sincerity that is sometimes very great with the cunning of an Apache in hiding. I've always had an intuition of his treason, without obtaining absolute certainty. Now, for the sake of artistic curiosity, I desire to have a flagrant proof of his infidelity."

"I don't see . . ."

"Listen, child. I love Victor with an enlightened, curious and indulgent amour. I study him with maternal smiles for his frightful rascalities, his felonies and his criminal hypocrisies, which double for him the joy of deceiving me, for men easily believe in our imbecility. Now, listen to me carefully. What would you gain by taking Victor as a lover? The pleasure of deceiving me?"

"How can you believe . . ."

"Once again, don't interrupt me . . . A few dinners, a few trips to the theater and a few bunches of roses from Nice, bound with woven ribbon. Victor is poor, he can't do any more. For myself, I offer you the pretty heart in rubies and diamonds that you like so much."

"How nice of you!"

"Except that it's necessary to give my lover a rendezvous, hide me in your drawing room and . . ."

"No, no, not that!"

"Don't worry; the preliminaries will suffice for me. It's agreed, isn't it?"

"So be it. Tomorrow, at five o'clock.

"Ah! Poor me! You've already set a day!"

✳

Victor is at Gabrielle's feet in her little lilac Perse drawing room, repeating to her what he said to Colette at the beginning of their liaison. These things always serve in similar moments; it is good not to fatigue the brain-cells.

The betrayed lover, like a statue of despair, watches through a gap in the curtains.

"Oh, Gabrielle," Victor whispers, "I love you! I love you! Other women no longer exist. Oh, the burn of your lips, the taste of your kisses! Give them to me, your kisses! All, all of them! More, more . . . !"

And Victor makes bracelets, belts and gags of profound kisses for Gabrielle. If all those kisses were congealed as precious gems, the adored would resemble a Hindu idol adorned for a sacrifice.

In spite of her anger, Colette cannot help finding that Victor, seen thus, is a trifle ridiculous. She has never noticed that shrill voice with the weakness of a sylvan flute and those feverishly impatient maladroit hands. Furthermore, her torture has been rather hard. She is suffering in her amour and in her self-respect; the observation of a false note in the beloved is almost as painful as his indignity. White with emotion, she parts the curtains, to the great joy of Gabrielle and the amazement of her accomplice, whose eyes shine with a hateful flame . . .

A great silence follows, more lugubrious than a Lent sermon and more poignant than a drama by François Coppée. Finally, the delinquent takes his hat, and then the door, with the natural dignity of bad consciences.

It thus that Colette obtains the proof of her misfortune, and loses, simultaneously, her last illusion and her first lover.

A MOTHER'S ADVICE[1]
(*La Presse*, 18 February 1899)

The studio of Marcellus, a young man who will impose himself when he has found a new formula of art, and who will become increasingly difficulty. Perhaps a time will come, in order to give proof of his great originality, for him to return to ancient pictorial errors, as writers have simply returned to the romantic novel. For the moment, Marcellus is seeking his path and is still lingering, here and there at rose-bushes that he strips, all the way to the delicate heart, in order to perfume his memory and his drawers. That Marcellus is refined!

In the painter's absence, Emmeline, Liane and Lydie, his pupils, have installed themselves before easels and are copying an Italian model who is posing on a platform. Madame Missa, sitting next to the model, is studying the young women while crocheting.

Emmeline (*fourteen years old, short skirt, hair down her back*): I've never been able to do a forehead and a nose in a straight line. People find that beautiful . . . it's the Greek type. Personally, I think it's the stupid type.

Lydie: You always find things astonishing.

Emmeline: And then, the low brow with hair planted above like the hairs of a brush . . . do you also find that intelligent?

Liane: Do you prefer bald heads, my dear Emmeline?

---

1 At this point in the series the heading "Contes Rapides" is abandoned, replaced here and for the next two items by the heading "Le Beau Marcellus" [The Handsome Marcellus]. The triptych looks suspiciously like the sliced-up opening of a much longer story that was abruptly abandoned.

Emmeline: Everything requires a just measure (*To the Italian*): Would you turn to your left, Madame?

Lydie: Oh, no, turn to the right.

Liane: I beg you not to budge.

The Italian: It's necessary to reach agreement. I can't obey everyone at once.

Madame Missa: Monsieur Marcellus is making us wait today.

Emmeline: We're also taking advantage. Three hours of lessons a week, when we know full well that we'll never be able to pay the teacher!

Madame Missa: What's that you're saying?

Emmeline: I'm saying that we're cluttering up Monsieur Marcellus' studio, that we're preventing him from receiving his friends, and that we aren't giving him anything in exchange for those bad procedures, no compensation.

Liane: What about the honor of having formed remarkable pupils?

Emmeline: Don't make me laugh. Look at your good women. There's one in nougat and the other in spiced bread. As for the design, I'd rather not talk about that.

Lydie: Show us your painting.

Emmedline: I've never tried to do an Italian; I'm aware of the insufficiency of my means.

Madame Missa: What have you done then, wretch?

Emmeline: The parrot on your hat, Maman, it's squawking. (*She shows her canvas.*)

Madame Missa (*with an approving smile*): She's funny, my daughter; I believe that she'll succeed in society.

Lydie (*getting up*): I've had enough! I come here for the painter, not for the painting. If our artist wants me, he can invite me.

Madame Missa: Are you mad? A man who hasn't arrived and who agrees to give lessons at three francs a time?

Emmeline: It's true that he could have asked for twenty; the result would be the same. Lydie has no ambition.

Lydie: Monsieur Marcellus is poor, but he's of the same breed as those who triumph. You say that he lacks talent? What does talent do, today? It requires flexibility, ingenuity in flattery, persistence and determination. It's necessary to know how to bend the spine, eulogize gracefully, nor recoil before any painful task and receive rebuffs with a smile on the lips.

Liane (*scornfully*): It's necessary to be flat and vile!

Lydie: Yes, until the day of triumph. Then . . . oh, then, what a revenge, Messeigneurs! Beware, the mild, the proud, the delicate! They'll be made to pay largely for all the humiliations one has received!

Liane: It's cowardly to avenge oneself in those conditions.

Lydie: If one didn't avenge oneself on the weak, one would never be avenged.

Liane. Personally, I think that there's nothing in life but amour.

Lydie (*laughing*): Maman! Is she out of date!

Madame Missa: Amour? That sometimes sickens the heart and always sickens the head. It's forbidden by mothers who have experience.

Lydie: And then, it's necessary first to think about the necessary before offering oneself the superfluous. Personally, I'm looking for a husband, nothing else.

Madame Missa: Marcellus won't marry you, because he's as positive as you are, except that he doesn't see as far. He doesn't know that an intelligent and intriguing girl brings more than a big dowry: a guarantee of success. Men think they're very clever, my dear; fundamentally, they have a rare naivety. Oh, if I hadn't beaten the drum for the late Missa, we wouldn't have had a sou!

Lydie: Don't worry, Maman; I know how to treat a husband. Unfortunately, Marcellus has a mistress. I've often seen her in a coupé at the door; she waits for us to leave before going into the studio.

Liane: A woman of the world?"

Lydie: Yes, very elegant.

Liane: Pretty?

Lydie: A very passionate air, big dark eyes, a pale complexion . . . it seems to me that she'll frighten me . . .

DISAPPOINTMENT[1]
(*La Presse*, 3 March 1899)

II

Lydie lowers her head, a hint of dread and jealousy spreads over her crumpled face of a Parisian doll; Liane puts down her brushes in order to listen to her sister more carefully; Emmeline, the scamp of the family, thumbs her nose at the somnolent model, still motionless on her platform.

Madame Missa (*in a severe tone*): Since you thought that Monsieur Marcellus had a mistress, why were you obstinate in struggling?

Lydie: For one thing, he can't marry her; she's married. Then, he's only seeking to break it off, that's certain. I know from the concierge that they quarrel loudly in intimacy.

Madame Missa: Lovers' quarrels. People get angry in order to reconcile better afterwards.

Emmeline: Oh, my poor sister. If you're counting on him to pick the wedding bouquet, the orange blossom will be oranges.

Liane: I'll have a better chance with Henri Saint-Leger. I'm certain that he wants me, and that he finds me to his taste.

Emmeline: He's the only one at his home. Not accommodating, Maman and Papa Saint-Leger. If you succeed, you'll be very clever, my dear Liane. A sensible young man, Monsieur Henri; he won't want to discontent the parents.

---

1 The original title, "Déception," is ambiguous; it could mean "deception" as well as "disappointment"; the double meaning is deployed deliberately.

Madame Missa: Do what you like, my daughters, provided that appearances are saved. Tell yourself incessantly that life is a battle and that victory goes to the most skillful. No sensibilities or weaknesses! If you knew how men mock you! Not one is sincere, not one is grateful or faithful. They only seek to trick us, to do us harm, in order to claim one conquest more. Oh, my children, if you heard them boasting about their good fortune in the indecent language that is habitual to them, you would no longer have any esteem or pity for them. Their appreciations of us would make apes blush! Protect your hearts with triple armor, my dears, arm yourselves with trickery, cunning and even cruelty. One wins those monsieurs with praise, one excites them by means of resistance and one retains them by means of . . . bad behavior.

Liane: Oh, Maman, I could never do that! (*She throws herself into the arms a of a beardless pink and blond young man who has just come in.*) Monsieur Henri! Monsieur Henri! What joy!

Henri Saint-Leger: Working again on such a beautiful sunny day?

Emmeline: It's in order to advance Lydie's affairs; she's hung up on Marcellus, the master of the establishment.

Liane (*blushing*). Have you spoken to your parents, Monsieur Henri?

Henri Saint-Leger: Alas! I make a new attempt every day.

Liane: And futile! But you swear to me to persevere, to fight with confidence and courage?

Henri Saint-Leger: I swear it.

Liane: It's good to be loved thus. You'll permit me, Maman, to abandon myself to joy?

Madame Missa: Well, if you have so much of it . . . abandon yourself with prudence, however; contemplate the abyss, but don't let go of the rail.

Henri Saint-Leger (*laughing*): What a terrible experience!

Madame Missa: When one has three daughters to bring up, campaigns count triple.

Liane: Shh! Here comes the great artist.

Marcellus, his moustache conquering, a smile on his lips and his eyes shining, makes his entrance amid the ecstatic silence of his pupils. The Italian model, who is asleep on the platform, her headscarf askew and her mouth open, resumes her pose resignedly.

The Italian: Can I go now?

Marcellus: How long have you been posing?

The Italian: An hour. That's five francs.

Marcellus: We'll pay in full next time.

The Italian: It's just that I have three children.

Marcellus. Bring them—they can pose too.

The Italian: That won't enable them to eat.

Marcellus: It will occupy them. Go on, my beauty, and sleep less—you're thickening your lines.

Madame Missa: These models are demanding!

Marcellus: They all want to be paid. As if painters were rolling in money! They're lucky; in a good studio they have the chance of seeing their features immortalized by the brush of a master, and they complain! If I earned five francs an hour I'd be very content myself!

Madam Missa: You'll have the glory!

Marcellus: Everyone has the glory today! There's a perpetual fanfare in the newspaper for color merchants, merchants of prose and hawkers of pills. The great men, Mesdames, are those about whom no one speaks.

Lydie: Why not assist more at our little sessions? What do you expect us to do without you?

Marcellus: Whatever you please; it doesn't matter.

Lydie: As much as to say that we're obscure daubers . . . But we don't hold it against you, Monsieur Marcellus, we're only too glad to see you occasionally, to admire your works, to count an artist of your value among our friends. It would be very kind of you to come more regularly to our Thursday and Sunday gatherings . . . I recite verses of the new school, which sing so delightfully the neuroses of the ardent and mysterious soul—and how! My sister Liane plays Wagner . . . and Emmeline knows popular songs . . .

Marcellus: Thank you with all my heart, but I scarcely belong to myself. In life, one can't always do what one would like to do. There are circumstances stronger than the will.

Lydie: And wills stronger than circumstances. Yes, we know . . .

Marcellus: Believe me . . .

Lydie: Nothing can bend you, then? Neither my arguments nor my prayers? If I told you that I'd be particularly flattered to see you . . . that you'd be giving me a greater pleasure than you think . . . ?

Marcellus: If you said those things to me I'd be very happy, very proud and very grateful . . . I'd promise, but I wouldn't keep it.

Lydie (*indignantly*): Yes, your time is taken! There are others who expect it, whom one fêtes, surrounds with attention and tenderness! Every day a carriage stops outside that door . . . a woman gets out of it . . .

Marcellus (*shrugging his shoulders lightly*): You're mistaken.

Lydie (*with tears in her eyes*): I've seen! I've seen!

Marcellus (*picking up a canvas turned to the wall and showing a ravishing head of a young woman*): I'm getting married, Mademoiselle; this is my fiancée.

While Madame Missa and Liane take the faint but superbly disdainful Lydie away, Henri turns toward the threshold of the studio.

Henri Saint-Leger: You'll permit me, dear master, to come and make a few nude sketches?

CONFIDENCES
(*La Presse*, 10 March 1899)

III

Marcellus, without a glance of pity for poor Lydie, has closed the door of his studio again and has stopped in front of the portrait of his fiancée, whistling a popular tune, when his friend Frédéric Monteil enters noisily, a cigarette in his lips and his jacket flowering with a sprig of lilies-of-the-valley.

Frédéric: What are the names of the three partridges guarded by that old hawk?

Marcellus: The Missa children. I'm giving them lessons in painting.

Frédéric: The mother could substitute for you. She has a glaze of ceruse and lacquer on her face.

Marcellus: They have just in fact, withdrawn their confidence from me, and I'm delighted by it! They're ruining me in models, paying me in compliments and taking an excessive place in my life.

Frédéric: With pretty women . . .

Marcellus: You're mistaken, my dear; those airs of an amorous she-cat hide a grim virtue.

Frédéric: At the exit, however, they enveloped me with an expert interrogative gaze that took away all my veils.

Marcellus: Yes, but they only undress with the gaze. They aren't only perverted morally . . . It was too dangerous: the demi-confidences, the demi-virginities; the mother has put good order into them. These demoiselles, nowadays, know absolutely everything—theoretically, of course. They even know so many things that they're wounded beforehand. That's education backwards: the preservation by horror from vice that has no more secrets. It's as if people who have a desire to commit suicide were taken to the Morgue.

Frédéric: That's the new method of mothers?

Marcellus: Well, science has always been the enemy of reproduction. But it's not a matter of the little Missas; I've found a genuine young woman, and I'm marrying her.

Frédéric (*stupefied*): You're marrying? What about Claudia?

Marcellus: Claudia can put on her mourning; our liaison has lasted long enough. I've been supporting her reproaches, nervous fits and cries of jealousy for three years. And what's worse is that I'm a friend of her husband, that he calls me continually, that he can't do without me. The poor fellow is consumptive to the last degree, condemned by the physicians; I no longer want to deceive that moribund, who has taken me in affection, doesn't know anything and doesn't understand anything. His confidence, makes me indignant, desolates me. I'm accomplishing a charity by remaining, and also a bad deed! In sum, I've had enough, and I'm reclaiming my liberty. (*Changing tone, with an affected detachment*): How do you like this sketch?

Frédéric: Charming. I know that physiognomy.

Marcellus: Certainly; you've seen Mademoiselle Raymond at my home, with her father.

Frédéric: Mademoiselle Raymond, the daughter of Baron Raymond, the Counselor of State? A large dowry and expectations . . . all my compliment! When is the marriage?

Marcellus: I adore her!

Frédéric: Yes, yes, the father has better than money. He's very big in the world of politics and business. He disposes of great influence. It's a medal at the Salon, decoration, the Institut. Lucky man!

Marcellus: I haven't given a thought to those advantages.

Frédéric: On the contrary . . . oh, I can see why you're dumping Claudia.

Marcellus: I'm not dumping her.

Frédéric: No, you're leaving her, that's more correct. If the word differs, the thing is the same. Your remorse with regard to the husband is very timely. I tell myself the same thing. If you knew how crafty we are with ourselves! When a dubious action is in our interest, we always arrive at convincing ourselves that it's our duty to do it; it's the most natural thing in the world. We don't put any malice into it, we're pure of all premeditation, and we hold to limpid reasons that stifle the feeble protests of our conscience.

Marcellus: Who would be grateful for my weakness? Claudia has given me a few years of her existence, because she loved me. She's been happy because of me, it's her who owes me gratitude.

Frédéric (*laughing*): It's a point of view. Have you the luck to please all women? I imagined that to approach and conquer one of those creatures, so much desired, it required infinite care, interminable attempts, a skillful siege made of gallantries, tender words, sighs and gifts. And behold, suddenly, at the slightest attack, the first one you meet abandons herself for good, for the worst motive. It's necessary to cherish that . . . A carriage has just stopped outside your door.

Marcellus: It's Claudia.

Frédéric: Good, I'll leave you. How long will it take you to inform her of her dismissal?

Marcelus: Oh, don't talk to me about that. I feel that all my energy is abandoning me. What a bore! My God, what a bore!

Frédéric: Come on—it's only a moment to pass. If you hesitate, you're lost!

As he withdraws, Frédéric crosses paths with a young woman clad in a discreetly elegant dark dress, the large frilly black tulle collar of which makes her pallor stand out even more. The regular and delicate features are imprinted with sorrow. She advances hesitantly and holds out to Marcellus, with a tender gesture, a large bouquet of moss-roses.

Marcellus: Bonjour, Claudia; you're too kind.

Claudia (*after kissing her lover, putting the flowers in a vase, and stopping in front of the portrait that Marcellus has not had time to cover up*): What, you have a new commission? A young woman? You didn't say anything . . . ?

Marcellus: What do you expect me to say? Yes, it's a sketch, as you can see.

Claudia: You have a singular expression. Why are you avoiding looking at me?

Marcellus (*laughing falsely*): Me? You're crazy! I am as I always am.

THE WITCH
(*La Presse*, 29 March 1899)

Sonia puts a long dark mantle over her periwinkle-blue silk robe and her golden corselet ocellated with turquoises; then, via dark alleys known to her alone, she goes in search of the witch.

Sonia has profound, hard and malevolent eyes, a red and fleshy mouth superb in its design, which is contracted hatefully, and her long hair floating behind her makes her a veil of darkness. Like unquiet souls wandering the earth, bats whip the sparse trees with their furry wings, brush the motionless branches and the eaves of mossy roofs, swirl over glaucous pools and disappear into the distance. A fateful church bell vibrates lugubriously. Sonia wraps herself more tightly in her mantle and hastens her steps.

The depths of the valley seems to hollow out infinitely. The clouds warring in the sky pass over an ultramarine firmament pierced by the cold light of stars; a light perfume of moss and damp earth floats in the air, with other aromas, more mysterious and more vehement.

Suddenly, at a bend in the road, a shack appears with a window tinted by a yellow radiance. Sonia pushes the door and penetrates into a low, sinister room filled with bizarre objects illuminated vaguely by the flame of a candle. She takes a step forward, and suddenly recoils with a cry before the menace of two phosphorescent eyes that are fixed upon her; she hesitates momentarily and repels, with all her force, an enormous owl that clutches at her dress. In a corner, an old woman is crouching, chanting in a hoarse voice the verses of an incantation. Her stiff arms are raised, holding above a pyre of dry leaves the bloody heart of an animal.

"What do you want, child?" she asks. "Why disturb me at this hour?"

Without responding, Sonia takes a piece of silk cloth from her bosom and hands it to the witch.

"Ah, yes," says the latter. "You desire to have news of a person who is dear to you: a friend? a relative?"

"No."

"You want to preserve by spells the person who wore that dress? You want to know her future?"

"No."

"Perhaps she is ill and you've come to ask me for remedies"

"No."

"No," says the young woman again, shaking her little brunette head with tight lips and a harsh gaze. "I want you to avenge me on my sister Lydie. This is her dress, her beautiful dress embroidered with pink pearls, which I've ripped up."

"Avenge you? Why?"

"Because I hate my sister, who is admired, and sweet, and ineffably beautiful, like the warm dawns of June when flocks of white pigeons pass over and the silence is woven of vague fading songs. She has, in her azure eyes, the splendor of a cloudless sky; she makes one dream of calm and florid landscapes, of all the joys and all happiness. I hate her, I tell you, because she is a person that people love."

"And why do you not love her too?"

"Because gazes turn away from me, who am pale and sad; because people flee me and fear me. She is the light that attracts, I am the night that alarms! Woman, avenge me on the one who confronts me and insults my pain . . ."

And Sonia's plaint trailed off into sobs, became the bitter and anguished confidence of a soul crucified by jealousy, which has suffered and wants to cause suffering in its turn, which, unconsoled and desperate, invokes and evokes a mysterious force, weeping in the shadow that envelops her like a shroud. She straightened up, madness in the depths of her dark eyes, launched like a gasp the satanic litanies of the spell-caster, and, picking up the throbbing heart, which had slid to the ground, wrapped it in Lydie's dress and pierced it with long golden pins. Soon, the pale cloth was covered in red patches, the thick blood sticking to the slender white hands of the young woman. But the old woman uttered a burst of laughter,

"Leave the heart, Sonia; it won't suffice to do the harm necessary to avenge yourself. You can render Lydie unhappy, but she won't be any less beautiful."

Sonia reflected, and replaced the bloody pins in her hair.

"However, I want to be more beautiful and more beloved than Lydie, you hear? Do you not have some powerful philter, some marvelous poison that will metamorphose me?"

"I possess venomous plants that cause death and rare essences that prolong life, but I will make you a more precious gift. You're young, the future belongs to you, and it only requires a ray of sunlight for the roses of election that are in your soul to flower. Listen: you have silk and velvet fabrics, robes of silver and gold, lace and precious stones. Return home, take what seems to you to be the most enviable, and beg Lydie humbly to accept it. Go, hurry, and when you have dressed your sister in your most precious garment, look at yourself in this little mirror that I'm giving you. You'll be satisfied."

Sonia took the mirror and departed, running through the night. In order to arrive more rapidly she tore her garments on the bushes and bruised her dainty feet, unused to running. A crazy ardor rendered her insensible to pain.

As soon as she arrived she opened her coffers of jade and ivory and brought out her necklaces, her rings, her fans of plumes, her perfumes, her scarves softer than moonbeams, her lace finer than spider-webs, and, curbed by the weight of all her wealth, went to offer it to her sister.

"Oh, dear Sonia," said the latter, very moved, "keep your adornments and your jewels. I only desire your affection."

And she embraced her.

Sonia felt a flood of flame descend within her. An unknown joy made her faint, and her eyes reflected what was happening in her being. Avidly, she took the little mirror and looked at herself.

A miracle! The face that she saw had a radiant and supernatural beauty, a beauty of faith and love.

She recognized, then, the sovereign philter and understood that what had metamorphosed her thus came from a divine sentiment that had entered her heart for the first time: Goodness.

THE HORSE-SHOW[1]
(*La Presse*, 12 April 1899)

Cloudy weather with sudden clear intervals that cast sashes of light over the steps, and caress the dead flowers of hats and the living smiles of pretty mouths open like flowers.

There is a big crowd to applaud the show, for it is the week of our frisky officers, the great military week of adultery and Cythera. In the smart stand, the blonde Baronne des Ablettes, in a low-cut lunar eclipse robe so tight that she can hardly sit down, is flirting with Comte Filoselle.

The Baronne: Not fun, the races! One comes because bad habits linger, and one catches cold conscientiously. Then, how sad it is to see the same faces every year, more wrinkled and more cleverly retouched, the beautiful ladies that one no longer attacks because they're disarmed!

The Comte: Personally, I'm in favor of the discharge of the troops. Your husband is absent, come and discharge tomorrow at my house.

The Baronne: Do you think so? I've promised my couturier to launch his completely adherent seamless bathing costume, with only one crease in the lower part. I'm a dutiful woman.

---

1 From this point in the series onwards the item in the features no longer appear under the headline "Contes Rapides." It is usually replaced by one of two headings, under which the stories are classified in accordance with their tone; this one is the first to be headed "A vol d'oison," an expression carrying the implication in this case of "a bird's-eye view."

*In the reserved stand, the daughter of Colonel X***, a tall thin brunette in a carob-tree dress, is chatting with the daughter of General Z***, in a very simple Belgian jacket.*

Mademoiselle X*** (*very emotional, while a genteel officer of hussars is getting ready to ump the first obstacle*): It's Oscar's debut! If you knew how I'm trembling! His mare is so violent! She'll never get over the water jump.

Mademoiselle Z***: It's going very well. Hup! Hup!

*Mademoiselle X*** utters a scream and clings to her friend's arm, Oscar has slipped in the saddle and, after a moment of disquieting lurching, has ended up recovering an unstable equilibrium.*

Colonel X*** (*to General Z****): Damn! How have I been landed with such a crock! No seat at all, and he wants to marry my daughter!

The Butte has taken up residence near the stables, as always, but as those ladies are fond of literature, a reserve of the highest tone reigns there; one could believe that one were at the Hôtel Rambouillet, my dear! Let the women of the world permit themselves brisk words and risqué implication! Yvonne de Givrae, in an aquamarine scarf encrusted with old guipure, is playing games with Tigrane de Chichi, who has surrounded her paltry beauty with a halo of lace and ideally foamy plumes. Old rakes are buzzing around urgently, extending elytra and antennae to the florid boat like cockchafers in the spring growth. B., the fashionable painter, is strolling with a financier whose wife he is courting with a view to a 30,000-franc portrait.

Yvonne (*to the financier*): Bonjour; how are you?

The financier: I saw you from a distance, and came running with my friend B., the great artist.

Tigrane (*perceiving the financier's rosette*): You're a military man, Monsieur, that's obvious,

The Financier: Pardon me, but I work in a bank.

Tigrane: We also have bankers, on my mother's side; as for my husband, who . . . navigated, he's dead, Monsieur, dead of a seizure on his return, after having sent me a bullet, I won't say where.

The financier: I congratulate you, Mademoiselle.

Tigrane (*scenting an exceptional affair*): Oh, you understand me! You sense all that there is in my soul of ungraspable tenderness and noble impulses compressed by base realities, aspirations and flights toward a bewilderingly distant ideal! (*Striking a pose*): I am the sphinx with the perverse blue eyes, the succubus dazed by morbid amour . . . I am . . .

The Financier: I'm pressed for time . . . excuse me . . .

The Painter (*amused, on examining the forty-two rings that climb over Chichi's variously-sized knuckles*): There isn't one for today's fiancé, then?

Tigrane: No, I like you too; you have something that pleases women and incites them to stupidities. I'd like you to make my portrait as a green spider. You understand, thin intersecting threads, entangled, tightening over a mysterious background, so as to form a hairy niche in which I radiate like a glaucous star! You'll make me a monster and a rare jewel: a prodigious, divine and terrible monster . . . !

The Painter: That would be very expensive . . .

Tigrane (*stretching herself in a feline manner*): I don't pay any attention to expense. No joking, you know; I want my spider!

The Painter: You'll have it!

And the conversations continue, with the game of little horses that turn and turn on the carpet of blond sand. That game is similar to life, which always brings back the same obstacles. There is nothing unforeseen except the bumps and the falls.

PRINCIPLES
(*La Presse*, 26 April 1899)

The sun, like a golden spider, parts the canvas of gray cloud from time to time, sending us the thin thread of its rays. The buds, swollen with sap, allow tentative sprays to burst forth, and the lilial clusters that prelude, in timid arpeggios, the splendid symphony of summer.

In a large provincial garden, between baskets of forget-me-nots and wallflowers, the Floc spouses are plucking caterpillars off the leaves and collecting snails. They bend down, self-important and congested, in the new grass, where their short and rude fingers dishonor the fragile daisies.

But Madame Floc has stopped for a breather.

"You don't know, Victor," she says, "that in order to give a dinner on the thirteenth so as to place us right away in the locale, I've made my visits, and I know who the people are that it's necessary to invite. We can choose among the useful relationships."

"The Durands, for example? The husband has a good situation in business; he might be able to push our son Joseph . . ."

"Pooh! All façade, their luxury. It's said that they're going to sell their property and that they've mortgaged their farm, La Crapaudière."

"The Dubois, then? They've come into an inheritance . . ."

"People remarried after divorce—fie! I even believe that they only divorced in order to arrive there. What do you expect? My principles don't permit me to receive households that haven't passed before Monsieur le curé."

"What if we were to invite Madame Aurélie Couvresse? She offered the blessed bread at mass the other day . . ."

"That's because she can't do otherwise, because she's flat broke. No profit in that direction. And then, it would be necessary to receive her niece, a poor girl who dresses like a whore."

"The young woman's reputation is intact."

"Intact? Mère Michu has seen her in the little wood with her cousin, a great Nicodemus who works in literature—a fine métier in which one dies of starvation."

Monsieur Floc has drawn closer, his eyes gleaming.

"What were they doing in the wood?"

And Madame Floc, indignantly: "Reciting verses! After that, how will the silly girl find a husband? All the more so since she has no dowry!"

"There only remain to us, alas, the Maire, the notary and the tax-collector. It's necessary, however, that our son is amused. If we can't offer him a choice morsel, he'll leave immediately after the coffee, as he did last Sunday."

"Yes, and when he goes out in the evening it's to go find creatures and lose his money gambling in all the bad places. By the way, I'm going to ask Abbé Sicard to change our places in the church. I don't want to find myself, at any price, next to that red-haired woman who poisons the atmosphere with musk and wears rings on all her fingers . . . a woman who doesn't wear gloves is a bad woman!"

"I've noticed her . . . she is, on the contrary, charming."

"Charming! With a triple layer of make-up on her skin, a head fluffed up as if she were a poodle and a skirt so clinging that she can hardly take a step! She'll surely seduce our Joseph. She's a slut, I tell you!"

Madame Floc stops, suffocated, and crushes with a vengeful thrust of her heel an innocent beetle with black velvet antennae and Florentine bronze wings. White corollas are falling gently, like pure snowflakes, incensing the pathways with perfume of amber and honey, while the first wasps circle and spiral, looting the hearts of little flowers,

But Madame Floc's face extends in a soft smile.

"I've got it, my friend; let's invite the Durandins; the wife is very seductive and . . . Joseph doesn't displease her."

"You think that our son . . . ?" says Monsieur Floc, thoughtfully.

"Yes, and it won't cost him anything. We'll leave them together, after dinner . . ."

LIAR![1]
(*La Presse*, 10 May 1899)

"Yes," she said, "I hit him!"

She had been put in the presence of her lover's cadaver, and, her face pale and her lips contracted by a bitter smile, she looked at it.

"I hit him," she repeated, "and you can condemn me. I don't regret anything; I've suffered too much. My story resembles that of many unfortunate women and you won't learn much from it. When that man took me, hypnotized by ill-treatment, sold by a venal father, I'd already fallen, but he was my sole amour; I loved him as I had never loved, as I didn't think one could love. He let himself go, flattered, fundamentally, by the sentiment he had been able to inspire, while conserving an obsession with my disgrace and making vague allusions to it I reassured him, explaining the sad circumstances that had led to my fall. He smiled with disdain: 'It was necessary to resist!'"

"'Yes, perhaps . . . but I didn't know; I was so young.' He shrugged his shoulders and I went on: 'You believe me, don't you? Oh, if you knew with what horrible disgust I yielded! Well, I've certainly been punished!'

"He didn't respond. I thought that he doubted my words and I wept for a long time, wanting to wash away my sins, to redeem them by means of a sublime devotion, an immense sacrifice . . . Alas, what could I do? What devotion, what

---

1 This story is the first in the series to bear the alternative headline *Contes inquiétants* [Disquieting Tales].

sacrifice, could I offer in the humility of my futile existence? He often forgot me for days on end, and I stayed at home, only thinking of him, waiting for him in anguish. However, when he came back, he interrogated me suspiciously, hostile, and before my protestations: 'Oh, a woman who has had two lovers always knows how to occupy her leisure. Haven't you admitted yourself that you weren't new when I met you . . . ?'

"'That proves, my love, that I'm honest, and you can believe me when I swear to you that I adore you, that I'd give my life for you . . .'

"He pressed me against him. Then, after our kisses, our most ardent caresses, his gaze became black again and his voice suddenly hissed: 'Say that you've been the same with others!'

"'Never!'

"'Don't lie, you're a whore, nothing but a whore, you hear!'

"'Louis, I beg you, forget the past. I submitted to him in shame and revolt, he horrified me!'

"'No, no, you regret it, certainly. The past responds to the future!'

"Discouraged, I hid my face in my hands and I sobbed. Then my dolor seemed to calm down. He consoled me, soothed me like a child, wiped away my tears, kissed me and left it. But his doubts soon assailed him again. In vain I cherished him, consecrated my being and my entire soul to him; he exhumed the mud of the evil days again in order to throw it in my face. However, I was young, I hoped even so. There was justice in Heaven, no doubt; it was sufficient to wait, to be compensated for all evils . . . and I waited with confidence, mild, affectionate and resigned.

"I wished ardently for a child to fill my life, to cheer up my hours of solitude, which became more and more numerous. My wish was granted. I brought into the world a paltry being whose little face seemed to reflect my anxieties and my discouragement.

"Louis showed neither joy nor annoyance; his eyes remained clear and cold in contemplating his son. After a month he sought resemblances among his friends. A horrible frisson had chilled my heart. He still suspected me! He denied that living proof of our tenderness; he even struck me, in my child. I wrung my hands in despair.

"'You'll never believe me, then? However, I only have you my life! Here, my eyes, my lips my body, everything is yours! Yours!'

"'Yes, today . . . but yesterday . . . and tomorrow . . . ?'

"The child died; he was so frail. I took him to the cemetery alone; Louis, because of his family, didn't want to compromise himself. When I returned home I wept inexhaustibly. My lover was surprised.

"'You loved him very much, then?'

"'Oh, yes, Louis, I loved him as I love you; that says it all.'

"'Bah! You've never had such transports for me; the affection that you had for him was different.'

"'Different, perhaps, but just as profound.'

"'Women have an answer for everything; there are naïve fellows who let themselves be taken in. I know you, you and those like you! Certainly, you're not fundamentally bad, and I know that in quitting you I wouldn't find myself any better off. But I don't trust you, and take your protestations for what they're worth.'

"I shut up. What was the point of struggling any more? Wasn't everything futile? I remained mild and submissive, because I still loved my lover, but I didn't abandon myself any more to that amour, which had ceased to be a consolation, a support and a guide in my poor existence. I was quite alone henceforth, desperately alone; nothing sustained me any longer except visiting the flowery field where my child was buried. Several times a week I went with bunches of carnations and roses, which didn't have time to wither.

"'I had told Louis about those frequent absences, which only happened at times of the day when his occupations kept me away from him. He approved, nonchalantly. However, one morning, a sort of presentiment made me hurry and return home sooner than usual. Louis was there with his nasty face.

"'Where have you been?' he asked.

"'To the cemetery, as you know very well.'

"'You're lying!'

"'Look, here are the flowers from his grave.' I showed him my sad bouquet. He took it and trampled it underfoot.

'You're lying!'" he repeated, violently. 'You've been with . . . someone else!'

"Then, Messieurs, I saw red. It was too much. The scissors were on the table. I picked them up and . . . I've said everything; condemn me."

She had related her story in a blank, indifferent voice.

The judge remained perplexed.

"But did your lover deceive you?" he asked.

"I don't know."

"Did he beat you, or maltreat you?"

"No."

"He didn't give you enough money?"

She shrugged her shoulders scornfully.

"In sum, you had some *interest*?"

She disdained to respond.

The judge scratched his ear. "One doesn't kill a man for such a trivial reason," he said. "The woman is lying."

THE ESCAPADE
(*La Presse*, 18 May 1899)

A very delicate odor of grass, amber and sap
The branches of the apple trees form a white parasol,
Quivering and silky, which comes to brush the ground,
To rebound lightly under the wind that is rising.

The orchestra of sparrows preludes the sin of Eve.
And in the hidden nests sing: Do, re, mi, fa, sol!
The old walls have the mauve tones of girasol
Under a radiant sky, a sky florid with dreams.

Trees of sensuality, hope and perfumes
You who are reborn of your defunct loves
With the same ardor, incessantly unslaked,

Shake over our heads your divine whiteness;
For the rose of April, the snow of our hearts
Only falls once from the tree of life.

Through the alleyways florid with lilac and hawthorn, Miguette and Vincent draw away from the familial dwelling. They are walking arm in arm, almost silently, their souls capsized by a strange emotion. Vincent is sixteen, and love-sickness has gripped him since the Easter vacation. Citing their young age, permission to marry has been refused by their parents, but they have sworn by by-pass their consent by uniting themselves before God, like the divine lovers whose caresses sing the eternal hymn within and around them.

A rain of white petals falls from trees swollen with sap; under every white corolla a sly leaflet appears, of an adorably tender green. Everywhere there are chirpings and wing-beats; the air has a flavor of honey and incense made of the sweetness of sylvan breaths. The furze preludes, in arpeggios of small flames, the great symphony in gold major that it will play for the heavens, the woods and the bees.

Vincent appeases his thirst for kisses on Miguette's cherry lips.

"Miguette, I love you!"

"I love you, Vincent!"

"Soon we'll be reposing next to one another."

"And that's very serious, it appears. After that grave sin, our parents will be obliged to unite us!"

"We'll ask for a room at the Lion-d'Or Inn."

"You'll ask for it, Vincent; I'd never dare."

"As long as they don't refuse us . . ."

"You think they might?"

"Well, I don't know."

"My dear Vincent, what if we sleep here, on the moss, until someone comes to look for us?"

"It wouldn't be sufficient. It's necessary to accomplish a very culpable action. When we've done something very bad, it'll be very good for us. On the moss, we'd get away with a scolding and an immediate separation. I don't want to quit you, Miguette."

"Nor me, Vincent; you'll be my little husband."

The girl picks an anemone or a wild orchid here and there, and makes a frail bouquet of them, which she slips into the blue ribbon of her belt, and butterflies follow her, like a great animate flower, drunk on the perfume of her radiant youth.

The path turns under the guipure of the delicate branches, which the buds, scarcely open, gem with a crop of emeralds,

On the frail trunks of the hazel trees, on a weave of tigella, the light flowers of honeysuckle pose like pink and white spiders,

The daisies in the mild grass show the little faces of novice nuns in their wimples, and for them, the lilies-of-the-valley sound the mass of amour with all their silver bells. It is good to live, to love and to believe.

Here is the village square, planted with lindens, the church at the back with its old cemetery and, at the bend in the road, ornamented with a naively painted zinc sign, the Lion-d'Or Inn.

"It's there, Vincent."

"It's there, Miguette. Come on, courage!"

They have taken one another by the hand and have entered the smoky hall where a few lads are emptying bowls of cider and breaking a crust. The hostess, a former dancer at the Moulin Rouge who has been put out to grass after having milled all the wild oats of the capital, welcomes the young couple with her most amiable smile; but they remain silent, intimidated, while Marianne, the maid-of-all-work who serves the clients gazes at them curiously.

"You desire, Monsieur, Madame?" asks the landlady, maliciously, winking.

"Speak," says Miguette, who is hiding behind Vincent.

"No, you."

"Come on, get on with it."

And Vincent, as red as a poppy: "We'd like a room."

"One room, my darlings . . . with one bed?"

Before the old woman's smile, Miguette feels faint. Unconsciously, in a revolt of irresistible modesty, she protests.

"A room for two, Madame."

And the hostess, beaming broadly, with the tone of her former days: "Marianne, prepare a room for two lilies!"

AN ANGEL!
(*La Presse*, 30 May 1899)

For three months Paul loved Thérésine and saw her every day in the fine property of La Frénaie, near Tours, where she lived with her parents. Immediately after breakfast he went to look for her, and while old Aunt Lise, who was supposed to watch them, went to sleep on a bench he wandered in the depths of the park with her. He talked to her about charming trivia, intoxicated by the pure air, and formed a thousand projects for the future to which she listened, smiling. Then, when they were tired, verdant hiding places near the pond, known only to them, offered them a reliable shelter. Beside one another, silent and languid, they watched water-spiders skating around the large leaves of the nympheas, and picked plushy irises and buttercups in the fresh grass.

She seemed to him to be very sweet and chaste; almost furtively, in the dread of troubling her, he posed his gaze on the double star of her eyes. But the little sidereal flame scarcely vacillated, so innocent and pure was she.

He would have liked to talk to her as his fiancée, to speak to her lightly, as if pulling the petals from roses, to find caressant and delicate expressions. But "girly" language was not what he was accustomed to speak, so he judged it unworthy—him, the blasé fun-lover—to crumple that great stainless lily.

However, the weeks went by. Friends and members of the family arrived from the depths of the province to witness Thérésine's marriage. Among the guests was a handsome youth who immediately made himself at home, addressing the domestics familiarly, questioning everyone, enchanting everyone with his wit and good humor.

"That's my cousin Roger," said Thérésine, indifferently.

And when Paul, vaguely jealous, persisted: "He's come to La Frénaie two or three times. My father and my mother have a great deal of affection for him, in spite of his somewhat dissipated conduct. I don't know any more," she concluded, lowering her eyes.

Paul thought that he understood that cousin Roger inspired a mediocre esteem in his dainty fiancée, and did not worry about it any more.

The time that preceded the day fixed for the ceremony was truly delightful, The young woman was transformed, like a corolla opening the fragile silk of its petals in the sunlight; happiness seemed to emanate from her, surrounding her with a celestial halo. Paul was madly smitten, burning with desire to place his mouth on Thérésine's forehead, eyes and lips, in order to respire her, to embrace her insatiably. But always, the young woman's great air of chastity retained him on the edge of a declaration. In his fearful worship, she appeared to him then to be hieratical, distant, like a saint in a stained glass window, which light penetrates and transfigures, but which cannot be animated by a frisson of amour.

On the eve of the signature of the contract, the sun set softly in waves of blond vapors, removed its diadem of rays, and behind the ashy line of the willows, no longer showed more than half of its ardent, congested face.

Paul, whom Thérésine did not come to rejoin because of a cruel headache—doubtless caused by emotion—was wandering on the edge of the pond, recalling the thin felicities of recent days. A light breeze passed through his hair, brought him the peppery perfume of carnations and vervain; acacia flowers were falling, spiraling down from the trees, making a snowy foam at his feet, which he stirred with the tip of his cane.

Suddenly, an almost indistinct murmur reached him, and, his heart beating faster, he approached a verdant hiding place that he knew well. With infinite precaution, he parted the braches, advanced his head and looked. Thérésine, the adorable virgin, the immaculate lily, the candid fiancée, was swooning in the arms of her cousin and extending the flower of her lips to him.

"Oh," the latter was begging, "when will you be mine . . . entirely mine?"

And in a faint voice, she replied: "Soon, Roger, soon . . . since I'm marrying tomorrow. Afterwards, you know, I'll have nothing more to refuse you, will I?"

A DIVORCE
(*La Presse*, 5 June 1899)

A hostile, aggressive rain that has been falling stubbornly since the morning is drowning desire and determinations, communicating its evil intentions to people; and the liquid sheets intersect, blurring, trailing sonorous pearls on umbrellas, escaping in cascades, seeming to imprison the pedestrians in sentry-boxes of spun glass.

The pretty Madame de Follavène has bravely sent her coupé home, in spite of the downpour and has headed at a brisk pace for the house of Maître Boutran, the celebrated Parisian advocate, who has for ten years pleaded for and obtained all separations between ill-assorted spouses.

The maître's study is hung with bottle-green fabric, as is appropriate, ornamented here and there with a few sumptuously severe *objects d'art*, and the young woman, reassured, installs herself as if at home, her soul open to confidences and her mind suddenly serene.

"What brings you here, dear and charming friend?" asks the advocate, with the forbearance of a confessor who has known the little secrets of his penitents for a long time.

Madame de Follavène lowers her eyes and sighs faintly, bearing to her nostrils a sculpted gold flask with an emerald cabochon.

"I'm so emotional. I could never . . ."

"But yes, yes . . . a little courage!"

And Maître Boutran imprisons the white hand and the flask in his own powerful hand. He seemed to be holding two rare and delicate jewels, which he presses gently.

His client's lashes descend like clouds over the double star of her eyes.

"It's difficult to say . . . it's a matter of a very special case."

"Truly?"

"I haven't come for a divorce, as you might think. No, I've come for . . . the opposite. It's not your specialty, I know . . . but you're my sincere friend, and I thought . . ."

"You were right to count on me, for, if I've understood correctly, you desire a reconciliation?"

"Yes, yes, a reconciliation . . . oh, how well you grasp things!" murmurs the young woman, withdrawing her nervous hand from that of the handsome advocate.

"Speak, dear Madame; I have a keen desire to be agreeable to you, and I shall do my best to do so. Tell me the details of the matter."

"You know that Lucien is deceiving me outrageously . . . ?"

"My God . . . you're exaggerating . . . a few little escapades of no consequence. All husbands do that."

"Oh, I've pardoned many caprices myself. Today, it isn't a vulgar fling about which I want to talk to you but a tenacious liaison."

"Are you quite certain?"

"Alas! Doubt is no longer possible. Lucien has a passion that dominates him and maddens him to the point of making him lose all restraint in my regard, all sentiment of propriety! I have only too many proofs of my disgrace."

"You don't desire a separation of bodies, nor of wealth?"

"I love Lucien! I love him all the more because I sense him irresistibly detaching himself from me."

"Yes, that's not uncommon."

"Then, I thought of being very malign . . ."

"And you've made a blunder . . . Come on, be fully sincere, admit that you've accused, threatened, insulted; then you've dragged yourself at the infidel's feet, and have implored him, moaning, and that tears, if it were possible, have removed a little of the charm from your delectable visage?"

"No, dear friend, I haven't wept—it's much more serious!"

"You're frightening me! A threat of suicide, doubtless, a melodramatic scene in deplorable taste, with disastrous effect?"

"Nothing is lost, thank Heaven!"

"Then I no longer understand. Please, dear beauty, deign to inform me."

"This is it, and don't scold me too much . . . Thinking to bring Lucien back to me by means of jealousy, I wrote passionate letters to myself."

"Poor woman! He perceived the trickery?"

"Immediately."

"Perhaps you have even confessed it?"

"Yes, in a moment of weakness, about which I blush, but he pretended to take the declarations seriously enough to ask for a divorce."

"Ah! The situation is very compromised."

"There are no more resources, are there?"

Maître Boutran reflected, scratched his ear, and looked thoughtfully at his pretty client, who abandoned herself naively to her despair, in an admirable pose.

"I have an idea, my dear Madame; perhaps you might be able to regain the love of your husband."

"Truly? Oh, speak quickly! Guide me! I'll follow your advice blindly. Speak! Speak! What is it necessary to do for Lucien to love me again?

With a gentle smile, the advocate said: "It's quite simple. Deceive him for real."

AYMIENNE
(*La Presse*, 13 June 1899)

He had seen her at the Festival of Flowers in a float of moss-roses and white irises. A moss-rose herself, with her soft white tunic garnished with Malines lace, her narrow corselet encrusted with enamel scarabs and the dewdrops of her diamonds, she had made a profound impression on him.

Several times they had crossed paths under the multicolored arches of the path of Longchamp. From her rutilant buggy, he had taken handfuls of broom and buttercups and had thrown them in her face like louis. She had closed her eyes under the caressant rain, and folded her arms, in a charming retreat, quivering, behind the plushy fan of a sheaf of irises.

He had stayed until the last minute in order to see the adorable vision pass again and again. The frail carts of mauve orchids, hives of daisies hospitable to amorous wasps, windmills devoid of galettes and innocent bonnets, tandem of blue hortensias, boats full of varied flowers, sumptuous caleches of crimson poppies, victorias of lilies and carnations, and immense baskets knotted with extravagant ribbons reminiscent of dream butterflies, had filed past in vain. In vain, tender gestures had been sent to him with flourishes, like *billets doux* signed with a smile, or a kiss between two petals, a voluptuous frisson in a perfumed jewel-case—he had had no desires except for the unknown woman of the moss-roses.

Having cleverly cut through the file of floats, under the flowery downpour, on the ardent, feverish, morbid carpet of all the mutilated corollas exhaling a hectic hymn to a murderous

Eros in their ultimate breath of intoxication, he had followed her all the way to her dwelling, and had sought information from her concierge—prudent and well-trained—who had informed him of the necessary.

The widow of a foreigner of distinction, her name was Comtesse Aymienne de Canthara. She received many select people, which was not astonishing, as she claimed to be descended from the Crusades. Very charitable, she gave on a lavish scale, in order to be worthy of visitors of high lineage. Operating in broad daylight, as her youth permitted her to do, she had nothing to hide from her friends, and, very skilled in all bodily exercises, delivered herself ardently to cycling, hunting and walking.

Utterly dazzled by Aymienne's luxury, he wrote to her timidly, not daring as yet to present himself at her home. Then gradually, the letters became more passionate, more pressing, desire living on abstinence and amour fattening on fictions.

Madame, he traced with a burning hand, *I love you madly. My lips have solid kisses, my heart is avid for tenderness. Let me touch a tiny corner of your dress, the one you wore at the Festival of Flowers and which undressed you so prettily! Let me, my dainty fay, my divine moss-rose, respire your lace and detach, like a calyx, the corselet with enamel scarabs! Eyes closed in my ecstasy, I can still see your pert gestures behind the great irises; your supple hair, so brilliant that the breeze spun sunlight in its golden distaff; your harmonious arms made for caresses, your waist, your fine hips that the cloth espoused so tightly; the blooming star . . .* [two pages of inflamed citations]. *Thank you for the visual feast that you have given me; may not my other senses also have their small share of joy? I wait and I hope . . .*

The response finally arrived:

My friend,

Yes, I believe in your love and I am ready to recompense it. But remember that if you have loved me, it is thanks to my irises and moss-roses. Don't be ingrate and pay the florist.

Cost: five hundred louis.

PLEASURE!
(*La Presse*, 21 June 1899)

Pale weather, as yet indecisive; in spite of the morose vapors there is nevertheless a kind of after-joy in the sky. It is Corpus Christi; the bells are sounding carillons for mass in the villages with the loquacious urgency of devoted old women; the crows are fleeing with a clatter of wings, a black cloud against the white cloud of first communions. Muslin skirts are quivering, seemingly emerging from the grass with the daises and buttercups, like large flowers blossoming in the wind of canticles.

Irma la Rouge, in a bright dress, still beautiful in the blaze of her ardent mane, has stopped, slightly emotional, and has pressed more tenderly the arm of Louis, her lover of the previous evening.

"I'm very glad to have come here, very glad! It's nice of you, my Loulou, to have brought me to the country! It reminds me of my childhood and the slow processions over rose petals, amid the songs and the prayers . . . oh, how long ago it was! How much has happened since!"

Irma sees herself again, very small, in the church square, in her stiff Sunday garments in raw colors. Her crazy hair, curly and rebellious, rutilant and superb, in spite of pomades, made her a halo of flames, and the boys, teasing her, were already calling her Irma la Rouge! She sees the square, planted with centenarian lindens; it seems to her that the bells ringing full tilt are passing over her head with the invisible wings of angels . . . Here are the children of the choir in scarlet robes, cantors with fine curly hair chanting in shrill voices under the great candles weeping wax. Here are young women holding banners studded with gold, hardened like armor. The incense unfurls in little iridescent swirls, drowning the ecstatic faces of veiled virgins with foreheads circled by light crowns. It is an archipelago of foamy muslins with the snowy islets of young daughters of Marie protecting the Paschal Lamb. The music of serpents and ophicleides rumbles dully like distant thunder, sustaining the drone of the cantors in creased rochets, accompanying the glory of the old curé under the scintillating awning, like a garden of gems.

All of that ends up in the soul of Irma la Rouge, penetrates it with forgiveness and caresses it so gently that she feels a desire to weep.

"Oh, my Loulou, how stupid you must think me! You, who doubtless expect gaiety and humorous remarks from me . . ."

He had encountered her the day before at the hazard of a stroll through the windmills of Montmartre, and, intrigued by her large eyes, by turns tender and anxious, by her physiognomy, suffering beneath the contrived smile, he had followed her to her narrow abode of the cicada of amour. Timidly, she had asked him not to quit her so rapidly, and in a persistent apathy he had accorded her a day in the open air, two hours from Paris, under real trees, in real sunlight.

"Why am I a whore?" she replied, when he interrogated her vaguely. "I don't know; it happened of its own accord. My first master, a rich farmer, took me while I was haymaking in a field. Then I had to confess a pregnancy and the farmer's wife threw me out. Having spent my last sous on the child, it was necessary for me to earn a living as best I could, ill-treated by some and solicited by others, who wanted to obtain what I had already given. Weary of resistance, I yielded again, and brought a second child into the world. To raise him, having neither parents nor friends, I came to Paris on foot—twenty leagues in the middle of winter, with my babies under my arm. I fell ill; I knew poverty and the hospital. Then, from fall to fall . . . Certainly, I would have loved anyone who took pity on me . . . but there you go—men have only ever demanded pleasure from me . . ."

And on the word "pleasure" she burst into sobs.

Louis looked at the poor girl, slightly annoyed by that crisis of tears.

"Bah! You're still beautiful," he said, a trifle ironically. "For a few years you can serve the charming god Eros devotedly."

"And *rosse!* Oh, yes, my Loulou," she concluded, without malice.[1]

----

1 The improvised rhyme is difficult to translate; the best approximation is probably "get beaten up."

WOODEN RABBITS
(*La Presse*, 6 July 1899)

If it is a benefit to live, why seek ferociously to "pass the time"? Passing the time is traveling toward death, hurrying up, selling cheap the delectable state of alert and blissful consciousness that is accorded to us so parsimoniously. But those who seek to *pass the time* and who go, always at a run, from one point to another without fathoming anything, without savoring anything, are precisely the pusillanimous, the uncertain, those whom the thought of the final disappearance frightens the most!

Oh, how the master of masters must be amused on high by our continual contradictions!

That evening in June, Guy found himself with one of those disturbances of existence that cannot support solitude, even *à deux*. They had dined, smoked and chatted about horses, gambling and women, without finding sufficient interest therein. The atmosphere was heavy and Guy let himself go to the mildness of dream. His thoughts took on substance: they were blue-tinted sylphs circling in the peace of the evening, whom speech alarmed. Speech, in any case, is a disagreeable thing; it disrupts the harmony of the countless ungraspable sounds of somnolent Nature. There is an unparalleled voluptuousness in living and keeping silent in order better to feel alive. Guy judged it thus, and the prettiest woman would have been wrong at that moment, because she could never have been worth as much as the ideal of his dream, which fled him or enlaced him at the whim of his caprice.

"Let's get away!" sighed his friend, yawning desperately. "I'm bored!"

"What do you want?"

"I don't know . . . to do something . . . to kill time."

"Kill time, fool! It's him who'll kill you."

"Let's not think about that . . . let's go out for a walk, let's go listen to the gypsies."

"Not worth the trouble; you can hear them from here. They're everywhere: in cellars, in the trees, in the gutters. They're all plying their bows to the distant princess who will take them away in her galley!"

"Let's go to the fair at Neuilly; there's Pezon and La Goulue,[1] a naturalist quadrille in a cage of wild beasts!"

"All right," said Guy, obligingly.

From a distance, the avenue seemed flamboyant. Interminable arches of colored glass extended from one sidewalk to the other, forming a luminous dome, a blossoming of huge multicolored flowers beneath the flowers of the sky, which were grouped disdainfully with unalloyed scintillations.

As soon as the entrance, there were roundabouts of little pigs and varied animals, circling to a grinding of vague notes, obstinately hoarse, unhinging the meninges. There were twisting wheels, aerial ships, vertiginous swings, a hundred homicidal machines for the usage of those avid for pleasure and suicide: a miniature of Dantean tortures accompanied by howls, convulsions and shrill cries. They saw games of massacre, celebrated executions, Vacher and his victims.[2]

---

1 Jean-Baptiste Pezon (1827-1897) was the most famous lion-tamer of his era, and was painted several times by Henri de Toulouse-Lautrec, but he was dead when this story was published, and the mention of a cage of wild beasts rules out the possibility that the reference is to his son Adrien, who worked as a fairground painter. Toulouse-Lautrec also painted the dancer "La Goulue" (Louise Weber, 1866-1929) several times while she was the star of the Moulin Rouge, although she had quit the cabaret in 1895 and opened her own traveling show, which was a disastrous flop; it is unlikely that she would have been performing at the Neuilly fair in 1899.

2 The serial killer Joseph Vacher (1869-1898), sometimes nicknamed

Marguerite de Bourgogne in her bachelor pad and Marat in his bath. They contemplated resigned lions and frenetic tamers, a philosophical crocodile and an agonizing she-monkey who gave them her hand with a mild gaze of distress. Then a little girl in a torn lawn dress with pink surah underwear took them by the arm, laughing.

"Leave us alone!" said Guy, sulkily.

But she persisted.

"No!" he growled.

"At least, my dear, if I displease you, take me as far as the rabbits."[1]

They pursued their route under the smoky Argand lamps, along the fortresses of spiced bread behind ramparts of nougat, in the reek of rancid grease and oil.

"Behold, Messieurs et Mesdames . . ."

Here is the flea-circus, the . . . melomane, the Prince Colibri,[2] the spider-woman, the human shark, the wrestlers in gold tights and female wrestlers in licorice sticks. Here are the obese Columbines and Pierrettes displaying their legs under white tutus and flesh-colored leotards, vaguely reminiscent of choice cutlets in their paper lace pricked by a rose.

"Behold, Messieurs et Mesdames . . ."

The girl squeezes Guy's arm more tightly.

"It's here, my love, look how nice they are!"

A roundabout of white rabbits sparkles superbly, dethroning the piglets of ancient fêtes. And, hoisted on to the backs of the innocent rodents, women are quivering joyfully.

"l'éventreur du Sud-Est" in honor of the notorious Englishman known in France as "Jack l'éventreur" [Jack the Ripper].

1 It is probably not irrelevant to this story that *lapin* [rabbit] was also a slang term used in the nineteenth century for a passenger or parcel carried *gratis* by a diligence or other conveyance for which a fee would usually be required. It is certainly not irrelevant that the term also features in *double entendres* of lewd implication, which have English equivalents related to the rhyming synonyms "bunny" and "coney."

2 "Prince Colibri" was a general pseudonym applied in French fairgrounds to midgets.

"Would you like a ride too?"

"Yes," says the girl, her eyes gleaming with covetousness. "You can offer me that! It's not dear, babe, and it kills bad luck . . . not to mention that I have nice underwear."

And the child leaps on to the symbolic rabbit, offering the pink bouquet of her flying skirts,

"Behold, Messieurs et Mesdames . . ."

THE OLD WOMAN WITH THE ROSES
(*La Presse*, 3 August 1899)

It was in the field of rest: a distant, humble, mysterious field full of broom, sweet marjoram and lavender around slightly neglected tombstones. A very old grandmother had come there to visit a very little girl who had died suddenly, no one knew of what, as saplings and little birds die when it pleases God to make faggots and singers for Paradise.

The minuscule mound scarcely protruded in the midst of others, punctuated by a cross of black wood bearing two dates and a name: Antoinette. That was all.

Often, during my aimless wandering, I passed along the path where the very old grandmother prated for the very little girl, and I assumed that the mother and father had died at almost the same time, distantly, no doubt, leaving the ancestor the care of weaving with her frail hands the garlands of roses that put a hint of beauty and sweetness into that lost corner every morning. Lost? Nowhere did the warblers chirp with better heart, and one might have thought, when the dew was suspended from newly opened corollas, that nature, coming to the aid of indifferent humanity, had spread tears in order to give illusion to the defunct.

When I saw the old woman coming at her unequal pace, wrapped in a tight shawl of black merino wool, with her vacillating eyes in their sunken orbits, I got up and saluted her amicably. She seemed confused, made herself even smaller, almost faint, sketched a ceremonious reverence and passed on very rapidly, stumbling slightly in the long grass.

The two flaps of her shawl, which caught the wind, were inflated like awkward wings; the flying wisps of her hair were silvered softly, and then she disappeared around a calvary.

We expected one another; we knew one another; we liked one another without speaking to one another. Our eyes had understood. In the countless wrinkles of her forehead and her temples, in the profound creases of her lips, sealed by an infinite sadness, I read an excessively long life of anguish and an excessively long desire for deliverance: the desolation of someone who has vibrated too much and no longer has anything but the dream of a dream, the shadow of a shadow, an obsessive and dolorous vagueness.

That year, spring had been clement, flowers everywhere: large periwinkles, open like blue stars of an ingenuous tenderness; new leaves filigreed with white gold, streaked with green gold, sprinkled every morning with fine pearls; climbing plants suspended in light arches garlanding the railings and the crosses, running in perforated arcades in naves, rose-windows and cathedrals of dream, built in a night by dryads who came there to weep amorously.

The old woman also gathered harvests of roses. She carried enormous sheaves of them, whose candid, grave, mad, melancholy, voluptuous, disquieting heads smiled in the light. There were white roses, modest in bonnets of pale foam, tea-roses vaguely nuanced with amber, with hearts of topaz; closed roses like the faces of virgins, whose eyelids—transparent petals—were lowered over the mystical dream; broadly blooming roses as insolent as a courtesan's laughter; and dark, almost black, roses in which the blood of a crime seemed to be concealed.

The contrast between the glorious flowers and that human ruin was gripping. The old woman shook her white tresses in the triumph of her larceny, the milky droplets of her eyes wandering in their orbits with an anxious joy, and her yellow, desiccated hands, in which all the bone-structure was precise, clung feverishly to the embalmed trophy. And I meditated upon the futility of hope, of resignation, of happiness, of pain and of lies before the futility of everything.

"Of what did she die?" I asked, one day.

She shook her head.

"How can one know? There are beings who cannot live, just as there are some who cannot die. Life is incomprehensible. In any case, it's necessary not to think about it any longer. The thought bites like acid, tears like iron, twists and destroys like fire. The only thing that desolates me is that, when I'm no longer here, no one will bring my sweet flower of heaven the sweet flowers of the earth."

And the ancestor went away, curbing her back more and more, as if to bring her lips, avid for infantile kisses, closer to the ground.

The summer passed, and then the autumn. The brown mantle of dead leaves fell softly over the sadness of things; large clouds began to travel doggedly, and it seemed to me that the nights became heavier, that the impenetrable veil of darkness would never again allow the sympathetic gaze of the stars to be divined; but the daylight was even more lamentable.

After an absence of a few weeks, when I regained my solitude, winter had taken away the last leaves; the woods, the meadows and the roads were similarly despoiled, under a persistent and glacial rain.

The old woman, for whom I went in search in the blessed field, no longer appeared. I no longer saw the two flaps of her shawl, in which the wind was engulfed, inflating like awkward wings, nor the wisps of her hair silvering softly; I no longer followed her with a tender gaze as far as the calvary. I learned that the old woman, having finally found the road to deliverance, and gone to join her little angel

And I put bouquets of white rises on the grave, for the two innocent souls . . . because the souls of very old grandmothers are similar to the souls of little children.

A FIRST TIME
(*La Presse*, 13 August 1899)

The sea is calm, flecked with orange and blue tints that extend, fading, toward the horizon, to fuse in a uniform sheet of deal turquoise with the opaline sheet of the sky. Near the shore, silver scarves quiver, latching on to the shingle, trailing threads of foam over the golden sand.

The beach is almost deserted; the faint echoes of the casino orchestra seem to cradle the rhythmic dance of the waves. Over there, lovely madames in the overheated rooms are sporting unprecedented marvels of linen and lace, and yawning quietly behind their fans. The little horses are turning, turning, offering modest gains to those cleaned out at baccarat, and feverish hands, scintillating with rings, are pushing silver coins over the green baize.

Isabelle de Praneuf, in a dress of pink Chinese crepe delicately embroidered with large storks with deployed wings, is sitting under a tent at the edge of the sea and chatting with the Comte de Praneuf, her husband.

"It's pleasant," she says, "and I'm happy."

"Dear little wife!"

"Isn't your intimate friend Max des Esquilles due to arrive in a few minutes?"

"Indeed; I'd forgotten him. But don't count too much on him, darling; Max is a conqueror who profits from all the hazards of war."

"Truly, he has so much success! You surprise me greatly."

"Women tear one another apart over him, and not the least beautiful. One could believe that he casts a spell on them."

Isabelle shakes her pert head and shrugs her rounded shoulders, which the birds of her dress are kissing devotedly.

"He's not as seductive as you seem to believe, your friend Max! If I could be taken, it's not him who could take me. In truth, you're infinitely better, my dear Raymond."

Raymond, moved, presses the hand of the adored blonde and envelops her with a long moist gaze.

Slightly nervous, Isabelle gets to her feet and takes a few steps with pretty undulations of the hips beneath her ultra-clinging skirt: a fashion she has of betraying everything without compromising anything, and which is a voluptuous and ironic poem, something like a satirical song of the gait. Her corset, straight in font, makes her breasts stand out in the silky fabric, and disengages her round rump under a narrow belt, which has a giant scarab in pink coral for a clasp.

"Here he comes! Here he comes!"

Raymond gets up in his turn, with a visible annoyance.

"Let him go to all the devils!"

"No, my dear, it's very nice on his part to come. Run to meet him! Let's go! What are you waiting for? He's certainly looking for us."

The comte hastens, and the young woman, to give herself countenance, seems to interest herself prodigiously in the fate of a jellyfish, which she turns over with the tip of her umbrella like a great withered flower with glaucous petals. A few minutes of delectable expectation, and Max is beside her, surrounding her with a halo of covetousness.

"Madame . . . Isabelle . . . my dear . . . !"

"Shh! Are you mad?"

"Bah! Your husband can't hear us; he's found acquaintances. Let's profit from this moment of solitude to arrange a rendezvous . . . tell me, tell me, when can I see you?"

"But . . . here . . . at the concert at the Casino."

"No, no. I want you differently . . . this evening, all to myself."

"That's impossible! How can I escape? People would know; I'd be doomed."

"I love you, I love you to the point of dying of it. Your kisses . . . oh, your kisses!"

"No, please . . ."

"Yes! I beg you, my adored."

Max is truly handsome: the feline moustache, the mat complexion, the sparkling pupil in the iris with red reflections of cornelian. A little frisson runs down the back of the darling.

"Remember that I've only been married a year and have never failed."

"It isn't failing to take pity on the man who loves you. This evening, this evening . . . will you? Oh, will you?"

"No, no, don't persist. It would be horrible!"

But Isabelle's eyes belie her indignation, and Max, who knows what great feminine resolutions are worth, shows himself charming to Raymond, finally returned, informing him about finance, politics and twenty other trivia that amorous women scarcely understand.

"A little more, my wolf, there's only the foam!"

Isabelle, beside her dear husband is having a snack, very politely, a savant snack, spicy and incendiary, washed down by nice amber and ruby wines that put a furnace of desire into the brain. Raymond, astonished and delighted, no longer recognizes his divine Isabeau, who kisses him ardently and huddles against him, seductive and solicitous.

They have forgotten the place, the time, the earth and the sky! They are no longer vibrating for anything but their very legitimate tenderness; the immortal canticle is flourishing on their spousal lips as if normally only flourishes on the lips of lovers. They are united in duty as they would be in sin! And Raymond, intoxicated to the point of ecstasy, falls asleep following his unexpected dream.

Hastily, Isabelle has covered herself with a long dark mantle and has gone at a stealthy pace through the ill-lit back alleys of the village.

Max, who has been lying in wait for her for two hours at a corner of a path, seizes her arm abruptly and leads her to the retreat that he has chosen for their embrace.

"You! You! I though you weren't coming! Why are you so late? I was gnawing my knuckles with impatience. Wretch!"

But she, with an adorable candor: "I would never have dared! Think about it . . . a first time! And then . . . then . . . I got carried away with my husband!"

SUNSET
(*La Presse*, 21 August 1899)

The Sea unfurls softly
Over the blond carpet of the strand,
And her song rises incessantly
Toward the vault of the firmament.

On the horizon of ashen gray,
Showing his face of light,
The Sun, in the immensity
Seems to be descending regally.

And the Sea is covered in her turn
By a sash of precious stones,
Raised by the florid breezes
Drunk on perfumes of amour.

For her lover she catches fire,
With languishing sighs,
And sunbeams like tender arms
Seem to extinguish every wave.

Then, when the enamored Star
Has reached the profound bed.
One sees, trailing on the water,
His great ripped mantle of gold.

It is a very quiet song that dies on the shore: the song of wavelets
to the pizzicati of foam, to the iridescent crests that murmur,

palpitate and caress small seashells, in one last note of crystal purity, while the sonorous basses rumble and the violoncellos of the open sea utter their amorous plaint untiringly.

On the horizon everything seems to dissolve into a glory of dream for the smile of the sun, which lies down in the waves. The sea shudders at the approach of the magnificent lover, covering herself with an incomparable cape of fulgurant gems, sown in profusion, overlapped, entangled and twisted in fiery serpents, woven into garlands of roses; here as white as a snowfall, there as crimson as a garden of tortures. A basket of corollas and fireflies, a rolling mosaic of unknown gemstones, a shredded carpet of nebulosities, fresh fluff, feathers of dead wings, massacres of stars. It is an incomparable spectacle of grandeur and beauty. And in the finesse of the air, the waves sing more loudly. All the voices fuse in an infinite chant, all the voices of desire and passion that celebrate the wedding of the Sun god!

Before that unusual spectacle little women pass indifferently, strictly corseted, their loins protruding under narrow dresses, fixed in a lascivious and dolorous torsion of the waist im- posed by society. It is the hour of flirtation, of prattling, of witty words gleaned in the lecture hall, of honey-and-lemon malevolence. They examine one another with rapid searching gazes, their smiles ironic; they assess one another, compliment one another, scratch one another with delicate claws, quickly retracted into velvet gloves. All the felinity of the mondaine purrs, stretches, fidgets and runs rings prettily around the ap- athy of men. The grand dames in quest of little shocks rub el- bows with whores wearied by Parisian nights, who can finally contemplate the sunset while not in bed. It is sometimes also, for them, the rise of a lucky star with the rise of a fine fortune.

But the King Star has dipped his tresses of light in the waves that he caresses with a tremulous lip, while awaiting the ultimate kiss. He descends into a blaze of topazes and rubies; he seems to exit through a portal of flame open to a sidereal furnace, a sky in fusion of an unsustainable splendor. Sheaves of light spring from that superhuman conflagration, extinguishing in a field of hyacinth, onyx and sardonyx, which extends, degrading softly, as far as the melancholy of dead turquoise.

The orchestra of the waves inflates, bursts, and is unleashed in a formidable gasp of amour. It is the intoxication the delirium of violins sighing over the shrill chanterelle, in the fanfare of brass recklessly sounding the eternal hymn of sensuality!

✳

In the depths of the casino, women who were once beautiful and who were once adored are pressing avidly around the baccarat table, parading their febrile fingers charged with rings over the green baize. Over their throats, which once knew necklaces of kisses, rows of inestimable pearls collide; over their shoulders, which once bent under mad embraces, arachnean lace is draped; from their thick, deformed waists, in spite of savant armatures, golden pouches and diamond-studded purses hang. And that is also a sunset; the sunset of Beauty, agonizing in the bed of forgetfulness, colder than a tomb, the apotheosis of futile wealth, possession without amour.

HAPPY HOUSEHOLDS
(*La Presse*, 27 August 1899)

The Duval and Dumont households have installed themselves, in order to forget the emotions of Parisian life, on a little Breton beach, quite unknown, in the sole company of amorously yawning mollusks.

Since the morning, sitting on the sand, with a huge pink-striped parasol shielding their heads and their skirts lifted up over tawny leather ankle-boots, Madame Duval and Madame Dumont have been contemplating the waves with the placidity of heifers in grass, and making one another small confidences. The former is pale and smooth, pulpy and flavorsome in her milky flesh of a blonde quail; the latter is brunette, sinewy, with amber skin, gilded like Muscat grape that the sun has caressed for a long time. They have been mingling the silky tangles of their floating hair and allowing the marine breeze to kiss their frail napes all day long. The soul of the waves espouses the waves of their soul, and in the blue of the horizon the blue of their dreams fades away. Azure everywhere, above, below and within! It is an orgy of azure, only troubled by the voracious sadism of the crabs, violating the innocent seashells in order to eat their hearts, or the agony of the jellyfish that are drying out on the shore, presenting the striped corollas of gelatinous orchids.

Sometimes, the ladies, in the company of their husbands, great lovers of fishing, go out to the rocks that extend over a long surface covered with seaweed, in which innumerable pools shine. Monsieur Duval holds Madame Dumont's net;

Monsieur Dumont offers his hand to Madame Duval in the difficult passages.

In the distance, the sea undulates behind the sticky gray plain of wrack. Little mounds of yellow sand, surrounded by white stones, resemble cardboard fortifications raised for the dolls of some children's game. Crabs maneuver there heavily, like lead soldiers, advancing obliquely in a sly manner and then, at the slightest alert, withdrawing their maladroit feet and remaining immobile, brown amid the brown pebbles, under the kite-like wing-beats of some marine bird,

They catch shrimps in the fissures in which pink and mauve tresses float, which seem to be swimming, and they find mussels covered with moss and ash-gray shellfish whose cooked flesh is delicate.

Madame Dumont, who is brave, pinches the tapering ends of the beards of crayfish, which she thrown in her basket, where they resemble a pile of little glass beasts of infinite fragility.

The two men repose, sometimes, in order to smoke their pipes or eat some charcuterie wrapped in newspaper.

The first days were charming. They talked about the mildness of nature and the felicity of simple hearts. They regretted not having discovered a virgin isle in order to spend days there exempt from domestic cares and political discussions; they have relaxed honestly, without afterthought, and even without any thought at all. Then, with the monotony of daily joys, came cruel tedium, followed by the desire to pass on to a new game. Monsieur Dumont has thought about the distant princesses of the Moulin Rouge, and Monsieur Duval has sought among the fisherwomen for an acceptable sinner. But the fisherwomen only fish in seawater, and the humor of Madame Duval—who senses her husband's culpable desire—bristles with as many barbs as the shrimps she has fished.

Piquant insinuations came in consequence to wounding words, and wounding words led to incurable animosities.

The frail wooden hut that they inhabited in common resonated from evening until morning with the noise of conjugal quarrels. Existence became intolerable. If they were to think of quitting the little Breton beach in order to return to the Parisian furnace, however, it would be necessary to abandon the project, the villa having been rented for three months, and no one having presented himself to take the succession.

At that moment, Monsieur Dumont, who that thus far respected the property of others, took it into his head to find that Madame Duval was ideally blonde, and Monsieur Duval whispered seguidillas and fandangos into the Andalusian ear of Madame Dumont.

The indolent Madame Duval did not want to annoy her husband's closest friend and ceded to Monsieur Dumont's solicitations behind an outcrop of rock, while Madame Dumont, a little further away, also sacrificed to the sacred laws of amity with Monsieur Duval. Monsieur Dumont deceived Madame Dumont with Madame Duval; Monsieur Duval deceived Madame Duval with Monsieur Dumont, Madame Duval deceived Madame Duval with . . . Monsieur Duval . . . Monsieur Dumont . . .

In brief, everyone was deceived and harmony was no longer disrupted!

THE CHAIN[1]
(*La Presse*, 8 September 1899)

I wanted, outside of your power,
To bring back my errant thought,
To weep under the dying breeze
Tears that you could not see.

I wanted, far from vain ardors
To contemplate other horizons,
And expel by means of my treasons
The fever that was burning my veins.

I wanted, by means of other kisses
To intoxicate myself as far as suffering,
To forget even the hope
Of our unappeased sighs.

But insult and outrage themselves
Enchain more solidly
The flesh of two lovers
Nothing cures that which one loves.

Nothing cures that which one flees.
I have rediscovered the noise of chains

---

1 This story is a revised version of the one published in the 17 September 1898 issue of *La Presse*, translated herein as "The Departure." The names of the characters are changed but the story proceeds in much the same fashion until the conclusion, which is markedly different and much sharper.

In the forceful breath of oaks
And the murmurs of the night.

Everything augments my torture;
For the noise of tempting iron
Covers the voice of the singing waves
And all the voices of nature.

My chain is riveted to you
And in an infinite anguish,
My heart gasps its agony,
A fiber in every ring.

The immense steamboat had emerged majestically from the port, drawn by a powerful tug, and the friends of the passengers, the relatives and simple curiosity-seekers massed on the harbor walls, on the beach and at the windows had cheered its departure. Handkerchiefs at the end of extended arms still floated in the distance like butterflies at the end of a thread. Then, the ship having crossed the narrow passage enclosed between two granite walls, had finally felt free, and had begun its frolics, like an enormous monster running over the water. It had drawn away at top speed as soon as it was out of the port, on a smooth sea beneath a lapis lazuli sky, and now it seemed very small, as if it had sunk into the ocean.

Sylvian's first emotion had been that of a man condemned to death to whom the commutation of his sentence has been announced. Once his exile had been decided, the rupture accomplished, he had sensed his anguish slightly appeased by the thought of this distant voyage over the waves, of this consented calvary from which he would perhaps never return.

Oh, if only the old man could change his soul, metamorphose like the water, the sky and the shore at the passage of the great errant ship!

He thought that the last split had annihilated his faculty of suffering, that he was only an inert body, since Hélène had expelled him and given herself to another. He saw again the slim young woman with the tawny hair and the delicate profile of wax, scarcely tinted by a reflection of life. He saw her ardent eyes, her sad and faunesque smile. She had taken his strength, had drunk his existence, playing with him, with his nerves and his blood, a tyrant avid for joy and gasps. A sorceress of vice, she had caused to vibrate, to please him, all the notes of the viol d'amour, had lavished on him, with a feline dilettantism of a succubus, the caresses that corrode, slowly and surely, laving him neurotic, exhausted, his marrows and his brain melted like lead in an alchemist's crucible. And he regretted the morbid sensualities from which he was about to be weaned. Never, in his hours of struggle had he felt himself plunged in such a cloaca of misery!

It was no longer a mental and obsessive dolor but the madness of a beast devoid of shelter, the distress of a lost being who no longer has a roof and all whom all the brutal forces of the world have come to assail. He had a desire to talk to the strangers with whom he was rubbing shoulders, to tell them his troubles in order to be pitied and consoled. He had, deep down, a shameful need akin to that of the pauper who is about to hold out his hand, an irresistible need to feel someone sharing his pain. But no one turned toward his misery; he remained desperately alone.

He made an effort and went into the lounge, where a few passengers were asleep in the corners. It was really a vast floating cosmopolitan hall where the well-to-do of all the continents had to live in common. Its garish luxury resembled that of grand hotels, theaters and all the public places in the world where money no longer counts. Sylvian went back up to the deck, and tried to occupy his gaze and his mind with the spectacle of grandiose nature.

The coast was blurred with lilac and blue, confounding its chimerical contours with the clouds. At his whim, he sculpted clouds, palaces, mountains, domes, columns, minarets, sinister prisons or glorious towers, erupting volcanoes, gibbets and crosses of torture; he contemplated images of joy or distress, and entire wild city on a sky in flower! And in the fugitive harmonies of the breeze, in the ardor of distant sands, he rediscovered the voice and the perfume of his mistress.

"Hélène!" he sighed, holding out his arms.

Lips aspired his ardent plaint, and hands were posed on his shoulders.

"Here I am!"

He thought that he was embracing the supple body of his lover and fainting in a profound caress.

"Go away!"

Abruptly, he had drawn himself erect, with a frightful pounding of his heart. The entire phantasmagoria of his dream had disappeared. He was alone on the deck, in desolation, in darkness . . .

He respired . . . but light laughter ran over the waves; the phantom was there, the implacable phantom of his amour.

THE OLD WOMAN
(*La Presse*, 21 September 1899)

She is dead, the old woman, and her oblique profile
Is outlined all white on the gray wall.
Outside, one hears the cold breeze passing
Which sweeps away the spread foliage, weeping.

Eyes wide open, full of the frightful mystery,
The children assemble around the mattress
Gaze at the meager, pale and weary face
Whose kisses are henceforth gone from the earth.

They are contemplating death for the first time!
Ignorant until then, they went into the wood
To pick vermilion fruits and white flowers,
Under the burning sun and the biting wind.

They went to collect pink shellfish,
Hair in the wind, bare feet in the nacreous sand;
It is the first time that their fearful hearts
Understand that all beings and things pass away.

Consternated and tremulous before the blue corpse,
They are still gazing, with eyes full of fear,
And when there is thunder, rain or wind outside
The anguish of oblivion shivers in their soul . . .

The fisherman's cottage near the strand seems to be leaning over to listen to the song of the waves. It is unsteady, dilapidated and corroded, by both the sun and the rain, covered with a brown leprosy, striped with long cracks, with a skewed roof that sustains itself as best it can; trickles dry out before the door; a few meager geraniums with crimson flowers languish against the wall and on the sill of the window with closed shutters.

Jean and Sylvestre, two little children, with bushy hempen hair and pale blue eyes—the ingenuous blue of streams and the April sky—gaze at the old woman, stiff in her big bed. They are astonished to find her with that jaundiced tint, like the candles burning in the dull candlesticks, and their awkward hands shift a twig of box-wood soaking on a plate.

Grandmother has the beads of a rosary in her fingers and a cross of black wood on her breast, on which a silver Christ shines. She is rejuvenated, devoid of wrinkles, almost pretty, with her white hair very smooth under a frilly bonnet. At the back of the room—the unique room, which serves as the bedroom, dining room and kitchen—a cradle surrounded by curtains shelters the slumber of the new-born, arrived a few days before the death of the ancestor.

Sylvestre and Jean speak in low voices, interrogating their mother, still very weak, who nevertheless has to supervise the final preparations.

"Why doesn't Grand'maman Rosine reply to us this morning? Why is she so beautiful with her Sunday bonnet, but also so pale?"

The mother sobs silently, shakes her head and takes the children by the hand.

"Go and play, my darlings."

"No, no, we want to know. We're not doing any harm. We're being very good."

"Your father will be coming back. Wait for him on the road. He's sure to bring back fine blue and pink fish with golden scales, and he'll give you deep seashells that sigh like the wind in the branches."

"When we're grown up, we'll go fishing with Papa, in a boat that will dance like a kite."

"Yes, my darling."

"Then we'll go down to the bottom of the sea, won't we, Maman? What's at the bottom of the sea?"

"Mountains, forests, animals and flowers such as one sees in dreams . . . marvelous and terrible things that no one knows."

"Why doesn't anyone know?"

"Because those who go down under the waves never come back."

"Is Grandmother going to go down under the waves?"

"No, she's going to go up to Heaven."

"Ah! She's going to fly away?"

"Yes."

"With the birds that disappear into the clouds?"

"Her soul has gone with the swallows."

"And what is there in all that blue? Is it as beautiful as the bottom of the sea?"

"It's even more beautiful. One can't imagine such magnificence,"

"Does one also find rocks and forests there, fish of all colors and flowering rose-bushes?"

"Much better; one sees the sun, the moon and the stars . . . and paradise, which is like a firework display."

"It's to paradise that Grandmother has gone?"

"Yes, my darlings."

A neighbor comes to look for the children while the old woman is carried away in a narrow marionette-box, for the old woman had diminished considerably in the last years of her life and weighs scarcely more than a bran doll.

When they return, Sylvestre and Jean weep with their mother, in mourning.

"Since it's so nice up there, why do we remain alone down here? We want to fly too, to see the fireworks!"

And the sobs are redoubed. The desolate mother can find nothing more to say, but then, in a sudden inspiration:

"Console yourselves, my darling; grandmother hasn't gone very far—it would be too painful for her to leave us. She's come back; she's in the white cradle. The good God, finding her infirm and broken, has made her a brand new body for her lovely soul of a little child. Go and kiss her."

Sylvestre and Jean, full of joy, race to the baby, who has woken up, smiling at them, with a toothless and funny ancestral smile that is very familiar. They press her to their hearts, put a thousand sonorous kisses on her wrinkled cheeks and cry, tenderly: "Bonjour, Grandmother!"

BIRD'S-EYE VIEW
(*La Presse*, 5 October 1899)

Between the Women

At the Château des Vignes. On the terrace, which is already traversed by the farandole of crimson and gold leaves, Madame de Murloff, Madame d'Effeuillée and Flora are chatting negligently, contemplating their rings or the tips of their little feet. The sun is setting discreetly behind the plane trees; the vervain and the tuberoses are exhaling their soul of perfume.

Madame d'Effeuillée is thirty years old; petite, dainty, plump, with hair the color of ripe corn and an artificial camellia complexion, a voluptuous and supple figure.

Madame de Murloff is twenty-five years old; not pretty, but less than that; sometimes red-haired, sometimes brunette, with eyes that also become green or black, passing through violet, gray, yellow and maroon.

Flora is twenty years old; a closed rosebud that only asks to blossom under the kiss of butterflies; reserved and proud in appearance.

Madame d'Effeuillée: What a nice day . . . it's truly very pleasant . . .

Madame de Murloff: Our hunters will be returning soon.

Madame d'Effeuillée: What a pity! Not amusing, our husbands.

Madame de Murloff: Nor the others.

Madame d'Effeuillée: Between ourselves, we can talk about clothes, music, literature, and insult the absentees politely—oh, those who merit it!—and the time passes without ennui. The men find nothing to say to us . . . they're polluted, the fools, by bad company. What do you think, Flora?

Flora (*with a detached air*): I don't know. When I marry, I'll marry someone very rich . . .

Madame d'Effeuillée: And you'll deceive him?

Flora: Oh!

Madame de Murloff. Yes, you'll come to that, like our little friends. The men one deceives are the only ones that love you. As soon as one forgets to take a husband or a lover seriously . . . they avenge themselves.

Flora: I'll profit from your good advice.

Madame d'Effeuillée: Don't listen to young Adolphe. He's nice, but he doesn't have a sou.

Flora (*feigning astonishment*): Adolphe?

Madame de Murloff: Would you believe it? He asked me for a rendezvous this morning.

Madame d'Effeuillée: Yesterday, he dirtied my mauve deerskin shoes under the table.

Flora: A little while ago he sent me verses in a basket of roses . . . the monster!

Madame de Murloff: What did we tell you? Among men, it's necessary only to see the useful side. You know my necklace of black pearls?

Madame d'Effeuillée: Superb.

Madame de Murloff: I chose it one bead at a time . . . but it's irreproachable.

Madame d'Effeuillée: Personally, I prefer precious trinkets, valuable paintings, terra cottas . . .

Flora: And it's your husband who . . . ?

Madame de Murloff and Madame d'Effeuillée (*laughing*): Naturally.

Between the Men

Out hunting, Raoul, Ernest and Adolphe are sitting in a clearing some distance away from Mesdames de Murloff and d'Effeuillée, who are sleeping peacefully beside their dogs.

Ernest: Yes, Madame d'Effeuillée isn't bad, but already slightly faded, and her make-up!

Raoul: Madame de Murloff has more going for her. What a mouth! What eyes! I pity the husband.

Adolph (*conceitedly*): He gets what he wants . . . he's content.

Ernest: In sum, women are insupportable, save for a few good moments. Parrots who only know one refrain and serve it to us indefinitely.

Adolphe: In the moonlight, with variations on the stars . . .

Ernest: I prefer whores. One knows immediately what's what, and it's less costly.

Adolphe: Get away! Beautiful women have never cost me anything!

Raoul: Really?

Adolphe: And if I wanted . . . one gets so bored in the country!

Raoul and Ernest (*enviously*): Not possible! Then, can one dare?

Adolphe: It's as I tell you.

Ernest: Even little Flora?

Adolphe (*boastfully*): Shh! Discretion, Messieurs . . .

Ensemble

Evening, in the drawing room. Mesdames de Murloff, d'Effeuillée and Flora are offering tea to the messieurs while the husbands play piquet.

Raoul (*in a whisper, to Madame de Murloff*): If you knew how bored I am away from you! Twenty times I was on the point of abandoning the hunt. I'll say everything, my secret is stifling me . . . oh, don't interrupt me . . . *etc., etc.*

Ernest (*whispering to Madame d'Effeuillée*): I never cease to regret your dear presence, my pretty blonde fay. Oh, you'll never understand how much I love you . . . ! Yes, yes, I adore you! For too long I've been trembling and suffering in silence . . . *etc., etc.*

Adolphe (*whispering to Flora*): It's not my fault if the women seek me out. For myself, there's only one in the world! I'm sincere, Flora, I swear to you! It's a fervent worship, an infinite and respectful tenderness that I offer you. I don't have anything, but I could become somebody if you help me . . . and . . .

The ladies, very emotional, blush, palpitate and, ingenuously, allow their fingertips to be pressed.

Who are the greater liars?

MAD
(*La Presse*, 15 October 1899)

The clarions sound; the fanfare bursts forth while the regiment passes along the white road in the thin morning mist. The sounds vibrate madly in the pure air, rolling and rebounding like the bells on the collar of a post-horse, unleashed in a triumphant tempest, and then fading, weakening, gradually dissolving in the distance, until they are no more than a vague rhythm, a skeleton of harmony, a sigh, a tremulous note more tenuous than a thread of spider-silk suspend from the calyx of a rose.

Mad, with her fingers in her eyes, is sobbing recklessly in the grass of the ditch, and I address a note of encouragement to her from my window.

"Don't distress yourself, little Mad; He's gone, but he'll come back."

The young woman parts the pale silky tangle of her hair, stands up, and wipes away the dew that is pearling in the ingenuous flowers of her eyes.

"For sure, if he doesn't come back, I'll have nothing more to do but die! However, he didn't look at me just now."

"He didn't see you . . ."

"Oh, yes he did . . . but he was ashamed, before the others."

"Ashamed of your smile, pretty Mad? It's foolish to be so difficult! There are other lads in the village, amiable and cheerful. A girl like you can't lack admirers!"

"I only have one love, Madame, and that's for life."

Mad is wrong; it's necessary, with eyelids closed, to accept everything that can fill the frightful void of existence for an hour, everything that has an appearance of amity or tenderness.

"If Jacques forgets you, my girl, it's necessary to love someone else."

Although very young, Mad has experience.

"I don't want to take a gallant, like Victorine or Louise. Jacques is my fiancé, you see. Lovers are like dogs . . . it always ends badly, and the best thing is not to have one."

She's right; the best thing is not to believe in anything or anyone, to have neither faith nor hope. Those who hang on desperately to their chimera fall lower than the average individual; it's true that they have departed from a greater height!

"Come on, little Mad, don't cry! Nature is beautiful and you're twenty years old! Another autumn, which will slide over you with the caress of dead leaves. Later, the winters will be leaden for your paltry shoulders! It's necessary to make a provision of courage for the future. You've quivered at spring blossomings, you've seen the great August sun rising over the horizon in the symphony of your heart and your senses. You've had the illusions of primroses and roses. What are you complaining about? Fortunate Mad, have you not seen the sheet of the ripe wheat turning yellow, like a sea of blazing gold that seems to reflect the flamboyance of the heavens, a sea rolling its ardent swell with all the breath of the passions? Sometimes, in the heat, a sudden calm puts the ears to sleep, a fecundating breath emerges from the earth, rising like a voluptuous incense as far as the pistils of the lilies, and all the corollas swoon at the same time.

"One senses the semen running in the warm and heavy seeds, springing forth in an irresistible sap! And before the giant crops, before the mystery of nature, have you not shivered with a new dread and a new joy?

"Then the reapers have come and, sheaf by sheaf, the golden rockets have been extinguished. Every thrust of the scythe bites into the living flames, and behind the curbed black men the somber and sad earth reappears.

"For you, too, darling, the reapers have come; but you have loved and you bear the glorious harvest within you. Don't envy coquettish women, the brainless and soulless dolls of flesh who are adulated, and don't curse the handsome, vain and egotisical lads, cruel in their indifference, who are cajoled; they ought not to be proud of being loved, since they have done nothing to deserve it. But you, the disdainful, the devoted, the tender, whose crucified heart is bleeding in the road, be proud of knowing how to love."

<h1 style="text-align:center">LÉO AND JULIE[1]</h1>

(La Presse, 3 November 1899)

They had met at a concert on a Sunday under the linden trees of the Place des Jacobins in Le Mans, and their gazes had expressed their happy surprise and their desire. Now, they saw one another almost every evening, in secret, their parents having effused energetically to unite them. By virtue of that rigor their caprice had increased, and had mutated into an amorous folly that excluded any other sentiment. They murmured endlessly those sweet stupidities that the heart invents and the heart alone understands. That is why the language of lovers, although always similar, has never been subject to the outrages of fashion.

"How have I been able to live without you?" she said.

"How would I be able to live if I no longer had you?" he replied.

"An infinite happiness comes to me from your presence. Do you love me as much as I love you?"

And she scarcely heard his response in the precipitation of the kiss with which he closed her lips.

It was necessary to separate. Léo had already received several pressing letters from his parents; the last one no longer admitted any excuse or suffering any delay.

The young man's baggage had been packed since the morning, and he had just made his adieux to Julie, almost decided not to listen to her pleas and to resist her tears. In any case, the absence would only be temporary; in autumn; in autumn,

---

1 This item is headlined "Idylles," a classification not used again.

he would return, still amorous, and they would resume their pretty duet, scarcely interrupted.

But she didn't want to understand anything, and to everything that he responded she shook her head obstinately, with a desolate movement.

"I don't want you to go."

"It's necessary, I swear. I've already delayed for too long."

"Take me with you, then."

"You'd be lost, my darling. What would people say about you? Your family would be indignant and would reject you if you tried to come back later."

"What does that matter? The world begins and ends with my tenderness."

"Have you thought that I'm not rich, that existence would be hard for you?"

She laughed, and became coaxing.

"Well, I'll work, if necessary. I know how to sew, embroider, and make lace. You'll see, we'll be able to get ourselves out of difficulty. Look, I'll write this tomorrow and leave my letter in clear evidence in my room:

"*My dear parents, You wanted to kill my amour, but I can only live by means of him. I'm going with my beloved Léo. Your very happy daughter, Julie.*"

Léo was not convinced, but she cajoled him, persuasively and passionately, with the faith of her sixteen years. He thought that it would be difficult to find such a pretty mistress again, and that it would be a joy to show her off at the theater and in elegant cabarets, that a little dressing up would reveal her royalty . . . for money, there was gambling and moneylenders . . . for everyone knew, since Romeo and Juliet, that parents all have entrails of stone.

She saw that he was weakening, that he was about to give in, and, letting herself fall at his knees, she took his hand and pressed it to her lips for a long time, with gratitude.

It was decided that they would leave the next day, in the middle of the night, like two criminals; and, that plan settled, they embraced, weeping with pleasure, madly happy, having followed their chimera.

She accompanied him out of the little garden into a sloping street that led to the river. When they had passed the last houses she drew aside the lace veil that hid her face, and took a deep breath.

The round orange moon, between the branches of the plane trees, resembled a colossal fruit hanging from an invisible stem. Its rays fell into the water, twisting all the way to the depths making the alleyways drowned in shadow even more mysterious. The placid night was displayed around them; a chained dog was barking faintly in the distance. They were no longer talking, lost as they were in the chaos of their thoughts. All their tenderness rose again to their brains, like an excessively generous wine, and their dream seemed to them to be more magical and more luminous than the moon, inclined over its fleeting mirror.

"Your lips," she said; "I'm yours, with all my submissive soul, with all my prostrate being. I adore you!"

She was no longer thinking about marriage. She felt too humble next to him to desire to become anything but his servant.

He took her in his arms, he lifted her up; never, never again would be quit her. All the rest was pale compared with that triumphant certainty.

Midnight chimed.

"Already!" she sighed. "Tomorrow, at the same hour, I'll leave with you. One more day!"

Their mouths joined for one last time and then he drew away, hastily. She adjusted her mantilla and returned home, her heart extended toward distant kisses, new kisses that she was about to collect, like heavy warm and perfumed clusters of grapes ripened in the sun of her amour. She would be his, he would be hers, ineffably; and their mortal remains would descend into the same tomb, embalmed with caresses, united even in death!

✳

A letter from Julie, three months later:

My dear parents,

We have been living on potatoes with a little salt water for a week. We only have a straw mattress under a cotton coverlet. The landlord is talking about throwing us out; my last dress is in tatters and I believe that Léo has beaten me. Quickly, quickly, come to fetch me!

Julie

*(Rue ***. Sixth floor, at the rear of the courtyard. Don't ask anything of the concierge.)*

SAPHO
(*La Presse*, 15 December 1899)

> *Powerful lion, lord of the jungle,*
> *Your gaze is grim and beautiful!*
> *When you juggle with the tamer,*
> *A great frisson wrinkles your skin!*
>
> *I love to see you roam the shadow,*
> *With regret for the desert;*
> *And in your ardent and somber face,*
> *Your eye is open more feverishly.*
>
> *But the roaring lionesses*
> *Have forgotten their hairy gods,*
> *Your caressant lovers*
> *No longer follow you in the night.*

Melcy, in a long robe of orange brocade, split down the side, allowing the sight of a dove-gray leotard and riding boots, whips her wild beasts, scolding them and cajoling them by turns, wild herself with her thick russet mane and the metallic gleam of her eyes. In the efforts that she makes, her shoulders shine with droplets of sweat, piercing the velveteen, and when she raises her arms, the golden moss of her armpits gleams softly beneath the flamboyance of her orange bodice.

Sapho, the black panther with emerald eyes and the long, supple and muscular body, comes to lick her fingers and lie down at her feet.

Sapho is splendid in her languid and voluptuous pose. No patch stars her tenebrous fur; she is as mysterious and as disquieting as the night.

For a moment, Melcy embraces her placing her head against hers and, putting her mouth on the clenched muzzle, seems to forget herself in a profound kiss, the panther closes her eyes, tips back her forehead, purrs like a cat and rubs herself on the warm and perfumed flesh of the woman. And they are truly two amorous beasts, as perverse as one another, claws withdrawn into velvet gloves, gazes lost in the infinity of a dream . . .

Then a blow of the whip attains the wild beast, and brings her to her feet, howling and terrible, her maw stretched, revealing all her teeth, in the regret of the interrupted caress and the rancor of the lying pleasure.

The woman laughs, scornfully, and the humiliated beast gathers herself, ready to pounce on her prey, to grip her in an unforgiving embrace . . . The two bodies roll, embrace one another and bite one another amid gasps and roars. A few female cries are heard . . . A second crack of the whip, a fascinating gaze, a curt order, and Sapho comes to crawl submissively at the feet of her mistress, imploring her for another gentle game.

People applaud, with the vague discontentment of an excessively facile victory, the unconscious desire for murder and bloodshed, the troubled cruelty that haunts the heart of every human being.[1]

The usual audience of menageries is there, a mixed public composed of socialites, known prostitutes, maids and workmen in the livery of laborers. The monkeys are agitating in

---

1 Erotic encounters with black panthers feature in several other stories and novels by La Vaudère, as this one makes up a pair with the one included herein in two separate versions, "Tamer" and "Red Lust"; the first of her several posthumously-published novels, *Sapho* (1908), is explicitly based on the present story, but has a very different conclusion.

their cages, passing the crooked hands of old women through the bars, seemingly insulting and imploring at the same time, in a faint exasperation. Philosophical bears sway gravely and ironic parrots drop coconuts on the plumed hats of female spectators.

In the first row, a tall, pale young man with prominent cheekbones under long side-whiskers is following all the movements of the tamer with the keenest interest; and the panther, who has perceived it, roars at him, rearing up furiously against the bars.

"Hop! Hop!"

Melcy has fired two revolver shots at Sapho's ears, and, holding out flaming hoops, excites her savagely with her voice. The animal traverses the garland of fire, bounds and rebounds, her pelt dolorous, her fur singed, seeming a fantastic beast herself, a monstrous chimera of flame.

The act is concluded; Melcy bows, quivering, and makes a sign to the pale young man to come and join her.

Behind the cages, in a sort of corridor hung with green cloth, the tamer smiles at the stranger and interrogates him.

"You love me? Yes, you love me, since Sapho is jealous and becomes more malevolent every day. For a month you've been present at all the performances, and the other evening I was nearly devoured. Are you rich?"

The stranger nods his head and Melcy draws him toward her, lascivious and seductive—as with the panther—and weighs her painted lips on his.

"Take me away, then . . . I'm afraid of Sapho!"

An indefinable smile distends the visitor's side-whiskers; he does not respond. Melcy repeats herself, offers in an ardent prayer of her entire being.

"Take me away?"

"No."

"You don't want to?"

"No."

"We can go a long way . . . I love you so much!"

And he, with a strong British accent: "Quit the menagerie? Never!"

"Why?"

"I've made a bet that Sapho will eat you."

"So what?" Melcy demands, with an indescribable stupor.

"I'm waiting."

FROZEN LOVE[1]
(*La Presse*, 31 December 1899)

Love lost, the bruised child
Has stopped before the door;
The pale bouquet he is carrying
Has flowered in his pale hand.

He is not cured of his dream;
The dolor of life is too great
When all hope is dead;
But he seeks a last refuge.

The winter and its chill is here,
For him the battle has been hard.
Saul, forgotten on the road

Will soon reach his final hour;
Would you like to take his hand
And shelter him in your dwelling?

In the Bois the sun, shining scarcely above the stripped branches, resembles an intermittent electric bulb in a cardboard sky. The isle, still cheered up by a little cerulean foliage, aquamarine gems and beryls, has the appearance, under its delicate layer of frost of being asleep in a glass case. And a few snowflakes scatter white wreaths over it: amorous regrets, memories of doomed kisses. A bitter wind conducts the

---

1 This story bore the unique heading "Arabesques."

mourning of voluptuous barcarolles, sermons and swirls of corollas and perfumes.

However, from the Allées de Longchamp, Madrid and Suresnes, elegant coupés emerge, warm and very discreet, which flourish in the mist of ice with roses from Nice, white lilacs and violets. The packed file of carriages stops near the lakes, and dainty young women, muffled in precious furs, descend briskly, hasten toward their favorite pleasure, neglected for such a long time, for the establishment in the Champs-Élysées can only offer relative satisfactions to fervent skaters.

Sympathetic groups of beautiful friends form around the braziers. People search for one another, smile at one another, and scratch one another with playful kittenish claws while purring, seemingly caressant.

Isabelle de B***, in an "ice-blue" velvet bolero skirt with turquoise and mat gold scarab buttons, has joined Francine de C***, her best friend, is a short costume of "water lily" woolen fabric lined with ermine, with broad flaps of silver fox.

"Bonjour, darling! How are you?"

"My doctor has prescribed exercise."

"What are we doing today? Speed or art?"

"Speed to begin with. I need to numb myself in order to believe that *it's arrived*."

"Let's wait for the gallery to be more brilliant. Have you noticed how late the men come."

"And how slowly they skate?"

"Legs of cotton."

"No more savant curves, outwards or inwards. No more serpentine virtuosity, poems in blade major."

"What do you expect? It's the fluctuations in the Bourse, or those of the Boers. Stock prices have gone down so much! An unfortunate reaction!"

"Personally, I've liquidated."

"For the cunning, my dear, it's the time to take a position. Long live the gold mines!"

"Oh, Francine, that's only too true!"

Giselle and Francine link themselves together, gliding and swaying harmoniously over the mirror of the lakes, departing like arrows, stopping, making complicated arabesques, impeccable eights, graceful interlacements, and then, with nostrils quivering, gazes lost and hair flying beneath skewed toques, hold one another tightly and boston recklessly.

The gumball sun sinks a little further and disappears in a sheaf of gray paper, the same gray paper that will later wrap all the gilded pastilles of the heavens and plunge the Bois into chilly darkness.

Foreigners, actresses and the elegant women of all strata of society pursue one another madly, calling out to one another, making efforts of the bust and the rump, leaning over as if to pick invisible flowers, straightening up again, spinning around, going, coming back and taking a few glorious falls. Correct and weary old messieurs, such as are found everywhere, amuse themselves watching from the bank, walking like clocks that are still regularly wound but no longer chime.

Meanwhile, the petty vicomte to whose obstinate lukewarm homages Giselle has been subjected throughout the autumn succeeds in speaking to her while she is putting on her long zibeline mantle frilled with English needlepoint. He has lilac cheeks, a mauve chin and a violet nose. He babbles a vague request for a rendezvous in a distant bachelor pad with a fake log fire warmed by gas.

And Giselle, having examined her frail admirer from the corner of her eye, responds, mockingly: "Impossible, dear friend! Visits, tea at the Palace Hotel, Monsieur X**'s lecture, fittings everywhere . . . oh, I'm much too busy to think about amour!"

PERFUME
(*La Presse*, 17 January 1900)

Perfume of a memory of my life enlaced,
Dream of a dead hour in that long embrace
Of which I retain, bruised, the irremissible imprint,
You haunt the road that I travel, wearily.

Perfume, subtle perfume of a dead amour,
You send into the shadow where my holy faith
Slumbers deeply, without regret or dread;
Why come to talk to me about the past?

I knew nothing more of myself, and nothing of Her,
I had forgotten everything; why, faithful perfume
Are you entering into my being and making me suffer?

I sense my ancient tenderness reawakening
To the breath of kisses, and sense myself dying;
O perfume, are you the soul of my mistress?

Marcel had taken a long silky lock of hair from a box, which suddenly caught fire between his fingers, palpitated on his lips like a golden bird and then fell back, inert, into its narrow coffin. Next to the Beloved's hair reposed a few dried flowers in melancholy colors, crumpled ribbons, a packet of letters and a white leather glove. And the penetrating perfume, the tenacious perfume of the woman, was disengaged by those things, enfevering with desire the languid being of the lover.

He revived, in those ardent effluvia, his happiness *à deux* in the depths of the nest of caresses, his poem, so sweet, that the death had interrupted . . . He saw her again, leaning over his shoulder, inspiring him, encouraging him in his labor as a poet, shelling out his sonorous rhymes and playing with his sunlit rhymes, like a child with a necklace of amber and topaz.

Everything in his thought was transfigured, mutating into a vision of dawn and dusk. It was his youth that passed with the smile of his belief, his pride and his energy. He was strong, he was twenty years old, with illusions and talent. His eyes reflected the azure of summer nights and the azure of his dreams. He marched, head high, happy in the chimerical kisses that were burning his lips.

How distant all that was! Marcel took the lock of hair from the box again and spread out the tenuous threads, which ran over his arm in a steam of light; then, plunging his face into it, he respired the evocative perfume again, with a great frisson— the perfume as precise as a caress—seeking the sensuality of an ultimate possession.

But everything went dark. After the hours of amour he had climbed the eternal calvary that leads—rarely—to glory or the hospital, his pockets full of manuscripts, copied in a bold handwriting of pride and dream, the poet had known humiliating stations in editorial offices, polite and scornful refusals, illicit favors, insults, injustices and, even more desperate, the frightful silence, the criminal silence that discourages the most valiant, kills the divine crop in the seed, devastates the fields of roses and the olive groves, and casts into the gutter those who had a little corner of Heaven in their soul, those who seek in the miry water, even so, the reflection of the stars.

> *The poet has found bitter sensualities*
> *To prick his flesh to the depth of the veins;*
> *The errant butterflies of enchanted noons,*
> *Which die slowly of their vain intoxications;*

At moments of regret he sometimes still seeks
A supreme frisson at the tips of golden wings,
But the dream soon agonizes and dies . . .
    Time passes!

Oh, one day to rediscover the lost intoxication.
To believe that all is not hollow, deceptive, fragile;
To abandon oneself again to the hectic lie
That puts its halo around the heads of gold of clay;
To swoon with faith, hope and forgetfulness!
But the sun is already sinking in the pale sky,
Will you not go soon, as everything darkens and fades?
    Time passes . . .

Marcel, his lips clasped to the tawny lock, to the warm and odorous fleece, weeping for his twenty years, his amour, his genius, his dead mistress, his fantasies of glory and the great breath of faith that carried his being away.

He wept . . . and wept . . .

Suddenly, his room filled with a violent odor of cabbages, and the red face of Zoe, the lady of the house appeared in the gap in the door

"Have you finished yet? The soup is on the table!"

Marcel sighed, wiped his eyes furtively, hid his box of relics and joined Zoe, the former brasserie waitress whom he had ended up marrying fourteen years ago because she had a few sous.

"What a face! Are you ill, then?" she said, when the poet was seated before the warm plate and the liter of cheap wine. "What's up with you, to turn you around like this?"

And he, with an indefinable smile, responded in a feeble voice: "It's the odor of cabbages."

EYES
(*La Presse*, 21 January 1900)

Under a light tent fastened with garlands of roses, little Princesse Cysta spent her days in vague meditations. Her pale eyes seemed to be gazing into a far distance, beyond terrestrial space; her red lips smiled and her nostrils inhaled avidly the perfumes that escaped from four long cassolettes filled with cinnamon, nard and myrrh. She was thinking indecisive things, her heart empty and her soul unquiet. When she was interrogated, she said: "Something is exhaling from the depths of my being warm gusts heavier than the vapors of a volcano; voices summon me; a caress envelops me, and yet I don't love anything or anyone."

Then she went to sleep. The ringlets of her hair spread out around her so abundantly that she appeared to be lying on a bed of black feathers, and her tunic embroidered in gold and silver with precious corollas shaped her from the shoulders to the heels, shaping the proud globes of her breasts, tucked in over the ridges of her hips, raised up slightly at the tips of her toes, which shone like pink seashells. Her royal mantle studded with precious stones slid to her feet, her diadem rolled away, but her hand retained a heavy necklace of strange, changing, unknown gems over her breasts, in order that she might still feel it, even in her sleep.

Were they bright amber gums and topazes, or iridescent opal waxes, glaucous aquamarine fruits, cerulean apples of beryl, amethyst grapes, little balls of agate, amaldine, olivine or chrysoprase? No jeweler would have been able to say. Every jewel, in its luminous depths, darted a pupil encased in a golden eyelid. At the slightest tremor of the supple breast that supported it, the necklace was animated, writhing like a living serpent of flames.

But when Cysta detached it from her shoulders, the stones became smoky and dull, and remained as inert as the pebbles of beaches, which the tide has ceased to roll in its flux; a sensation of dusk and chill descended from the tent fastened with garlands of roses and the vaults of foliage that only filtered a violet light seemed to be lowering gradually in order to stifle the sleeper . . .

In their hermetic dementia, did her dreams have a meaning? Darkness and light came to her from the occult contact; her hours of intoxication sang in the fiery beads of that amorous rosary. So, she scarcely ever took it off; their two splendors appeared to live on one another. Precious fabrics, brocades woven with argyrose, studded with multicolored silks and watered silks stiffened with pearls and constellated with emeralds, did not weigh upon Cysta's desire by comparison with her jewel of election. She often made it slide between her slender fingers, and the ardent pupil that lived in every gem stared at her in an ecstasy of adoration of which she fainted delectably.

A year before, beautiful and free, under the nostalgia of the mystery of amour, she had taken a lover. Soon weary, however, of learned and ever-similar kisses, she had sought other embraces, without ever finding satisfaction. And while the men who had possessed her remained dazed by regrets, she remained haughty, icy and indifferent to all despairs. None of those masters of one night reappeared, and dogs chained up in the distance howled mortally, endlessly, in the darkness.

Every evening, however, a new lover, chosen among the proudest and noblest, crossed the threshold of her bedroom, and departed in the morning, never to return.

The last to be seen was somber and sad, but his voice had so much music that Cysta was moved in the very fibers of her being. Avid for profound sensations, she smiled at the elect of her dreams and admitted him to the royal banquet.

In the morning, however, as he lingered in her caresses, she wanted inexorably, to dismiss him like the others. Then his eyebrows had contracted over a gaze of hatred. "Yes," he had murmured, "I shall quit this abode of death and treason; yes, Cysta, you will never see me again, but you will remember me by this present. Here, look; they are the fixed eyes of your lovers of a single evening!"

For a long time she had remained immobile in the moisture of the last embraces, devoid of thought, indifferent, even forgetting the mysterious gift. Then, having finally raised herself up on her feverish couch, she had summoned her women and, before their long wonderment, had considered the jewel.

It was composed of a triple row of the disquieting stones, similar to glacier tears, the gazes of nixies or sirens fixed in eternal splendor.

"Oh," she moaned, "I recognize them. He was speaking the truth! They're eyes, eyes that are contemplating me!"

But her servants had started to laugh.

"Look, Madame, at these onyxes striped with golden brown, these sapphires streaked with green gold, these topazes, these emeralds speckled with silver, these amethysts flecked with red gold . . . oh, and these two dazzling pebbles . . . one might think they were black diamonds . . ."

The little princess trembled slightly; however, her hand knotted itself to the strange necklace and gradually drew it over her breasts and her lips in an increasing ecstasy.

She had had no other lover. The dead eyes that rolled over her flesh, supple and warm, were sufficient to enfever her desire.

She lived thus, in the radiation of her futile and superhuman beauty, enchained by the amorous necklace.

Then, one day, she saw a snowy thread quivering on her temples. She wept with rage, and it appeared to her that the jewel was paling.

Gradually, the white grains became numerous in the black crop; sinister daisies flowered on her desiccated temples and everything became desolation in that rapid autumn, which had been an enchanted spring. Shivering, Cysta gazed at herself in her tall looking-glass, and, with the folds of her veils drawn back over her breast, she dared not interrogate the excessively faithful necklace. One morning, one of her women put her hand on it.

"These stones are dead, Madame; it's necessary to get rid of them."

The princess stood up, livid, chilled by horror, and dragged herself to her mirror.

Over the yellow, withered skin of her breast the somber beads rolled lugubriously.

She wanted to pick them up, to kiss them one last time, but when she unfastened the golden chain that retained them, they crumbled to dust.

She understood then that Amour had finally avenged himself, since the fixed eyes of her lovers of an evening no longer desired her.

THE BEDAYAS[1]
(*La Presse*, 2 March 1900)

In the shade of varigniers, taks and tamarins, near strange flowers with heavy and delightful scents, three Javanese dolls are walking, dancers of Sousouhounan, "the implored," who is the Sultan of Solo. These bedayas are adorable in finesse and grace, with their onyx is framed in the blue-tinted nacre of the eyes, beneath long irises that one might think bordered with plumes, frayed at the tips, their minuscule mouths, always serious, and the amber skin of heir slender bodies. They advance slowly, holding one another by the waist, whispering trivia to one another in light voices.

The wind agitates the silver lotuses that each of them wears in her hair, rolled into large ebony shells and cupped in front, in such a fashion as to form seven gilt-edged triangles over the forehead. Behind their napes float clusters of white and mauve clochettes, and their faces are tinted with yellow *boreh*—the imperial color.

Their names are Soakia, Wakiem and Taminah.[2] Soakia, the eldest, is fourteen years old; she is the most reasonable of the three and the most adorned. Large golden flowers, with

---

1 This item is headed "Conte javanais" [Javanese Tale) and was adapted as the first chapter of La Vaudére's novel *Trois fleurs de volupté* (1900; tr. as "Three Flowers of Sensuality"), the first of a series of exotic erotic fantasies.
2 These were the names of three Javanese dancing girls who had performed with a troupe at the Paris Exposition of 1889. They were borrowed by other writers, notably featuring in *Les Belles du monde: Javanaises*, the third volume of a series of chapbooks by Catulle Mendès and Rodolphe Darzens, published in 1893.

hearts of precious stones, bloom on her red velvet blouse, which leaves the arms free. Her waist is tightened by a belt of plaques, alternately mat and shiny, sealed by an emerald clasp. A back silk sarong embroidered with fabulous animals and flamboyant corollas falls all the way to her ankles, circled by rings with cabochon gems.

Wakiem is in dark blue and Tamnah in white. They leave in their passage a mild odor of *melati*, which is the jasmine of the region, and that perfume, in the mystery of the beautiful garden, seems to be their little soul flying over the bushes.

"I'm bored today, Wakiem," sighs Soakia. "Our life is sad!"

But Taminah protests: "What does it lack then? You're the most celebrated of Sousouhounan's dancers, and none of us have received as many presents. Look, your bracelets and amulets are worth a fortune, and I'd give all my jewels for that emerald!"

Soakia, in nostalgic voice, goes on: "Something like hot gusts heavier than the vapors of a volcano are exhaled from the depths of my being; breaths brush me with a voluptuous caress that envelops me continually. Don't you feel anything similar?"

"No," say the girls, fixing their anxious gazes and curious on the bedaya, "but then, we don't yet know . . ."

Insouciantly, they have collected lotuses, scarcely opened, from the edge of the pond, with which they have ringed their shoulders and their frail hips, sometimes stopping to follow the flight of a migratory bird in the turquoise sky. In the distance, a pastor modulates on his reed flute the tune of an ancient *gending* of which he does not know the meaning, but which he repeats religiously. And the little dancers listen, thoughtfully, to the plaintive notes, which resemble the amorous appeal of a turtle-dove.

The heat increases and weighs more heavily, making chameleons and tiger-spiders drowsy on the trunks of the coffee-plants, causing the calices by the roadside to open wide, and immense butterflies with quivering wings settle at the hazard of kisses.

"I'd like," Soakia continues, "to wander in the somnolent countryside, further, ever further . . . to know caresses and embraces, to inspire a new tenderness in all those I encounter and who are worthy of it . . . in sum, to be loved forever, to make an offering to Boro-Bondour, who accomplishes the wishes of virgins."

"Boro-Bondour, the supreme Buddha, no longer protects us . . . Allah alone is great!"

"Personally," Wakiem affirms, "I believe in the legends of the spirits and the benevolent gods. I've often prayed to the enchantress Kidoul to emerge from her coral palace guarded by djinn in order to bring me pearls and those pretty red sea-shells that go so well with dark hair."

But Tamimah, the skeptic, ripostes, laughing: "And Kidoul has never come. She's asleep in the algae and doesn't care about Sousouhounan's little dancers."

Without responding, Wakiem opens her sarong of blue silk embroidered with chimeras over her breast and shows her companions a bizarre stone with opal and aquamarine reflections, sustained by a golden chain.

Soakia slides the jewel between her frail fingers, gemmed to the knuckles, and exclaims, laughing: "What a strange thing? Is it a sacred scarab with a metallic carapace, a moonstone found in the pale rushes haunted by malaria, or a jellyfish from some distant shore?"

"It's a fetish that the enchantress Kidoul brought me while I was resting next to the pond of the pink lotuses, because the enchantress comes at dusk to frolic in the fresh water."

The other girls consider Wakiem respectfully.

"Since Kidoul wishes you well, it's necessary to as her to favor our escape."

"Oh, Soakia! We'd be caught and condemned to death, eaten by wild beasts, burned, crucified or sewn into a goatskin with a snake and a cat. In any case, our master is good."

"He's a master. Liberty is preferable."

"Liberty is poverty."

"Bah! We'll dance along the roads like the public *ronggeng*. Let the fay protect us. I can mime the legend of amour for her."

And Soakia, on the velvety grass, has taken off her light sandals; then, her bare feet laden with rings with tintinnabulating circles around her ankles, she begins to glide softly, a hieratic and passionate phantom, a charming and capricious idol. Inflamed breezes agitate the silver lotus of her coiffure, the odor of melati is exhaled more forcefully from her saffroned body; the seven gilded triangles are stacked fatefully on her forehead and her ecstatic eyes are half-sunk beneath her voluptuously lowered eyelids.

Wakiem and Taminah have each taken up their rebab—a sort of viol in the form of a calabash with a long ivory shaft, turned in the decorative style of Indo-Chinese temples— and they are making the two brass strings vibrate with a resin-steeped bow.

Kidoul, the enchantress, has heard the prayer of the dainty dancers and has sprung forth like a scintillating pistil from the heart of the pink lotuses.

"Little bedayas," she says, "why wander the world? Believe me, stay in Krampong. Free, it would be necessary for you to dance for everyone, whereas here, you only dance for one man!"

"That's true," say the poor things, "but we're Sousouhounan's slaves!"

Then the enchantress concludes, with a benevolent smile: "A woman's role in all countries is to turn for the pleasure of men. It's still better only to have one master!"

POLYGAMY
(*La Presse*, 22 March 1900)

All is calm around the hut of Manou Tatambo, the powerful king of a tribe of black men who live in the Blue Mountains, not far from Warragamba, the river of the deep waters. It is an uneven site, covered with tenebrous forests and menacing rocks suspended in the void. The mountain has been torn by some subterranean revolution and pink sand streaked with silver runs incessantly from its large wounds. The uprooted trees are clad in interlaced climbing plants extending from one trunk to another, forming arcades, domes and perforated naves of a dreamlike delicacy.

Manou Tatambo's subjects, lying in a circle in the grass, have only an opossum-skin thrown over their tattooed ebony bodies shiny with coconut oil. The camp is composed of a series of huts made of bamboo branches and dry leaves, pierced by a narrow opening covered, like a curtain, by a flowering liana.

Little children, as naked as worms, are performing the "corroboree," which is the warrior jig of the savages, around the remains of a feast—doubtless the succulent flesh of some enemy killed on the battlefield.

Young women pass by, a parrot feather in their somber chignon, a wooden ring in the nose and a coral button on the upper lip. They are carrying little javelins terminated by a barbed hook, and are making one another small confidences while the males hunt cranes and pelicans on the edge of the foamy waves.

In his hut, a little wider and taller than the others, Manou Tatambo is reposing next to his six wives: six women with slender bodies chosen among the most agreeable of the tribe. On their still-firm breasts they wear singular necklaces made of little bones, which are the piously-collected fingers of glorious ancestors, and they have metal rings almost everywhere. Pink ibis plumes bristle over their loins and form a kind of elegant bouffant apron.

The chief speaks: "Narra-warragarah! Tattawah ousminah!" Which means: "Come to me, lotus of the feverish pools."

"Master of infallible judgment, here I am."

"Prepare my plug of betel and mash me a kaava root for my grog."

The six wives prostrate themselves three times, get up again, cut the aromatic root with thick knots into thin slices, which they cook delectably, and they chew it repeatedly while performing a bizarre dance, slowly at first and then more and more rapidly until it become a frenetic bamboula. By this time, the pellets of kaava have been subjected to a sufficient mastication and are offered to Manou, who plunges them into a skull filled with water and savors them with delight.

But Rata-Gabou, the favorite wife, having readjusted her apron of plumes, advances to the threshold of the royal hut.

"Master, it's the missionary from the land of fog who has come to civilize us."

"Send the pretty white man in, Rata, and let him be welcome among us."

Full of emotion, the good Father sits down, accepts a small infusion of kaava in a well-rinsed skull and speaks in a soft voice.

"My brother, I have half-converted you to our holy religion; I have preached to you about generosity and forbearance, and you have already marched valiantly in the road of enlightenment. Your mores have been fortunately modified, you have harvested the divine crop. But I want to do more, and today I shall treat a delicate subject."

"We're listening to you, sympathetic white man."

"Well, my brother, it's with pain that I see you lost in the errors of polygamy. A Christian worthy of the name must only have one wife."

"Only one wife!" says Manou, consternated, while his companions utter a long ululation of dolorous surprise.

"Yes, sage monarch, only one wife at a time, and he must only contract another in licit marriage after the death of his previous wife. Do you want to reach paradise and savor the eternal joys that efface all terrestrial pleasures?"

"I want that, venerated white man."

"It's necessary, then, to obey the divine laws of Christianity and renounce the work of Satan."

"I'll renounce them. I swear it on the head of Rata-Gabou!"

The Father got up and took his leave, while the favorite led the round-dance of the weepers and tore out large handfuls of curly hair. The pale fingers of the ancestors rattled on their breasts, and the coral buttons in their lips rose and fell in the spasms of sobs.

The good Father hastened toward other conversions, which bore the balm of his evangelical speech a long way, and it was only several months later that he returned to visit Manou Tatambo. Great was his triumph when he found him with a single companion.

"You see," he said, "the Lord has heard me and taken pity on you. Here you are, in accord with the precepts of our Holy Mother the Church."

"Yes," said the chief, "and I thank you. Old age has arrived, and I feel truly fatigued."

"Oh, my son, be blessed! May God heap you with his favors and watch over your tribe, which, I hope, will follow your example. But tell me, what has become of your former wives?

"You affirmed to me that one can only remarry after the death of other wives?"

"Certainly," said the Father, suddenly anxious. "What have you done with yours?"

And Manou, his mouth cleft by an enormous laugh, said, ingenuously: "Pretty white man, I've eaten them."

THE RED EGG[1]
(*La Presse*, 14 April 1900)

Gontran, on that fine Easter Day, had a desire to make a gift to Paquerette, one of those ingenious and magnificent gifts that remain in the memory of your lovers. But if the first of April permits foolish imaginations to surrender to all deregulation, and it is good form on that joyous date to present oneself to the memory of friends under the appearance of the more baroque and terrifying aquatic vertebrates, holy Easter is only symbolized by a modest container of unesthetic ovoid form.

Having racked his brains, uselessly, Gontran bought an egg, a vulgar egg; only he wanted it in gold in order to insert worthily five pretty thousand-franc bills. The precious case being carefully screwed down on a little wad of thin paper, our gallant finding it similar, save for the color, to all the eggs in the world, had the idea of daubing it with vermilion in order to play a joke on his darling.

Although Gontran was not an artist—far from it—the operation succeeded marvelously, and the most expert eye would certainly have been deceived by it.

Before the Gâtisme-Contagieux theater, where Paquerette was all the rage, a tall pale lout with a disquieting appearance of vagabondage and abstinence came to open the door of the

---

1 This item is headed "*Conte de Paques*" [An Easter Tale]. It is necessary, in order to appreciate the story, to know that hard-boiled eggs sold by French grocers at the time the story was published were routinely painted red in order to distinguish them from fresh eggs.

coupé where the young man was dozing and offered a dubious but humble hand.

"Have pity, handsome monsieur."

"No, leave me alone."

"Give me my Easter gift, Monseigneur, enough to buy a little red egg? I'm hungry, I assure you."

Gontran, who has just put five thousand-franc bills into a golden egg for Mademoiselle Paquerette of the Gâtisme-Contagieux, did not have two sous for a pauper who might not be lying.

"I don't have any money."

"Oh, *zut!*" said the gamin, "it's not my lucky day."

And philosophically, without any further acrimony, he headed for another carriage door.

In her minuscule dressing-room, hung with Japanese silk with solar fans on the ceiling, Mademoiselle Paquerette was making up her cheeks with the aid of a hare's foot mounted in a blond tortoiseshell bearing her monogram.

"Bonjour, you."

" . . . *Soir*, mon amour."

"And has the hen the lays golden eggs laid for me?"

"I believe so. Here's its latest."

Paquerette pulled a face. "Oh! A red egg!"

"You can eat it at home."

And Gontran favored her with an extremely ironic wink, which was wasted on the lovely child, very occupied in elongating her eyelashes with an ivory wand coated with kohl.

However, she replied negligently: "In truth, it's not a famous feast!"

"I'll indicate to you a new fashion of eating hard-boiled eggs. You'll see, it's very amusing."

"Pooh!"

"In the meantime, I'll run away. It's absolutely necessary that I put in an appearance at the home of my aunt des Glïeuls, who has put me in her will."

"Go, my friend."

"You can take the coupé that's waiting outside the theater, and I'll join you at your home."

"Understood."

Gontran went out, his soul luminous, and Mademoiselle Paquerette poured out for the leader of the orchestra, in her "little chauffeuse" costume, her trickle of provocative gasoline. It is true that the robust incendiary opened her mouth above a triple row of authentic pearls—yes, my dear!—and a few trinkets in diamonds, which always disposes an audience kindly.

On returning to her dressing-room, the divette, having decided to break that night with the friend who was so ungenerous, wrapped herself in her large white coat lined with chinchilla and picked up the unworthy present with a distracted hand.

At the door the pale lout opened the door of the coupé and moaned what he had been moaning all night, uselessly, to men and women alike:

"Have pity, beautiful demoiselle . . ."

"Go away, and quicker than that!"

"Give me my Easter gift, my infanta! I'm hungry! Just enough to buy a little red egg!"

"A red egg," said Paquertett, bitterly, holding out Gontran's egg. "Eat that, my lad; it will bring you luck."

And that is how one recognizes the hand of Providence.

LARGESSE[1]
(*La Presse*, 20 April 1900)

From every bud, a delicately ragged leaflet of a tender, ingenuous hue is emerging; anemones of thin taffeta and daisies with cheerful faces frilled with white muslin protect nests of violets and wild strawberry bushes; a snow of petals is falling from the trees.

He and *She* have quit the racecourses where even the horses respond to the most baroque and despicable idioms of our beautiful French language. He and She have followed charming pathways in the Bois, which are only shaded by a fine green lace over the transparent azure—a slightly pale azure—of the convalescent sky.

He is thirty years old with the appropriate appearance, the eye, the hair and the consciousness of his value. She does not yet count twenty-two Aprils, but has already made a name for herself in foot-stamping society.

"Did you notice," she says, "Prince Kothiko-Kan-In and his retinue?"

"Yes, he's very sympathetic,"

"I've seen women of all lands, women of the Exposition exhibiting necklaces to make us die of shame."

"Oh, very often fake."

"Not at all—the purest Oriental peals. I know what's what! If you were kind, my Loulou, you could offer me—I'm not demanding—that pear-shaped emerald that I saw the other

---

1 This is the first of a group of stories headed "*Contes d'Exposition*" [Tales of the Exposition].

day . . . you know, the one that emerges from a sheath of thirty-two brilliants."

"You're mad, my dear."

"Why? I'm not asking for the impossible."

"I've just lost again on Merry Boy, who shied away from the wall, as well as on Fénélon II, who fell at the brook."

"But you won with Miss Fleurie, beating Tendre Amour, Pétard and Fragola . . ."

"Meager compensation."

"Be nice, my Loulou, give me my emerald."

"No, no, it's necessary to be reasonable."

"Look, there in your wallet there are two pretty silky bills."

"A trifle, I assure you."

"Oh, my little pear isn't very dear."

"Later."

"Truly, for a chic man . . ."

"A chic man, precisely, is obliged to stricter economies than others. He has to monitor his budget very carefully if he wants to make all the expenditures that a reputation for elegance provokes. Now that society has its eyes fixed on us—the kings of fashion—it would be vexatious to fall."

"When I think that you haven't yet offered me anything but a poor ring with a sick turquoise that is dying today . . ."

"I was unaware of the poor health of turquoises."

"It's necessary to give me a diamond or a ruby."

"You'll have them, my darling . . . after the Exposition."

The darling pulls a face and does not unseal her lips during the return journey. Half-closing her eyelids, leaning back on the cushions of the victoria, she waxes quietly indignant against her Loulou and caresses little projects of revenge, of feline perversity.

At the Champs-Élysées, the couple has made the choice of a table much in view, in a renowned cabaret, and has ordered a distinguished menu that the gallery, above all, will appreciate,

The child is much to her advantage, and does honor to her Loulou, with a plumed hat coquettishly posed on the foam of her tawny hair, and a pastel blue skirt with silver wands lined with old guipure, similarly shadowed with silver. Admiring gazes study the harmonious contours of her bust, her undulating waist—in spite of the excessively-hooked corset—and her slender fingers ringed to the knuckles.

"They find you lovely, my dear, even without the pear-shaped emerald, which would add nothing to your native charm."

Still angry, she remains silent, disdainfully nibbling pink crayfish, a contraband partridge wing, a lettuce leaf and fruits.

Cosmopolitan diners animate the hall with garish costumes and varied clucking; the waiters circulate, hasty and congested, their mouths pursed and their eyes haggard.

"It's hot," says the darling, finally. "Let's go."

On the plate, augmented by a bill more copious than the meal, the young man has placed a thousand-franc bill with a noble gesture.

"Quickly, we're in a hurry."

The waiter flies away and comes back with two blue bills and gold coins, and carries away a generous tip very ostentatiously.

"You're still sulking?"

The young woman smiles, shakes herself, divining the sequel, and casts a sideways glance at the plate, still full.

Then he, sliding toward her the stream of gold: "Here, darling; keep the money."

And the darling, very red: "Pointless, my Loulou; you'll only ask for it back tomorrow."

SPECTER D'AMOUR
(*La Presse*, 2 May 1900)

The almahs are singing:

> *Here come the dainty dancers,*
> *Flowers of the harem, flowers of spring,*
> *With subtly exciting perfumes,*
> *Roses, jasmines and tuberoses;*
> *Here come the little charmers,*
> > *Flowers of spring.*

> *To the slow rhythm of chants,*
> *Their doll-like bodies sway;*
> *Dance, crimson and gold lotuses,*
> > *Dance again!*

It is nine o'clock in the evening. The Rue de Paris is animated, transformed into a garden of dreams. Monstrous red and yellow corollas with electric pistils open in the tender foliage of chestnut trees, pouring mysterious jets of flame over the passers-by.

A few days hence, crowds will walk this privileged pathway, in which, along with the blonde roses of May, the founding spirit of joyous Montmartre is flowering, where laughter sparkles like a light foam in the precious cup of harmony.

Yesterday, at the Exposition's *Roulotte*, the All-Paris of elegant premieres assembled to applaud *Kadidja*, an extraordinary Turquerie animated by the shrill chant of black eunuchs.[1] While frail Parisiennes opened their eyes wide in order to fill the memory with the melancholy vision of those guardians of the seraglio, a foreign woman with tenebrous hair and heavy eyelids ringed with kohl came to sit down beside Pierre, and spoke to him boldly.

"Well, you know, it's necessary not to laugh at these things."

The astonished young man contemplated the brunette spectator, whose entire being seemed to be quivering with an intense emotion.

She went on, confidentially:

"It's necessary not to laugh, because that story really happened."

"The story of Kadidja?"

"Yes."

Pierre, rather incredulous, placed a sympathetic finger on the bare hand of his neighbor, scintillating with emeralds and turquoises.

"With you," he said, "anything might happen, if you desired it. Who is the mortal who could oppose a refusal to your caprices?

On stage, Kadidja was singing to the exquisite music of Charton:

> *To love is the law of the world;*
> *Not to love is sinful,*
> *No longer to love profound night;*
> *To love is the cherished dream!*

---

1 Kadidja was the name of the Prophet's first wife, and thus became a common given name for Muslim daughters. On 28 April, the Exposition's traveling theater, the Roulotte, did put on a dramatic piece, advertised as a "fantasy," the title of which is given in the *Almanac des Spectacles* as *Radidja,* by Jane de la Vaudère and "Charton", presumably the composer Georges Charton (1862-1929). I assume that the R is a misprint, but I cannot locate any other reference to the play.

To love is pleasure on earth.
Not to love is dolor,
No longer to love is misery,
Always to love is happiness.

"To love!" sighed the unknown woman. "You Frenchmen are terrible men whom women follow blindly. Your voice opens all doors, even those of the harem."

"Who are you?" asked Pierre.

"I am one of the temporary companions of Loti," she said, "the one who inspired his sweetest books: *Aziyadé* and *Fantôme d'amour*.[1] Aziyadé is not dead, since she is speaking to you."

"Aziyadé?"

"Yes. Could I live with a decrepit master, after such delights? I fled the seraglio, and here I am."

"The eunuchs were no longer watching, then?"

"The eunuchs have followed me. It is them who are exhibiting themselves at the *Roulotte* theater, and I have come to applaud them out of gratitude . . . do you understand?"

"Certainly. Then you are the one that the charming poet is celebrating?"

"In person," affirmed the foreigner, proudly. "He sang of me in two volumes, which is rare for a French writer."

"Very rare," said Pierre, marveling at such a subtle observation of the character of our men of letters.

"See, in spite of the fourteen years that have gone by, I'm still beautiful. In any case, I have only counted fifteen Aprils."

When the performance of *Kadidja* had ended, Pierre took his conquest into the shadow of the chestnut trees, not far from the electric flowers of the Rue de Paris, into a ditch propitious for secret conversations.[2]

---

1 *Aziyadé* (1879) was Pierre Loti's first book. The other reference is to his *Fantôme d'Orient* (1892), which was combined with it in a later edition.
2 The ditches of the Fortifications were routinely employed in the Belle

Crouched in the rubbish, he allowed to rise toward the idol of amour all that his imagination suggested to him of voluptuously provocative images. His lyricism even attained unsuspected heights . . . but for once, he encountered a true believer.

"O woman," he concluded, emotionally, "you who were without bitterness and without caprice, you who were the loyal, intuitive, caressant, silent, submissive, tender and disinterested lover, I adore you among them all!"

But she, tipping back the young man's head in order to contemplate him in a pale moonbeam and posing her beautiful velvet gaze on his, said: "Friend, before going any further, I want there to be no misunderstanding between us. Will you give me the wherewithal to pay for my toilette and hotel expenses? Life is Paris is so dear!"

Epoque by the cheapest Parisian prostitutes for their swift transactions.

A GOOD FRIEND
(*La Presse*, 10 May 1900)

Monsieur and Madame Ducotel, in the company of their friend Bernard, had visited the Exposition in a fragmentary fashion, in order to make the pleasure last longer.

Madame Ducotel was charming; friend Bernard had perceived that fact more every day, and the husband, increasingly, had lingered over the marvels of exotic displays.

They were in the Tunisian section: roses, nougat and pistachio pastries on stalls and on trays.

"Good, that, Monsuur, for the little lady . . . Buy me, Monsuur; only two sous."

White teeth, like almonds, sliced through the faces of spiced bread, with eyes of blue-tinted enamel that spun like balls.

The air reeked of vanilla, incense, pepper, and other things that Parisian nostrils could not define very well.

The Rue du Souk saw a flood of amazed visitors spreading out among its multicolored shops, and commerce was truly prospering.

"Nougat! Nougat! Nougat!"

Bernard and Ducotel admired the Porte du Keif, the mosque of Sidi-Mahres, the Manouba, as perforated and precious as an Oriental jewel of silver and turquoises.

A young woman, with thick black hair, spread out like a mantle of darkness, her hips mobile under a sash with multitudinous yellow and green stripes, a proud bosom covered with a tinkling rain of sequins, was smiling in front of one shop, and without saying anything, had more success than the others.

"She's lovely!" remarked Madame Ducotel, drawing closer to friend Bernard.

Then, as Ducotel forgot himself before the attractions of the shop of the hairdresser Ahmed-ben-Harfa, she became emboldened to the extent of brushing the young man's arm.

"You prefer brunettes, don't you?"

Bernard protested. "No, I prefer blondes."

"Why?"

And, with a coquettish gesture, she lifted up the golden stream of her fine tresses beneath her large black hat.

"Only the blonde is the entire woman," Bernard replied, "because she possesses an infinite variety of nuances and expressions. Almost all brunettes resemble one another; they are the majestic, splendid and monotonous skies of the Midi. How much more troubling, for the poet, are the soft tints of our horizon, with its milky dawns and roseate sunsets. In the land of blondes, even the storms are benevolent, making the flowers scintillate without curbing them."

"Then I . . . ?"

"You are the realization of my dream, the woman seductive among them all—the Parisienne, in sum."

Madame Ducotel, who was from Le Mans, was flattered. In any case, she merited friend Bernard's eulogies, having a delicate, slightly fleshy face beneath her pale golden fleece, traversed by yellow gleams, eyes of changing color—glaucous in the shade and violet in the slight—and a shiny, swollen mouth that one would have liked to crunch like a praline.

In a candid manner, she took possession of Bernard's hand, squeezed it gently, and retained it momentarily in a velver caress that made the young man feel faint.

However, by means of an abrupt effort of will, he pulled away from the temptation, and suddenly put on his iciest expression

"Oh," she said, blushing. "I thought you were my friend?"

"Yes," he replied, sadly, "but I'm also Ducotel's."

She uttered a shrill, pearly, nervous, slightly anxious laugh; and as the husband was returning with rose and citron pastries, she said: "Let's go back; I'm tired."

They returned sullenly through the phantasmagoria of multicolored palaces, as brilliant and deceptive as the scenery of a fantasy play—the great fantasy play that France offers to attentive and curious nations.

Madame Ducotel quit Bernard with a cold conventional politeness, and did not invite him for the following day, as she was accustomed to do.

And in the evening, at dinner, when Ducotel talked abundantly about everything and nothing—the Rue du Souk, the belly-dancing, the Manouba and friend Bernard—she said, disdainfully; "Oh yes, the dear friend!"

"What? What a funny expression you have."

"I didn't want to tell you, but since you mention it . . ."

"Did I mention something?"

"While you were looking at Ahmed-ben-Harfa's shop, Bernard took me by the hand and squeezed it very hard . . ."

"Oh! I'd never have thought that of him!"

"Indeed! But I made him understand that he was on a false path. If you wish, we won't see him again."

"Dear little wife!" And Ducotel concluded, bitterly: "So much for friends!"

ROLLING WALKWAY
(*La Presse*, 20 May 1900)

Lucien, motionless, leaning on the rail, allowed himself to be borne along as if in a dream, through the phantasmagoria of pink, blue and green palaces flourishing with arabesques, interweavings and astragal arches, gemmed with rose-widows, cabochons and olives. There was a prodigious accumulation of colonnettes, niche statues and scroll-work excavated like a precious guipure. He was living in a *conte de fées*, and when he closed his eyes he continued the charming dream; palaces descended from the clouds, with towers ringed with crenellations, domes reminiscent of crushed fruits and sheaves of obelisks as slim as golden pistils. In the light of the stained-glass windows the bas-reliefs sweated ardent corollas, a dew of honey and murder. Foliage of flame was climbing everywhere, with shiny dangling clusters of amaldines and chrysoprases.

Lucien, intoxicated by light, remained dazed in that orgy of colors, which seemed to him to e excessive, and even a little cruel, under the bleak Parisian sky.

And the rolling walkway kept rolling . . .

Branches appeared to be holding out Japanese paper umbrellas delicately tinted with lilial hues. Then, behind a window, the young man suddenly saw a bright face, which smiled at him. He was now going past gray houses with modest entresols, ornamented with prints and furniture in painted pear-wood. The young woman who was looking at him with such an evident interest seemed to him to be ideally pretty in the half-light of the room. He blew her a kiss, but did not have time to notice her emotion in the rapid glide that carried him away.

The next day he returned at the same time, and then the day after next, and the following days. The coquette was always sitting at her open window, watching out for him and blushing delicately when her gaze encountered his.

"Bonjour, Mademoiselle."

"Bonjour, Monsieur."

They exchanged a few words, brief phrases, as if they had known one another for a long time.

And the rolling walkway kept rolling . . .

She ended up having the effect of seeming absolutely adorable in the soft shadow of spring foliage in the florid frame of her window. Her eyes widened, radiantly, with a particular glaucous gleam; her harmonious upper body was displayed like a hieratic calyx. That woman, certainly not similar to others, had an enveloping and mysterious charm that he was encountering for the first time.

He would have liked to speak to her at length, and ardently, to throw amorous words at her like rose petals, spelling out his passion like the beads of a golden chaplet. But the rolling walkway, as implacable as destiny, kept rolling, and Lucien whispered to himself the sweet things that he would have liked to murmur to the beloved.

Above his head, the fragile clusters of the chestnut trees shook opaline confetti under the lacy screen of ingenuous, infantile leaves, so tender that one would have liked to crunch them like lettuce hearts.

One day, he became emboldened while passing before the young woman, and, in a determined tone, requested a rendezvous for that evening. She inclined her head in a sign of acquiescence, and as the rolling sidewalk was still rolling, it seemed to the amorous young man that he was navigating on the unctuous and pure waves of an ocean of oil.

She and He met at dusk and sat down on a bench behind a wall, in the acrid dust of fiacres and trams. And suddenly, for poor Lucien, the ideal fiction took on the features of some woman, white and plump, with an upper body that was too long, on unesthetic legs. He searched in vain for the inflamed speech that he had prepared in the smooth glide of his hours of ecstasy, but remained as coy as a young hawk before its first little bird.

That was because the rolling walkway was no longer rolling.

IN THE CHINESE STYLE
(*La Presse*, 1 June 1900)

In a sad voice, Robert requested celestial tea from a very French waiter who was obstinate in offering him extra-dry champagne.

It was the inauguration of the Chinese pavilion at the Exposition. The amusing constructions, capriciously adorned with wooden guipures and precious interweavings, opened their doors to an undulating and select public. In the vari-colored fireworks, frail Parisiennes seemed to be stirring Loie Fuller's veils[1] and juggling with large luminous balloons, which the wind, a trifle frisky, was swaying in the branches.

Everywhere, in the halls, superb fabrics were resplendent, heavy with gold and silk embroideries, standards jeweled with shiny roses and decorated with chimeras and dragons with glaucous eyes, rare items of furniture incrusted with nacre, ornaments of ivory and jade, pot-bellied vases, lacquer screens, terrible weapons and perfume-burners.

In the mist of Celestials with long tightly-woven pigtails, in the spectrum of brightly-colored Chinese robes, the ideally blurred costume of Jane de Chichi had caused a sensation. It was an entire poem of lace and lawn, signed—but not with gratuitous renown, times being hard! In any case, Jane never wore the same poem twice, and her inspirations, true genius,

---

1 The spectacular dancer Loie Fuller had her own pavilion at the 1900 Exposition, which boosted her publicity considerably and made her "serpentine dance" and "fire dance" world-famous. She applied unsuccessfully to patent her much-imitated choreography.

were virgin of all plagiarism: no copying in the underclothing of a beautiful pure and firm figure; regular seams, no amorphous fantasy or needy rhymes. Robert furnished to the poets of couture the paper necessary for their lucubrations, and the paper of the Banque de France represented fifty thousand francs: fifty thousand francs for thirty dresses more perfect than the sonnet of Arvers, in which the most academic of academicians would only have seen sturdy consonants supported by impeccable nickeled feet!

In all frankness, it was a gift.

Jane's good friends dried up with jealous rage, and Robert's good friends were exultant with impatient covetousness.

Nevertheless, Robert was morose, even more morose on this evening of inauguration in the phantasmagoria of the lights and the scenery.

"Why that careworn brow?" asked the child, pressing the young man's arm against the lace of her bodice.

He turned toward her his expression tragic.

"Look at me," he said, "and admit frankly that I have no more than a few days to live."

She uttered a burst of sincere laughter.

"A few days to live! But my dear, you're as plump and florid as a novice monk!"

"Plump and florid!"

"Take it from me. Well, you have changed in the last month."

"I have changed, haven't I?"

"When I met you, you seemed less . . . dashing."

"I hardly had the breath . . ."

"And I said to myself that I'd be your last mistress, so . . ."

"We've led a joyous life . . ."

Robert uttered a groan and asked for a cup of celestial tea from the very French waiter, who continued to provoke him with the offer of extra-dry champagne.

"My pretty Jane, I'm very unhappy."

"Unhappy, at your age, with your fortune, your health and my amour?"

"It's precisely for those good reasons that I'm suffering."

"I don't understand."

Robert supported his flourishing double chin on his white hand, ornamented with a superb emerald.

"Such as you see me, darling, the physicians had abandoned me, after having cared for me though a dozen mortal maladies . . . indelicate heirs you understand? I had swallowed all the mixtures, followed all the treatments, submitted to all the operations. I only had a month to live, at the most. On that point, the diagnoses, divided until then, came together with a touching unanimity."

"So?"

"So I said to myself that after two years of drugs and vivisection, I could amuse myself a little, since, one day or another, the fatal fall was imminent."

"My good dog!"

"I liquidated my fortune and partied. We've had a great party, an exquisite party!"

"My darling wolf!"

"But I wasn't very rich . . ."

Jane went very pale, suddenly grasping the awful truth.

"You're cured and ruined! Wretch!"

"Yes, ruined and cured. Nothing remains for me but suicide. Oh, those physicians . . . !"

And Robert, decidedly unable to obtain his celestial tea, sighed and emptied a glass of extra-dry.

THE FINGER OF BUDDHA
(*La Presse*, 14 June 1900)

While visiting the Dutch Indies at the Exposition, I was surprised to encounter, near the Buddhist temple of Chandri-Sari, three dainty rong-geng, who are the pythonesses and loose women of the high roads of Java. Little poor princesses of legend, they were as pale and light as moonbeams with "yellow boreh" and "blue lotus" sarongs tightened at the waist by barbaric metal belts with turquoise clasps.

Over their dark hair, mingled with exquisitely-scented clusters of melati, were warrior helmets representing a garonda of green gold with its wings deployed. That was their ceremonial costume, and I asked them in honor of what god or goddess they had gone to so much expense.

The eldest, who might have counted a dozen Aprils, told me the following story in Javanese, with the musical, seemingly distant voice that is reminiscent of the sighing of the wind in branches.

"We are, as you know, a vagabond tribe that has remained faithful to the ancient religions, part Buddhist and part Brahmanic, around the craters and on the slopes of the great volcanoes. Every year, in the land of fire, we go into the ruined temples to implore the beneficent spirits, to ask them for advice and protection. Around us rise heaps of sculpted stones, guarded by tall figures that the moonlight frosts with fantastic gleams. They are terrible Buddhas, squatting or upright, grimacing of blessing. They reach seven or eight times human height, and the aureoles that surround their heads seem to emerge from the azure vault, detached like a little dead star from all the wandering stars of the heavens.

"Often, the same statue, charged with several attributes, evokes a complex being endowed with multiple powers, and we tremble before the menace of the gods as before the anger of the volcanoes, whose eternal rumbling fills the air."

"But little rong-geng, this doesn't tell me why you're here."

"Patience, you'll understand everything soon. Look at this superb Buddha with the face of a woman, with two open eyes of strange and mysterious beauty."

"He gives the impression of springing from his golden lotus like a sheaf of flame from a volcanic mouth!"

"It's him who spoke to me in the temple of Tjambi-Seou and ordered me and my sisters to come to Paris. We distinguished him immediately. He dominated, like an omnipotent master, the groups of idols with four arms, and the monsters with the heads of goats or elephants in formidable and puerile attitudes. We prostrated ourselves before him, after having burned a few pinches of aromatic herbs and imitated, with our reed flutes, the buzzing of bees and the babble of loquacious streams. If you knew how scared we were! The divinities around us grimaced more and more, showing enormous bellies or flattened breasts, opening toothless mouths, holding out forks, balls or javelins . . ."

"And Buddha reassured you?"

"Not right away. We had already torn our breasts and covered our faces with our hair as a sign of desolation when an invincible torpor threw us to the ground. Soon our pupils vacillated. There was no longer anything but a fog in which we saw fantastic images loom up against the walls like an infinity of panting beasts, swollen or emaciated, bristling their claws and darting out their tongues. Serpents had feet, pigs had wings, gigantic fish with human heads were holding apples in their mouths; bulls lifted up their horns crowned with flowers, and crocodiles devoured tigers. We no longer knew what was real or artificial in that décor. All the strangest forms—creations of delirious brains, nightmare and madness—were there, in heaps, mutilated or still standing in profound niches. Paws, skulls, eyes falling from their orbits, terrifying and obscene symbols lay everywhere . . ."

The frail rong-geng shivered at the evocation of those terrors, but soon a happy smile illuminated their pale amber faces.

"Finish, finish quickly," I said, very interested.

"It was then" my interlocutor continued, "that we had an adorable vision. At the place of the high crater that dominates the temple of Tjambi-Seou, we saw your Eiffel Tower rise up."

"The Eiffel Tower?"

"Yes, Madame; it was lit up as no volcano has ever lit up in our homeland!"

"It was lit up . . ."

"And that is how," the child finished, lowering her long gilded eyelids, "we knew the will of the gods . . ."

A CRIME[1]
(*La Presse*, 1 July 1900)

The handwriting is the man, says the graphologist.

Madame Ida de Royalment did nothing in life without consulting Mademoiselle Sibylla, chiromancer, pythoness, prophetess and graphologist.

"Never link yourself with anyone without coming to see me," Sibylla had recommended her client. "It only costs, as you know, a petty louis every time, and what is a louis for someone who desires to encounter the dreamed-of friend, delicate, constant, submissive, ardent and generous?"

"Certainly, my dear, but you need a lock of hair to consult the oracle, and how can I ask a man for hair other than in intimacy?"

Sibylla smiled with slight disdain.

"An obsolete custom, my beauty! A line of handwriting is sufficient for us today . . . two words on a card or an envelope, the slightest thing . . ."

It was thus that Madame de Royalement, charming but excessively credulous, allowed herself to be taken in by a seductive voice, a nice gesture and a few elegantly traced fly-spots.

He and She had met at the Egyptian theater before the Sudanese, Abyssinian and Syrian dancers. It was amid the drone of derboukas, the sighs of flutes and the hum of bees and cicadas that they had exchanged their initial skirmishes.

---

1 Although it continued the series of tales of the Exposition, this item was headed "*Conte Graphologique.*"

Tattooed girls, with their eyes immeasurably widened by kohl, made sequins leap on their bellies in extraordinary tremors, agitating their heads like the pendulum of a clock, listing their breasts in cadence to the every-more precipitate rumble of barbaric music. The provocative poses of the odalisque of the bottle had authorized a few light remarks between the young man and his neighbor. Then he had brushed her hand, negligently enabling her to see a superb diamond that he wore on his little finger.

"What a beautiful ring!"

"Oh, it's the gift of a Highness . . . I have others."

Very impressed, Ida had assumed a graver attitude, a meditative expression that was not habitual to her.

Now the Arab women on stage surrounded the stout Antar, their hero, awaiting the Persians. There were knife-jugglers and wrestlers; Aïssaouas swallowed a few scorpions and sank long iron spikes into their skulls.

"You're exquisite," modulated the stranger in Ida's ear. "Where do you live?"

"Shh!" she said, as the brunette fiancée of Antar emerged from the group that was emitting such odd trills. "She's being abducted . . . let's go."

"What if I were to abduct you too?"

Ida knew that it was necessary to mistrust Exposition conquests.

"Tomorrow, if you wish . . ."

"Tomorrow, truly?"

"Yes, and if you please, write your name and your address here, in this notebook."

"What's the point? We'll meet again tomorrow, here, at the same time . . ."

"Write anyway, and I promise to be punctual at the rendezvous."

With a golden pencil, the stranger wrote a few words on a piece of Bristol and Ida lost herself in the crowd, retaining the memory of a fiery gaze, a seductive voice and an exceptionally large diamond. Mademoiselle Sibylla, consulted the same evening regarding the stranger's handwriting, immediately waxed ecstatic:

"Entirely remarkable characters! You see, there are two sorts of handwriting: upright and inclined. All weaknesses and moral flaws, as well as all qualities of the heart and the mind, are indicated by various involuntary angles. The more distant the handwriting is from the perpendicular, the more intellectual flights and sentimental nobility there are in the author. Straight and stiff downstrokes, on the contrary, indicate the most revolting egotism. When incoherent downstrokes incline alternately in one direction and the other, overlapping the little letters, it's the most evident sign of cerebral derangement or criminality. In the present case, nothing similar; the handwriting, I affirm, indicates an exquisite sensibility, an admirable grandeur of soul, an excessive generosity and a passion and tenderness that nothing can weaken. That's two louis, in view of the late hour . . ."

Delighted, Ida met her noble foreigner again . . . you know the rest. The chambermaid, on arriving a few days later to open the shutters of the luxurious room in which Madame de Royalement was reposing, recoiled uttering a cry of horror. Ida, dressed adorably but insufficiently, in her hair alone, with a curtain cord around her neck, was making an even whiter patch on the white carpet and no longer giving any sign of life.

The murder is too recent for it to be necessary to go into more ample detail. The murderer moreover, arrested the following week as he was attempting to sell his victim's jewels, is languishing at present in a cell, awaiting the supreme expiation.

That is how a very amiable demi-mondaine, too confident in the science of graphology, was assassinated on the night of the second of June, between midnight and one o'clock. Mistrust handwriting, therefore!

BUREAU DE TABAC[1]
(*La Presse*, 20 January 1901)

Familiar tune

Little bureau, little bureau
Come recognize the services
Of veteran errand-runners
Who reflect their hearts in the floor
Fulfilling two offices
In the minisses!
Little bureau, little bureau,
Temple of charming delights,
To obtain your benefits
You need to have a good tip;
If not, no chance!

One day, Monsieur Pottier-Pellerin, paper-pusher, while appending vague signatures, saw a little woman come into his office; she had a halo of blonde hair under an immense black hat, with gleaming eyes and a minuscule pink mouth, as appetizing as a praline.

---

1 Appearing after a long interval, during which the short fiction feature was dropped from the paper and its space taken, in part, by a political cartoon, this item was headed "*Dans la coulisse*" [In the wings]. In France, the government retained a monopoly on sales of tobacco, and its agents routinely distributed Bureaux de Tabac [licensed tobacconist's shops] to retiring civil servants and soldiers wounded in the line of duty, but competition led to notorious corruption.

Without allowing herself to be intimidated by the dignity of the place and the majesty of its occupant, she explained that she was the milliner opposite and that she would be infinitely happy to coif the minister's wife. Only, she had no protections and, being a wily individual, she had said to herself that it would be better, in order to avoid any false intermediary, to "seize the bull by the horns" by addressing herself directly to the husband.

Mademoiselle Frigolette, who knew good form, did not, of course, make use of that unsavory phrase, but the significance of her little speech, wrapped, like a sweet, in the sugar-coating of her Parisian cynicism was almost identical, and, with the aid of her pretty face, she had no difficulty in making herself heard.

Monsieur Pottier-Pellerin was all ears and all eyes; his ears went red and his eyes were flamboyant, which announced the ravages of an intimate conflagration impelled by the breeze of culpable desires.

"So, Mademoiselle," he pronounced in a high-pitched voice, "you work in hats?"

"Yes, Monsieur, I fabricate a trivial knot here, a feather there; in a foam of illusory tulle in a nest of little birds of paradise; that gives you an inimitable chic."

"A knot here, a feather there . . ."

"Yes, it's a very reliable and very varied art."

Pottier-Pelletier no longer knows what he is saying. He draws closer to the darling, who describes the model of a new coiffure that she destines for Madame Pottier. To coif the minister's wife is her entire ambition.

How can one resist so many enveloping graces? Nine months later, Monsieur Pellerin found himself the happy father of a very well-constituted brat, and, not knowing how to recognize such pleasant services, offered Frigolette academic palms!

But ministers pass and milliners remain. After Madame Pottier-Pellerin, Frigolete coiffed Madame Duranton, which was worth a second baby, as welcome as the first, and the authorization to put on her sign: *At the caprices of the minister.*

A numerous clientele frequented the discreet shop that Frigolette, blooming like an autumn rose, animated with her savant grace. She coiffed respectable but difficult women, who often made her recommence the same frilly cabbage or inverted cooking-pot ten times over.

Whatever peevish people allege, all trouble has its recompense. Today, Frigolette, whose reputation is well-established in the quarter, has just brought a fifth brat into the world and the government, grateful for so much loyal service rendered to the fatherland, has granted her a *bureau de tabac.*

A KING[1]
(*La Presse*, 18 February 1901)

King Bilan liked the high life, as everyone knows. During his numerous sojourns in Paris he courted blondes and brunettes, passing through all the intermediate shades. Little and great ladies could scarcely resist the prestige of the crown and the scepter, all the more so as the man was good looking and did not lack, at times, a certain majesty.

It is said that, thinking that he was unknown to the regulars of the place, he strayed one evening to the Moulin Bleu, and had a conversation with a little dancer with a strange child-like face who was known as Comet Flower. As dainty as you could wish, Comet Flower had a stellar gaze underneath a luminous fleece, scattered like the tail of a wandering star—hence her gracious pseudonym.

Many a time during that memorable evening she took the king's hat off with the tip of her agile foot, dazzled him with the perfection of her splits and spinning entrechats, so well that he took her back to his temporary nest, lined with silk and, she thought, pretty banknotes.

The king was primarily generous with caresses, but he involved the beauty in a splendid business affair that he was in the process of launching, with the complicity of a subtle banker and a few suckers full of confidence. It was, I believe, a matter of a copper or gold mine, and the joyful Comet Flower

---

1 This item and the remaining ones published in *La Presse* appeared under the heading "Fantasia"

opened enormous eyes in which the astral nuggets already seemed to be shining.

"Truly, sire, you've put your hand on a vein? But then you'll be better off than all the presidents of our Republic! At least you'll give me a slice of the cake?"

And His Highness, with an unctuous tone in which a few distant Danube pebbles were rolling, said: "I'll give you a golden gondola with oars of nacre and a sail with more pearls than an early morning lily."

"That would be nice! Only, since you're being so kind, I'd like to ask you something else . . ."

"Speak."

"I have a brother . . . a brother who's been out of work for weeks . . . Anatole, nicknamed Frizzy. Oh, a very good lad, you know. Couldn't you do something for him too?"

But the king did not like to get mixed up in the family affairs of his "flings." He kept silent, and became very sulky. Comet Flower, who was tenacious, resolved to invite Frizzy along one morning, without sounding the alert, and to soften her friend with opportunistic caresses and eloquent words. It was a big risk, but too bad. One can be a dancer at the Moulin Bleu and still fight for a noble and generous cause.

The day before the one fixed for Anatole's visit, Comet Flower launched, in honor of her lover, one of her most suggestive steps, revealing herself to be unrivaled for her "Cockayne mast" on points, her "Gargles" and her "Bankrupt splits." The spectators at the Moulin Bleu formed a circle around her and applauded frantically.

Bilan, very happy with that triumph and certain of his incognito, took the little one away without perceiving that a bald monsieur who had not ceased to follow him all evening had watched him depart with dolor and amazement.

That bald monsieur was none other than a powerfully rich sucker who had furnished important capital to the prince's financial scheme. Without hesitation, having learned by chance that the protector of the pretty Comet Flower was also the protector of the affair in question, Monsieur D***, full of suspicion and resolved to get out, presented himself the following day at the royal domicile, followed closely by the dancer's brother.

Anatole, alias Frizzy, was delivering himself in the dressing room into which he had been introduced to the most ardent protestations of respect and devotion when the sucker's visit was announced.

"Skin of Serbia!" said the prince, "That's torn it. When Monsieur D*** sees that Comet Flower's friend and King Bilan are one and the same person, he won't want to know any more . . . We're in the soup! I no longer have anything but my crown, and I've just put that . . . how do you say it . . . in hock."

"That's annoying," said the girl.

Frizzy pranced and smiled, while the prince put on a wonderful plum dressing gown with a multicolored floral design and the star of the Moulin Bleu stuck a rose in her hair for her only garment.

Meanwhile, august gazes detailed, under Anatole's suit, his rather advantageous physique.

"You'd make a fine Nero at the Neuilly fair," said Bilan, "but put on my dressing gown."

"Oh, Sire!"

"Put it on . . ."

"There you are, Sire . . ."

"Now, go find the clown that's bothering us, and tell him that the King . . . is you!"

CONFETTI
(*La Presse*, 4 March 1901)

Irma Flavian, one of the prettiest girls in the studio of Pascal, the painter of refined elegance, a fervent admirer of sunsets and moonrises, had spent the evening of Mardi Gras with the master. One generally saw a joyful company there, but the invitations, very rare and much sought-after, sent to disciples, friends and postulants of distinction, only permitted entry on showing a pink card and a white paw, just like a marriage of our charming President de la Chambre; only here, there was no crowd to dread; the vicinity of the temple and the corridors were deserted, with the consequence that the deserving faithful, some of who had, over their lilial nudity, only a simple mantle lined with ermine or rabbit, were able to penetrate discreetly, without rejoicing gazes or offending modesty. Public morality, which would have no outrage to display that day, was greatly chagrined and morose, while everyone in the painter's hermetically sealed little town house enjoyed themselves greatly.

When Irma Flavian nonchalantly allowed the sumptuous zibeline garment that enveloped her blonde beauty to fall there was only one cry of admiration. Her nacreous body, like that of the Anadyomene emerging from the waves, was adorned with the divine dew of a frail diamond necklace—the fruit of her first economies. In truth, Irma scarcely possessed anything except for her necklace and her zibeline, but she retained the faith of her eighteen Aprils and the good humor of creatures of joy who, no longer having anything to lose, have everything to gain.

The ball was exquisite, in the large studio flourishing with a profusion of tea-roses, anemones and mimosas, which the delicate electric pistils dissimulated in the sheaves caressed with febrile gleams. Japanese masks with gilded eyes and teeth grimaced amid the ivories and jades on the silk of Mikado wall-hangings; nude studies, borrowed from the adorable models who pressed around the master, appeared, by contrast, a trifle static and dull, not being, like the living masterpieces animated by the desire for dancing and kisses.

At the first smiles of dawn, Pascal and his pupils had the amiable fantasy of dressing their lovers in a tunic of confetti, a rain of roses having become too expensive since the days of Roman orgies. There was then, from the top of the painter's long ladders, a hail, an avalanche, a deluge of light gummed roundels that settled in rosettes arabesques and splendid mosaic on the moist bodies of the women, with the most bizarre effect. Serpentine girdles and the headdresses of barbaric chieftainesses completed the metamorphosis.

Only the Tanagrean beauty of Irma still remained in its initial splendor when a student decided that the lilial body required an immaculate fleece of white confetti, and within a minute, the darling personified well enough the fay of the frosts, crowned with snow and girdled with long ribbons of frost.[1]

At first she laughed like a madwoman at her paper royalty, but then, without knowing why, she felt infinitely sad and, weeping like a spring, wanted obstinately to go home. A friend took it upon himself to put her in a fiacre, while a

---

1 The opening of the story, up to this point, was adapted as the opening sequence of La Vaudère's novel *Les Androgynes* (1903; tr. as "The Androgynes"), which also cannibalized characters and motifs from several of the author's other newspaper stories, including the dancer featured in the previous item.

348

belated mask threw her full hands into the collar of her long cloak a further snow of confetti.

On returning home Irma found pushed under her door a telegram announcing the death of her sister Zizine, deceased in the village home of her grandparents in a lost corner four hours from Paris. She imagined the grief of the old couple, left alone with a little girl six years old, Toinon, too young to sympathize or console, and she resolved to depart immediately. She put on a woolen dress devoid of adornments, a simple black garment, and took the first train with little pieces of paper rebellious to the thrusts of the comb still in her blonde hair.

Now the funeral is passing slowly alongside denuded slopes and apple-trees garlanded with mistletoe; the procession of women, bearing candles, zigzags awkwardly in the rocky path, which the snow covers with an ever thicker layer, slippery under feet clad in large clogs. Toinon, the child, is hanging on to Irma's skirt, while the old wives mutter, with indignant expressions, a few disobliging reflections.

"Is it permissible? She still has confetti in her hair, the slut!"

"Why, that's true! Doubtless she's coming back from a ball; it's obvious that she's been dancing all night!"

Toinon has heard without comprehending. She does not understand very well, either, what death is; she has only been assured that her sister has gone to paradise, and her naïve gaze follows with interest the snowflakes that fall relentlessly upon the silver-fringed cloth of the little coffin that four men are carrying like a toy.

Suddenly, a light dawns in her mind.

"Of course," she says. "Zizine is going to the angels' ball, since Heaven is throwing confetti."

IN HEAVEN
(*La Presse*, 12 March 1901)

The Earth, floating in space,
In the sidereal light,
Like a ship that passes,
Disappears in the immensity!

It flees, an ephemeral atom,
And perhaps, in spite of the effort,
It will be a phantom vessel
By the time it reaches port.

An old, bald Monsieur who occupies all the moments of his life with astronomy is recounting before Toto that a dainty planet with opaline reflections has come, without warning to undertake its frolics in the telescopes of scientists. Toto, who is five years old, listens with an expression all the more wonderstruck because he does not understand. But the beautiful story is as troubling as a *conte de fées*, and little children, like old men, are very close to Heaven.

It is an amateur, Monsieur Witt,[1] who, while photographing double stars in their most suggestive poses, has discovered that crazy star and has baptized it Eros. Eros was teasing a comet, which enveloped it with its crazy golden tresses, and only appeared vaguely in its luminous waves. Doubtless wea-

---

1 The German astronomer Carl Gustav Witt discovered two asteroids, the first of which, spotted in 1898, he named Eros.

ry of flirting with the nebulousness of our petty actresses, he preferred to pester the stars of the great celestial stage, whose soft eyes blink so prettily on the blue curtain of the night in the beautiful evenings of Messidor.

However, the mischievous god has not yet disinterested himself completely in our carnivalesque adventures, and from time to time he approaches curiously, neglecting Mars and Venus. Venus, too incomparably adorable to be vindictive, consoles herself by wearing robes gemmed with rubies and sapphires, but Mars, vexed, is shooting artificial fireworks at us, launching monster petards and roman candles that risk overturning the chariot of the Great Bear.

"Oh," says Toto, delighted. "You'd be very kind, Monsieur, to take me to Mars."

"Pooh! Mars is a planet of little importance, which doesn't present either the ludicrous appearance of Saturn, surrounded by his lifebelts, or the sumptuous appearance of big Jupiter, which, with his fluttering satellites, seems to be taking a harem for a walk in the heavens,"

"What is a harem, Monsieur?"

"It's a boarding-school of young women directed by an old professor."

"Shall we go to Jupiter, then, Monsieur?"

"It's too far away, my little friend. I can only take you to see the Moon."

"Oh, yes, the Moon! Show me the Moon."

Toto, who is well-behaved, had his wish granted. For an hour he thought he was wandering delightfully in the lunar star, and hung on to the umbrella of his aged guide in order not to be cast away in the Ocean of Storms or the Sea of Humors.

It is affirmed that in that singular land there is neither vapor not vegetation, nor soil, nor water: nothing but terrible rocks with the monstrous profiles of grimacing giants, with long stratified lava flows between their black lips.

Toto believes that he is passing through the midst of micaceous crystallized ferns: a dead forest with brilliant trunks of quicksilver, with clear cold lakes like immobile mirrors. He traverses the Marsh of Putridity on tiptoe, in order not to stain his new socks, for his mother has recommended him to avoid dirty places; but the marsh, of a dazzling whiteness, is like the ground beneath cherry-trees in April after a violent wind.[1]

Here, on one side, is the ridge of Mount Haemus, overlooking the Sea of Serenity, on the other, the chain of the Caucasus and the edge of the Lake of Dreams. Toto passes through a crystal tunnel and then traverses the dried-up Seas of Fecundity and Nectar. In the distance, bizarre mountains zigzag, which seem to be crumpled in old gray silk with extinct reflections; a few are pierced by holes, like madrepores, but there are some that stick up like needles of jade and stucco, or seem to be rolled up in balls like hedgehogs.

But the magical projections are concluded; Toto falls back from the beautiful dream into muddy reality and goes home in a rain shower and a malevolent wind.

"Tell me, Monsieur, are they very high, the little candles that dance in the sky? As high as the Moon?"

"Much higher," says the old Monsieur, paternally.

"Are there flames there? Are there? And who blows them out?"

"God, my little man, as he blows out our souls; for the soul is a flame that is relit in paradise when one has been good on earth."

---

1 Toto is presumably being shown a slide show; Georges Mélies' famous film *Le Voyage dans la lune* (1902) had not yet been released. The aged astronomer that the author has in mind is Camille Flammarion, the brother of La Vaudère's principal publisher, Ernest Flammarion: she had undoubtedly been acquainted with him for some time, given their mutual interest in spiritism, and the visionary fantasy that provides the title story of the collection of translations, *The Double Star and Other Occult Fsantaies*, is based on his theories on interstellar reincarnation.

"Are all souls alike, then, Monsieur?"

"Yes, my child."

Now Toto, in his narrow bed, remains very thoughtful, and as his nursemaid, having tucked him in beneath his white coverlet, leans over to snuff out the candle, he says:

"Wait. I want to say a prayer, in order that the soul of the candle will be happy in Heaven."

END OF LENT
(*La Presse*, 17 March 1901)

In the garden of the convent, Germaine and Giselle are strolling slowly, their arms linked. All along the avenue, couples of girls are circulating thus, passing back and forth before a Holy Virgin in plaster, girdled in blue, whose face, shoulders and hands, open and blessing, are covered by minuscule green mushrooms. On the edge of the path, in the moss and the moist ivy, violets have accumulated under the golden feathers of the first cowslips. Behind the plane trees, the façade of the convent is perceptible, built in the style of the seventeenth century, with its twenty-two sequential windows and its fronton, the tympan of which lodges a powerful clock.

Germaine is fourteen years old; she is thin and pensive, with a transparent complexion of paschal wax and hair as bright as gilded crumbs of true incense. Her bosom is scarcely inflated, her figure as slender as a delicate pillar.

Giselle is fifteen. She has rosy skin, with hair the color of freshly-peeled chestnuts and fiery blue eyes that only have mystical ardors as yet.

They are both wearing the uniform of the boarders of Notre-Dame du Crucifix: a black dress traversed by a silk ribbon knotted on the left side; on the breast shines the silver medal of the Enfants de Marie.

"Oh," says Germaine, "how beautiful Père Frumence's sermon was!"

"Yes, very fine."

"It seemed to me, as I listened to it, that I was drinking a warm and smooth celestial liqueur."

"Père Frumence has preached in the Holy Land; he has the perfume of the olive groves of Gethsemane."

"A little while ago," Germaine continues, "Sister Zéphirine summoned me to the chapel and we decorated the altar, for it appears that the Père only speaks well among flowers. Oh, nothing but serious plants, as befits these days of penitence: shiny holly with berries of crimson coral; mistletoe enameled with glaucous pearls, laurel and ivy. But the odor of the branches moist with sap was so violent that I almost fainted."

"That's like me; I nearly fell ill at the end of the sermon. Sister Pulchérie makes her own incense with cinnamon and myrrh. We're all intoxicated when we leave the chapel."

"Perhaps it's also the languor of renewal that penetrates us, unknown to us."

"I'd like," says Giselle, opening her nostrils, as nacreous as small seashells, "to pick all these little yellow flowers, so tender, respire them slowly, and make a golden cushion for my lectern, and plunge my arms and lips into it all day long."

"Have you savored the first buds of the trees? It's as good as frangipani or angelica."

"And the lilies-of-the-valley? Oh, a salad of cowslips and forget-me-nots!"

The sparrows have become frisky again; this winter they had the air of old messieurs hunched in their quilted dressing-gowns!"

"And the wood-pigeons! They're puffing up their quicksilver chests with a pink sheen, and seem to be dancing a flowery pavane with their mates. They're cooing and asking for something."

"Undoubtedly. We too desire something vague and mysterious that we don't know."

"Yes; my heart sometimes beats as if it wanted to break out of my breast; then without any reason, I want to weep, and my prayers are much more ardent then."

"It seems to me that Père Frumence, who loves flowers and incense so much, doesn't talk to us enough about natural things. We understand them all so well!"

"These trees, these corollas, these herbs, enable us to comprehend bounty, devotion, charity . . ."

But a band of sparrows with bristling plumage, making warlike clamors, lands on the path, pursuing with thrusts of the beak a fearful little bird whose injured wing is trailing on the ground.

"Ah!" says Germaine. "Nature is malevolent too!" And she adds, laying down her woodland flowers at the feet of the plaster Madonna: "Good Virgin, these are for the little Boers."

X-RAYS
(*La Presse*, 28 May 1901)

Radiography has been generating talk for some time, and a lady too "ardently" treated has demanded five thousand francs in compensatory damages from her cruel physician, which have been accorded to her by the civil tribunal of the Seine, on the basis of a report by the dean of the Académie de Médecine.

Since 1895, X-rays have upset the world, and we have all contemplated anxiously photographs of translucent legs and hands—like ferns or the feet of antediluvian lizards—and thoracic cavities garnished with gelatinous lungs reminiscent of crushed jellyfish. Under the baleful apparatus the prettiest woman resembles an Ann Radcliffe heroine in her glass coffin, or Edgar Poe's Berenice! Nothing is more hideously macabre than the deformed images of that which is life but already seems to be death. Science, under its coaxing appearances, is becoming more and more ferocious, and our vivisector surgeons recall well enough the artistic torturers of the *Jardin des Supplices*, carving flesh into red lace, in long curly ribbons, making "patients" into great inverted lotuses or chrysanthemums with a thousand petals.

René loved Louise and Louise loved René.

They were both young and charming, of equal fortune and birth; nothing, it seemed, could oppose their legitimate union. Besides which, the families had known one another for a long time already, and René's mother had experienced a real chagrin when Louise's mother died as a consequence of an unsuccessful operation.

Or, rather, if I'm not mistaken, an operation always succeeds, according to the *Bulletin des Médecins*, but the patient sometimes has the bad taste to perish, without reason, an hour afterwards. It was surely uniquely her fault, for the savant practitioners had opened, extracted, scoured, scraped, raked and sewed up everything again in accordance with the rules of the art.

René, very smitten, therefore wanted to marry Louise, who was languishing like a flower deprived of sunlight; but his parents only responded to his pleas with evasive phrases, which gave evidence of little enthusiasm for his future projects.

"Oh," wept Louise, "what have I done to them? They surrounded us with so much care when we were children! Did they not let us play together for entire days, and did they not smile approvingly when you called me your 'little wife'?"

"I still call you that, my dear Louise, and the wish of the children we were then will be accomplished now we're grown up!"

"Thank you, René; I love you even more, if that's possible, for that sweet promise . . . but let's search together for what might have modified your parents' favorable opinion of me. Am I less pretty?"

"Oh, no!"

"Have I unwittingly committed a reprehensible action, which you don't mention to me out of delicacy?"

"You're perfection itself!"

"Have I not been respectful and attentive to your parents?"

"They render justice to your charm and goodness."

"Finally, my fortune . . ."

"Not another word, my dear Louise! These considerations wound me, and you have no doubt, I suppose, of our complete disinterest?"

Louise, blushing, her heart contracted, lowered her head. "Then I don't know . . ."

"Have confidence, and ask your father to take a step that will no longer permit my parents to avoid the issue."

"So be it, although the roles appear to me to be inverted, and it costs my self-esteem to submit to that supreme proof."

Louise's father decided, therefore, against all custom, to ask for René's hand, in order to console the poor girl, rendered nervous and unhealthily impressionable by uncertainty.

"Yes," was the response, "but on one condition."

"What?"

"It's rather difficult to say . . ."

"Oh, for the sake of my daughter's happiness, I'm ready to hear anything."

"Certainly . . . however . . ."

"Is it a question of interest? Louise possesses . . ."

"We'd take her without a dowry."

"In that case . . ."

"Well . . . well . . . we want to see through her stomach!"

EFFLUVIA[1]
(*La Presse*, 13 April 1901)

They stand up sparkling,
The knotty and deformed apple trees,
And their enormous crowns,
Make white petals snow.

It is an odorous scatter,
A carpet of pink velvet,
On which the sun has reposed
Softly, its errant splendor.

Beneath your great bright vaults,
Flowery trees with gray roots,
You seem in the incense of breezes
To lead the celebrations of spring.

A little sunlight, and every bud sheds its corset, showing its green surah chemise; imprudent little flowers part their gamine collarets for the stings of the first wasps. Sap flows in the heart of old trees and desire sings in the breath of the breezes.

Elisa and Léon, married for three years, are insensible, at least in appearance, to the effluvia of renewal. They have been seen at the racecourses, at the show-jumping arena, at the little private exhibitions where it is good form to be seen. But a few flirtations, followed by jealous scenes and temporary

---

1 This item was headed "Fantaisie d'Avril" [April Fantasy].

quarrels, have soured their relationship. They are desirous of avenging themselves on one another, but without pushing things too far . . .

They would like to scratch the surface of the skin, to give one another the anguish of danger by suspending one another above an imaginary gulf and shouting loudly that they are doomed!

Léon is twenty-eight years old; he is tall, elegant, a rather handsome fellow, although a little too thin and pale, with indecisive, myopic bespectacled eyes, always frayed at the edges, which seem tearful.

Elisa is twenty-two; she is blonde, curvaceous and aware of the prestige of her glaucous peridot irises flecked with gold. Many a dream passes through those eyes, but the Dream is not demanding, and usually requires no more than a slight shock to fly away into the azure, like those soap bubbles that are adorably nuanced and end in an apotheosis of light.

Elisa, a faithful reader of the discreet and gallant correspondence of a worldly periodical, has responded to an offer of amour written in the usual form of five-sou announcements of ennuis for sale, hire or loan on a weekly basis, which are displayed brazenly on the back pages of fashionable newspapers.

Among those labor-free tendernesses in quest of the pity of passers-by, in a telegraphic style, she has distinguished one less economically expressed, the words of which have stuck to her heart like the feet of bees coated with honey:

Young man of the best society, educated, distinguished, ardent, delicate, sensitive and understanding, desires union of soul with pretty young woman having, like him, rare and sentimental aspirations and artistic sympathy for all who suffer in beauty. No agencies; sterility and discretion. Write Noël, etc.

Elisa had read and reread those few lines, which seemed to dance like the blue flames of a punch, and the divinely scintillating name of Noël had put all of Heaven before her eyes.

Noël, Noël! She had dictated to her best friend long and caressant letters to that mystical lover, who had responded in a large, tormented handwriting that revealed the intellectual storm of a miner of the ideal. It was about Noël that she was still thinking on that melancholy evening in April, while Léon, also pensive, was nonchalantly smoking a blonde khedive cigarette and drinking the green tea of Si-a-Fayoune.[1] Thin arabesques of blue smoke were rising up momentarily and then, impelled by an air current, returning toward Elisa, who dispersed them with a wave of her hand.

"You have nothing more to say to me, then?" she asked, after a long silence.

"What do you want me to say? Our thoughts are in discord and we each live in a different sphere."

With a discouraged gesture, Léon took out a handkerchief to wipe the misted glass of his spectacles, and caused a piece of paper to fall from his pocket, which Elisa picked up with stupefaction.

"This note!"

And he, untroubled: "Well, yes, it's a letter from Asile, a woman who understands me and loves me."

Elisa has gone very red. She interrogates Léon with a fearful gaze. But he goes on, in a plaintive voice: "Asile! A bizarre and hospitable name! A woman who bears that name must be a creature of election! 'Asile' comes from Paradise!"

"While 'Elisa' has not quit the earth?"

"Perhaps."

Then, the young woman smiles.

"Asile, my friend, is me. That pretty name, which make you mystically ardent, is simply Elisa backwards. But in that case . . . in that case . . . ?"

---

1 The tea of Si-a-Fayoune features in Joris-Karl Huysnans' Bible of decadence *À rebours* (1884) but does not appear to have had any real existence.

She has put under her husband's nose a letter from the unknown friend whose burning declarations sing incessantly in her memory, and she reads, emphasizing the words: *To you, my adored, your Noël for life.*"

And he, writhing: "*Noël, that divine word, which contains all amour!* O neurasthenic, ludicrous and perverse imagination! Noël, my dear, is Léon backwards. Let's go, come and embrace me! We'll reread these follies and we'll love one another more truly, as we've loved one another in dreams!"

PRIVATE VIEW
(*La Presse*, 2 May 1901)

Lucie Punir—Lulu to her friends—is coiffed in a golden crest, like Félicien Champsaur's heroine, the clownesque Lulu who unhooked hats, brains and hearts with the tip of her dainty foot.[1]

It is the day of the private viewing, and it is necessary, as a good private viewer, to exhibit a spring dress and put on a drolly strange baby-face that will bring the beautiful ladies at ten thousand apiece—in either direction—out of the woodwork.

Lucie, in any case, knows her métier, having posed for Carolan, the master cultivated in large and small town houses, who has no peer for perching a black hat on a blonde fleece, rendering the latest creation of Taquin and making a expensive jewel shine on white skin. Madame de C*** and the Marquise de B*** having only been able to give rare moments to the artist for their portraits, it is Lucie who has "completed" them by lending her shoulders and her arms, enveloping herself in arachnean, velvety fabrics whose creases are so tender that they espouse all womanly mysteries.

The petite, facing forwards or seen from behind, her fingers abandoned to the kiss of rings with bezels more ardent than amorous mouths, dreamed for hours, her eyes half-closed and

---

1 Félicien Champsaur's *Lulu, roman clownesque* (1901) was a novel based on an 1888 pantomime. La Vaudère and Champsaur collaborated on some work for the stage, and he was one of the first critics to praise her literary work.

her cheeks enfevered, and her dream went toward an honest, calm, loving life. She saw herself as the wife of a painter, already arrived, enthroned for good in one of those sumptuous and hospitable studios where she had posed languidly in the dizzying warmth of a heater.

On the morning of the private view, Colombel Vermillon, one of Carolan's pupils, had taken her to the Salon of painting, and seemed to find pleasure in being seen with her. They had wandered disdainfully this way and that, and had then installed themselves in front of Colombel's canvas, a fantasy in a very modern style representing the Lulu of Champsaur's novel, with her golden crest, a paper hoop in her hand, only clad in a tutu of black gauze. That audacious composition, worse than nude, very adroitly spiced, attracted the elegant public, and the women uttered amused little laughs on recognizing Lucie Prunier in the svelte clowness with the voluptuously dilated pink nostrils and glaucous peridot eyes speckled with silver. Colombel smiled and strutted, savoring the sidelong glances and compliments like nectar.

"Do you know that you're truly lovely, my little Lucie?"

"Is it the first time that you've perceived it? I've posed for you in Lulu's costume, though, and you know me entirely."

"I've always found you delightful, with an ingenuously mischievous air and a tender hint of sentiment, uncustomary in the rapacious, vulgar and stupid girls who make a métier of modeling."

"Oh, there are exceptions. Carolan must not be content, for he wanted to keep me to himself, and you painted that clowness in secret."

"Yes, a commission from Champsaur, who, like many poets, is in love with his heroine. It is thus with him for all the women that have featured in his novels, brunettes, blondes and redheads, taken from nature or created in accordance with the fantasies of his imagination. He spends long hours contemplating them and they're the only ones he has truly loved."

Lucie felt warm; the attention of which she was the object embarrassed her somewhat; she would have preferred to go down to the sculptures, but Colombel retained her with passionate words, an arm around her waist and a knee against her own.

They dined frugally, like two lovers, and then returned to sit down before the clowness, who interested the crowd more and more by virtue of the perversity of her enticing smile, her sunlit crest and the undulating lines of her body, undressed in a black gauze tutu.

Lucie, tired but happy, attracted all gazes, which only cease to caress her in order to pose on her blonde image.

"It's a true likeness," said one woman.

"The mistress of the painter or the writer," whispered another.

"Doubtless both; she's pretty enough."

"Eighteen years old?"

"But eyes that have seen everything!"

Colombel was exultant. His seductive phrases were singing to the choir of the girl, who firmly believed that she had seized the chimera of her dream. Until the hour of closure, it was an enchantment.

At the door of the Grand Palais, he bowed with a slight irony.

"What, you aren't going to see me home?" she asked.

"No time; a rendezvous with a woman of the world."

"What?"

"She looked sideways at us sufficiently! I'm going to ask her for eight thousand francs for her portrait."

"You don't love me, then?" sighed Lucie, her heart constricted. "I thought . . . you've been so nice to me until now, and you've kept me by your side all day."

"Well, that permitted people to compare the painting with the model."

"Ah!"

"Yes, it was an advertisement for me!"

OFFERINGS
(*La Presse*, 17 May 1901)

Benares, the holy city; it is night. On the steps of the Ghats, which descend into the Ganges, psylls—snake-charmers—are exhibiting king cobras, swollen with venom, coiled around their necks and their wrists. They are hissing in a plaintive fashion, and the reptiles raise their small flat heads, extending their forked tongues in a desire for caresses. The shore displays, under a fantastic light, its temples, its palaces and its ruins. Garlands of roses, offerings of the faithful, dangle in the water; the smoke of odorous resins rises in light swirls and semi-naked men bring wood, balms and coconut oil for funerary pyres. Immense crows are flying all around, croaking imperiously, awaiting the human remains spared by the flames. The clamors of mourners mingle long ululations of dolor with the joyful cries of he birds of prey. Those women, enveloped in white veils, resemble large snowflakes fallen at random, and children are sometimes detached from their foam of gauze, muslin and silk, who sometimes go to plunge into the water of vases of red clay or copper.

A group of natis—sacred courtesans—has formed near the Ghats. The beautiful young women, with pale amber breasts and burning eyes elongated toward the temples by streaks of kohl, under proudly arched eyebrows, are carrying to the goddess Dourga grains of rice, coffee, mhowa flowers and perfumes contained in little vials of jade and ivory. Necklaces of peridots and aquamarines with glaucous gleams descend as far as their waists, which are gripped by metallic belts studded with gems and fringed with pearls.

They are laughing, and recounting the week's gallant prowesses: many good deeds agreeable to the goddess, which would otherwise be considered as black sins.

Ourvasi (the Nymph), Ruanvili (Gold Dust) and Schahabalu (Glory of the Moon) have taken the road back to the temple of Dourga. Before them, the great sacred apes are gambling from one column to another, throwing peelings and making countless graces in order to obtain treats, which the visitors of the goddess do not fail to distribute to them. In the lateral galleries, sustained by green and yellow monolithic pillars, the cows sacred to the religion are wandering indolently. Ornaments of glassware surround their powerful necks and silver-painted horns. They are the guardians of the place.

But the Nymph, Gold Dust and Glory of the Moon have prostrated themselves before the idols, scintillating under the convergent glare of lamps, and are annihilated in mysterious adorations. Then, the first has placed three almonds in a triangle on the copper table supporting the image of Dourga, and has arranged crimson cardamom berries around them the number and placement of which are determined by the ritual. The other two have given, after her, grains of coffee and rice, which they have disposed so as to form complex figures, and have spread essence of Ghazipour roses over everything while intoning, in unison, a bizarre chant that trails off and dies away on a shrill note.

Other natis surround them and display with pride their noses and ears laden with rings, and their red-tinted toenails ornamented, like their fingers, with precious rings. "Now," says one of them, "let us offer to the goddess our malicious acts and our treasons of the week. The most ingenious will receive from each of us an Oxus ruby and a Sambalour gem."

"I," declared the Nymph, "invited the prettiest devadassi to a fête that lasted two days. Men begged at our door, but we did not let a single one in."

Gold Dust spoke in her turn: "I went on a pilgrimage to Djagganath and I found new tortures for remarkably handsome and well-made young fakirs. They'll remain mutilated until death!"

"I was with her," said a little girl eight years old, with large ingenuous eyes and supple and lively movements. "I dipped my little finger in the blood of the victims and I still have a little red under my fingernails."

Glory of the Moon came last.

"I made fun of two Chinamen. The adventure is amusing; that's its only merit."

"Oh, tell us."

"The Sons of Heaven, who wanted me ardently, approached me here, and as they seemed sumptuous to me, I took them to a 'sugar house' to interrogate them as to their intentions. They offered me cucumber and ginger cakes, washed down with a little cinnamon and pink lotus wine, sprinkled with gold, very refreshing! My gallants laughed with the ends of their yellow teeth and ran their impatient claws over my shoulder.

"Behind them were spread, on a sandalwood table, trembling jellies in large bowls, unctuous creams and flower-syrups of all colors.

"Then, while teasing my Celestials, I attached their long pigtails, very quietly, to the perforated edge of the table; then I assumed my most lascivious poses and I mimed a few scenes from the Kama Sutra for them.

"They were exultant, stamping their feet with joy, begging me to choose between them, for those singular men don't like sharing. Then I took the tuberose from my belt and threw it at their feet. They hastened to drop to all fours; the shelf with the syrups tilted and . . . oh, I'm still laughing! If you had seen them in the jam . . . !"

"Glory of the Moon," the courtesans said, "the goddess will be content, and you have performed a meritorious action."[1]

____

1 A version of Glory of the Moon's anecdote is incorporated into La Vaudère's best-selling novel, *Le Mystère de Kama* (1901; tr. as "The Mystery of Kama"). Whether the fact that it is in such rank bad taste has anything to do with the fact that it was La Vaudère's last story to be published in *La Presse* is purely a matter for speculation.

OPERATED!
(*La Lanterne* Supplement, 5 October 1901)

Emmeline, twenty years old, blonde, plump, pretty . . .

Marthe, her best friend.

Emmeline is lying on a small lacquered bed painted with bouquets of roses; her bare arms are resting on a velvet coverlet constellated with gold, which shines like a firmament.

Marthe: How are you, since the doctor operated on you?

Emmeline: Well, very well.

Marthe: How do you feel?

Emmeline: Immensely appeased. I wouldn't have believed it, because that physician, with his broad shoulders, his long arms and his hairy hands, inspired a certain terror in me.

Marthe: And you fell asleep just like that, immediately, without resistance or anguish?

Emmeline: My anguish could not resist the coaxing of that devil of a man. His gaze, fixed on me, shone in a singular fashion, like that of a cat. His pupils seemed to me to be two ardent fireflies that attracted me and fascinated me until I lost consciousness. His voice had particular modulations too, sometimes dull and sometimes sharp, which vibrated in my nerves delightfully. I even think I laughed in my abandonment.

Marthe: Yes, a frightful, hysterical laughter . . . How you must have suffered, poor darling!

Emmeline: But no. One has a truly exaggerated idea of these operations. They'll soon arrive at cutting up the human body as one cuts up an apple, and withdrawing the principal organs at the end of a silver fork, very gently, like little pips.

Marthe: You make engaging comparisons.

Emmeling: The lyricism of gratitude. I've never been as perfectly happy as when I was made to submit to this redoubtable proof. It's unbelievable! Voluptuous waves ran over me; I disappeared into a foam of the Milky Way. In sum, I can't describe such sensations with words sufficiently . . . suggestive. You can grasp . . .

Marthe: No, my darling; how can you expect . . .

Emmeline: If one weren't risking one's life, as it appears, at this little game, it would be agreeable to me to be operated on every day!

Marte: That's unusual!

Emmeline: What am I saying, every day? I'd even like to recommence several times a day. Perhaps, in martyrdom, one experiences similar delights . . . I now understand the first Christians, who smiled under the claws of beasts . . . one of the mysteries of nature! There are abysms that can only be filled in dreams . . .

Emmeline shakes her delectable face over her lace pillow, flourishing in a spray of pale gold the cornflowers of her eyes and the minuscule poppy of her mouth. She has never been more beautiful, and her hand, which is caressing Marthe, is as fresh and supple as a lily petal. The frightened confidante wonders, however, whether her friend is in full possession of her senses, and whether the shock might have been excessive for the organism of a frivolous socialite, slightly unhinged and neurasthenic, as they all are nowadays. She collects herself momentarily, singularly moved by the troubling sensations evoked by that surgical confession.

Marthe: We're assured, however, that the attempt is one of the most perilous; that it's necessary to dig into the flesh profoundly, claw, cut and suppress; that the blood springs forth in floods, and that even when the operation has succeeded perfectly—this is affirmed in the physicians' reports—the patient

is extinguished by exhaustion, like a lamp emptied of its oil.[1]
For you, my darling, there's no more danger, you're respiring
joy and the wellbeing of living. All the same, you've deployed a
famous courage; in your place, I wouldn't have consented.

Emmeline: It was necessary.

Marthe: Was it truly urgent? What was wrong with you,
then?

Emmeline: Vapors, anxieties, dizziness and continual
toothache . . .

Marthe: And now?

Emmeline: I told you: a great appeasement.

Marthe: How did you find out about this Merveille?

Emmeline: It was a colleague at the waters who indicated
him to me. He no longer operates himself because his sight
is weak and he's too enfeebled by age. It appears that it's necessary to be very vigorous to bring complicated work to a
successful conclusion.

Marthe: Doctor Merveille is a skillful practitioner.

Emmeline: Truly, it costs so little to have . . . you know
what . . . taken out! I don't understand why women still hesitate to get rid of that compromising superfluity! Think about
it, darling: no more risks to run, no more ridiculous anxieties
that poison our existence! On emerging from the hands of our
benefactors, we're really the equals of men. One can't pay too
dearly for such an advantage!

Marthe: There are, from time to time, a few deaths at-
tributed to criminal operations. Public opinion is stirred up

____

1 In her novel *Les Demi-Sexes* (1897; tr. as "The Demi-Sexes") La Vaudère
did not seem to understand what the sterilizing "operation" she was
describing (very coyly) actually entailed; she has obviously found out in
the interim, perhaps by virtue of having read *Le Mal Nécessaire* (1899;
tr. as *The Necessary Evil*) by the physician André Couvreur, which gives a
much fuller and gorier account of a hysterectomy, adding a cruel twist that
might well have inspired the present story, which might have been rejected
by the editor of *La Presse* for being too scandalous.

. . .

Emmeline: Leave off . . . jealous colleagues have put that rumor about. Have not powerful intelligences always had their detractors and enemies?

※

Nine months later.

Emmeline is lying on the same small lacquered bed painted with bouquets of roses; her face, which retains a slight pallor, sometimes turns toward a cradle veiled with English needlepoint, which her friend Marthe is rocking with a resigned patience. A confused wailing resonates in the room.

Marthe: My poor Emmeline!

Emmeline: Oh, my dear, these physicians . . . Do you understand? Not only didn't he take anything out, but he . . . added something.

Marthe: And you paid for that?

Emmeline: Five thousand francs!

Marthe: That's the progress of science!

NINOCHE
(*La Lanterne* Supplement, 12 August 1902)

The dressing room of an actress in a féerie theater. Ninoche, as a "Seaweed Fay" is passing around her waist a belt studded with aquamarines and amethysts, closed by a golden crab, while Zizinette is reddening her ears and blurring her eyelids. They are both clad in pink leotards and coiffed with large nacreous seashells, wearing water-green corselets fringed with silver sheets forming a cascade, and showing the slender shoulders of little girls under a triple row of pearls and coral beads.

Ninoche: I can't fasten my crab. Will you help me?

Zinzinette, *tugging with all her strength on the belt in order to fasten it*: You know that it's beginning to show?

Ninoche: Damn; it'll soon be six months. I'll need to ask for a leave.

Zinzinette: You're sure of the prince, at least?

Ninoche: He's in the hall every evening, devouring me with his eyes . . . in the second row of the armchairs, to the left.

Zinzinette: A very chic fellow. You're lucky!

Ninoche: When he can't come he sends his negro with bonbons and flowers.

Zinzinette: Superb, that negro! When I'm rich, I'll hire a negro too. That's what poses a woman.

Ninoche: Everything about the prince is becoming: the horses, the carriages, the private train . . . and if I continue to exhibit myself in this inept play, it's for my pleasure, because I'm a pretty girl and men look at me.

Zinzinette: Your prince must be flattered, anyway, by your success?

Ninoche: He never complains. He's under my charm, ever since the memorable evening when I figured in the living tableaux of the Princesse de S***.

Zinzinette: What were you playing?

Ninoche: The Muse, and he was the sweet poet. I descended from the friezes to place a crown of laurels on his head, and the princess, in the wings, recited *La Nuit de Mai* in an emotional voice: "Poet, take your lute and give me a kiss."

Zinzinette: And it was in consequence of that kiss that you listened to the prince's lute?

Ninoche: Oh, no, for Maman had told me that it was necessary not to let myself be kissed, especially by poets who had nice lutes, because, when they can play well they no longer want to play anything else and become gypsies of amour.

Zinzinette: Oh, girls who still have their mother are very lucky.

Ninoche: She also said to me, the worthy Maman, that almost all men are liars, and that before playing the "little fool" it's necessary to choose carefully among the gallants the fellow infatuated enough to take a girl seriously and chic enough to make her a situation.

Zinzinette: Sage advice; for you were still a little white goose, an immaculate lily.

Ninoche: I waited for a favorable opportunity. At sixteen, one has time to have some fun.

Zinzinedtte: Since the prince was the first, he'll recognize the brat, and if you're clever . . .

Ninoche: All would have gone well without that pest Irma.

Zinzinette: The Irma that you replaced in the *pas de trois?*

Ninoche: It's not my fault that she was sacked; she muffed all her entrechats and her glissades failed. As for her points, they were cotton, and I prefer not to talk about her turning gargouillades and her beaten jetés.

Zinznette: A tortoise, eh?

Ninoche: Well, she hasn't forgiven me for having more spring than her.

Zinzinette: She's a bad lot!

Ninoche: I understand her tricks now, but then, I let myself be taken in by her demonstrations of amity. I thought she had a sure and disinterested affection. I confided my little affairs to her.

Zinznette: Poor kid!

Ninoche: The slut didn't take long to perceive that the prince came to the theater almost every day and that he had a crush on me. So, one evening she said to me: "No stupidities, you know, Ninoche. Let your old man be convinced that you've never had anyone before him, that you're only yielding because he inspires such a mad passion in you, and that you're infatuated with him. That way you'll attach him definitively. It's an assured fortune."

As Maman had sad the same thing, I was devoid of mistrust and an utter idiot. I replied: "My good Irma, it's necessary to arrange things, and since you know the prince, do me the service of talking to him for me; show him the head, make him believe that I adore him, that I'm ready to sacrifice my treasures of innocence to him. In sum, you know men; I put my fate in your hands."

The stage manager, *passing by like a gust of wind*: On stage the Seaweed Fay! If you're not on cue, I'll fine you twenty francs!

Ninoche: What a boor!

The stage manger: What did you say?

Ninoche: Nothing.

The stage manager: That's a fine of sixty francs.

Ninoche: ****!

The stage manager draws away, exasperated.

Zinzinette: Perhaps you went a bit far . . .

Ninoche: So we can't even chat now!

Zinzinette: Finish, quickly!

Ninoche: After a few days Irma whispered in my ear: "It's for tonight!"

"Oh," I said, very emotional.

"Yes, I've arranged everything with the prince; you only have to climb into his carriage after the performance, and don't refuse him anything . . . nothing, you understand!"

"In spite of the consequences?"

"Certainly."

"And if you-know-what arrives?"

"So much the better."

"However, Maman told me . . ."

"It's necessary not to spoil this affair, my little Ninoche. Your good mother, I'm certain, would be of my opinion. A mature man who's smitten with you and has so much money! Think! You'll attach him for life!"

Zinzinette: Well, then?

Ninoche: Alas, alas, I did everything that that poisonous Irma had recommended. The carriage was waiting for me outside the theater. I got in, slightly surprised not to see my lover, but I thought he was waiting for me at home, in the midst of his charming preparations.

Zinzinette: Get on with it! Honorine is recommencing the shrimps' dance. That will warm up the direction!

Ninoche: Oh, my dear, I had no sooner crossed the threshold of the little town house than two arms embraced me with a delightful ardor. The antechamber was plunged in darkness, but I didn't have time to pull myself together or protest, so irresistible was the embrace!

Zinzinette, *listening with increasing interest*: Bravo! Who could ask for anything more? Fortune, situation, amour . . . not to mention that your imminent maternity might well enable you to be espoused in legitimate marriage. Who would have supposed it, at the prince's age? And you've always been as . . . lucky as that first time?

Ninoche, *weeping*: Alas, my dear, that first time was . . . the negro!

RED LUST[1]
(*La Lanterne* Supplement, 18 December 1902)

The menagerie, empty of spectators, is asleep in a strong mist of respiration and the bitter odor of pelts. The sand, freshly raked, forms slight whirlwinds around crates in which the large reptiles marbled with ocher and cinnabar are torpid. It is the hour when the wild beasts half-veiling their shining eyes, lie down nostalgically, their claws retracted into velvet gloves. One senses, however, that they are armed for defense, ready to bound at the slightest alert, and even in sleep, their fangs glisten menacingly behind the turned-back chops.

After the evening meal, the last performance will take place, the most important one, which will join to the ordinary exhibitions the emotion of the struggle, the dance of the lions in the central cage, where the tamer Stephano will deploy the whip and the revolver, making the terrible beasts pirouette like circus clowns, and redden their bellies with the fire of burning hoops.

Myrta, the black panther, always in revolt, roars dully in anticipation of the imminent visit; her paws clench feverishly and her fur bristles in voluptuous frissons; she is believed to be amorous and jealous. Twice, already, she has thrown herself upon Stephano and, standing up, dominating him with her massive head, she has rubbed her muzzle against his cheek. But the tamer has mastered her with a glance, conquered her

---

1 This story is a revised and expanded version of the story first published in the 13 August 1897 issue of *La Presse*, translated herein as "Tamer."

with a caress, and, with his boot on her spine, has maintained her there, panting, under the enthusiastic bravos of the public.

It is ten o'clock. The assistants turn up the gas, bring baskets full of meat for the carnivores' meal, distribute fruit to the monkeys and wake up the parrots, living flowers brightening the monotony of the dark pelts, and erecting in the corolla of their open wings the pistils of their irritate crests.

But a young woman has come in, escorted by an ageless and sexless governess, to exchange a few words with the lads, who know her, accustomed to seeing her every evening, since the installation of the menagerie in the suburban quarter. She is Antonia, the daughter of a rich businessman from Madrid, who comes furtively to intoxicate herself on the odor of circuses, in the unacknowledged and almost morbid desire to caress her soul with a little suffering, to see blood flowing and bones breaking.

She experiences the murderous passion that leads señoras to the *plaza del toros* and puts in the puerile heart of virgins the ferocity of inquisitors and torturers. She is, however, as frail as a reed, her voice is soft and her onyx eyes, speckled with gold, crackle in the paschal wax of her skin; she seems a mystical being of grace and bounty. But she comes from the land of the matadors, where amour seems better after the red vision of an arena strewn with spilled entrails, where the troubling perfume of woman mingles with the bitter reek of abattoirs.

For the moment, her *espado* is named Stephano, the superb tamer who juggles with the great lions, and appeases the jealous fury of the black panther with caresses and seductive words.

Antonia has stopped, pensively, before the beast's cage, and her golden gaze, aimed at Myrta's fiery gaze, interrogates it for a long time.

The panther has risen to her feet, her muzzle puckered over the sharp teeth, her tail thrashing; then, stretching herself along the bars, her entire body vibrating with a lascivious spasm, she yawns nervously, and is convulsed by a hoarse gasp. The regret of the desert and free amours grips her in the solitude of her prison; her flanks agitate, and her claws scratch the ground in a desire for caresses or murder.

Antonia has slipped her umbrella between the bars, and the beast, twisting the whalebone like flexible stems, is gnawing the ivory sleeve, having passed her head through the zinzoline silk, which makes her the collar of a female clown.

"Oh, look Gertrude, see how crazy Myrta is today!"

"It's necessary not to excite her," advises the governess. "Something bad might happen to Stephano."

A strange gleam passes through the young woman's eyes. She does not reply, but her heel taps the ground impatiently and her nostrils dilate in an ardent aspiration.

Gradually, the public arrive, the habitual public of fairground marquees, composed of bourgeois, workers, idlers, good-time girls with scented hair, little vagabonds and suspect louts.

The obstinately swaying bears, the hyenas, the foxes and the torpid boas in the crates, and the consumptive or mock-ing monkeys captivate attention at first; then everyone groups around the central cage for the exercises of Stephano, the hand-some tamer whose breast is adorned with flattering plaques and who flexes his harmonious muscles in a bright leotard.

In the front row, Antonia remains motionless, her lips dry, her hands burning. She does not know exactly what she expects, but she senses that something is going to happen, because she wants it to, and because her criminal anguish has communicated itself to the black panther, whose fur is glistening like a velvet robe as her flesh quivers.

Here comes Stephano. Proud, nervous and agile, his whip held high, he has entered the cage and, before the fixed gaze of the women, has made the lions twirl, which come to lie down at his feet, licking his hands, superb and gentle. The pistol shots, the burn of the fiery hoops and the effort of the singular tricks have not been able to irritate them. They crawl in a servile fashion, and the royal fleece of their spine makes a soft seat for the tamer.

Hands applaud furiously, while Antonia's pretty mouth sketches a disdainful moue. Stephano, charmed and surprised by the young woman's assiduity at his exercises, contemplates her with a vainglorious assurance.

She smiles, and her imperious gaze fixes upon that of the tamer, descending into him as if into a mysterious well, and causes all the fibers of his being to vibrate. He goes pale, and the anxious expression of his features reveals that he is conscious of Antonia's tragic desire. His energy is sunk in that of the unknown enemy; he loses the personality of his free and thinking self.

"Stephano," she says, "the black panther is waiting. Only her conquest is worthy of you.

Myrta is now in front of the tamer. She seems to be plunged in a rigid immobility, and, like a cat dazzled by the light, she extinguishes beneath her weary eyelids the double star of her pupils. The young woman standing up in front of the cage is a human panther far more implacable than the captive beast. She utters a scornful laugh at the hesitation of the man, whose instinct is perhaps warning him, and murmurs through clenched teeth: "Coward!"

Stephano put his arms round the beast for the habitual games; but she resists, roaring, embraces him in her turn and knocks him down. The two bodies roll, bound and twist, in the midst of cries and gasps. Women faint, while the employees, armed with pitchforks and pikes, hasten to the bars, mastering the panther, whose muzzle is red with blood.

Antonia, her eyes capsized with ecstasy, has detached the triple row of pearls that adorn her gracious neck, and she hands it to the vanquished man.

"Thank you," she says, in the slightly guttural voice of a Madrileno virgin. "That was almost as good as the *plaza del toros!*"

THE FIRST STEP[1]
(*La Lanterne* Supplement, 6 January 1903)

Isoline: Twenty years old, dainty, droll, frail shoulders, hips scarcely developed, air undulating; reminiscent of a curious boy, but perversely suggestive for some. Has married a businessman who has treated her as a "legitimate wife" and has only permitted to her to savor the regulation joys of marriage. In her drawing room, soberly furnished, correct and cold, she yawns furtively behind her Malines handkerchief. An obese valet de chambre introduces the visitors.

Guy de Sainte-Genèse—twenty-four years old, brown hair and velvety "bitter curaçao" eyes, sympathetic lips, appetizing teeth—advances with the slightly gauche timidity appropriate to his youth.

"Alone again, dear Madame? It's true that in October one makes few visits. I am doubly fortunate . . ."

"Why, it's the dear vicomte! I've resumed my day, even so, in the hope that people might take pity on my good will and come to relieve my ennui."

"What a nasty word! What, at your age? And so pretty?"

A brief silence. A slight blush colors Isoline's cheeks. She thinks that Guy is not bad, but that he must be very inexperienced, and scantly comprehending. She reads in his eyes as clearly as in an advertisement for soap that he is foaming with

---

1 This story was reprinted from the 2 March 1902 issue of the humorous military periodical *La Vie en culottes rouge*, where it appeared under the title "Saint-Cyrien."

desire, but that amorous words are sticking in his throat and will not emerge . . .

Come on, then, lad! Get on with it! For want of speech, there are gentle gestures, very enveloping, very respectful, for it is unnecessary to go any faster than the violins, and put the woman in the awful necessity of being offended.

Saint-Genèse, who has a vague intuition of things, and does not know yet what one can risk on such occasions, prefers to examine floral patterns in the carpet, in order not to commit a gaffe. He will catch up later.

"It's very kind of you," he says, "to have permitted me to come assiduously to your Wednesdays. So, you can see that I never miss one, and that . . ."

Isoline comprehends that the child does not want to take a risk. She cannot, however, dictate his declaration to him. She advances a dainty foot, sheathed in mauve spidersilk, edged with a frill of old ivory lace and replies, with a provocative gaze:

"I'm always delighted to receive you; I beg you to believe that yours is the first name inscribed on the list of my intimates, which isn't long."

Guy, very troubled, goes on, as if his head were exploding: "Were you at the Duchesse's play?"

The Duchesse now! thinks Isoline. *Eh! What do I care about that old battleaxe? Are we going to go astray in society gossip? Oh, how I'd love to have other cares than the cares of my stupid life! To be able to relax in a bath of caressant memories as if in a milky liquid in which my skin would be continuously tickled! How good it would be to plunge into it entirely! However, the little vicomte seems to be made of wood today. Perhaps he thinks that his bachelor pad isn't worthy to receive me, or that I have a debt to pay. I shouldn't have had to show him my underwear. I'm certainly frightening him with my contained passion; he's only encountered as yet the banal complaisance of girls or the complimentary provocation of dowagers. It's impossible, however, for me to tell him what I want; it's necessary that he vanquish adroitly, without wounding me and without letting me believe that my defeat was premeditated. It's also necessary that I can resist until the end, clinging to my virtue, without, however, putting up a necessarily ridiculous struggle. It requires ardor and adoration, wit and tact, gestures of undressing and stroking, neither too much nor too little: a contained but devouring fire, a bold but docile manner, lips that seek and find with a seductive skill, hands that grip playfully, eyes that demand everything but are neither insolent nor joyful, nor mocking, nor skeptical. My God, how difficult this is! Sainte-Genèse will never be able . . . but get on with it, lad! Let's go . . . boy . . . let's go . . . ah!*

Guy, intimidated by the absorbed expression of his interlocutor, asks, awkwardly: "Do you follow politics?"

Politics! Lord! It's a complete disaster.

And Isoline, no longer vibrant, postpones the education of the young man until the following Wednesday.

THE BEAUTIFUL HOUSEINI
(*La Lanterne* Supplement, 4 April 1903)

"So," said Caravadek to Sadik-Beg, "you're marrying the beautiful Houseini tomorrow? You don't know the rumors that are going around on her account, then?"

"Yes," replied Sadik. "I know that her humor is indomitable, as indomitable as that of her cat Yahin, the black angora that never quits her. I also know that all the gallants have recoiled, until now, before a request for marriage, and that, in spite of Houseini's fortune, the most smitten and the most resolute have not dared to brave her wild character. Personally, I find her charming."

"Certainly," Caravadek concluded, "I don't know of anyone more accomplished in body and face! I wish you good luck, Sadik. May your wife comport herself more worthily than mine—for, alas, my conjugal misfortunes are no secret to anyone."

Sadik smiled discreetly. He was tall, brave, well-built for fighting and pleasure; the conquest of a rebellious beauty did not seem so very difficult to him.

On the day of the wedding, the amorous man waxed ecstatic about the grace of the bride, whose large green eyes were scintillating like emeralds. He would have liked to wrap himself in the warm and profound mantle of her hair and pick amber clusters of kisses from all the niches of her flesh; but he contained himself, for it is necessary not to show young women too much admiration; the best means of making oneself cherished is still to feign indifference.

Houseini had retired to her apartments to await the master's arrival. Crouching on an onyx step on the edge of a basin, she had lifted up her broad sleeves behind her shoulders, and slaves were commencing the ablutions methodically, in accordance with the sacred rituals. The moon was shining through the high window, and the faint sounds of little flutes and tambourines arrived, like the sighs of turtle-doves.

Houseini unfastened her necklaces, her bracelets, her veils fringed with silver and the savant shells of her incomparable tresses. Swaying her entire body, she intoned prayers, and her last garments fell around her like April snow. Then her favorite slave passed layers of balm over her breasts, with subtle and fresh effluences. The perfumes floated around her, like an aura, and evaporated from her flesh in gusts, sometimes agile and sometimes heavy. She was naked, supple and perfect. Her hips rounded out softly above her polished, strong legs tapering like pale bronze colonnettes. One of her servants tinted the palms of her hands vermilion, passed antimony over the rims of her eyelids and elongated her eyelashes with a mixture of gum, musk and ebony.

Yahin, his spine supple and his ears pricked, prowled around the slaves, purring, and his glaucous eyes, flecked with golden dots, had the same cruel and caressant gleam as Houseini's. With multitudinous feline gymnastics, he seemed to be defending the entrance to the gynaeceum, watching over the brown beauty of his dear mistress.

When Sadik, clad in his military uniform and armed with his sword, went to his wife's chamber, she was sitting in a solemn attitude, and her gaze launched lighting flashes, precursors of storm. Yahin, all his fur bristling, uttered hoarse miaows, teeth exposed and claws extended. As he made as if to throw himself upon Sadik, the latter, with a single thrust of his weapon, cut off his head, and, swinging that head, from which blood was escaping in impetuous jets, like a somber flower with a crimson pistil, he offered it to the tremulous beauty.

It was, it appears, an adorable night . . . !

A few days later, when Sadik related the adventure to Caravadek, the latter thanked him warmly for having informed him of the means of subjugating women, and, recalling that his wife also possessed a superb angora, he disappeared in order to consider an idea that had just occurred to him.

As soon as darkness had drowned beings and things, Caravadek went into his companion's chamber armed with a scimitar and a bellicose expression. The favorite cat of the house advanced to meet him, in order to wish him welcome, but, instead of caressing it, as usual, he took it by the head and severed its neck.

While he bent down to contemplate his victim, he felt a violent blow to his head and he fell to the floor, semi-conscious.

When he was able to open his eyes, he saw his wife before him, as terrible as Vengeance and as implacable as Punishment.

"Imbecile," she said to him, with a disdainful snigger. "It was on the day of our marriage that it was necessary to kill the cat!"

A PARTIAL LIST OF SNUGGLY BOOKS

ETHEL ARCHER *The Hieroglyph*
ETHEL ARCHER *The Whirlpool*
G. ALBERT AURIER *Elsewhere and Other Stories*
CHARLES BARBARA *My Lunatic Asylum*
CHARLES BARBARA *Stirring Stories*
S. HEZOLNRY BERTHOUD *Misanthropic Tales*
LÉON BLOY *The Tarantulas' Parlor and Other Unkind Tales*
ÉLÉMIR BOURGES *The Twilight of the Gods*
ADA BUISSON *The Baron's Coffin and Other Disquieting Tales*
CYRIEL BUYSSE *The Aunts*
JAMES CHAMPAGNE *Harlem Smoke*
FÉLICIEN CHAMPSAUR *The Latin Orgy*
ARMAND CHARPENTIER
　　　Claustrophobic Madness and Other Stories of Death and Love
BRENDAN CONNELL *Metrophilias*
BRENDAN CONNELL *Spells*
RENDAN CONNELL (editor) *The Zaffre Book of Occult Fiction*
BRENDAN CONNELL (editor) *The Zinzolin Book of Occult Fiction*
RAFAELA CONTRERAS *The Turquoise Ring and Other Stories*
DANIEL CORRICK (editor)
　　　Ghosts and Robbers: An Anthology of German Gothic Fiction
ADOLFO COUVE *When I Think of My Missing Head*
RENÉ CREVEL *Are You All Crazy?*
QUENTIN S. CRISP *Aiaigasa*
QUENTIN S. CRISP *Rule Dementia!*
LUCIE DELARUE-MARDRUS *The Last Siren and Other Stories*
LADY DILKE *The Outcast Spirit and Other Stories*
CATHERINE DOUSTEYSSIER-KHOZE *The Beauty of the Death Cap*
ÉDOUARD DUJARDIN *Hauntings*
BERIT ELLINGSEN *Now We Can See the Moon*
ERCKMANN-CHATRIAN *A Malediction*
ALPHONSE ESQUIROS *The Enchanted Castle*
ENRIQUE GÓMEZ CARRILLO *Sentimental Stories*
DELPHI FABRICE *Flowers of Ether*
DELPHI FABRICE *The Red Sorcerer*
DELPHI FABRICE *The Red Spider*
BENJAMIN GASTINEAU *The Reign of Satan*
EDMOND AND JULES DE GONCOURT *Manette Salomon*
REMY DE GOURMONT *From a Faraway Land*
REMY DE GOURMONT *Morose Vignettes*
GUIDO GOZZANO *Alcina and Other Stories*
GUSTAVE GUICHES *The Modesty of Sodom*
EDWARD HERON-ALLEN *The Complete Shorter Fiction*
EDWARD HERON-ALLEN *Three Ghost-Written Novels*